Two Cousins of Azov
Or
You Can't Pickle Love

As a teenager, Andrea Bennett wanted to be an artist. When
that didn't work out, she decided on academic adventure, and
eventually gained a degree in Russian & History from the
University of Sheffield. *Two Cousins of Azov* is her second novel.
She lives in Ramsgate, Kent, with her two sons, partner and
dog, and divides her time between writing and charity work.

 @andreawiderword

Also by Andrea Bennett

Galina Petrovna's Three-Legged Dog Story

TWO COUSINS
OF AZOV

OR

YOU CAN'T PICKLE
LOVE

ANDREA BENNETT

THE BOROUGH PRESS

The Borough Press
An imprint of HarperCollins*Publishers*
1 London Bridge Street
London SE1 9GF

www.harpercollins.co.uk

This paperback edition 2017
1

First published by HarperCollins*Publishers* 2017

A catalogue record for this book is available from the British Library

ISBN: 978–0–00–815957–3

This novel is entirely a work of fiction.
The names, characters and incidents portrayed in it, while at times based on
historical events and figures, are the work of the author's imagination.

Set in Bembo 11.5/15 pt by Palimpsest Book Production Limited, Falkirk, Stirlingshire

Printed and bound in Great Britain by Clays Ltd, St Ives plc

MIX
**Paper from
responsible sources**
FSC˘ C007454

Find out more about HarperCollins and the environment at
www.harpercollins.co.uk/green

For Mum and Dad

CONTENTS

THE DISAPPEARING EGG

A fortnight after the rabbit incident, Gor was standing at the table in his kitchen waiting for water to boil for his lunchtime egg, and scratching his head with a thoroughly chewed pencil. The crossword before him lay unresolved, the fluffy white cat at his feet virtually ignored. The egg nestled, still cold, in his palm. He was distracted, gazing out of the window with unseeing eyes, the gloominess of his inner thoughts reflected in their murky depths. A dog howled. A crow cawed. He shuddered, brows drawing tight. Perhaps he should fetch his jerkin?

This was it: autumn was moving in all around him – its bags unpacked, its toothbrush already in the glass above the basin. The daylight that splashed across his thin canvas slippers held an unhealthy pallor. He sniffed: the essence of the rain-washed ground was percolating the walls. A chill would not do. He was letting himself go. The pencil dropped to the table and he strode from the room. He would unearth his autumn slippers a few weeks earlier than usual, and gain a drop of solace from mildly cosy toes.

Gor did not mind autumn so much. He was not sentimental

about the seasons, and neither missed them nor anticipated their return. Each dawn came later, and the days seemed worn out, fading to dusk before the birds had finished singing. This put a strain on his light-bulb supply, but it rarely strained his nerves. Autumn was a quick and mucky deal, transforming summer's dust to cold dirt within a matter of weeks. The alchemy hinged on a drop of three degrees and some extra millimetres of rain. But it was just the cycle of life. It was good to be rid of summer's heat, Gor muttered to himself. The humidity had been stifling, especially at night.

Sometimes, tossing and turning in the fug of summer's stillness, he had the strangest feeling, as if he were in the wrong place, and were the wrong kind of creature. It was a different sense, not hearing or taste or smell, but a physical memory, printed in his bones. He almost felt he had wings; could feel them unfurling from his back, the effortless rise and fall as he swooped above the earth. He sensed he should be someone else. It made his stomach contract, like a long-forgotten promise: yes, I will be good; yes, I will be true. It made him yearn to nest somewhere high and stony, bone-dry.

Perhaps it was his Armenian roots finally tugging him back to the landscapes of his forefathers. The southern Russian town of Azov, his current domicile, was not his natural habitat, after all. It sweated or shivered on windy, salt-marsh flats where the mighty River Don emptied into the shallow Azov Sea. From the top of the ancient ramparts, you could see the water glisten and heave in the distance under a fierce sky, while Azov steamed under a cloud of midges. And Armenia itself had nothing to do with the sea, sitting noble and remote, glorious and resplendent in separateness, its barricades the mountains that

2

rose up on each side, while its sinuous back arched to heaven, veined with dusty roads that twisted into the very sky.

He sat in the hall, rummaged in the shoe box and eventually tugged on the autumn slippers, their leather outers shiny with age, the inners enveloping his soles in the softest lamb's wool.

Maybe one day he would return to the land of his ancestors, well, one half of them, and sit on an Armenian mountain. He would mark out the spot with his graphite eye where a tree would be planted in a pebble-strewn valley. On a stretch of flat earth by that tree, he would fashion an Armenian house, with high brown walls and elegant arched windows. He would grow vines and till that difficult soil to bring about a richness of fruits, juicing the earth.

But then again, maybe not. He had visited the country only once, in his youth, to meet strange, distant relatives and see what he was missing. He had enjoyed the trip, as far as he recalled, but had never made the journey back despite his intentions. Life had got serious, and his priorities had changed. Take his career at the bank, for instance. It had flourished quickly, weaving roots that would keep him firmly embedded in the local soil. And now, many of those he had met would no longer be walking souls: they were probably buried under the trees in the valley, resting in that dry, sandy earth. For him, time was getting late to be building a house and learning a new language.

He sighed and returned to the kitchen, the bold figures of the wall calendar catching his eye, smirking at him as Pericles twisted at his ankles. A timid X marked that first Friday in September, when he had made his move and taken fate into his own hands. A deeper slash of an X denoted the day, two weeks later, when things had gone very wrong. Now, he stood before the calendar, tugging hard on his goatee beard and, with a frown, took the pencil to mark another X four days after that. The date of the rabbit incident. The day he met Sveta.

He shuddered, despite the lamb's wool slippers, and realised he had been ignoring both the crossword and the egg. He could not abide a dry egg. He went to remove it from the pan and stopped short, mouth dropping open. The pan was empty, boiling away merrily to itself with no sign of an egg in it at all. But he had put the egg in there just moments ago, before going into the hall. He had heard it gently boiling away! He was sure his fingertips still felt cold where they had rested on its smooth, hard surface. He looked around, feeling stupid: where could it have gone? Pericles opened an eye and observed his master probing the oven, the cabinet, the larder, the empty biscuit jar, all the cupboards: all for nothing. There was no egg. Gor's eyes strayed up to the light fittings and down to the floor, not searching, but wandering. He stood motionless and unsure of himself, staring into the pan of boiling water as it giggled back at him, winking.

What was going on? Things did not just disappear. There must be a logical explanation. He opened the heavy fridge door: yes, there was the egg container, and there was the space left by the egg he had removed precisely six minutes before, or a little longer, come to think of it. Tuesday's egg was definitely gone. He slammed the fridge with more force than was necessary and shut off the gas under the pan. He didn't care for this at all.

The last thing he could afford was the loss of a nutritious egg. To hell with it: he'd just have to have tea with a piece of buttered bread. After all, he'd survived without eggs before, and much besides, although admittedly a long time ago, back in Siberia. He was about to sit down to his meagre luncheon when the telephone changed his plans with a harsh and repeated bleeping. He hesitated, buttered bread in hand, wondering who it might be. Still it bleeped. He hurried out into the hall.

'Good day!' he pronounced grimly, his deep voice booming off the walls.

His bass was answered by a slightly scratchy contralto. 'Ah, Gor! It is I . . . Sveta.'

'Oh, yes.' He winced and swallowed a sigh, relaxing minutely against the wall. 'How may I help you?'

'We have a rehearsal shortly at your apartment, if I am not mistaken?' She did not pause, despite the implied question. 'However, I have to say Albina, my daughter, you remember? Well, she is really not at all well, and I have had to keep her home from school. I cannot leave her, obviously.' Gor's chest heaved with inaudible relief as the idea settled into his mind that Sveta was about to cancel their rehearsal. 'But I was wondering . . .' she continued, in a more intimate tone, 'I would hate to miss the rehearsal, when we've just started, so do you think you could come to my apartment, and we could do it here instead? Albina will be very well behaved. She has promised.'

Gor's black eyebrows locked for a moment and he chewed on his cheek, surprised by Sveta's determination, and also disappointed by it, truth be told. 'If there is no other option, Sveta, we will have to do what we can. I can come to your apartment, if it is absolutely necessary: that is, if you think I should.' The woman did not detect his lack of enthusiasm, and thanked him

5

for his flexibility before ringing off with a contrived tinkle of a laugh.

He had noted her address on the first piece of paper that had come to hand; the bank statement of the Rostov Regional Magic Circle. How he wished he'd never become treasurer. He chewed on his cheek as he stalked back to the kitchen to tidy, and fret.

Today, the convoluted tricks and the cabinet of magic, once his diversion of choice, held zero appeal. He felt tired, uninspired; preoccupied, perhaps. He coveted time to himself, to play the piano and ruminate on these problems of his disappearing memory, the strangeness of life, his burgeoning conscience, and the piles of doubt surrounding him, reaching to the ceiling, sometimes crowding out the daylight.

He did not sleep. The hands that combed through his hair sometimes shook. Odd events had been occurring, and it wasn't just the stupid egg or the hideous rabbit. An afternoon at the baby-grand might give him peace to sort through his thoughts. An afternoon with Sveta surely would not.

As he came to the doorway, humming softly to himself, a movement in the window drew his glance. He looked up automatically, expecting to see a pigeon wing, or scrappy paper in the wind. Instead, to his astonishment, he glimpsed the imprint of a face, features clouded by the steam that clung to the cold glass, but definitely a human countenance – just hanging there, peering in – four floors up. He froze, dumbfounded as the face faded into the clouds, and then dashed over to the window. The hinges scraped as he pushed the frame and craned his head out and down, raking the view. There was nothing to see: no human, no bird, nothing at all except an empty wash of sky and the pitted courtyard below. Somewhere a dog barked, and a door slammed. Leaves fell to earth from a skinny silver birch. He stood, panting into the cold, damp air, watching his steam dissipate and waiting for his breath to slow to normal. When it did, he rubbed a bony hand across the cavities of his great, dark eyes, and shut the window.

Returning to his bedroom, he stood at the mirror for a long time. Was he sick? Was he losing his grip? He looked the same as before: there was no sign of dementia or confusion in his face. But then, what did they look like?

He held out his hands: they were solid, strong, ready for work. He could stand up tall and straight. He remembered everything he had done so far that day, and he absolutely knew what day it was, what year, where he stood and what he should be doing. He grimaced at his reflection. What he should be doing, he acknowledged, was packing the car with props and going over to Sveta's.

There was nothing to be done: he must carry on as normal. He shrugged his shoulders, and pulled on his jerkin.

A MOTHY MOUTHFUL

Once Gor's little tea-chest car had been loaded up with his basic prop requirements, the short drive out to Sveta's presented no problems. He switched on the radio, enjoying the heavy thunk of the solid black buttons as he progressed through the stations, searching for something mellow, wordless and reassuring. He eventually fixed on Rachmaninov, the notes bubbling in his blood like oxygen as he navigated massive pot-holes and waved with a swift, jerking movement to the newspaper seller on the corner – a man whose name he did not know, but who was a staple of his day. Later he would stop and buy a paper, and exchange nods and worldly wise shakes of the head: this he knew. He passed through the main square, bustling and full of business, and saluted the traffic policeman keeping order at the crossroads. He crossed the metal bridge over the River Don and drove on towards the newer side of town, increasing his speed as the road, if not the tarmac, broadened. He eased around a couple of rights and a left, past encampments of kiosks and packs of shaggy, mud-encrusted dogs, and set about the artful business of hunting down the correct boulevard, corpus, building and flat number for Sveta.

Despite the Rachmaninov and the wide, sw[...] [...]
thoughts dwelt on his new assistant. He was no[...] [...]
do. Gor had not practised as a magician for a nu[...]
but his previous experience was relevant: he [...]
demeanour, and a fitting temperament; he could be [...] [...]us,
and instil belief. If required, he could take the audience with
him on a journey that could confound and perplex. In his own
estimation, he was a master, if very rusty. But this Sveta: could
she ever be an effective foil? If they were laughed off the stage
he would get no further bookings, and if they simply weren't
very good, well, the bookings would be unpaid. And that
would be bad news. Indeed, he nodded grimly to himself, the
pay was the whole point.

A cloud of steam hissed from a pipe by the roadside, and
Sveta evaporated from his thoughts, replaced by recollections
of the empty pan, and the steamy face. Had it been real, or a
hallucination? Were his nerves really that bad? Maybe neither
he nor Sveta belonged on the stage. Maybe he should forget
his plan. Would he really be able to confound and perplex and
command a paying audience, if he couldn't successfully boil an
egg? Did people these days even want magic? What with their
pop music, private enterprise and foreign holidays . . . He
rubbed his chin and nodded as her building came into view,
allowing himself a quick 'rum-pum-pum-pah' along with
Rachmaninov to raise his spirits.

When Sveta opened the door to Flat 8, Building 4, Corpus
6 on Turgenev Boulevard, Gor was taken aback to see that the
apartment behind her was entirely in darkness. She looked
dishevelled compared to previous weeks, her blonde hair puffy
and tufted around her hamster-like cheeks, and her make-up

,ed. They stood facing each other, him nodding good ,y and she seemingly frozen.

'Good—' Gor began and was immediately quelled with a 'sssh!' that rattled his bones. 'What is it, Sveta? Is something wrong?' he whispered, still standing in the doorway.

'Quietly, Gor! As I told you, my little girl is sick today. She must have absolute quiet. She is . . . she is a highly strung girl, and suffers, you understand?'

Gor thought he did not understand, and frowned. 'I have to get my things from the car. That will, I am sure, make a little noise, but I will be as careful—'

'Oh no! You must not bring the magical cabinet into the apartment! No, no, that would be too much! The noise and excitement! We must just rehearse, as if we had it with us. No equipment, thank you.'

'Make believe, Sveta? I am not convinced. Maybe we need to have a talk.' He raised his eyebrows. Still Sveta stood in the doorway, stepping uneasily from one swollen, slippered foot to the other, not inviting him in. The warm smell of the apartment rolled into his nostrils: furniture polish and something edible – gravy, perhaps.

He cleared his throat. 'May I?'

'Oh, of course, of course, come in, how silly of me!' She stood away from the door and flicked the light switch. A blowsy ceiling lamp trickled pinkish light along the narrow hallway. 'Please, take off your shoes! Here we are, some slippers – for men!' Sveta, her face beaming in a way that made Gor uncomfortable, handed him a pair of navy suede slippers with grubby woollen insides. He had the impression they had been waiting a long time for a suitable pair of feet, although they were not

10

particularly dusty, and gave no home to spiders. There was something about them that reminded him of the pleasure boats down on the river: abandoned.

She bade him sit on the bench by the telephone table to remove his shoes, and stood over him as he did so. She repeatedly glanced down the corridor to a room at the end, where a door lay ajar. He guessed the daughter must be occupying that wing, and must be suffering: her mama was clearly anxious. Perhaps he should have brought melon.

As he pulled on the second slipper he heard a flapping, followed by a whistle of wings through the air. He raised his head as an avian screech rang out, followed by what sounded like a series of muffled oaths, deep within the apartment. Sveta giggled, her fist pressed into her mouth, pushing down on her small, receding chin. She turned to him.

'That's Kopek, our parakeet. Albina loves him, and she's teaching him to talk. I think Albina has a special relationship with animals – an affinity, I think it's called,' she confided with an air of pride.

Gor raised an eyebrow, but said nothing. The bird had sounded as if it were in pain. The screeches continued, becoming louder and more insistent, and then interspersed with a series of thuds that made the light fittings rattle. Gor and Sveta looked at each other. The latter dropped her smile, sighed and pursed her lips.

'Just one moment,' she said, raising a lone index finger into his face before hurrying down the corridor and through the open door at the end, pulling it closed behind her.

'Be my guest,' he murmured to himself.

He turned to the bookcase as he waited, perusing the familiar

11

titles and shaking his head occasionally. Scratchy sibilants hissed from the door at the far end of the hall, followed by a storm of shushing. He hunched his shoulders into his ears as the unfortunate bird continued squawking. He dropped the book in his hand – *The Mother*, by Maxim Gorky – and leapt inches into the air when the mysterious door clattered open and a shrieking girl-cum-devil came dashing into the corridor. A round, pink face framed rolling marble eyes under ropes of hair, fixed into pigtails by two enormous shaggy pom-poms, which flew fiercely about her. She was laughing. Or crying. He wasn't sure. She was definitely running – towards him.

The shrieking noise the girl was making morphed into an extended 'ahhhh!' of terror as her foot caught in the edge of the runner and she started to tumble. In that moment, as she sought to regain her balance, she reminded Gor of a bear cub in a hunter's trap: her half-grown body out of her control, its constituent parts flailing around her haunches, the fore-paws and hind-paws huge and silly, but also full of menace. It was in the last moment before impact that Gor noticed she was carrying a small, brightly coloured bird in her right hand, its beak stretched in a soundless, endless squawk of terror. He raised his hands.

He heard the impact before he felt it. The air whistled from his lungs as he dropped backwards onto the bookcase, the girl felling him like a tree in the forest. For a moment he was in blackness as a mass of hair, smelling of gravy, furniture polish and pom-poms, claimed his face. He was aware of pain in his back and a tightness in his chest. There followed a second of absolute quiet, and then a roar as if a shell had struck the apartment. The girl began heaving sobs, coughing and spluttering

12

as she fought to right herself, all the time not letting go of the small, still bird in her hand.

'Kopeka! My Kopek-*chik*! He's deeeeaaaaaddddd!' The words erupted from her.

'Oh, *malysh*, shush now, collect yourself, and let's have a look at you.' Sveta huddled over her daughter, trying to heave her up from the tangle of rug and bookcase and Gor, yanking ineffectually at her arm. 'I've told you not to run in the house, haven't I?'

'He's deeeaaaaadddd! You made me kill him!'

'No no, I can see his eyes are gleaming – look! He's just stunned. Let's get you up and check on our poor guest. Are you injured?'

'I hate you!'

'Now, now baby-kins! Mummy didn't mean to make you fall over.'

'But you diiiiiidddddd!'

'I just want you to behave—'

'Ladies – I can't breathe,' Gor broke in as the discussion became heated. The girl crushing his chest glowered at her mother and snivelled at the limp bird cupped in her hands. They carried on arguing. A flutter of panic rose in his throat and his hands flew into the air.

'Help!' It was the only thing he was able to say.

Albina squinted into his face, sniffed behind her trembling hands for a moment and shifted her weight up and sideways.

As she did so, the bird made an utterance in a high-pitched, acid voice. Gor's eyebrows met his hairline and Sveta's jaw dropped. Albina grinned as she wiped her nose on her sleeve, and then gazed into the globe of her hands.

13

'He's alive! Oh, Mama!' She pulled the hapless Kopek close to her face to nuzzle his electric blue feathers.

'Oh! That's wonderful! I told you he was fine. But mind his beak, baby-kins. You know what happened last time,' cautioned Sveta. 'Now let's get you up—'

'Did that bird . . . I mean, did the bird just say—'

'I told you she had an affinity for animals,' beamed Sveta, pulling the girl up from the floor with one hand under each armpit, and then reaching out to Gor with a sunny smile.

'Gor, this is my daughter Albina. Albina, say hello to Mister Papasyan.' The girl regarded Gor sullenly. 'Albina is not well today, are you, munchkin?' continued Sveta, 'so she really needs to go and rest and be quiet in her room. But you wanted to meet Mummy's guest, didn't you, darling? Gor is a magician. And we are going to rehearse. You don't mind, do you?'

Albina said nothing, but looked along her lashes at Gor and chewed her lip. The bird made a guttural clucking noise.

'I'll put him away,' said Albina, raising her head with a smile, 'and then I can help you.'

The rehearsal that followed was, perhaps understandably, not up to scratch. Without props or a stage, and with both of them distracted by the day's events, neither was in a magical frame of mind. Instead, they discussed various possible programmes for shows and the range of illusions they could offer, where they might stand and how they might move their arms and legs about. The list of meagre bookings so far taken was reviewed amid worried sighs from Gor. Sveta suggested some murky-sounding venues in depressing nearby towns that might be persuaded to have them. When she began chattering about organising a variety spectacular of their own, Gor succumbed to a cough, drowning out her words.

He observed her misty eyes, and asked her what the profit margins would be.

'Well, er . . . I haven't got that far, yet.'

He nodded his head knowingly, and Albina sniggered behind her hand.

Indeed, the girl was a continual distraction to Sveta, as she refused to leave the room. In fact, she refused to leave Gor's side, and followed him around at the space of half a pace all afternoon; trailing him in the kitchen, huddling into him on the sofa, and even insisting on showing him into the bathroom when he enquired as to its whereabouts. Gor had taken a deep breath and bolted the door firmly as she waited for him in the hallway.

'What sort of costume will you be providing?'

He issued her with a puzzled frown.

'I must have a costume, must I not? Assistants must always be well presented – a sequinned bodice, I was thinking, with feathers at the shoulder, and a net skirt, with fishnet tights underneath. And a feathered tiara. It is traditional, is it not?' Sveta laughed deep in her throat as Gor harrumphed and looked away – directly into the probing gaze of Albina.

'Are you planning to use Kopek in your show, Mister Papasyan?' she asked, sliding her feet over and over the nylon covering of the couch and setting Gor's teeth on edge as she did so.

'Ah, no, Albina, I don't think that would be a good idea.'

'Magicians use rabbits though, don't they?' she asked, and then, 'Ouch, Mama, I caught my toe-nail.'

Gor shuddered as she picked at it. 'Yes, some do. But I have not used animals in my magical expositions, ever. I find, when we are confusing and confounding the human mind, that animals are neither necessary nor advantageous.'

'But they're cute. Kopek would be cute, in a top hat or with a wand or something. He could hold it in his beak. Go on, Mister Papasyan, you could use him.'

'No, no, Albina, really, it's not necessary.'

'Mama, tell Mister Papasyan he should use Kopek.'

'Well, Gor, it is a good idea, don't you think?' Sveta beamed at him and wound a finger through her brittle blonde hair. 'After all, people like animals—'

'No, Sveta, it is out of the question. That . . . bird, can play no part in my—'

'*Our!*' interjected Albina.

'*My* magic show. And that is final.'

Sveta drew in her lips and began to fiddle with the cuffs of her cardigan. Albina eyed Gor for a moment and let out a low chuckle.

'You thought Kopek was swearing, didn't you?'

'Yes, Albina, he was swearing.'

'No, you see, that's where you're wrong! He's a very clever bird. He was speaking Japanese.'

'Albina, really I think our guest—'

'Shut up Mama! Let me tell Mister Papasyan.' Albina stared at her mother as the latter avoided her gaze and dropped her eyes to her hands, which were now pulling on a scrap of fluff in her lap. 'Kopek was speaking Japanese! He's very keen on karate. So am I.'

'She is,' smiled Sveta, looking up at Gor and nodding.

16

'I'm a yellow belt. *Fu kyu* is a karate exercise.'

'It is!' Sveta smiled again. 'Albina learnt it at school.'

'So you have a dirty mind, Mister Papasyan,' said the girl, and she sent Gor a look from the curving corner of her eye. He could imagine her causing havoc in a hen-house.

'I don't know about that, Albina,' simpered Sveta.

'Are you a millionaire, Mister Papasyan?' the girl lisped eventually, 'because Mama says you can't be, but Mister Golubchik in the bakery says you owned a bank—'

'Albina!' shrieked her mother, 'we do not gossip here!'

'Ladies!' Gor began, his face closed, blank eyes on the floor. 'It has been an interesting afternoon, but I fear I must leave you. I don't think we will get an awful lot more done today.' He was determined not to be drawn into a foolish conversation about karate moves, his finances or anything else with a twelve-year-old, or whatever she was.

'Oh, but Gor, I can't let you leave just yet,' cried Sveta. 'Here we've been planning all afternoon, and I haven't offered you anything at all. Let me make you some tea and a little sandwich, before you go. I insist!'

When he thought about it, Gor had to agree that he was famished, especially as there had been no egg at lunchtime, so he gratefully allowed Sveta to trot into the kitchen to prepare a little something. He was relieved when Albina, after some minutes of further staring, stumbled out to help her mother. He took a turn of the room, briefly opening and then closing the purple curtains that shut out a view of the neighbouring block.

Sveta returned with a small tray on which stood a glass of tea, a rye-bread sandwich stuffed with cheese and parsley, and a painted oval dish of congealed boiled sweets.

17

'Here, Gor, please help yourself. Albina and I will eat later.'

The women sat on the sofa opposite his armchair and watched as he began his snack. The tea was perfect. 'Ahh!' A warming glow spread throughout his belly. 'This is wonderful, Sveta!'

'Thank you. It is Georgian. You can say what you like about the Georgians, but when it comes to tea, they know what they're doing.'

'Indeed! And stew, in fact,' agreed Gor. 'Georgian cuisine is most satisfying!' He bit into the sandwich, the coriander seeds on the crust adding a sweet lemony aroma to the sourness of the dark rye. He was suddenly ravenous, and chewed quickly.

'I don't know about that, to be honest. I don't eat out much. Home cooking does for us. We like cutlets and stewed cabbage – you can't go wrong with that.'

'Oh yes, nothing wrong with that. Cutlets are a fine food. I didn't mean to—' Gor took another bite of the sandwich and started to chew. It was at this point that he noticed something odd, and it slowed his mastication. He felt something that was neither cheese, nor parsley, nor bread. Something with a strange texture – a crunch, slightly papery, slightly hairy, and slightly mushy, all at the same time. His jaw stopped moving and his teeth rested together, the food un-swallowed. Some sense was preventing his tongue from pushing the bolus to the back of his throat for the next stage. He gagged, and looked down at the sandwich.

'Albina here likes *ukha* fish soup,' carried on Sveta.

'I like the heads,' the girl agreed.

Gor nudged the two leaves of rye bread apart to view the filling more closely.

'Oh yes, the fish heads, you do, don't you?'

'The eyes and brains are the tastiest bits,' smiled Albina.

He squinted, and frowned. There, squashed between the cheese and the parsley, lay the partial remains of a huge, hairy brown moth. Its wings were spread wide, and covered most of the area of the bread. Only half its mottled, brown body remained.

'They are full of vitamins, aren't they?' laughed Sveta, catching Gor's eye as he looked up, his face pale, his twisted mouth still full of chewed up cheese-moth-parsley. Albina was watching him closely, her face twitching.

'Is something wrong?' Sveta's face still curved with a smile, but her brow was creased with concern. Gor's great eyes watered as they swiftly searched the room for any opportunity to get rid of the unwelcome food. There was none: no napkins, no plant pots. And still the women stared. There was nothing else for it. He manoeuvred his tongue underneath the mothy mouthful and swallowed, with steely determination.

'No,' he squeaked when he was sure it was not coming back up, and he cleared his throat before taking a thankful gulp of the hot, sweet tea, 'Well, yes, actually. I must go.' He shuddered at the thought of the moth flushing into his stomach, struggled out of the chair and hurried from the room, placing the unwanted tray back in the darkened kitchen on his way out.

'Oh no, tell us what is wrong, please!' implored Sveta, a note of genuine concern in her voice.

Gor sat on the bench to turf off the navy slippers and shove on his own comfortable brown boots.

'I . . . well, I don't know Sveta, maybe it's all nonsense, but things keep . . . I don't know, it's just so strange . . . I must admit, I'm a little bit frightened.' He looked up into her face.

19

'But why?' Her hand was on his shoulder.

'There was a huge moth in my sandwich just now.'

'A moth? Oh . . . dear!' cried Sveta. 'But that's nothing to be scared of, Gor—'

'It's not the first odd thing, I assure you! There was the rabbit—'

'Oh yes, the rabbit was dreadful!'

'What rabbit?' cried Albina.

'And phone calls . . . at all hours of the day and night. Endless, silent phone calls! Knocks at the door too, when there's nobody there. And then this morning, an egg disappeared from the pan, as it was boiling—'

'Disappeared? Well, that's magic! That's . . . supernatural!'

'Yes! No! And that's not all. You won't believe me but . . . there was a face at the window – a face!'

'But you're on the fourth floor!' cried Sveta.

'Exactly!'

'Creepy!' chimed Albina.

'Yes,' agreed Gor. 'I find it quite . . . quite creepy, as you say.' He frowned.

'Who was it?'

'No one,' said Gor at last, the words pushed out through gritted teeth. 'There was no one there. I looked . . . there was just thin air.'

'We should look at the sandwich, Mama,' directed Albina, 'I think we should . . . be sure.' The girl trotted into the kitchen and returned moments later with the dishevelled plate held out in front of her at arm's length. The three looked down on the remains of the meal.

'But it was there. I saw it!' Gor's long, thin index finger

prodded into the bread, cheese and parsley, spreading out the food, probing for the winged intruder. There was nothing there.

'It was there!' His voice wavered as he looked into Sveta's reassuring blue eyes. 'What is happening to me? Do you think . . . I'm sick?'

She pursed her lips. 'How long has this been going on?'

'Two weeks, approximately. Since around the time we met, in fact.'

'Is that so?'

'Ooh Mama, what can that mean?'

'Shush, Albina. I think I can help you, Gor. I have a friend, well – an acquaintance. She may be able to assist in . . . resolving all this.'

'You have?' Gor asked, surprised and relieved. 'Is she a doctor, perhaps?'

'No,' said Sveta, 'much more useful. She is a psychic.'

'Ah,' said Gor quietly, and his eyes dropped to the floor.

'*Fu kyu!*' screeched Kopek from his perch in the kitchen.

TOLYA TALKS

The yellow ball of the sun hung like an egg yolk in the milky sky, spreading no warmth, exuding no glow – simply suspended. Anatoly Borisovich, or Tolya for short, swallowed a rich blob of saliva. Egg in milk, like his baba made on special mornings long ago, when he had been small and blond, able to charm the crows from the trees, the snails from the buckets. When he had been young. He whisked his thoughts, scrambling the sun-egg, hankering after – something edible, something nurturing, something good. He realised, with a grunt, that he was very hungry.

How many pairs of eyes along his corridor were resting on that sun, he wondered, how many of his fellow patients – is that what they were? – were still breathing, waiting for pancakes and milk, porridge and death. He knew there were other patients. He heard them sometimes. He hadn't been out of his room, couldn't remember how he'd got there or what lay beyond the door, but he knew there were others. He turned his head, bushy grey hair rustling on the pillow. The door was opening, the green of the newly painted corridor seeping into his room. A young, athletic-looking man entered and stood at the end of the bed, fidgeting, paper and pen held to his chest. The man appeared to be speaking to him. Was he real?

It was very odd, being spoken to. It hadn't happened for, well, quite a while. Anatoly Borisovich screwed up his eyes. Yes, the young man's mouth was definitely moving, the chiselled jaw jumping up and down, teeth winking. There were lots of words coming out, a jumble of sounds. He decided to listen, and did his best to tune in. He recognised the familiar crests and dips of the letter clusters, the sounds of syllables, but the words themselves seemed to be running into each other, racing, charging, leap-frogging even. He screwed up his nose.

The young man stopped. All was quiet. Anatoly Borisovich licked his lips, and his left eye twitched.

'So what do you think?' asked the young man. Anatoly Borisovich snuffled with satisfaction. He'd found the end of the ball of wool, the start and end of the phrase. Things were improving. 'Is that something you might be able to take part in?'

Anatoly Borisovich hesitated. He hadn't understood anything else the boy had said. And although he wanted to speak, he couldn't marshal his tongue: it flopped shyly about in his mouth and hid behind his gums. Eventually he managed a smile, crinkling up his eyes, and let out a small groan.

The young man spoke again, more slowly. 'It is very simple. You tell me about your dementia . . . well, I mean your forgetfulness, erm, your loss of memory and how it happened that you ended up in here, er, when was it . . .' Grey eyes danced across the notes. 'Thursday eighth of September? Almost a month ago. Anyway, I will analyse the information you give

23

me, make a diagnosis, and then find a way of reducing your confusion, and your fears. So that you are happier. And maybe, you know . . . you can go home, at some point. You had some kind of physical breakdown, didn't you? And a mental cataclysm of some sort? You were raving when you first came in?'

Anatoly Borisovich nodded and flexed his mouth, preparing to speak, but the boy, sensing a positive reception, was quick to go on.

'Your file is quite sparse, but potentially, I find you an interesting subject . . . and anything you can tell me will be useful. I'm a medical student, you see, and I'm in the middle of my gerontology module. You will be my case study.' The paper pad crinkled in his hands. 'I have to get it in by the end of October, so . . .' He looked into the old man's eyes. 'It's not just decrepitude, is it? There was something – dramatic?'

Anatoly Borisovich tried to speak, but the boy went on. 'You are willing to take part? Wait, turn your head to the light please?' The young man paused, and squinted. 'Actually, I want to ask you about those scars. Scars can be a very good place to start. I have learnt, you see, they cause trauma not just to the skin.' Anatoly Borisovich nodded, the corners of his mouth pressed downwards with the weight of his visitor's insight. The boy went on. 'Maybe I can ask questions, and you can answer either yes or no, if that is all you can manage?'

The boy finally stopped talking. Anatoly Borisovich gulped in air and pushed out some words.

'Your name? What is your name?' The sounds crawled across dry vocal cords.

'Vlad,' said the young man, passing him a beaker of stale water from the bedside cabinet.

24

'Vlad?' He sipped and coughed. 'What kind of a name is that?'

The young man smiled and fidgeted with his pen, but made no attempt to answer.

'I mean,' the old man took another sip of water, 'Is it short for Vladimir, or Vladislav, or what? I can't talk to you . . . if I don't know you.' He spoke slowly, waving his fingers in the air to underline the words. If Vlad had been blessed with an imagination, he might have likened Anatoly Borisovich to a wizard.

'Vladimir,' the young man replied with a smirk.

'Good.' Anatoly Borisovich heaved a great sigh. 'You want to hear my story? I have never told it. Can you picture that?' The young man was about to respond, so he went on swiftly, gathering pace. 'Truth be told, I'd forgotten it. It was lost somewhere, somewhere in the trees, for so many years. But it has been coming back, while I have been lying here, seeing no one, being no one.' His voice was almost inaudible, soft and dry like the whisper of grasses at the end of summer. 'I forgot my present, but remembered my past. Well, well . . . And since you ask, so nicely . . . I will tell you. But it's strange to hear words in my own voice! Imagine that!' His eyes lit up with dazed wonder: eyes that shone too brightly. 'Did you know what my voice sounded like? I'll bet you didn't. You're the first person to show any . . . interest. They feed me and wash me and prod me with sticks but . . . but no one talks, no one listens.' He pushed himself upright in the bed and bade Vlad shove another pillow behind his shoulders. 'What day is it?'

'Tuesday.'

25

'Expand?' Anatoly Borisovich crinkled his face at Vlad.

'Fourth of October. 1994.'

'Ah! Autumn already.' He took another drink, and smacked his lips. The voice got louder. 'They never ask me how I am, you know: they just look at that chart, and ask me if I need the toilet,' he carried on. 'They think I'm a piss pot!' He took childish delight in the word, chuckles hissing from his throat like air from an old tyre.

Vlad smiled and scratched his curly, chestnut head. Anatoly Borisovich noticed how the biceps quivered under the knit of his foreign-looking jumper.

'I will put that right. Would you like some tea, perhaps? I can get an orderly to bring you some?'

'Ah! Tea! Yes!' The old man's eyes shone, as if tea were a long-lost son.

A few minutes later, with the aid of some fragrant lubrication, the words tumbled briskly on his tongue.

'Thank you, thank you!' He stirred in a fistful of sugar cubes. 'Is that a pine tree out there? Beyond the fence?' He took a sip, and sucked in his cabbage-leaf cheeks. 'These eyes are worn out with looking. I have looked long and hard, at many things, in many places. But I can't make it out. It moves, you see: sometimes nearer, sometimes further away. One night it was at the window. I think it's a tree. It must be, mustn't it? If not a tree, well, I . . .' the old man stuttered and stopped, turning wide eyes to Vlad. 'There isn't a forest?'

Vlad straddled the visitor's chair by the old man's bedside, pen and paper dropping to the floor.

'No forest, Anatoly Borisovich. I don't know about trees: I am a medical man. It may be a pine.' He glanced out of the

26

window. 'I would say it is definitely a tree.' The old man smiled encouragingly. 'No forest, but lots of water. Because we're by the sea.'

'By the sea? Oh really?'

'Of course – just a few kilometres further west.' Vlad pointed into the grey. 'That way: the Azov Sea.'

'Ah! Yes! That rings a bell . . . maybe. Is Rostov far?'

'Not far. We're more or less half-way between Azov and Rostov. You are from Rostov, no?'

'No.' The old man nodded. 'Not Rostov.'

'Ah. Well, you seem to have found your voice, so talk, Anatoly Borisovich. Tell me what happened to you. The more you say, the more detailed my case study will be, and the more helpful to you. I've plenty of time: my shift has officially ended, so I'm free all afternoon, more or less. Do you remember being brought here?' He smiled, generous lips drawing back to show the clean faces of straight white teeth. The old man's eyes rested on them for a moment: they were sharp and huge and strong looking, like those of a horse. His tongue probed the stumps and pits in his own worn gums.

'No. Not at all.'

'Ah, well, maybe we can start a little further back?'

Anatoly Borisovich took a sip of tea, slurping joyously.

'Very good. I was born in Siberia—'

'Maybe not that far—'

'—a little village not far from Krasnoyarsk. You know Krasnoyarsk?' The old man waited, and fixed Vlad with a stare that demanded an answer.

He thought for a moment. 'Yes, of course – it has a hydro-electric dam. Wait, have you seen . . .' he fumbled in his pocket and drew out a large, crisp bank note folded neatly in half. 'See? It's on the back of the new ten thousand note. The dam.' He held it to the old man's face for a moment.

'Ten thousand rouble note? Are you a millionaire, Vlad?' Anatoly Borisovich was incredulous.

'Not yet, but I'm hoping!' He flashed a smile. 'But seriously, ten thousand roubles is nothing: about two US dollars. That's Yeltsin's inflation for you . . . we're all millionaires now!' Vlad winked as he re-folded the note and placed it carefully back in his pocket.

'Two dollars? Millionaires?' The old man's mouth flopped open and a furry, pale tongue poked out. 'But what would we want with US dollars, eh? We have our health and this Soviet Union, I mean, um . . . what's it called now?'

Vlad shrugged and bent to pick up his pen and paper. 'What indeed? But continue with your background. You were born in Siberia.' He leant forward on the chair, thrusting his chin towards the old man. 'Do you remember your childhood?'

'Oh yes, it was all to do with being a child. I remember, you know, out there in the forest, everyone had to work. In the forest, with the trees . . . hard work! Everyone had quotas. You had to fulfil your quota, or your pay was cut. It was piecework. My papa, he over-filled his quotas. All the time. He was a hero, you know! They put him on a flag – for a time. We never saw him.' The old man's eyes wandered as his mind strayed back to reach out to his papa.

'Freezing cold all the time, I should think? And what about the gulags, the political prisoners? Did you see them? It must have been the 1930s?'

Vlad's questioning seemed vulgar to the old man. He wanted

to think about his papa, and his baba, and the pine trees. He didn't want to think about the camps. He frowned.

'You may have thousands of roubles, Vlad, but you know little about people. Listen,' he coughed and sipped his tea, 'I was a child. I was happy. I didn't know about any camps. Comrade Stalin was our friend, our protector!' His eyes glowed. 'It was just a little village, a straggle of huts with pigs and chickens, hard workers, lazy drunks. It *was* cold, in winter. But Krasnoyarsk is in the south: we had a summer, oh yes . . . hot and humid and heaving with midges! Midges so bad they sent the cows mad . . . or so went the story. There were lots of stories.' He rubbed his eyes. 'Stories come out of the forest, you see . . . come out of the bark of the trees, to eat up your mind like an army of ants!' He stopped, grinning. 'Let me tell you a story.'

'Is it relevant?' Vlad answered meekly. He knew he should be drilling for facts, perhaps working through a structured Q and A about the weeks leading up to the old man's admission. He also knew Polly would be waiting for him after work. She'd probably have sex with him – joyous, sweaty, slippery sex – if she was in a good mood. Which she wouldn't be, if he was late. He checked the Tag-Heuer watch strapped to his wrist.

'You said you would listen, Vlad! Please listen!'

The old man wanted to ramble, to go way back. Maybe it would be good for a bit of practical analysis. Maybe, even, he could write it up as a 'talking cure'? It depended on what was said, of course, but . . . He had thought the old man would cough up some story about a fall, maybe TB, too much vodka or maybe some old war wound . . . But a spot of psychoanalysis might be worth a try. A story was a story. And to be honest, he had always loved a good story. Just not as much as sex.

'Yes, of course, go ahead, Anatoly Borisovich.'

'Once upon a time, in a forest far away, there lived a young lad: green eyes, impish smile, and cow-lick hair. A simple-clever lad called Tolya—'

'That's you?'

'You're sharp! A boy called Tolya, simple-clever, who lived with his granny, whom he called Baba, his dog called Lev, and his papa. Away in the East, where the bears prowl and the pine trees sway. Where the saws bite the trees day-in, day-out, and where little boys learn about life . . .'

Vlad rested the pen nib on the paper, ready to write.

Tolya wrapped his hands around the mug of broth waiting for the warmth to flow through his sore, grubby fingers into the bones of his hands. He was sitting in his corner on the wooden bench, swinging his feet under the table and leaning against the wall. The lamp was lit but his eyes strayed to the blackness beyond the window next to him and his breath steamed up the glass. Not seeing was worse than seeing. He put the mug on the table and wiped the steam with his sleeve. He peered into the hole he'd made and moved the lantern away, the better to make out what was outside.

For a handful of heartbeats there was nothing but darkness and the noise of the wind chasing through the sky and the trees. Then he saw something move near the well. He strained forward, feet nearly touching the floor as he pivoted. He watched the rectangle of black, holding his breath. Nothing materialised into a shape. He slowly breathed out and sat back down to slug the last mouthful of broth. It was good, salty and hot, and he felt cosy with the mug in his hands. He observed his own reflection in the bottom, all fat nose and tiny bug eyes. He chuckled: Tolya the monster, *RARRRRR*! King of the forest! He roared and nearly choked, coughing broth back into the mug and spluttering barley grain down his chin. He wiped his face on his sleeve. As he turned his head to do so, again he saw a movement in the corner of his eye, far off in the yard: a fluttering, maybe at ground level, maybe in the arms of the pine trees reaching out like giants when the wind blew. It had not been a figure, but a flicker. A flapping wing, perhaps. He shivered, and swung his legs under the table to keep himself brave.

'We are marching . . . we are marching . . . and we march to vic-tor-y!' he sang in a wobbly, high-pitched, keeping-his-spirits-up voice, determined to sit it out until Baba's return. He would keep watch, and not be scared. Although being scared was one of his favourite thrills. Just not *too* scared.

'Where's she got to, eh boy? Don't be scared: there's nothing to be scared of.' He addressed Lev the dog in comforting tones. Lev wasn't scared: Lev was never scared. He was stretched out under the table resting his bones, dreaming of rabbits. Tolya rubbed his ears. 'She'll be back in a moment. Or Papa. And he'll bring some sausage. I'm sure he will. And cheese. And maybe a drawing pad, like he said he would. Hmmm . . . We are marching, we are marching, and we march to—'

The singing ended in a squeak. A thump had rattled the window. He'd been lying belly-down on the bench, stroking the dog under the table, and had forgotten to keep a look out. Now he dared not look up, dared not move. There was something monstrous in the yard. His heart thudded. There it was again! A tapping on the window, faint but insistent, as if hard, icy fingers were reaching out, piercing the glass, and if he sat up . . .

'Lev . . . Lev!' His voice squeezed between taut vocal cords, his body stiff like washing left in the frost. 'Lev . . . come here, boy!' The dog looked up drowsily, puzzled by the child. He licked the empty hand proffered to him and flopped back down with a groan.

'Lev! listen! There's something outside. I can hear it. It wants to get in!' Still Tolya bent under the table, now pushing his head and shoulders down and tipping himself off the bench to the floor. He lay alongside the dog. 'It's coming for us . . . we must be brave . . . we must shut our eyes, and cross our fingers. That's the drill. The boys at school told me. Cousin told me. And we must ask Comrade Stalin—'

Tolya's head cracked the underside of the table as the door opened and cold air washed into the cottage. He cowered. Lev thumped his tail.

'Tolya!' A voice like a pistol shot. 'Come help me, son! I've got a lot to carry. Come on now, pet, help Baba!'

Lev heaved his tired bones from the floor and ambled towards the owner of the voice, tongue lolling as she cuffed his ear with a large, reddened hand.

'Lev, you old rascal, what do you want with me, eh? And what have you done with my grandson?'

'Baba, I'm here,' Tolya scrambled out from under the table, pulling hair and dirt from his baggy grey trousers as he did so. His hands shook. 'We heard a scary sound. It was the moth boy, fluttering in the trees. He tapped on the window! I was . . . I was petrified!' The boy looked up from his trousers and a single tear escaped each of his bright green eyes as he blinked.

Baba's hands stopped still on the dog's nose and she regarded the boy. 'You heard the moth boy, you say? And what did he sound like, eh? Like wind in the trees, or like me walking in the yard?' She raised an eyebrow and waited for Tolya to reply, but the boy avoided her gaze, and instead fiddled with the buttons on his jerkin, running his fingers over their smooth surface again and again. 'Did Lev hear the moth boy?'

Tolya shook his head. 'I don't think so, Baba.'

'You've been scaring yourself instead of doing your jobs. Hiding under the table with the dog – you should have been drawing water from the well, or clearing ash from the stove. You're a rascal, young Tolya, and Papa will have to be told!'

She put down her bag and handed him a solid brick of black bread. 'Food in our stomachs, son, that's what you need to worry about. The real – the here! You've scared yourself, and now no one will sleep.'

'But I'll sleep with you, Baba, and with Lev here, and I'll sleep well. No matter what the moth boy does.'

'Ha, maybe you'll sleep well with some food inside you, we'll see. But you mustn't get between me and my sleep, I've a lot to do tomorrow. Now, help me get the dinner ready. We won't wait for Papa, he's going to be late.'

'He's got a quota,' said Tolya in a serious, grown-up tone.

'He's got a quota,' echoed Baba, nodding her head.

The pair washed their hands in the bucket by the stove and began preparations for the evening meal.

'No sausage tonight, Baba?' Tolya searched through her bag.

'Ha! Sausage? No sausage tonight. I've forgotten what it looks like. They say things will get better but . . . but there, we will wait and see. I haven't forgotten the taste!'

33

'Ah, the glorious taste!'

'Pure heaven,' grinned Baba.

'Like eating sunshine,' said Tolya.

'You know, we could always try making sausage out of Lev. What do you reckon?' Baba's worn cheeks glowed red as she chuckled.

'Baba! That's not funny!'

'No,' she agreed wryly, after a short pause, 'it's not. You're my sunshine, boy. You are my joy. Don't ever change.' She hugged him close, bread knife in hand, and breathed in the familiar, warm smell of his hair, his neck, his young life.

They set about their tasks, and swapped stories of the day's events.

'Did you draw me anything today, young Tolya, eh?'

'No, Baba. I need a new piece of chalk. That one's all worn away, I can't hold onto it.'

'Akh, again? Well, we'll see what I can do. Maybe up at the school house we'll be able to beg a piece of chalk. We'll keep trying. I love your pictures. You've got a gift there, son. Much good it'll do you.'

The well bucket clanked as the wind whipped out of the trees and across the yard. The boy dropped his spoon. 'So, Tolya,' said Baba slowly, 'now you've told me about school, what's this talk of the moth boy? Where's this coming from? Old stories, boy . . . not good Communism.' She observed him from the corner of her eye as she began to cut the black loaf into slices. Tolya stirred the buckwheat porridge with an inexpert hand.

'We were talking after school, Baba. Pavlik has seen him. And Gosha. He came to their windows, in the night. He was tapping for the candles. And cousin Go—'

'He should know better!' Baba tutted, and shook her head.

'It's true though! He said the moth boy wants to get into their houses, to get near the light, and lay eggs in their ears. They've all seen him! All of them! He waits at the windows! Maybe he wants to eat them! Suck out their brains—'

'Enough! On with your jobs!' Baba scowled over the bread. 'Those boys with their stories! I'm going to have a word with that cousin of yours!'

Tolya pretended to get on with his jobs, but his eyes strayed back to the window. In his head, he could really see moth boy: his moon-washed face, pale as the northern summer night, pale as milk, luminous as ice; his huge eyes, round, bulbous, staring from his shrunken skull like twin planets, empty and dead; his stomach, round and furry, grossly blown up and dissected into two pieces – thorax and abdomen, both parts moving and throbbing; worst of all, his wings, fluttering, green and brown and blue, vibrating, shimmering, huge and furry: inhuman. He could see him flitting amongst the trees, shivering, diving, a puff of moth-dust from his vibrating wings, projecting himself, aching to cross from the trees into the village, from the dark to the light, fluttering over chimneys and into window frames, knocking on the panes, reaching out with limbs that were withered and ice-cold, frond-like . . . were they wing-tips, or antennae?

'Is that done?'

He sucked in air with a jolt. The spoon in his hand was hovering over the pan, not stirring but making useless round movements in the air. The porridge looked stodgy, and was drying at the edges.

'Yes, it's done, Baba.' He nodded and smiled, and carefully

scooped a good serving into each of their bowls, adding a peck of salt as he went.

'Eat well, Tolya. We have a *Subbotnik* tomorrow: you will need your strength for the voluntary work.'

'Another *Subbotnik*! But Baba, it's Saturday! I want to play, and help Papa in the yard, and teach Lev how to march!'

Baba gave Tolya a tired look, and sighed into her lumpy porridge. 'Tolya, that's the point of a *Subbotnik*. We do good works on our day off. Well, we who have no choice do. And everyone reaps the benefit. It is our duty.'

'But that's not fair!' The boy's bottom lip started to tremble.

'Life's not fair, Tolya, life's not fair. Now eat your porridge, and grow big and strong. Then you can tell them what to do with their *Subbotnik*.' She laughed, the sound gravelly and low. Tolya cuddled up closer to her, sharing her warmth, and chewed on his black bread and buckwheat, determined to grow big and strong.

Later that night, as they lay side-by-side in the big wooden bed in the corner of the room, Tolya listened to his baba's breathing. Steady, big breaths whistled in and out of her chest, making the quilt rise and fall, rustling slightly. She was warm and solid, like a living stove. He knew she wasn't asleep.

'Tell me a story, Baba.'

'Get to sleep, boy – it's late. Too late for stories.' She turned onto her side towards him, plumping up the straw pillow with her shoulder, and tucking down her head so that her nose and mouth were under the covers.

'Tell me the moth boy story, Baba.'

'Akh, I wish I'd never opened my mouth. Moth boy . . . what nonsense! There is no story. It's just a myth; tittle-tattle.

36

I've never seen him . . .' Baba's voice trailed off and she yawned, 'And it was all so long ago.'

'Not that long ago, Baba. Not like when you were a girl.'

'Ha!' She chuckled and opened her eyes. 'No, not that long ago . . . yes, when I was a girl . . . that was another century! There were no radios, no mobile cinemas, no electricity, not anywhere – and no one could read! No one like us, I mean. There were no communes, no soviet councils . . .'

'But that was before moth boy?' prompted Tolya.

'Akh, moth boy. No, moth boy's not that old – although, if he's a spirit then . . . he's as old as water, as old as the stars. Maybe the shaman knows, eh? You know the local people believe, don't you? And who's to say they're wrong.'

'What did you see, Baba?'

'Nothing. It was a dream . . . a story. The story got into my dream. Some words people were saying.' She began to doze off.

'But what about the story?' He pressed his elbow into her chest.

'A boy ran away to the forest; a strange boy. He wanted to be a shaman, that's why he went. He hid in the trees, shaking the leaves . . . but the moonlight slid into him, through the cracks round his eyes.' Tolya felt around his own eyes with soft fingers, looking for cracks. 'It shone in his brain, you see. And once it got into him, he couldn't come back, no matter how cold and lonely he was. He was moonstruck; a lunatic, half boy . . . and half moth. He taps at the windows, but he can't come back.' Baba's voice was becoming thick with sleep.

'I've heard him, Baba!' Tolya rocked his blond head into Baba's shoulder to rouse her. 'He's real.'

'Oh, my boy! Real, not real: what's the difference, eh?' She smiled and patted his hair with a heavy hand as her eyes fell shut. 'Nothing lasts forever, except stories.'

'But we believe in him, don't we Baba?'

'Go to sleep. We believe what we want to. And what we believe must be real, mustn't it?' Tolya nodded. 'Maybe you'll be a scientist when you're grown up, and you can tell me if spirits are real or not.'

'I will, Baba. I'll be a scientist. Then we'll know.'

'Good. But now it's time to sleep. Papa will be home soon, and he'll be angry if we're awake.'

Tolya closed his eyes and pressed his nose into the pillow, nestling into the warmth of his babushka, and imagining how his laboratory might look, when he was grown and big and strong. He would get to work in a flying machine, and eat only sausages and sweets.

'Next time you see moth boy, Baba, you know what to do?' She did not reply, but he carried on talking, looking down into his own hands. 'Just close both your eyes, and cross both your fingers, and say to yourself, as loudly as you can, "Comrade Stalin, protect me!" and all will be well. That's what the boys said. All will be well. Just believe. That's what they told me.'

Baba grunted and stroked his head. The warmth of the bed spread through his limbs and over his mind as he fell into the velvet nest of sleep. A sleep so deep, he heard nothing, sensed nothing. Not even the lonely sound on the windowpane.

tap-tap-tap

The old man's head snapped up.

'You see, Vlad, moth boy is as old as the wind, the water. The story . . . I didn't make it up! Ask anyone!' He rubbed his eyes with a sticky, squelching sound. 'They go to the flame, they get too close and – fssssst!'

Vlad stared at the old man, puzzled, and then turned his eyes to the fine grey mist rising from the mud flats beyond the window. He blew out his cheeks.

'We didn't really get very far, did we, Anatoly Borisovich?'

'I was too young . . . too young to know the half of it! I thought Comrade Stalin would protect me! What did I know?'

Vlad glanced at his watch.

'Indeed. Anatoly Borisovich, I'm sorry, I have to go.' It was gone four o'clock. He licked his lips at the thought of Polly. 'I am sorry to leave at such an interesting moment.'

'Interesting?' Anatoly Borisovich yawned. He felt warm inside. He hadn't talked at such length for a long, long time, and had forgotten how energising it was to converse with another person, instead of muttering to himself. He also felt extremely tired.

'I'll come again, maybe later in the week? Perhaps then we can get to the research part? What you've told me is fascinating, thank you, but I can't use it. It doesn't help me understand what has been troubling you recently, you see, and what caused your collapse, and your memory loss. That is the point of my research.'

'Research?' repeated the old man absently. 'Collapse?' He frowned. 'Oh yes.' He cleared his throat. 'You couldn't see your way to bringing me a little morsel to eat next time, could you? We don't get much that is sweet here, Vlad, and I do find talking exhausting. Do you like a bit of cake, yourself?'

'Cake?' Vlad looked hurt. 'I don't eat cake. I'm an athlete – or at least, I was.'

39

'Oh really? That's a story!'

'Not really.'

The old man's eyes rested on Vlad's arms as the muscles flexed under his sweater, then travelled to his legs, slim in their close-fitting jeans.

'I'll see what I can do to find you something sweet. And hopefully next time we can make some progress on how you got those scars. It will help us make sense of what is . . . going on now.' Vlad was shuffling his papers and jangling his keys.

The old man reached a wrinkled hand up to his cheek to feel the marks with dry fingers.

'I loved my baba. It wasn't my fault, you know, what happened to her.'

A STUDY IN BISECTION

Gor drove home through the autumn mist, back across the bridge, past the newspaper stand, past the busy, bustling square, past the kiosks and the lights, hurrying for a little peace. On arrival, he bolted the door behind him, put on the safety catch, and cleaned his teeth, twice. The second time, he used rock salt and oil of menthol, slicing through the film of moth that clung to his canines. He flossed with a piece of white cotton, and examined his mouth in the bathroom mirror, grinning back at himself with a mirthless growl.

A visit to a psychic: he couldn't believe he had agreed to it. But Sveta had been keen to help, and what was more, her concern had seemed genuine. He hadn't expected it. When they first met, two weeks before, he had not found her a promising prospect. She had been hesitant and largely displeased, full of sighs and fussy questions: not the best properties of a magical assistant. Their second rehearsal had been little better. But today she had smiled, laughed even, and turned into a real person. A real person who served up giant, hairy moths in her sandwiches. Gor shuddered. Was he losing his mind? Had the moth even been real? No one else had seen it. He ran his tongue around his teeth as he sat in his armchair, the cats twisting around his ankles, mewing.

But the rabbit – there were witnesses to that. It had been very real, and very disturbing. A rabbit and a moth: there must be some logic to this. He leant down to tickle Pericles' chin and thought back to his first encounter with Sveta, searching his mind for clues, trying to remember everything, exactly as it had happened. It had been warm and sunny in the morning, with a fine rain setting in at lunchtime. The headlines on the radio were of the rouble plummeting against the dollar, savings disappearing, huge rallies in oil stocks, the threat of war in Chechnya. And in his own apartment, he had been invaded by a woman who had answered his advert – fluttering on a lamp post in the leaf-strewn street – the day it had been put up. She had come in, fully unprepared, and fussed.

'Mister Papasyan—'

'Call me Gor.'

'As you wish. Mister—'

'*Gor*, please,' he repeated politely but firmly. He was hunched away from her, grunting slightly with the effort of doing up the box clasps. She chewed on her red bottom lip, and then remembered her lipstick.

'All right. Gor . . .' Her voice trailed off.

She had forgotten what she was going to say. She strained her neck to observe the outline of his shoulder-blades through the old, thin cotton of his shirt, listening to him grunt, and wondered if he suffered from asthma. Her own chest felt tight with a sudden edge of panic. She breathed out noisily and tried to relax.

42

'It would make what we have to do this afternoon much easier if you could just call me Gor. And breathe in.'

'I see.' She breathed in again, trying to make herself smaller, but resenting the implication of his words. She was not a large woman, although equally, not birch-like. Who needed twig women? What good were they? And who was he to tell her to breathe in? He had her at a disadvantage, and she wondered for the tenth time if this afternoon had been a mistake. All she could do was close her eyes, patient and saint-like, as he huffed and puffed.

'And I will call you Sveta, if that is permissible to you?'

'Oh yes, very good.' Her voice fluttered and she did not open her eyes.

'There, that all seems correct.' He made a vague 'rum-pum-pum' sound in his cheeks and stood up tall, towering over her. 'Where were we?' He scratched his head, the silver hair ruffling as his fingers played a trill against his skull. He appeared more fuddled than she had expected.

She pursed her lips, unknowingly pushing her red lipstick further along the crevices that radiated from her mouth, out into the soft, doughy pallor of her face. Suddenly, she brightened.

'You ask me to wiggle my toes?' she asked hopefully, arching one heavy brown eyebrow.

'No, not yet. It's far too soon for that. We have a little way to go. Just . . .' He positioned her hand higher, pulling on her fingers, and paused to observe the effect. 'How do you feel?'

'Um, fairly . . . normal. Not magical, at the moment, I have to say.'

He turned away tutting to himself, hands on hips, shaking his head.

43

'Is something wrong?'

He did not reply, but turned slowly this way and that, scanning the room.

'Gor?'

'The saw . . .' his voice came from between tight lips.

He turned back towards her and his eyes, large as the moon and dark as night, rolled slowly from one side of their sockets to the other, and back again. She felt a sweat break out on the palms of her hands and a fluttering in her stomach: he really was a fright to look at. 'The saw, Mister . . . er, Gor?'

Gor spun away. He was annoyed with himself and what he considered the rather slow-witted woman before him. He took in the windowpanes, the rain behind them threatening to dissolve the sky and the land and bring everything to a smudgy, dripping halt. He took in his living room, bathed in the brown, honest glow of the books and sheet music that lined its walls, exuding a scent of permanence. He took in his baby-grand piano, dark and shiny as polished jet, perfectly tuned to be played at any moment. He took in the fluffy white cat reclining over its lid, one claw-prickled paw raised as if to strike at the polished perfection of the wood. And there, in the middle of it all, he took in the corpulent middle-aged woman, in a box.

He sighed, and removed his eyes from her: she upset him. The lipstick was too sticky, the hair too blonde, her understanding of magic zero and . . . and the rasping sighs that plumed and flowed from her like lava would have singed his tired nerves at the best of times. This afternoon was definitely not the best of times, despite the comforting rain. And now he couldn't find the bloody saw!

'It's on the table, by the door,' said Sveta quietly. He started at the words, coughed and refocused his eyes. They came to rest on the small table by the door. He shook his head.

'Ah, I see, madam, I see. My eyes are . . . tired.' He crossed to collect it, hips and ankles clicking as he went. He examined the blade in the puny light of the lamp.

'Yes. The saw: good! We'd better move on, before I forget something else. Do you feel . . . stable?'

She considered briefly, and nodded carefully. Gor did not respond. He was stroking his chin and staring through her. She swallowed.

It wasn't that his face was old: no, any face can make you wonder how it once belonged to a baby. But this – it was a face that was so mournful, so haggard and frayed, with such huge eyes, it could make a priest cry. Sveta shuddered, and the box rattled softly. On top of the piano, the white cat lay in abandonment, upside-down, and eyed her with mild interest.

'Svetlana Mikhailovna, hold fast. All will be well. I have to pause to think . . . I am an old man – you may have noticed. We take our time, in all things.' As he spoke, he waved a large, thin hand in the air, and then let it flap down again, the gesture both artistic and defeated. He did not smile. In fact, he looked exceedingly morose. 'Strange, you may think, as time is against us, but there it is.'

Again Sveta pursed her lips, and tried not to look at Gor or the cat, which now seemed to be winking at her with its sapphire eyes.

'I am holding fast. *You* may have noticed – I have no choice.' She eyed the window and the rain swirling against the murky sky. The light was fading, and it made her anxious: she had a hair appointment at six. 'Do please hurry.'

45

The old man stood beside her, the top of his head not far from the ceiling above.

'You may feel some vibration, I fear. But there should be no more than that. It is a long time since I have attempted this action, so I have had the saw cleaned and sharpened. There will be no rust. My last assistant, God rest her soul, was quite against rust. She had an allergy.' Gor shrugged.

Sveta offered him a tight-lipped smile. 'I am not against vibration.' Her chin rose. 'And I have no known allergies.'

He nodded, and rolled up his sleeves. 'When we attempt this action on the stage, of course, you will not be balanced in the box between two chairs. I will have my whole magical cabinet at my disposal. It is just our misfortune we cannot use it today.'

'That's a relief. But why can't we use the cabinet today? I think I would feel a lot more "in character" if I were in a magical cabinet rather than balanced on two chairs. It was a lot of fuss getting into this box. And it seems quite unprofessional, to me.'

Sveta did not feel in character, or professional, or magical, at all. In truth, she did not know what the character of a magician's assistant should be, but she was fairly certain that it should be more glamorous than this. What was the point in her lipstick and her impending hair appointment if she were just to be packaged up in a musty apartment in the suburbs, laughed at by cats and repeatedly observed by an off-putting old man with a face like death? She chewed her lip.

'Since you ask so directly . . . we cannot use the cabinet, dear Sveta, because Dasha, my queen cat, had a litter of kittens in it, and they cannot be moved for a few days yet. She would tear you to pieces if you tried. She is a very . . . protective mother.'

Sveta felt the blood drain from her face.

'How unhygienic!'

'It was a safe place for her, I suppose. I don't worry about these things. We have bigger things to worry about, you and I.' He flicked a switch and the room was bathed in an acid lemon light. 'That's better! Now I can see!' He engaged the saw into the metal groove at the centre of the box and Sveta gritted her teeth. The light reflected off the blade and stabbed at her eyes as the saw's angle sharpened, and it made her angry, like a blow to the head.

'You're not . . .' she couldn't get her words out.

Gor began with a few experimental swipes of the blade. It made a noise like hell. She persisted.

'. . . you aren't seriously expecting me—'

Metal on metal rang out across the apartment; sharp and piercing. She gulped in air.

'. . . to engage in magical expositions . . . in a cabinet . . .'

The saw twanged and Gor muttered under his breath.

'. . . in which a cat has had kittens?' Sveta shouted, voice yodelling with the effort. The sawing stopped.

'Oh yes, Sveta. I expect that: most definitely,' he said softly. He examined his handiwork and the blade, and added, 'But do not fret. I will sweep it out, and administer some disinfectant. All will be well.'

Sveta's eyes bulged. He took up the saw and again worked its blade forwards and backwards, beads of sweat gathering on his forehead. It screeched and sang into Sveta's ears.

This was not what she had envisaged when she answered

47

the advert on the lamp post. There was no glamour here, only vibration and screeching, dark eyes and cats: on and on it went. She began to feel ill, stomach clenching, like that time she had rashly decided to take the ferry across the Kerch Straits to Crimea shortly after lunching on a basket of cherries and a litre of *kvas*. So long ago . . . She began to pant.

'Be still, Sveta. Don't wriggle.'

'Oh, but . . . the noise! The vibrations . . . they are going . . . straight through my . . .' Sveta's face turned pale olive.

'Sveta?' He ceased sawing. 'Is everything . . . ?' She groaned and waved her hands weakly in the holes at the side of the box. 'No, not hands at the moment, Sveta, move your feet: it's your feet everyone will be interested in.'

She groaned and made vague twitching movements with her big toes.

'Yes, that's it! Waggle away! Keep it going. Is everything else . . . normal?' His tone suggested concern, but his face remained unchanged, intent on the saw.

'Ugh . . . yes – no . . . I don't know!' She gritted her teeth and smiled, her expression manic. 'Am I cut in half yet? That's the main thing!' Colour, of a sort, was returning to her cheeks.

'Erm, more or less. You require quite a good deal of sawing.'

She did not know whether this was a compliment or not. 'I see.'

'I think that will suffice for the moment.' He drew out his handkerchief with a slightly trembling hand and mopped his brow.

'Oh! That's all? But you haven't drawn the two halves apart.'

'No. To be frank, I don't think we have sufficient stability to draw the two halves apart. And, again to be frank, I am not sure I have the strength. It's been a long time since . . . Well, would you be distraught if, on this occasion, we just assume that you have been bisected? After all, there is no audience here to please, apart from Pericles.'

Gor reached up a hand to fondle the cat and it puffed into his palm, a translucent globule of spit rolling from its open jaw onto the parquet below in an expression of feline ecstasy. Sveta shuddered.

She was disappointed by the whole experience, and felt an odd urge to cry. She had been cut in half, and it had been most unpleasant, but he couldn't even be bothered to draw the two halves apart! This mysterious magician, this person about whom she had heard so much gossip and legend, was turning out to be a disappointment. His apartment was clogged with books and cats and pianos, his demeanour was morose, and as for the rumours of wealth and fortune and gold in the cistern: well, frayed shirt collars and darned trousers told their own story. She found no evidence of treasure, of any sort.

'Very well, Mister Papasyan,' she said in clipped tones. 'If that is it for today, could you release me? I really have to be going – I have other appointments.' The old man nodded and bent to undo the clasps, stopping short as a sharp rap rang out on the apartment door.

'What now?'

'It was the door,' Sveta explained, still in clipped tones.

'Yes, I know, I—' Gor began, but thought better of completing the sentence. The woman seemed displeased. 'Bear with me, Sveta. I should see who it is. I won't be a moment.'

'But—' she rattled slightly in her box, and then, as it rocked on the chairs beneath it, realised stillness was the better option. Gor patted down his hair and headed for the front door.

He thrust an eye to the spy hole before opening up, and saw no one. But it had definitely been a knock, and definitely his door. He stepped back, released the safety chain and pulled the door open. The empty hallway lay before him, dark and silent. He peered left and right, sniffed the air, scratched his head and shrugged. There was no one. He was about to shut the door when a scrap of something on the floor caught his eye, and he looked down. There, on his doorstep, lay a huddle of brilliant white and damson red. He touched the object with his foot, stirring it slightly to better make out what it was. His breath caught and, ignoring the disgruntled rattling coming from the living room, he bent to his haunches for a closer look. Eventually, he realised: before him lay the body of a white rabbit, an oozing straggle of tendons marking the place where its head had once been.

A door slammed along the corridor and he shot to his feet, trying to make out who was there. Had it been the door to the staircase? He squinted into the gloom, but saw no one. He held his breath as he listened to the stillness: the patter of rain on the windows, occasional notes from his neighbour's TV. The headless rabbit made no sound. Gor gazed down on it and rubbed his chin.

'Help!'

Sveta's cry forced him back to movement.

'One moment!' he called, and stooped to gather the limp body from the doorstep, noting that it was still softly warm. Its nose must have been wiffling up until about an hour before.

Taking one last glance down the corridor, he turned and shut the apartment door.

He made for the living room with quick steps as the cause of Sveta's discomfort became clear. She was twisting and turning her head, writhing this way and that as best she could, trying to escape the attentions of Pericles. The naughty cat was seated on top of the box, clinging on with the sharpest claws of one paw and fishing for the whites of her eyes with the other. As she twisted, the box rattled and tipped, working itself towards the edge of the chairs. Gor swore under his breath and dashed across the room.

'Pericles! Away, sir!' He took a threatening stride towards the cat and brandished the body of the rabbit like a rolled-up newspaper. The cat dodged the blow and sprang from the box, arcing through the air to land with a thump in the doorway before retiring from the room with an indignant flick of his fluffy white tail.

Gor stood panting as he observed Sveta with a deep grimness: she was still in the box, and the box was still balanced on the chairs. But now she had a trail of sticky rabbit blood stretching from ear to lipsticked mouth, and her eyes, round and wet and shivering, were fixed on the contents of his right hand. There was a moment of silence.

'My dear Svetlana Mikhailovna—' he began in his business baritone. It was interrupted by a high-pitched shriek.

'Let me out of here! Let me out!'

'Yes.' He concurred, and placed the rabbit corpse in the nearest suitable receptacle – a fruit bowl on the sideboard – before approaching the box. 'I am sorry about this, Sveta. This is most peculiar.'

Her response was a mixture of words and sounds and water-iness, unintelligible and upsetting. Gor undid the clasps with tacky fingers and lifted the lid, offering Sveta his hand so that she could climb out safely. She stared at his bloody fingers, tutted and turned away, instead making her own route out of the box, backing out, behind first, wobbling, sniffing and shaking her head.

'You may want to, er, freshen . . . your appearance, Sveta. I am sorry . . . this is most unfortunate. Please, follow me – the bathroom is this way.'

She nodded and he led her to the hall, pointing out the way to the bathroom with a gentle, blood-stained hand. Sveta locked the door behind her. He heard her shriek as she looked in the mirror, but her snuffles and cries were soon masked by the knocking of the pipes as water ran in the sink. He washed his own hands in the kitchen, rolling them over and over in the stream of cold water and the froth of the soap.

Back in the living room, he sat on the piano stool, shoulders hunched, and observed the small, furry corpse in the fruit bowl. It was a domestic rabbit: someone had owned this little creature, most likely as a pet, not for food or fur. The rain beat on the windows and thunder rumbled in the distance. He observed the rabbit, and wondered why it was not wet. There was a movement in the hall.

'Do your cats always knock on the door when they bring you a trophy?' Sveta asked. She already had on her coat and scarf. Gor couldn't blame her. She eyed the fruit bowl with curiosity and disgust. 'You're not going to eat that, are you?'

'What? No! Sveta, really, what sort of man do you think I am?'

'Well, I'm not at all sure. You hear all sorts of things.' She pulled a face. 'Each to their own, I suppose. It's been . . . well, anyway, I must be going.' She tightened her headscarf, and added, 'But where's its head?'

'That is the oddest thing. I have no idea! My cats do not go out: they are far too valuable. So the perpetrator of this act was not my cat. I really don't know why this creature was on my doorstep. Or who saw fit to alert me to it. Or how it met its end. Or where its head might be.'

'It's a mystery,' said Sveta, pulling white faux gloves over hands that shook very slightly, and still eyeing the rabbit.

'Yes. But not one that I find attractive. In fact, there have been a few things lately—'

'Honestly, in other circumstances I would willingly stay and chat, but I have to go,' she broke in. 'I have a hair appointment.'

'Oh yes, of course. Well, thank you for your help today. I think it went well, all things considered.' He coughed and paused, but she did not respond. He would have to try harder. While she was far from perfect, he needed an assistant, and with bookings starting to come in for the new year, he needed one now, to get things in order. She would have to be charmed. 'I hope you are, um, uninjured, by your experiences? I am sorry about the rabbit and the, er, consequences – I was trying to prevent Pericles from doing something he'd regret.'

Sveta's mouth twisted, and she nodded, but again said nothing.

'We have the whole of the autumn to rehearse, and I was very impressed by your . . . by your . . . determination, today.' He struggled to find kind words. 'So, if you are willing, I think we can be ready for the new year.' He spoke slowly. 'I think we can become a convincing magical act, if we rehearse. What do you say?'

She looked into the shadowed pools of his eyes, eyes that were so full of sadness, eyes that were asking her a question: could she, would she? He needed her, that was clear. She hesitated, and pursed her lips.

'Very well.'

He smiled, the skin stretching over his cheekbones and making him look even more like a corpse.

'Although I have to say, I won't stand for any more funny business. And next time, I really insist – no chairs, and no cats!'

'Yes, Sveta, very well. I think next Tuesday afternoon, at around four p.m., if you can spare the time, would give us a golden opportunity to perfect your . . . your fine performance under the saw? And I will try to make sure that the magical cabinet is ready for you by then. On reflection, I agree – we would be more "in character", as you say, with the cabinet in use, and with the cats quartered in the kitchen, perhaps.'

Sveta suppressed a shudder at the thought of the kitten-infested cabinet, but said nothing. Instead, she opened her mouth as if to yawn, and ran her finger and thumb across the corners of her mouth – a movement originally designed to remove excess lipstick, but now a nervous habit. 'I look forward to it,' she said when she'd finished, her hamster-like face embellished with a smile.

After one more shriek and tussle as she spied Pericles perched on her hugely bulky brown handbag, she was gone, leaving only a vague impression of lily-of-the-valley and mothballs. Gor took a seat in his old armchair, stroked the worn leather of its familiar arms, and stared at the body of the rabbit. He would have to dispose of it somehow – but the rubbish chute did not seem fitting, and anyhow, it was blocked again. He'd better take it to the *dacha* and give it a proper burial in the soft, brown earth of his rambling vegetable patch. It would have to be tomorrow, though. Night was falling, dropping with the rain out of the lowering sky.

Usually, damp weather made Gor feel content. But not today. The drumming on the windows was making him uneasy, making it impossible for him to hear anything else. Still the rabbit lay in the fruit bowl, the cats circling on the floor below, tails raised like shark fins, their eyes disappearing as their faces creased into silent mews of desire. The rabbit would have to go now, he realised. He pulled himself out of the chair and headed for the kitchen, intent on finding some paper to wrap the body. Lightning flashed across the sky as he moved and he counted for the thunder clap: one-Yaroslavl, two-Yaroslavl, three-: a boom shook the apartment block. Only two kilometres away. It was odd to have a thunderstorm in the autumn: there had been no real heat today.

He gathered up the body and wrapped it in the brown paper, tying up the package with an abundance of string found in a kitchen drawer. He then placed it in the long-empty freezer compartment, so that it was out of the way of the marauding cats, and safe from the effects of decomposition.

Back in the living room Gor shut the old yellow curtains and pulled out the piano stool. He cracked each knuckle in turn, placed his fingers over the keys, closed his eyes and began a finger race up and down the notes. Today was no day for music – his quarry was the scales: every scale, every key, major, minor, arpeggios, contra-motion, two-three-four octaves.

These were sets of notes that could only be one way. They held no surprises, and were beautiful in their perfection. He played until his fingers ached and his heart pounded. He played until he forgot about the rabbit, and the thunder, and the woman with the wobbly cheeks and the lipstick. He even forgot about the mewling kittens in the cabinet. His fingers burned and his hands began to shake as each scale and its every variation was practised, and mastered. He didn't hear his downstairs neighbour knocking with a broom on his ceiling in disgust: for this was what baby-grand pianos were for.

He didn't even hear the phone ringing, trilling on and on as the thunder crashed. Ringing with persistence. Ringing to be heard. Ringing as if somebody was desperate: desperate he should know they were there.

A SHIVER IN THE TREES

The steaming tea was placed at his elbow just as before, but this time Vlad had brought a small parcel tucked under his arm. The old man's teeth chattered with anticipation as he pulled away the brown paper. Within, there lay a nest of honey-brown buns, fragrant with ginger and cloves. They shone in the cold glow of the strip-light.

'*Pryaniki!*' Anatoly Borisovich clapped his hands. 'How I love *pryaniki*! So very kind of you, Vlad! May I?' Without waiting he took a bun from the top of the pile and stuffed it into his mouth, lips stretching around the splitting shards of icing. His eyes closed in rapture.

'My landlady makes them,' said Vlad, unable to look away, revolted and fascinated by the bun-induced ecstasy as pastry crumbs writhed in the old man's mouth. 'She bakes every night, for no one. I don't eat them.' He patted a hand on his lean stomach and smiled, shrugging. 'So they're always going spare.' Vlad was determined to be business-like this time. They would get to the salient points quickly: this was research, with a purpose; he was a professional, and he needed only facts.

'She takes good care of you?' the old man grunted, 'this landlady?'

Facts, facts, facts. Don't get distracted, thought Vlad. 'She washes and irons very well,' he said. 'And there is always good food. She's lovely, really, but I don't get much privacy. I can't have my girlfriend round, for example. Anyway—'

'And your family?'

'Family?'

Anatoly Borisovich's eyes slid from the second bun, which he was now pushing into his mouth, to Vlad's grey eyes. 'Family,' he repeated with difficulty.

'Oh.' Vlad shrugged. 'In the country, forty kilometres or so from here. Mother, sister: I see them on holidays. We're not close. They're not like me.'

'No?'

Vlad perched on the visitor's chair, heels bouncing against the worn lino of the floor, impatient to start. He ran an eye over his subject. He looked better today: there was less puffiness about his face, his eyes twinkled and the knobbled toes that poked from beneath the bedclothes were pink. It was a turn-around. Maybe having someone to talk to was doing him good? You could never tell with the elderly: that was one reason Vlad found them increasingly fascinating. He hadn't imagined he would find gerontology interesting: his focus at the start of medical school had been purely the physical – the body, how it worked, how to make it stronger, how it collapsed. But the more he studied, and the more patients he met, the more absorbing he found their thoughts, their backgrounds, the sum of their lives. He hadn't quite got the gist of how it all worked yet, but he was fascinated by the idea that he could influence those thoughts, to promote a change, and achieve a goal, through stimulation. Facts, facts, facts, thought Vlad, fiddling with his pen.

'They're farmers. They live on a collective, in the middle of nowhere. We've been apart a long time.'

'How's that?'

He definitely had a good appetite: a third bun was now disappearing within his cheeks.

'I went to residential school: sport and science. Up in Rostov. I haven't lived at the farm for ten years or more. I've been lucky.'

'Sent away to school? How fascinating! And now you're going to be a doctor, because you must help your fellow citizens!'

'Well, I suppose . . . I was going to go for physics, but the girls in the medicine queue were much prettier.'

Anatoly Borisovich smiled as he chewed, and nodded. Surely the boy was joking?

'But enough about me,' said Vlad, 'we're here to talk about you.'

The old man was eyeing a fourth iced bun when a loud, low howl resounded in his belly. A steady diet of soft brown boiled things had left his digestion ill-prepared for food that was rich or easily identifiable.

'Drink your tea, Anatoly Borisovich,' directed Vlad with a smile as the old man clutched at his side and winced. 'It will help them go down. There is no need to hurry. The *pryaniki* have no legs, they will not run away.'

'That is good advice, thank you. Are you sure you won't have one?'

'No.'

'No sweet things for athletes, eh?'

'I'm no longer an athlete.'

'Why not?'

'Injury.'

'Ah, a pity!' Anatoly Borisovich tried a different tack. 'If oral delights don't interest you, what does?'

A steady green stare captured Vlad's eyes and all other details of the old man's face, including the smear of crumbs and the lattice of scars, melted away.

Vlad coughed. 'Well, you know: sport, cars, girls. Money.'

'That all sounds very . . . And how old are you, if you don't mind so bold a question?'

'Twenty-two.'

'You're not married?'

'Married?' Vlad's curls shivered as he laughed through his nose. 'No. Like I said, I have a girl, she's really . . . I really . . . Her name is Polly. She's beautiful. And she loves me. But marriage is not a priority.'

'So what is, tell me?'

'Well, you know: a car, an apartment, textbooks, travel. And I want to buy shares, get into investment, but I lack capital . . .'

'How romantic. And the arts, Vlad?'

'The arts?'

'What makes your heart soar? What makes you shiver with delight? What fills you with angels' breath? A painting, a piece of music, a modern ballet perhaps, you're an athlete, after all—'

Vlad thought for a moment. 'BMW.'

'BM-what?'

He snorted with a smile. 'It's a make of car. Big engines, broad.' His hands shaped the car in the air. 'Leather seats; German engineering.'

'German? I see.' Anatoly Borisovich nodded and turned his gaze to the lone pine on the horizon. 'Drawing is my particular love. I find it deeply calming. I can lose myself for days . . . I spent my life in illustration. They gave me a beautiful watch when I retired – a *Poljot*, the Soviet Union's best. I believe it's in here.' He turned to open the drawer of the bedside cabinet but it jarred, the cabinet rocking on its feet as he tugged.

'Don't worry, Anatoly Borisovich, show me another time. We really should—'

'I keep asking them for crayons and paper, Vlad. I know it would do me good. *You* know it would do me good. But they shrug and tell me maybe tomorrow . . . I need to get my thoughts straight. I am hoping to be discharged, you see, before the frosts set in. I might go south – the Caucasus, maybe, or further. Somewhere warm – Angola . . .'

'Angola?' Vlad stifled a laugh and glanced at his watch. 'That's as maybe. But Matron won't refer you to the doctors for sign-out until she's had "consistently good reports", will she? Like at school, you remember? And at the moment your reports are not consistently good. So, that's what we must work towards.'

'Oh yes, I remember our little school. That's lovely to remember! I received a rosette. Baba pinned it to the wall. She was very proud. And so was I. It was for drawing.'

'Good. So, perhaps if you are ready . . . You were telling me on Tuesday, back in Siberia, you lived with your baba, that is, your grandmother . . . ?' Vlad referred to his notes lying in scratchy blue lines across the notepad and read as the old man began humming.

'You were telling me about the thing that made you afraid.

61

The boys at school told you to close your eyes and cross your fingers if you heard the moth boy at the window? Remember?'

'Baba?' the old man burped quietly. 'Oh, I know what happened to Baba! I remember! It wasn't my fault! It wasn't me! Don't blame me!' His voice rose to a shriek and the feet under the covers began to kick.

'I'm not! My dear Anatoly Borisovich, don't get agitated! I'm sorry. I was just trying to move us along. I'll say no more. Just let the words flow. As you want to tell it.'

The old man slurped from his cup, but said nothing.

'Your grandmother told you that she'd seen something, or dreamt something . . . she talked of the shaman, and a boy going out into the forest . . .'

'The moth boy and the moon!' Anatoly Borisovich leant forward, coughing with the effort and scattering *pryaniki* crumbs over the bed. He wagged a short, fat finger in Vlad's face, so close it grazed his nose. 'It wasn't just talk, it wasn't a *story*. There was a creature – in the woods.'

'Did you see it? What did it look like?' The joints of the chair cracked like frosted wire as Vlad leant forward, and his pen wobbled the words *'imagination, or hallucination – childhood psychosis?'* on his notepad. He forgot about drilling for facts. 'Go ahead! Talk!'

Tolya's favourite chore was sweeping the yard. Baba stood at the doorway watching him as he stumbled around, twig broom in hand, running after the blackened, soggy leaves, chuckling to himself as the wind threw them in the air around his head. He tried to catch them, as if they were butterflies and the broom a net, scattering gravel and laughter as he went. Lev followed at a slower pace, flicking his tail this way and that and occasionally mouthing a low woof. Baba clucked her tongue and left them to it.

The leaves danced around Tolya's head and he dropped the broom, arms outstretched, pink fingers curling into the air, feeling the swell of the breeze pushing out of the pine forest across his corner of the earth. The world felt mysterious. How many thousands of kilometres had the wind come, and where was it going? What was it carrying, this rush of air: whose voices, animal or human? What smells were being swept around the pine trunks, over the streams and rocks, across the bed of brown needles and stumpy cones that covered the forest floor? Lev raised his head and sniffed the air, blind to all but the visions brought to him by his black, wet nose. Tolya did the same.

'What is it, boy? A bear? A wolf? A wood spirit?' Tolya crowned the dog with a handful of mashed leaves. 'You and me, we are hunters.' He imagined jumping over the fence into the trees, leaping from the branches onto that fragrant carpet of needles and tumbling into the wooded gloom, deeper into the forest, where the only sound was you and the crunch of twigs beneath your feet. He would hunt down the smells, the voices, the history. He would hunt down the shaman. He would track him to his hut hidden in the gloom and tell him about Stalin. No need for magic now, comrade shaman. We, you and me, we are Communism! We have the new magic, in Stalin's word. It will cure our ills, and keep us safe. Your forest belongs to us all now. Tolya gripped the top of the gate and stared out into the trees, looking for movement.

'Come on, Tolya!' cried Baba from the porch, 'there's work

63

to be done. Where's your broom, eh? Forgotten on the ground, and Lev is going to chew it up – watch out!'

Tolya knew damage to the broom would be punished and jumped down from the gate to retrieve it. The trees sighed and waved. He was lucky he had trees to look at, and not some neighbour's house. Take Comrade Goloshov, for example: if his house was opposite Comrade Goloshov's, all he would see would be an old man with a red nose sitting by the window all winter and on his porch all summer. And his house smelled funny, like the inside of Lev's ears.

He looked down the track towards the village. Smoke straggled from every crooked chimney. Chernovolets was little more than one road lined with wooden houses on each side, all higgledy-piggledy, not a straight line between them. To Tolya, it seemed a busy, people-filled place – after all, there was a school, and a shop, and a village hall, his auntie and uncle – even a doctor. The houses were ancient: indeed, not one was under fifty years old. The climate moulded the dwellings: the wooden walls and floors gradually bowed and buckled and sank in on themselves, producing façades as individual as the faces of the tenants. This was his village: four thousand kilometres east of Moscow, and home to five hundred and eighty-nine people, various chickens, some dogs, cats, rats, a few pigs, a riot of boys and girls, and a bucketful of stories and myths. Baba called his name. He leant the broom on the fence and joined her at the well.

'When will Papa be back?' he asked as they drew the water up.

'Late. He's busy.' The words came out like whacks of an axe as she puffed. When they'd finished with the water she

64

added, 'Comrade Stalin needs more paper, to print more information, and for that the paper mill needs more trees, and for that Papa needs to work more, to make sure the trees are ready and the paper gets made. Otherwise he gets in trouble. It's all in the plan, and we don't want any trouble.'

'Baba, will I work in the forest when I'm grown up? Is that in the plan?'

She laughed and wiped finger trails on her apron. 'Well, Tolya, I don't know. Maybe.' Kind eyes crinkled under a frown.

'That's good. I like trees.'

'Boy, it's hard work. You've seen Papa when he gets home: he can hardly walk. You won't have much time to like trees if you work in the forest. You'll be cutting them up.'

'But it's good work, Baba?'

'It's work. But you . . . you're different, Tolya. You're not like your papa. With your drawing and your writing, and all that . . .'

'But I could do it!'

'I'm sure, I'm sure, my treasure,' she said, smiling at him suddenly, the cracks in her face deepening. 'But we'll see. They're moving people out here to help with the work. Outsiders, from Moscow, and out that way.'

'Really? I've not seen any, Baba.' Tolya was intrigued by the idea of outsiders: what did they look like? What did they smell like? What language did they speak? Would their children go to his school?

'They don't live in the villages. They are kept to themselves: they have their own camps.'

'Our teacher told us about Pioneer camps, where children go for holidays if they've been very good. Are they like that?'

'Something like that, son, something like that . . .' Baba turned away and headed off back to the cottage, shaking her head. Tolya patted Lev on his soft, brown neck and tugged at his ears.

'Hard work, Lev-*chik*, hard work is required! We will work hard, and Comrade Stalin will be pleased, and say thank you to us! We will make him proud. That's what Papa does, and that's what we will do.' He looked around the yard with a critical eye. 'Where's the broom? There are leaves in the yard, and we must get them all! Every one! Not one leaf will be left!' He grabbed the broom and darted around the yard, chasing down the leaves and pushing them into the black wooden bucket.

Dusk quilted the trees, blurring their outlines as Tolya waddled about, pretending the leaves were goats and he was herding them. Baba had lit a lamp and it glowed orange in the window, but still Tolya stayed out. He was bending down, talking to himself and stuffing handfuls of leaves into the bucket, when a crackling sound, close by in the trees, made him stop. Something heavy had moved. Between his legs, looking back towards the house, he could see Lev. The dog was no longer snuffling around the feed bin. Instead he stood rock still, ears clamped to his skull and tail tucked between his legs. He was staring past Tolya into the trees. The wind disappeared, and for a moment all there was in the world was silence, and the thud of his own heartbeat.

A snap shot into the air and the blood surged in Tolya's veins. He swallowed and dropped the two fistfuls of leaves to the sodden earth. Lev churned out a growl. The wind blew a flapping sound into Tolya's ears: like sheets on a line, or maybe wings.

With eyes squeezed shut he drew himself upright, fingers crossed like the boys had said. He began to pray to Stalin for help. Before he'd got a word out, Lev's bark ricocheted off the trees, snapping Tolya's eyes back open. He stared into the gloom, groping in the darkness, dreading to see, but unable to turn away. At any moment, he knew, moth boy, with the throbbing, hairy thorax and wavering antennae, would reach out for him. For a moment he saw nothing but leaves and clouds and shadows. Then, among the lower branches of the nearest pine, something stirred.

Floating in the darkness there was a face, sharp and pale, with black-ringed eyes that glowed like fireflies. A human face? Maybe . . . he could make out two arms, perhaps, or were they wings? They flapped against the figure's sides as it hovered in the under-growth. Tolya raised his chin. He should be brave. He should protect Baba. He was about to speak when he saw the figure was not looking at him at all: its eyes reflected the lamp, in the house. It was looking past him. It might not even have seen him. He took a step backwards, then another, and felt the wall of the well behind his heel. The creature did not react. He couldn't go backwards all the way to the house. But if he turned and ran, it might give chase, swooping onto his neck with talons sharp as knives. What if it caught him, or worse, followed him in? He creased his eyes towards the cottage, face taut. The thing in the woods began flapping again, and a gurgle spewed from its mouth, somewhere between laughter and choking.

'What are you?' Tolya called out, his voice small and fright-ened against the wind.

It did not reply, but hunched down, almost hidden in the shadows.

'You can't hide! I've seen you! And . . . and I have a fierce dog! Baba will be out any minute. She knows about the old ways, and she won't be scared! She'll give you a good hiding!'

There was no reply. Tolya could see nothing, but Lev knew more, and a growl shuddered through him. A twig snapped not three metres from Tolya. He turned and fled, dashing on ship-wrecked legs back to the house as a tempest of barking filled his ears.

'Baba, Baba, there's something in the trees!' He burst through the door. 'A spirit! Moth boy! He's flapping in the trees – I saw him!'

She was busy, knife in hand, a pile of bloody bones resting on the table in front of her. 'What are you on about, boy? I've bones to boil, and you're shrieking about spirits?' A pot was already bubbling on the stove. 'And look at this kindling – it won't split itself!' Baba jabbed her knife towards the stack of wood in the corner. 'You and your stories—'

'Really Baba, I really, really saw it! Look: Lev is still out there, he won't come in! He's growling at it. It's in the trees! Look!'

He grabbed Baba's arm and tugged her towards the window. She pulled away from his grip.

'I see nothing, boy. Get the dog in. If he gets in the forest we won't see him for a week.'

'But he won't come, Baba!' cried Tolya, desperate. 'Please!'

'Akh!' she spat, and grabbed up the lantern from the window-sill. Together they hurried out into the yard. 'Lev! Come!' shouted Baba, but the dog was at the gate, intent on the trees, still growling, ears back and dagger teeth shining. Baba made towards him with swift strides but stopped short at the well, head cocked to one side, sniffing the air.

'It's there, Baba!' Tolya pointed into the darkness, where the eyes had glowed and the arm-wings had flapped. She said nothing, but held the lantern higher. Still Lev snarled, front paws coming off the ground in fierce jerks.

'Show yourself!' she bit out at last. 'We know you're there.'

Nothing stirred but the wind and the leaves.

'No harm will come to you, that I promise. We are good folk.'

Tolya looked up at her, questions bubbling to his lips.

'Hush!' she commanded.

Lev growled, then split the dusk with a volley of barks.

In the darkness below the pines, a greyness rose, shaking the air like a mirage. A wretched, flapping, scarecrow figure emerged, cloaked in rags; an apparition as thin as paper, filmy like the skin on a pond. Baba eyed it carefully, frowning and squinting, and clicked her tongue, muttering under her breath.

'Come closer, come here in the light – slowly, mind!'

The figure flickered, taking form out of the green and grey, solidifying from apparition to . . .

'You're no spirit. There's no magic at work here,' she said to Tolya, and then more loudly. 'You're no moth, are you? Who are you?'

The apparition moved closer, and in the soft light of the lantern, Tolya could see it was, in fact, just a boy. Older than him, taller, maybe sixteen or seventeen, but thin and strange. The boy stood still a while, then slowly raised his hands and flapped them in front of his face, in and out, in and out. Yellow-white teeth like standing stones split his mouth in a strange grin.

'Hey!' shouted Baba, and the flapping stopped. He shivered,

round eyes standing out from skin as pale as milk, as pale as the moon. He reached out a hand, emaciated and ground with dirt, as if to touch the rays from the lantern in Baba's hand. 'Come closer!' she said. 'Come see! We won't hurt you.'

The boy shuffled through the long brown grass until he stood at the fence on the edge of the yard. Again the hand reached out to the lantern, and this time gently tap-tap-tapped on the glass.

'Baba!' whispered Tolya, eyes round.

'Who are you?' asked Baba.

'Yuri,' answered the boy, his voice coming slowly to his lips, stilted and hoarse, pushed out on a sigh.

'Where are you from, Yuri?'

The boy said nothing, and simply pointed over his shoulder in the direction of the forest.

'Where are your people?'

The boy shrugged and stared at the lamp.

'Are you hungry?'

He reached out slowly with the same emaciated hand, and nodded. His gaze hadn't left the lamp, but Tolya saw his eyes were never still, flickering across-across-across as he looked into the light.

'Is warm, your house?' Yuri asked suddenly, smiling his strange toothy grin as his eyes oscillated in their sockets.

Lev sniffed at the boy's calves, jaws hanging open, but made no sound.

'It's warm. And you are welcome.'

'No, Baba! He scares me!' Tolya pulled on her arm, but she flicked him off with an angry glance.

'Quiet, Tolya! Come, we'll have some broth, and you can

warm yourself by the stove, Yuri.' Baba's eyes were watchful, and she peered in every direction as she strode back towards the cottage. Over the yard a silver moon rose, bright as a frozen sun, bathing the boys in its cold, blue light – one flapping, and one creeping behind.

The forest sighed, and wood smoke rose to meet the heavens.

'Anatoly Borisovich!'

A jolt thumped through his chest. Strong hands clamped his shoulders and his head snapped back and forth.

'Wha—? Who— oh!' The shaking stopped. Green eyes stared into grey.

'Did I fall asleep?' Wings were flapping in his mind, shifting memories like leaves in the wind.

'Yes,' said Vlad, releasing his grip and easing himself back into the visitor's chair. 'I thought maybe . . . Well, you gave me a fright. You stopped talking and made a choking sound, like you couldn't breathe. Like you were . . .'

'Sleep, Vlad. There's nothing to fear in sleep. It brings relief. You'll learn that, as you get older.'

Vlad snorted and slowly smoothed the blankets across the old man's bed.

'Maybe so. But I'm glad it was just a . . . nap.'

'I must sleep more. But I feel we made progress, don't you?'

'Well . . .' Vlad pushed the chair onto its two back legs and regarded the old man with a small smile. 'I can't really see it, myself. Hearing about your childhood in Siberia is very interesting, and I can see that just talking, just reliving things, is making you feel better. There's colour in those cheeks, Anatoly Borisovich!' The old man returned his smile with a grin. 'But

71

I need to know about your breakdown in September, and I'm still interested in those scars, for my case study. I have to write a report on you – for my medical degree, and for your best interests.' He leant close to the old man's face, seeking his eyes. 'And my report can't really be about your babushka and Lev, and this moth boy, can it? Do you understand?'

'Ah.' Anatoly Borisovich's hand floated up to his face and his fingers felt into the relief of his cheek, following the crevices and smooth patches: the map of his past. 'But it's all related . . . you need to understand . . . family . . .'

As the old man spoke, the kindly orderly appeared in the doorway.

'You're wanted,' she said to Vlad with a coquettish grin, 'in the office. It's your girl again, and I think she's in a temper!'

'*Blin*,' said Vlad, looking at his watch. He lurched from the visitor's chair, its feet squealing sharply across the floor. 'I'm going to be late.'

'Tsk! Even with your fancy imported watch?' She shook her head with a laugh and walked away up the corridor.

Anatoly Borisovich pulled a face as he closed his eyes. 'Your girl is cross. That won't do.'

'I think it's all the stress! I thought a date would be different, but she's . . .' Vlad sighed, grabbing up his pens and paper.

'Anywhere nice?'

'Palace of Youth.'

The old man grunted. 'You'd better go then!' His shoulders shook momentarily with silent laughter. 'But come back,' he gurgled eventually, 'as soon as you can, and I will tell you all: everything you want to hear! We will get your case study complete!'

He sank back on the pillows, feeling as if he had been sweeping the yard all day, catching the leaves above his head and breaking the ice on the well with his knuckles; exhilarated, and exhausted.

'Very well. But listen, please.' Vlad's voice was hurried. 'I will bring more *pryaniki* next time, or a cake perhaps?' Anatoly Borisovich opened an eye. 'Cake? You like cake? OK, so next time there will be cake, and you will get to the point, and answer some questions, and we will both be happy.' He turned for the door, and then looked back. 'You've spent almost the entire session talking about leaves and trees today, Anatoly Borisovich, and it won't do: they're not what caused your breakdown, are they? I need to know about *you*. I'll be back when I can.' The door slammed.

The blinds were still up. In the distance, Anatoly Borisovich could make out the lone tree beyond the fence shifting in the wind, its branches outstretched, shivering.

A knock at the door accompanied the scrape of its opening.

'Do you need the toilet?'

It was the grumpy orderly.

'No, thank you. But I would like some paper and crayons.'

'Matron said no: said it might excite you.' The orderly stomped towards him and held out a small steel cup filled with a viscous green liquid. 'Drink this, and settle down. You shouldn't get excited. That Vladimir shouldn't be exciting you. He's only a student.'

'Maybe so. But talking . . . is much better medicine than this.' He took the cup and swirled its contents. She drew down the blinds with a clang.

'Come on, drink up! I've got others to be seeing to,' she snapped, returning to stand over him, hands on hips.

Anatoly Borisovich held his nose, gave the orderly a wink and gulped down the medicine. 'I drank it all.' He grinned. 'Do I get a prize?'

'There's no need to snatch,' he whispered, after she had slammed out of the room.

THE PALACE OF YOUTH

'My dear Gor!'

'Good afternoon, Sveta.'

'I am sorry to disturb you.' She didn't sound sorry. Her voice was warm and husky, like fresh rye bread.

'That is quite all right.' Gor frowned at the receiver.

'But I wanted to know how you were.'

'How I am? I am quite well.'

'No ill effects at all? From the moth, the other night, I mean?'

Gor considered for a moment, and ran his tongue around his very clean teeth.

'None,' he said firmly. 'All residue was swept away when I returned home. I have had no problems with my stomach, or anything else. All is well.'

'That is good. I have to say, Albina insists it was nothing to do with her.'

'Of course.'

'And I believe her.'

'Of course. We must all believe her. She is a child.'

'Yes. So . . . I was curious. Well, not curious. I was worried . . . has anything else happened to you, since Tuesday?'

'Since Tuesday?'

'Since, since the moth incident.'

'Of course, the usual has continued.'

'The usual?'

'The phone ringing out in the night. Generally around midnight, sometimes earlier, sometimes later.'

'Do you answer it?' Her voice was quick.

'Occasionally. I don't know why.'

'And?'

'Nothing. No one.'

'How odd. Anything else? Any other foodstuffs disappeared?'

'Thankfully, no.' He paused. 'But I got a letter.'

'A letter?'

'A letter.'

'Who from? What did it say?'

'I did not read it.' Gor did not want to discuss the letter, shoved into his mailbox down in the foyer. How had it been delivered? Not by the postal service, that was clear enough. Someone had got in through the locked front door, delivered their message, and left. The dusty pot plants and the shiny brown floor tiles could tell him nothing. Baba Burnikova, nodding behind the desk, could also tell him nothing, apart from that a hand-delivered letter could not have come without her knowing. The empty courtyard, glistening with last night's rain and a thousand snail trails, could tell him nothing. He had opened the letter there in the foyer, leaning against the solid mass of the radiator, warming the backs of his thighs as he read. His name and flat number had been written in a childish hand, no doubt to disguise the writer. Inside it contained six words in an ugly scrawl.

'You didn't read it? But it could have given us clues, Gor! It might have been a spirit letter!'

'Too late, I'm afraid. It has gone down the chute.'

'Oh dear!'

'This is no criminal investigation, Sveta. It's just some no-good hooliganism.'

'Well, you were upset, no doubt. My news is good though – I have telephoned my contact.'

'What contact?'

'The psychic lady. Remember, I told you about her on Tuesday?'

Gor closed his eyes and swallowed before he spoke.

'And?'

'She can do it a week today.'

'Ah.'

'Is that too long? I'm afraid she is all booked up until then. Something to do with Greco-Roman wrestling at the Elderly Club. I couldn't really tell: she can be a little vague on the telephone.'

'No, no, that is very good. Next Friday it is. I do hope you haven't gone to a lot of trouble on my account, Sveta, I'm really not—'

'No trouble! I want to help. And Madame Zoya can certainly help us divine what, exactly, is going on here. She has a marvellous gift.'

'Quite.'

There was a pause.

'You sound low. Like you need cheering up.'

'I am quite cheery.'

He grimaced into the mirror by the telephone table, baring

77

his teeth in an attempt at a smile. It looked more like a snarl. He could almost scare himself with those eyes and teeth.

'Come to the theatre with us!' Sveta's voice bounced off his eardrum. For a moment he was speechless.

'Wh . . . what?'

'I just . . . well . . . you seem sad, Gor, and lonely, and well, Albina is in a dance show, with lots of girls and boys from school, and she asked specifically if you could come, and I thought, well, why not? It will be fun! And there's a craft show going on in the foyer at the same time. And pensioners get in for free.' Her voice crumbled to quiet as she reached the end of the sentence. A long pause followed.

'Hello?' whispered Sveta.

'That is kind of you, Sveta, to think of me.'

'It's the least I can do, after giving you such a scare with that nasty sandwich. You'll come?'

'Very well: I shall be pleased to escort you both to the show. What day, and at what time?'

'Ah, hurrah! Albina will be so pleased! It is actually tonight, at seven thirty p.m., at the Palace of Youth.'

'Tonight?'

'Yes!'

'At the Palace of Youth?'

'You know where it is? Just past the circus, and then the bus station, but before you get to the brick factory. It's opposite Bookshop No. 3.'

'No. 3? Where they sell stationery and records?'

'That's the one.' Sveta took a breath. 'You're not busy, no?'

Gor looked at the cats, the piles of music, his lunch tray still lying beside his armchair.

'No, I'm not busy. But I can't promise to be good company.'

'Your presence is company enough! We shall not burden you with conversation if it's not welcome, dear Gor! Albina will be so pleased. She is not so confident in dance, and it will be nice for her to have the extra support!'

Gor nodded and said his goodbyes and, looking up in the hallway mirror, noticed the vague shadow of a smile playing across his face. The calendar on the wall behind him winked. The smile faded, his face became set, and he stalked off to the bedroom, avoiding gambolling kittens as best he could, to select a clean shirt for the evening.

He didn't feel like driving, so took a trolleybus as far as the centre of town, and then walked.

Long strides brought him quickly from the central crossroads to the wide boulevard named after Mayakovsky, where milk-bars and furniture shops turned wide, hungry eyes on trudging shoppers and workers. He averted his gaze from the windows and the price tags. He hurried on, away from town, heading past the circus, which shone like paste jewellery half-way up the hill. Round, almost majestic, its curved concrete walls were bathed in jagged, multi-coloured reflections thrown by the glass of its windows. It looked like a space-age Colosseum with a giant Frisbee for a roof. Gor took in its curves and its perma-nence as he hurried on. He had heard that, years before, circuses had been travelling affairs, housed in huge tents borne by troupes of gypsies from town to town. They entertained the masses, taking stories and characters from place to place, ferti-lising minds and more with ideas and characters picked up and scattered across the continent from the Baltic to the Sea of

Okhotsk. For generations, travelling circuses had roamed like this, tossing ideas like seeds on the wind. But Stalin didn't like it. The travelling circus meant danger. He ordered permanent circuses to take their place in all major towns, staffed by troupes trained in state circus schools. So circuses were tamed: tethered in one place, telling one, state story, and doing one show . . . the one that Stalin liked. They were cleansed of magic and mystery, and made safe for the masses. No more tents and ideas blowing in the wind; no more transience. The circus was castrated, to become a harmless eunuch, no danger to anyone.

Gor had no love of the circus. He could not abide a white-faced clown or a leering, drug-addled lion. It was all fake, all manufactured, with a predictability that bored him rigid.

He snorted as he passed the queue snaking out of the door. He shook his head and tutted, but despite himself, remembered a night more than twenty years before, when he'd been there, to this very building, and laughed. How he'd laughed. Not at the miserable animals and their antics, nor at the lackey clowns, but at his own daughter as she sat beside him, her face a delight as each act had unfolded. Such a young life: such a happy child. He had loved the circus that night, because she had loved it; little Olga. A smiling face in the queue caught his eye and he glowered, turning away sharply. He huddled his shoulders further into his coat, and quickened his steps. The circus was rot.

He came to a halt outside what he surmised was the Palace of Youth. It was not a place he had been before. Great columns rose from the crumbling wash of the pavement to hold a canopy of dark grey concrete above windows that shone with a fizzing orange glow on Azov's youth. An abundance of small girls with buns and huge pom-poms flocked in and out of the lights in front of the building, their anxious mamas in tow, blocking the doorway and holding up the traffic as they alighted from buses and communal taxis. They were a myriad fluff-encrusted fledgling birds, shrieking and dashing, peppering words with pi-pi-pi noises as they came and went through the warped double-doors. Gor stood very still, towering above the faeries and their mothers, silent, grey, dark. He held his arms stiffly by his sides and every so often made a little hopping movement to one side or the other, attempting to avoid a collision. Still they flocked, an occasional mama looking up at him with startled concern as she steered her charge away from his shins and elbows. They seethed and rolled around him, a throng of girls in pink and white, chattering like sea-gulls. Gor's brow began to sweat.

'Gor! Coo-eee! There you are!' Sveta came breaking through the crowd like a steam tug, dragging an unwilling and extraordinarily gangly Albina in her wake. The girl bumped off every available surface, tangling limbs with her ballet-dancing colleagues, the tiny speckled waifs crumpling to the floor as Albina bobbed past in her grubby moon-boots, walrus grey. Her hair was piled into an elaborate bun, much like a nest. Gor smiled to the ladies and held out his hands in greeting. They drew together in the sea of fluff.

'Good evening, Sveta. Good evening, Albina. I am glad to see you! But whatever is the matter?'

'I don't want to do it! Don't make me! Please!'

Together they ploughed through the dancers, heading for the clogged doors. They pushed their way through with elbows held high and struck out for the cloakroom.

'But I've come specially to see you, Albina,' said Gor with some concern, as they took off their coats and handed them to the stout woman behind the counter. 'I am sure you will be . . . spectacular.' His goatee twitched as he attempted a kindly smile.

'But I hate it, and I don't feel well.' She gripped her stomach under her bright blue jumper.

'Now, now, *petuchka*, we've had all this at home. Gor has come here specially to see you dance, so don't disappoint him. No one is going to laugh at you. I promise!'

'But I can't even see properly! My hair is in my eyes!' said the girl, screwing up her face to squint around her.

'Look, Albin-*chik*, there is your teacher, waving – see?'

The girl pretended she was unable to see and crashed heavily into yet another dancing nymph.

'Now Albina, that is enough! Go over to Madam immediately, or I shall get cross. She needs you in the dressing room.' Sveta's brows were drawn into a tight furrow, and her eyes bulged. She was wearing blue eye-shadow and large amounts of mascara, Gor noticed with concern.

'I hate you,' Albina hissed.

Sveta blinked, sniffed, smiled brightly, and pushed the girl sharply between the shoulder-blades in the direction of her dance mistress.

'She's so glad you've come, Gor. And so am I. It is difficult, when we have no man around the house.' She smiled up at him, eyes wide, and wiped imaginary lipstick marks from the corners of her raspberry red mouth. 'Shall we take our seats? We're in the balcony. I can't wait!'

Gor stared after her receding form as she made her way up

the glistening concrete steps. He frowned. He was not sure he should have come at all.

Row B2 was very full. The short battle to claim their seats combined with the damp heat of the auditorium brought a glow to Sveta's cheeks and nose. Once roosted in her rightful place, she pulled out her compact to repair the damage and, angling it for a suitable light, spied the most beautiful man she had ever seen, sitting just behind her. A young man with curly brown hair, full lips and a strong, angular jaw. She wiggled her mirror for a bit more. She observed his neck: smooth pale skin stretched taut over muscular flesh, sporting what appeared to be a love-bite. She squinted and adjusted the mirror once more: his eyes were the clearest grey, framed by long, dark lashes, so sensitive . . . almost feminine. His gaze bounced off hers in the mirror, and she snapped it shut, almost bursting into a giggle. Here, just behind her, was a sentient statue straight from the olive groves of the Roman world: a living David-cum-Hercules. She stowed her mirror, and, after waiting a few seconds, turned her head to have a proper look. Yes, there he was, not more than a few metres from her, a living god bursting out of a cream-and-grey patterned roll-neck sweater. He must be a swimmer, she thought, or a gymnast, perhaps. He was reading the mime-ographed programme and holding the hand of a dark-haired girl, his thumb stroking the inside of her wrist. Her face was turned away, dark locks hiding her expression, but Sveta could see a strong nose and her jaw, set firm. She felt her own brittle hair with her fingertips, and her small, soft chin. The man spoke and played his fingers through the tips of the girl's hair as if to discover her face.

'I'm sorry,' he murmured. 'I know how much it means to you.'

'Oh really? I'm not sure you do. You're just not trying hard enough!' the girl replied loudly.

'I'm doing my best,' he said.

'Well, you need to do more.'

His programme dropped to the floor, and Sveta turned back in her seat. She smiled to herself: young love could be hard work. She could well believe the gorgeous young man wasn't trying hard enough.

Gor turned to her, humming a little tune, vague 'pom-pom-poms' escaping his mouth. He looked a little less severe than usual.

'Isn't this nice?' She wiped imaginary lipstick from the corners of her mouth.

'It is certainly different,' he nodded, looking around the auditorium. 'Such excitement! Such babble!'

The young couple behind her were still at loggerheads, now embarking on an exchange of urgent whispers. She sighed contentedly and turned her attention to the stage.

Fifty minutes later, Gor looked at his watch for the sixth time. They had so far endured ballet, folk dancing, a spot of folk singing, folk rock, some sort of modern expressionism, and something noisy and energetic that Sveta informed him was 'disco', beloved of black people in America. Gor harrumphed and expressed a hope that the black people in America performed it with more aplomb than the children of School No. 2 in Azov. At this point, Sveta had dug him in the ribs with her elbow, and tutted loudly.

Albina had looked miserable throughout her eight minutes

of the modern expressionist segment. She was supposed to represent 'technology'. Her hands had flailed and her feet had stumbled as she tried to convey the positive global outcomes of mechanisation. Things got worse when she caught her toe in a thread hanging from her costume. She wobbled and fell, crushing the white papier-mâché dove placed centre-stage to represent world peace.

'Oh, that's a poor omen,' said Sveta, 'I don't think we want technology to do that, do we?' She smiled a brave smile, and waved to her daughter as she stomped off stage, sniffing and carrying pieces of mashed dove.

At the interval, Sveta propelled Gor towards the ice-cream queue, where their stoical patience was eventually rewarded with a pair of stubby brown cornets. They were squished, chewy looking, each with a small paper disc stuck atop an ice-cream permafrost, becoming part of it. Sveta sucked hers off quickly and bit into the ice-cream, while Gor hesitated, looking perplexed, then applied long fingers to peel off the disc with a great deal of care. Sveta watched, strangely enthralled, as he took a tiny wooden spatula from his pocket and began to chip away the ice, flicking milk crystals onto the steps where they stood on the edge of the heaving foyer.

'My teeth,' he explained as he caught her gaze. 'They are all my own, which I sometimes think is a disadvantage. Cold or hot, it can all be a problem.' He curled his top lip to reveal fangs that went on and on, right up towards the base of his nose, almost like those of a rodent. Sveta shuddered and looked away, straight into the dark eyes of the Roman god's girl. She was staring at her, across the room, really looking at her this time – with the ghost of a smile on her lips.

'This séance—' Gor began.

The bell clattered for the second half, and Sveta jumped.

'Tell me later,' she mouthed and turned away, hurrying back up the stairs to the comfort of their seats.

'Give me strength!' muttered Gor as he wiped his whiskers and trod slowly behind her.

They pushed themselves back along the crowded row like toothpaste in a tube. A copy of the programme, pink and crumpled, lay on Gor's seat. He picked it up, sat himself down, and offered it to Sveta. 'It's not mine,' she said, 'I didn't buy one.'

'Neither did I.'

He opened it, stared for a moment, and then dropped it as if it had burnt his fingers.

Sveta looked from Gor to the paper and back again. His eye was twitching. She bent to retrieve it and flicked open the pages. There, in the middle, scrawled across the fuzzy purple lettering, was a message just for Gor:

THERE WILL BE REVENGE, PAPASYAN!
YOU'RE NOT SAFE IN YOUR HOME!

SVETA'S ACROBAT

'Here we are, now you sit down and have a little brandy. In fact, I think I'll join you. Watching one's daughter perform is always nerve-racking.' She fussed around, finding glasses. 'And what with the dove and everything . . . Yes, a tot of brandy will help us both! What a trying evening!' Sveta pulled the cork out of the ancient bottle on Gor's sideboard, and poured two large measures. 'There, a taste of the old country for you!' she said with a smile, and handed a glass to him.

'Sveta, I'm not really Armenian, I'm—'

'Not to worry!' she said brightly. 'Down the hatch!' She drained her glass in a single gulp without the slightest shiver or cough, although her hands trembled. 'Oh! There's nothing like Armenian brandy!'

Gor took a tiny sip and coughed as the richness burnt the back of his nose and slid like embers down his throat. It was a welcome sensation, replacing the cold of the street and the bone-rattling of the bus. He was glad to be home, glad to be away from the Palace of Youth and the crowds and the faces and the hidden threat that lurked behind them. Something about that message, and the way it had been left, had chilled him to the core.

'Are you sure you will be all right this evening, Gor? Shall we stay with you? I could make up beds?' She sat opposite him, curled on the sofa.

'No, no, Sveta. I shall be quite all right.'

'We can stay as long as you like?' Her eyes were on his face, determined, probing.

'No, no, really. Albina needs her own bed, I can see. She too has had an exhausting evening.'

The girl lay next to her mother, a collection of tiny white kittens cradled against her belly. She was already asleep, but every so often snuffled slightly, rubbing her face.

'Yes, she is a tired baby-kins. But we needed to get you home, safe and sound. You had a nasty shock.'

'Yes, I did. But now all is well, and you have to get home. Sveta—' He frowned, and stopped.

'Yes?'

'Well. I, er . . . um, you have no man, around the house, or . . . Albina's father, I mean? To look after you?' He cleared his throat.

'No, no, Gor. We have never had a daddy.' Sveta stroked Albina's foot.

'Ah. How – never?'

'Well, now Gor . . .' Sveta giggled and reached for a top-up from the brandy bottle. It glugged in her hands. She took a sip, sighed and let her eyes wander along Gor's neat, book-laden shelves. 'He was not the marrying type,' she said eventually, her face stretching out in a broad smile.

'Why?'

She shrugged. 'He was an entertainer. Here today, gone tomorrow. I knew that, from the start.'

Gor frowned. 'But he cared for you?'

'Oh yes, he cared very much. He would have stayed.' She took another sip. 'But I made him go.'

'You made him?'

She nodded, still smiling. 'Yes. I wasn't a young girl, Gor: I was a woman, a teacher already. It was my decision. I knew I'd be all right, and I knew it wouldn't work with him. He wasn't designed to live in a flat in Azov. He needed the wind in his hair.'

'What sort of entertainer was he, if you don't mind me asking?'

She grinned. 'Can't you guess?'

'Erm . . .'

'No?'

Gor felt a sinking feeling in the pit of his stomach. 'Not a magician?' he ventured, creasing his forehead.

She threw back her head and laughed, the sound brassy like a trumpet in the quiet of the flat. Albina muttered in her sleep as a kitten crawled over her neck for warmth, dabbing at her face with a tiny white paw.

'Ha! No, Gor! Whatever gave you that idea?'

He shrugged his shoulders uncomfortably, and felt a flush burn his cheeks.

'He was an acrobat, of course!'

'An acrobat?'

'Yes! Oh, how he flew through the air!' She gazed up at the murky ceiling, as if she could see her lover flying there. 'That's how we met.'

'How? In the air?'

'Oh Gor, you're being silly!' She giggled and took another sip of brandy. 'I took a party from the school, for an evening performance. Year 4s, I think they were. He was a visiting artiste – not the usual that we get here, day-in, day-out. He was a special, just for the season. High-wire, trapeze . . . He had a wonderful Cossack costume, I remember it all: long black boots, military jacket with shiny brass buttons, a tall fur hat – real fur, you know—'

'On the high wire?'

'No! Gor, really! Listen: he'd jump into the circus ring – I can see him now – a dark jewel of the Caucasus: the cheek-bones, the flashing eyes, that chin, such a nose! Akh! I knew from that first moment . . . I went to the circus every day after that. Very soon, he picked up on my passion . . . he could feel it, from where I sat. And he returned it – four-fold! How my heart would leap! He would stride to the bottom of the ladder and disrobe, very slowly. That in itself was a performance, Gor! He would place each item of clothing on his upturned shield. And do you know . . .' she leant forward, eyes dancing, 'he did that in the bedroom for me, also.'

'Oh no, Sveta, really!' Gor jerked in his chair, spilling brandy down his front. 'Now look what's happened!'

She chuckled, ignoring Gor's discomfort, her voice a low, sing-song melody. 'I was under his spell: it was the spell of love. You know how they sing about it? Well, it's true. He was amazing . . . not just beautiful to look at, but so tender, and funny, and just . . .' She sighed. 'But I knew it could never last. That was my bargain: supreme happiness, for a few months. And it was worth it. In the end, he had to go. I saw him off at the station. He went back to Leningrad. Of course there were tears, he could barely tear himself away. But it was for the best. And now, I have my Albina: I look at her every day, and I remember the day Bogdan and I met. And I remember how we created her, in that magical cauldron of our love, when—'

'Quite,' muttered Gor, and took a gulp of brandy. 'I'm sure you—'

'And what about you?' she cut in, an inquisitive smile lighting her face.

He raised his eyebrows, but said nothing.

'Have you known love, Gor? Have you a family? I can't help but notice . . . You have no photographs on show . . . is there anyone? Or are your piano and your cats enough for the master magician?' Sveta reached out a hand towards Pericles, who ignored it and proceeded to lick his fluffy white behind.

'Well, I . . . It's a long story, Sveta.'

'We have all night,' she replied in a sing-song voice, putting her head on one side.

'Well, ah. I—'

The phone rang out in the hallway, its bleeps rattling off the doors and windows. For once, Gor was relieved to hear it.

'I must get that,' he said, bracing his arms, hands gripping like crab claws on the chair to lever himself up and out: he felt seized up.

'No, no, Gor. I will get it. If it's your phantom caller, I'll speak with them.' Her tone was determined and she jumped off the sofa, stockinged feet knotting slightly, and made for the hallway with quick, uneven steps.

He heard her lift the receiver, wait to listen, and then bellow into it. Silence followed, then again the sound of Sveta's voice, huge and hard, as if in a school hall or a playing field, eating the distance, loud in every ear. The clunk of the handset going down echoed through the flat.

'No one?' asked Gor, rolling his eyes across the ceiling.

'No one. But I gave them what for.' She winked at him as she came back in.

'Right. Well, thank you for trying. I should call you a taxi, Sveta. It's getting late.'

'I could hear them breathing, you know. That's the creepy thing. They were listening, breathing, waiting to hear what I would say.'

'You must have surprised them.' He smiled slightly. 'You're a brave woman. I'll call that taxi.'

'If you're sure,' she said, her voice soft again, getting sleepy as she curled up on the sofa next to her daughter.

'I'm sure.'

'But do you know what?' she called out. 'I could hear something else, in the background.'

'Really? What could you hear?' Gor flicked through his directory for the taxi number.

'I don't know. It was just when I put the phone down. It was something like the wind.'

'The wind? They were calling from the street, then?'

'Maybe. But it was a strange sound . . . as if they were calling from the forest.'

'The forest?' Gor laid the directory aside.

'I could hear it: the wind, rushing through the trees.'

OPEN FLAME

His physical health was returning. He felt in charge of his body, the master of his limbs. However, he still slept poorly. It was as if the weather had slipped inside him: the wind blew on his thoughts, heralding the ice that would eventually solidify his veins, the bog that would form where his heart still beat. His dreams were filled with the roar and rush of forest air, the snap of twigs, and always the smell of wood smoke.

After two bad nights and an empty, lonely day, Vlad came back. He launched into the room on a Sunday afternoon, all energy and muscle, smelling wholesomely of baking and washing powder, grey eyes bright under his mop of dark hair. He stood by the door a moment, observing the kindly orderly's backside as she leant forward to replace the notes at the end of the bed.

'Come in, come in! Don't stand on ceremony! Is that for me?'

Vlad laid before him a folded newspaper in which reposed a voluptuous serving of creamy torte Napoleon. Anatoly Borisovich licked his lips.

'Well how lovely!' Excitement made the words jump. 'What a treat!'

'She was thumping about in the kitchen half the night making that. I told her about you, you see. And then I couldn't sleep, she was making so much noise. A lot of work, apparently!' He was walking around the end of the bed, talking to Anatoly Borisovich, but his eyes were mostly on the orderly, slipping to her bosom as she pressed past him on her way out.

'Nice jumper,' she said.

'Italian wool. Feel it.'

He offered her his arm to touch. She trailed her fingers across it, the cracked skin snagging on the fine knit.

'Lovely. Must have been expensive?' Her lips twitched as she pushed through the doorway, not waiting for his reply.

The old man found himself frowning, mouth open, but didn't know why. Vlad turned to him, and he pushed his cheeks into a grin.

'Well, I do appreciate it! Look at this!' He raised the paper to his face to inspect its contents more closely, fingers scooping up the layers of fluffy, fragile pastry enveloped in rich yellow custard. Delight dropped into his mouth and he savoured it, eyes closed, indulging the sweetness with every cell of his tongue, the sugar saturating his being and making his teeth itch. The clatter of the blinds going up brought him back to the moment. 'The weather is against us today, Vlad. It won't be long until the first frost. But the heating is working again. It has quite a gurgle.'

Vlad did not sit down but paced the room, twisting on his heel with a fierce squeak as he did so. He stopped by the bedside.

'Is something wrong?' Anatoly Borisovich stilled his hand half-way to his mouth.

'No!' He squealed away, pacing the other side of the bed as

Anatoly Borisovich chewed. Again he stopped and looked at his watch, its face the size of a field mushroom.

'Eat your fill. I'm just a bit . . . Well . . .' He grabbed the visitor's chair and whirled it round to sit on it backwards, thumping his buttocks down onto the worn plastic. The old man winced.

'Thank you, Anatoly Borisovich!'

'What for? Eating cake?'

'For agreeing to take part in my study. It really is good of you. Let's get started!'

'But I'm still eating!' The old man fired out crumbs with the words, studding Vlad's midnight jumper with a hundred creamy stars. 'You can't hand a man a plate of torte Napoleon and expect a miracle! This is so good. Are you sure you don't want to try?' He held out the paper and Vlad recoiled. 'Please give my compliments to your landlady, she is a huge culinary talent. And you are a lucky boy!' He stopped to smack his lips and dabbed at a trickle of dribble with his fingers. Vlad checked his watch, wiped custard specks from its face and, tutting, took it off, stuffing it into his trouser pocket.

'Very good, Anatoly Borisovich. I will talk, you will listen. Yes, and eat, that's fine. But to remind you: today is our third meeting. I need to get writing my case study. So what I need to know is what happened to bring you to this place. OK? That's all. A clear indication of what set off your . . . Collapse? Breakdown? Dementia? Which phrase do you think best suits your symptoms?'

'I don't care.'

'Very well. I have a theory – well, a few different theories, to be honest – about what is afflicting you, but I need more

95

facts. And then, well, hopefully I can help you to go home. You want that, don't you?'

Anatoly Borisovich could not, as yet, remember where home was, but he nodded enthusiastically.

'So, let us begin.'

Vlad cleared his throat and sat upright with pen poised, a serious look on his face.

Anatoly Borisovich sighed. 'You are behaving oddly,' he said eventually. 'What's wrong?'

Vlad ground the pen nib into the blank page.

'Nothing is wrong, I—'

'So what's the hurry?' He scooped more torte Napoleon into his mouth, and then sucked each finger.

The pen flipped into the air and landed under the bed.

'I . . . it's just—' Vlad scratched the back of his head viciously. 'The exams are approaching, and I'm worried. I still have a lot of work to finish.'

'Exams? Is that so?' Anatoly Borisovich chewed thoughtfully. The wind rattled the window.

'It's not just the exams.' Vlad leapt from the chair and took up pacing. 'Polly and I—'

'Polly?' Again a fistful of torte paused in the air.

'My girlfriend.'

'Ah, oh yes.'

'You probably wouldn't understand. She is also a student. She's very stressed. It makes her very demanding. I think she's a little . . . anyway, I don't know what to do—'

'You're right, I wouldn't understand,' the old man agreed and mumbled more cake into his cheek. 'This really is quite delicious. Delectable!'

'Is it?' Vlad's breathing was ragged, his expression pained. Their eyes met.

'You do, Vlad, what is right. It's very simple. Trust your heart.'

'Right.' He stared at the lone pine tree as Anatoly Borisovich chewed laboriously. 'Modern life, Anatoly Borisovich, is not so simple. If only you understood . . .' He shook himself, and issued a dazzling smile. 'Anyway, we must finish today. Your story—'

'Yes, my story. So, where were we, let me recap . . .?'

'Oh . . .' Vlad sat back in the visitor's chair and rested his head in his hands.

'Yes, yes, I think we'd met me, and Lev, and Baba . . .'

'And the moth boy,' Vlad added quickly and loudly, without raising his head.

'Yes! Oh yes. Yuri moth boy! So you *do* believe me!' Anatoly Borisovich chuckled, and turned his eyes to the horizon. 'He came out of the forest. He was real, you know.'

'If you say so. But has anything else come back to you?'

'Oh, it all came back to me. The day they brought me in here. It was all there, in fragments, like a ripped-up letter. I've put it back together, talking to you.'

'That's very good, Anatoly Borisovich.' Vlad nodded and smiled, hope glinting in his eyes. 'So you remember, now, the day you came in? What preceded it?'

'Not really. You see, it's moth boy – he's pushed everything else out.'

'I don't understand.'

'Neither do I. But let's pretend we do?'

'Finish your story, Anatoly Borisovich. Just finish your story.' Vlad ran a hand over his eyes.

★

Yuri followed Tolya and Baba into the cottage, hesitant at first, nervous of Lev's friendly, soft-pawed attention. He huddled by the stove for an hour or more, leaning against its warmth, his ill-fitting, pock-marked skin gradually blossoming from ice to milk to a soft honey hue. He crossed his arms over his chest each time Lev passed by to sniff at his boots, and said little. Occasionally he stood, as if drawn to the light of the lamps, intent on moving towards them, flapping his arms, his hands wavering at shoulder height. All the time he was smiling to himself, a secret smile, thought Tolya, while his teeth chattered.

Tolya helped Baba start the soup before taking a seat on the other side of the stove, observing the new creature from a safe distance.

'Are you a spirit?' he whispered, curiosity getting the better of fear. He wanted to look into Yuri's face, to see what mysteries lay there, but couldn't hold his gaze: the boy's eyes shivered in their orbits, seldom settling on any object apart from the lamps. This wasn't a proper boy. But he wasn't a moth either. Whatever he was, it seemed to Tolya that Yuri wasn't interested in him. Yuri wasn't his friend. Just like the boys at school.

'Hey!' Tolya tried again, whispering fiercely and prodding Yuri's leg with the poker. 'Are you a moth? Just say!'

'Moth! Moth . . . moth,' repeated the boy in his husky voice, not looking at Tolya, but instead leaning down to peer at the fire in the stove.

'He is a moth! He said so!' Tolya shrank back from the other boy as Baba clucked indifferently. Still Yuri's hands shivered and flapped around his face as he smiled.

'Tolya, come help me with these bowls. Yuri!' She waited for the older boy to raise his head. Out of the corners of his eyes he scanned the table, Baba and the bowls, back and forth. 'Here's some broth for you. Come to the table! Come now!' She spoke loudly, beckoning with her hands.

Yuri pressed himself to the warmth of the stove for a second, and then shuffled over to the rough wooden bench, opposite Tolya's place. Baba was still ladling out soup when his hands curved around the nearest bowl and he raised it to his lips. Tolya stared in disbelief.

'Hey! Steady boy! You'll scald your gullet! Use a spoon, boy, use a spoon!' Baba's words shot around his head and Yuri looked dazed, the bowl still in his hands, half-way to his lips. He smiled.

'Spoom,' he repeated, voice thick and eyes blank, and then, with recognition, 'Spoom!'

'Spoo*n*,' said Tolya, forehead creasing. 'The word is spoon!'

'Like this!' Baba bid Tolya demonstrate. He lifted the spoon to his lips and noisily sucked up the soup.

A laugh erupted from Yuri, loud and uncontrolled, full of joy.

'What is he laughing at?'

'They don't use spoons where you come from then, eh?' Baba chuckled, ignoring Tolya's question.

'Where *does* he come from, Baba?'

'Shhh!'

'But why is it funny?'

The boy picked up a spoon and, with great concentration, dipped it into the broth and then manoeuvred it to his mouth. He did it twice more. Soup splashed around the table in puddles as he slurped and coughed, barley grains showering the air. He laughed and choked with a gurgle, soup shooting out of his nose.

'Eh, Yuri, maybe your way is better for you? Just wait until it's a bit cooler.' Baba took away the spoon. Again, he went to lift the bowl to his mouth and Baba laid her hand on his arm to slow him down.

'No!' he shrieked, pulling free, his eyes on her, round and defiant, before they returned to the bowl in front of him.

'You were going to hurt yourself!' Baba shook her grey head and clucked her tongue, but she hadn't taken offence. Tolya frowned into his broth as Yuri licked the spillage from the table, strange yelping noises of enjoyment, half animal, half human, escaping him as he did so.

'Ha! He's a fine one, this Yuri,' Baba tutted to herself as she went to fetch a cloth. 'You'll get splinters in your tongue that way! You won't like that!'

Tolya gazed at the boy, his eyes narrowed. Yuri began to flap his hands in front of his face.

'You shouldn't do that. We have good manners in this house. And we like quiet!' Tolya looked down into his broth, and saw his face reflected there, all big nose and little bug eyes. Why had Baba invited him into their home? It was all strange, all wrong. He swilled the broth around, the grains twirling and floating like leaves on the wind, and tried not to cry.

'I don't like you,' he said quietly, looking up at the boy across from him. Yuri's gaze fell on him briefly, and he smiled. He didn't seem to care whether Tolya liked him or not.

'Well Yuri, you'd better be off now. You've warmed up and had a bit to eat, and Tolya and I have to finish our jobs before we get to our beds.' Baba was heaving about under the big bed, trying to reach something stored there. Dust swirled in the air around her.

Yuri wiped his fingers around the inside of his bowl and

100

sucked them clean. Then he stood up from the table and nodded, shifting from one foot to the other, flicking his fingers. The tapping and twitching was making Tolya cross. He couldn't wait for this Yuri to leave.

'You can take this with you. We don't need it.' Baba handed him an old padded jacket, patched many times, and bursting white wadding like foam along one arm.

'But that's for me, Baba!' yelled Tolya indignantly, dropping his spoon and leaping to his feet. 'Papa promised it to me! When I'm grown up! It's mine!'

'Tolya, you have years to grow into it, and Yuri needs it now. We'll make you a new one when the time comes. Let Yuri have this, eh?' Her tone was firm, and the other boy was already at her side, grinning.

Tolya sat down with a thump and kicked his legs under the table as Yuri took off his own frayed rags and put on the new coat. He stretched out his big, toothy grin and laughed. 'It's good! Mmm!' He wrapped both arms around himself and rocked from side to side. 'Good!'

'That will help you on your way.' Baba stood back and looked at him, patting him on the arm. 'Good travels now then, Yuri!' She led him to the cottage door. 'Goodnight!'

She stood and watched as he made his way across the moon-silvered yard, over the fence and out into the undulating forest beyond, disappearing into the darkness as his footsteps crunched on the grass and fallen leaves. It was a cold night.

'You gave him my jacket,' glowered Tolya as he stood to take his bowl to the bucket, once Baba had bolted the door. 'That was my jacket, and you gave it to some . . . some boy who can't even speak properly, or use a spoon!'

'He needed it more than you, son. It's cold out there, and he has so little.'

'But why has he got so little? Maybe he doesn't need anything, Baba? Maybe he's a wood spirit and he doesn't need our clothes, or our food? Maybe he's moth boy, and he doesn't need to come in here and sit by our stove!' Tolya shouted, hands clenched.

'For the last time,' Baba rolled her eyes as she rinsed the bowls, 'he's not a spirit, he's a boy. I don't know why he has nothing, and I'm not going to ask.'

'Why not?'

'Because sometimes it is better not to know! Now enough!' Baba turned and raised her hand above Tolya's head, as if to strike him.

He backed away, surprised and panting. 'I don't like him!' he shouted, 'and I don't want him in my house!' He thumped the log wall with his small, angry fists.

'A fine Communist you're turning out to be,' said Baba, shaking her head.

'Stalin would hate him too! He's weak and thin and stupid and laughs at nothing and steals things that are mine!'

Baba stood by the bucket picking barley grains out of her hair, her movements jerky and swift. She stopped and looked up. 'Not everyone can be equal, Tolya: not everyone is the same. Some have no family, no friends: they are weak. We must look after those people. It is our duty.'

'No! He took my coat! He's stupid and dirty and I don't want to do my duty!'

'You have no choice, eh? It's the right thing to do. Your conscience will tell you. And you'll have a new coat, when the time is right.'

Tolya spun away from her and leant his forehead on the musky-smelling wood of the wall. He shut his eyes as Baba put away the bowls and swept under the table. He poked his fingers into the knots of the wood and sniffed. She didn't understand the feeling he had, in the pit of his stomach, gnawing at him. It told him Yuri did not belong. It told him to be afraid.

'Come, be a good boy, and don't sulk. It's been a long day, and you've worked hard in the yard. Help me with the bedding, and wash your face and hands. That's it!'

She smiled as he peeled himself away from the wall and, silently, came to help her with the bed.

'Where's my lovely Tolya gone, eh? Chased away by a messy wood spirit? I don't believe it! He's in here somewhere!' Baba enveloped him in a bear hug that turned into a tickle, her fingers digging into his ribs.

'No! Stop!'

He chuckled despite himself, unable to be cross with his grandmother as they wrestled at the foot of the stove, laughing and twisting and tumbling. Lev jumped around them barking and nipping their boots, trying to join in. She could always make him laugh, no matter how cruel the boys at school were, or how much he missed his mama and papa. Baba could always make it right. And now the stupid boy had gone, she was all his again.

'Don't tell anyone about Yuri,' Baba warned before bed.

'Why not?'

'It's hard to explain. Talk brings trouble. And we don't need trouble. So let's keep him to ourselves, eh? Our secret?' She tweaked his cheek.

He wanted to brag to his cousin and the other boys about how he'd tamed the moth boy. He wanted to be important.

He wanted to make them see that he could be one of them. But still, he nodded.

Yuri didn't just come that night. He appeared every so often, melting out of the forest into the edge of the yard as dusk fell and the lamps were lit. He would stand, hands flapping gently at his sides, with a huge happy, otherworldly grin, laughing into the wind and the snow, tapping at the window, waiting for Baba to hail him in for a bite to eat. They'd sit at the table telling stories or playing games: card games at first, but Yuri couldn't get them, and the cards would fly through the air to fall in autumn patterns across the floor as he gurgled with laughter. So they thought up better games, like guessing the first letter of the things they could see, or taking turns to hide an object for the others to find. Baba would conjure up a bit of bottled fruit to savour, or maybe a piece of black bread smeared with honey. As the weeks passed, Tolya forgot to distrust Yuri, forgot that he was strange. The clutch of fear in his stomach when he appeared at the window melted away. He almost looked forward to Yuri's visits.

One night, around New Year, Tolya came home from school, frozen and famished as usual, to find the cottage brightly lit and the stove roaring. Baba and Yuri were waiting for him, standing in the doorway, their cheeks flushed, eyes shining.

'Surprise!' cried Baba, kissing Tolya on both cheeks. 'Look what Yuri has made for you! Look!'

'Ha ha!' cried Yuri, 'Look!'

They led Tolya to the table, where lay a wooden spoon, roughly cut and uneven. Along its spine, in blotchy poker work, he made out a moon and star, and the words

'He did that all by himself!' said Baba, beaming with pride.

'Friends!' said Yuri, and flapped his hands.

Tolya picked up the spoon and rubbed his thumbs over the words.

'Friends,' he nodded, smiling to himself.

Baba squeezed his cheeks. 'My good boy. My treasure, Tolya.'

The old man broke off and raised a trembling hand to his wet forehead. His past was hanging on his shoulders like a sack of kindling. He could almost smell it. 'I'm not sure—'

'Anatoly Borisovich!' Vlad reached out to take his hand, eyes pleading. 'Don't back away now. Take a moment to gather your thoughts, and go on, please!'

Green eyes rose to meet the hope and frustration radiating from every pore of Vlad's handsome, upturned face. Anatoly Borisovich nodded.

He took a sip from the glass by his bedside and blotted his lips on the sleeve of his robe.

'Everything has an end, even the happiest story, and sometimes without warning.'

'Yes?' Vlad leant towards him.

'It was a few nights later. I was in bed, sleeping above the stove, on the tiled shelf up there – it was a bitter night, blue and hard, and it was the warmest place, warmer even than the big bed with Baba. I remember . . . well, I don't remember. It is just a feeling; a smell like a bonfire, or shashlik smoking in the courtyard. A smell of danger.'

He stopped and passed a hand down the back of his neck,

tugging on the straggly ends of grey mane hanging there. 'I was in blackness, the depths of sleep. There was a smell and a noise, breaking into me. Crackling, fierce and sharp, prodding into my ears, and a stench blooming up my nose. I felt it all here.' Anatoly Borisovich pressed two fingers to his forehead. 'There was darkness in my brain like the end of the world. Something was wrong, but I could not move.

'Mama was calling me. I heard her voice and it made me shiver. I knew she was dead, you see. She called in my ear, called me to come. I opened my eyes, and all around me was black and orange – leaping shapes, shivering, snapping. Fire! I sat up on the stove, and flame and fire was all I could see, eating up our cottage, bursting over the table, rushing like rats, dropping from the curtains to the floor, racing up the timbers to the roof. My lungs bucked in my chest. I cried out and scrabbled to get down the side of the stove, but my legs tangled in the sheets and blankets, and I fell like a sack to the floor.

'My eyes were streaming holes in my face. When I forced them open, I saw only black and orange, black and orange leaping and crackling and tearing up the roof. My eyelashes fizzed and the hairs in my nose scorched. I stood, but the smoke and heat knocked me off my feet before I'd taken a step. So there I crouched, crying on the floor.

'I didn't know what to do. I was choking. I thought my lungs would bake. I coughed and retched as the smoke bit my throat and tried to call out to Baba, but my words came out a scream. I screeched like a pig being killed.

'I cried. I didn't want to die with the sound of my screeching in my ears. A roof timber came crashing down in the middle of the house, again I was knocked onto my back. Lying there,

I opened my eyes to see my last, and there was the night sky above me, cool and distant like the forest. I wondered about Stalin and heaven and all the stars that must be the souls of good children. I prayed for Stalin's help, the way we did it – crossed my fingers, shut my eyes, breathed to speak the words – and gulped in clean, fresh air. The smoke was flying through the roof. Maybe I could live!

'Adrenalin flowed through me then, drowning the terror. I leapt up. The front door was blocked where the roof had caved in, but the stove – the brave stove stood like a rock in the back, propping up the roof, protecting me, giving me an escape route. There was a back way, you see – a little side door where Baba got the pigs in, before they were taken away. I scrambled for the stove, to save myself.

'But then I thought of Baba. I looked back to her bed, and I saw arms in the shadows: arms, Vlad, reaching out to me, fingers moving, scratching the air. Fingers.' The old man looked down at his hands, the fingers twitching with claw-like movements. 'I couldn't scuttle away. I went to save her. I did! I jumped through the flames and thrust myself forward. But it started raining fire. I looked up and—'

Anatoly Borisovich looked up, a mess of tears trickling from his luminous, childlike eyes. 'I looked up and flames fell into my eyes. They stuck to my cheeks. I heard a scream, but it was just me, scrabbling in the muck and soot to get away. I was pain, not a human being. I had no control!

'When I came to myself, I was rolling around on the frost in the yard, rubbing dirt into my face. People were coming, running from their houses up the track: I heard them, knew their shouting and swearing. Comrade Goloshov, he came first, then my cousin, and my uncle. I was on the yard floor as they knelt above me, their faces glowing with the fire. They were all crying, my cousin was screaming . . . I saw the horror in his face: the horror of looking at me. The whole roof collapsed, and the flames leapt to the clouds. No one could save my baba. I'm not sure they even tried. They just all stood around shouting and scratching their arses.

'I was wrapped in a blanket: it took all my skin off. And they carried me away. They carried me away and I don't remember what happened. There was a fever. They thought I would die. I didn't.'

Vlad picked up the plastic water jug and emptied it into Anatoly Borisovich's glass. The old man took it, and sipped.

'That's how I got these scars.' The old man rubbed a hand over his cheeks and smiled, chuckling to himself as his eyes remained stark. 'I was going to save Baba, but I couldn't help myself. I couldn't do my duty. I scuttled away.' He drew a shaky breath.

'I'm sorry, Anatoly Borisovich. That's a . . . a sad tale indeed. But look how much you've remembered!' Vlad placed a large, warm hand on the old man's forearm. 'And do you recall what happened next?'

'What happened?' the old man grunted softly. 'They sifted through the wreckage, to gather up the bones before the animals got them. That's what happened next.'

'And . . . To you, I mean?'

'Me? Little Tolya? They buried my baba next to my mama in the cemetery on the lane going out of town. There was no priest, no service. I was too sick to go, and Papa couldn't attend: he was on a quota. In fact, I don't think I saw Papa again. It was just the way it was. My uncle and aunt and cousin all went, paid their respects along with Goloshov – ha! I saw the wooden marker, a few months later, there in the soil – crooked!

'I went to live with my cousin's family, and we moved to Krasny Bor, a few kilometres away. It wasn't the same. I wasn't like them. My cousin spent weeks crying like a baby every time he looked at me, and then, well, he avoided me. In school, and in our shared room. Our mothers were sisters but, you know, my mother had already gone, and his mother was a funny kind of woman. She chose to marry an Armenian. Not a bad thing in itself but . . . they're secretive people, you know? Look after their own. I felt . . . apart.'

'That's really . . . very interesting!' said Vlad, scribbling into his notepad.

'I'm not saying they mistreated me, but . . .' Anatoly Borisovich sniffed, and ran a finger around the bottom of his right eye. 'I was sent away to military school. Imagine me – in a military school! Ha! Wrenched from the forest and sent away to barracks, where they tried to teach me to follow orders and put together a gun. Me, an artist. I was there a long time, but they gave up in the end.' He smiled and sat silently for a while, eyes fixed on the air, on nothing. 'When I came back, my cousin had taken over the entire room. There was no space for me.'

'So, do you have . . . living family, Anatoly Borisovich? I've found no family record in your file. This cousin—'

'Yes. Cousin Gor. He's still living . . . around here, somewhere.'

'Gor?' Vlad stopped writing, mouth open. 'Er, that's an unusual name!'

'Goryoun Tigranovich Papasyan: a good Armenian name, my boy. As I recall . . . we both moved to Rostov. He came

109

first, and I followed. I still hoped to connect . . . for family ties, for something.'

Vlad had dropped his pen and was making a meal of picking it up.

'You're quite the butterfingers today,' observed the old man, his eyes closing as a great sigh pushed its way out of his chest.

'Ha! Yes!' Vlad chewed a fingernail and frowned. 'That's amazing . . . but, no . . . are you sure he's your cousin?'

Anatoly Borisovich opened an eye. 'Is that really a question?'

Vlad chewed a second nail. 'No. I'm sorry. It's just . . . oh, never mind.' He scratched his head. 'Nothing you need to worry about. And Yuri?' he said finally. 'What became of the moth boy? Did you ever see him again, after the fire?'

The other eye opened and directed a bright gaze into Vlad's expectant face. 'Yuri?' he said with a puzzled smile. 'He was gone. No one saw him again. He'd started the fire, you see, and he fizzed in the flames. He'd fried, like moths do. That's what happens, isn't it?' He leant forward suddenly, hands gripping the bedsheets. 'They die, if they get too close to the light. What else could happen?'

Vlad stared open-mouthed at the old man, and then leafed back through his notes. 'But how do you know? You didn't mention him being there, when you woke. Did you see him?'

Anatoly Borisovich's eyes burnt silently into Vlad's, his cheeks crinkling like weathered paint as he smiled.

'I am confused: that's why I'm here. I don't know what you're . . . You're trying to blame me? Of course! I knew you would! But it was him: Yuri moth boy! He started the fire. He killed my baba. He didn't mean to. But he was always trying to get to the light. You must believe me!'

Anatoly Borisovich yanked the covers up over his stubbly, crumb-strewn chin.

'I still hear him tapping, poor dead Yuri. Tapping on the windows, waiting to get in. He was tapping for days when I . . . when I—' The old man broke off and wiped a hand across his eyes.

'Tapping?'

Vlad looked from the old man to the window and back again, and something in the grimness of the face sent a soft chill across his skin. He pulled the sleeves of his jumper down over his hands and chewed on the end of his pen.

He read over today's notes: *vivid childhood imagination, coupled with possible early psychosis, led to hallucinations and projection of feelings and fears. Story of Yuri the moth boy an obvious fabrication / hallucination: the fictitious character an invisible friend.* He added the words: *blamed in retrospect by AB for the fire and death of grandmother, now those events have been recalled following long period of, what's it called – Post Traumatic Stress Disorder? Need to look it up. So, could have been arson or accident? Murder, or just manslaughter? In conclusion, likely triggers for physical / mental collapse on or around 8th September 1994: hallucinations brought on by fever and bout of 'flu diagnosed on arrival, coupled with malnutrition and sudden, uncontrolled recollection of the traumatic childhood event, due to the above and . . .* He tapped his pen nib against the paper.

'Was it the tapping that brought on your . . . recollection and collapse, do you think? You heard it, just before you came in here? Was it the trigger?' he asked eventually. 'We need a trigger.'

'Ah . . . Yes! Maybe?' The old man's eyes lit up. 'I'm not sure. It's such a blur. I remember a tree . . . I couldn't sleep! Such tap-tap-tapping!'

111

Vlad smiled to himself, jotting down: . . . *a trigger: the repeated tapping of a tree on the window, echoing the mythical moth boy tapping. The result: a frenzy of self-recognition, guilt and denial, resulting in a loss of all faculties and an inability to care for himself.* Then he added an asterisk and the words, underlined: *Amazing coincidence – Papasyan is his cousin!!! Estranged, however.* He sat up straight in his seat trying to hold down a triumphant grin. 'Superb, Anatoly Borisovich! That's just what I needed to hear! It's all clear to me now!'

He shook the old man's hand, pumping it up and down. 'You'll be relieved to hear we can end these visits now. You have told me what caused your collapse – and now I can write it all up and . . . er, sort it all out! That might take some time – I have to consult my tutor and all that, but well done! Well done! I'll be back, at some point . . .'

He hummed as he slammed out of the room, still smiling, not looking back. He could hardly wait to get started on his case study. It all seemed straightforward now. And he'd have to tell Polly about it. She was sure to be surprised. She might even be impressed! He looked at his watch, and thought of her peachy buttocks.

Alone in his room, Anatoly Borisovich covered his face in his hands.

'What have I said?' he murmured. 'Does he really have it right?'

DILL AND DOUGHNUTS

A sweet scent of dill and doughnuts threaded the air at the Golden Sickle cafeteria, not far from the centre of town. A squat middle-aged woman with frizzy orange hair, a square flat face of a similar colour and tiny, apple-pip eyes was enjoying a pastry stuffed with boiled condensed milk and chewy chopped nuts. Her companion sat opposite sighing into a plate of shredded grey cabbage – and dill.

'Honestly, Valya, this vegetarian diet will kill me.'

'No, Alla, it will save you. Listen to what your doctor said. Blood pressure is a killer. Meat is a killer. Dairy is a killer.' Valya smacked her lips and set about removing nut chunks from her back teeth. 'You've spent your life eating poison and now it's time to put it right. Get that cabbage down you and you'll feel better.' Teeth picked clean, she padded her finger around her plate, collecting up the last crumbs and sucking at them with noisy gusto. 'I could eat that again. Not as good as what I make, though. I did a torte Napoleon Saturday night – for Vlad. It was magnificent.' She smacked her lips.

'He was?' Alla's grey head bobbed up.

'*It* was. He was as well, but then . . . you know that.' Her

113

eyes disappeared as she grinned, leaning back in her chair, and stretched out her arms. 'Akh, my aching limbs. Six hours straight at the *dacha* I did on Sunday! But it's all done now: all ready for winter. You want to see another winter, don't you?'

Alla's eyes dropped to her cabbage salad and she turned over the pallid, speckled leaves with a bent fork. 'Of course I do,' she muttered, 'it's just—'

'Then eat your salad, and stop complaining. Do you want tea?'

Every feature of Alla's face drooped downwards, as if mouth, nose, eyes and brows might melt into a grey, watery puddle on the plate below. A sob rose in her throat. 'I can't have it!' She almost choked on the words. 'I can have compote, or birch cordial. No stimulants.'

'He-he!' Valya laughed gruffly and slapped her on the back. 'Look on it as "you-time": it's a treat for yourself. A real treat. I'll be back in a minute.' She bustled over to the counter to get the drinks.

Alla wished she had never started visiting the doctor. But once you start, and they find something wrong, it is difficult to kick the habit. One thing leads to another, you feel beholden to them, and before you know it, it's part of your weekly routine. It was bearable when there were just pills to be swallowed but now her whole life revolved around keeping herself alive. She skewered a piece of cabbage and placed it on her tongue. At the next table, a small girl was eating a sausage in pastry. Alla could smell it, every grease-laden, fat-drenched molecule. Her stomach howled.

Valya returned with a glass of steaming tea for herself, and a glass of hot water for her friend.

'*Na zdarovie!*' she laughed, chinking the glasses together as she pushed her ample backside into the small wooden chair. She took a slurp and screwed up her face, gold teeth flashing. 'Ah! That's better. Sorry, no birch or compote, so . . .' She leant forward. 'Are you going on Friday?'

'Going where?'

'Madame Zoya's?'

'The tea leaves? Nobody told me!'

'Not leaves: a séance,' Valya hissed. 'I just heard today.'

'Ooh! I wonder . . .' Alla pulled a dog-eared diary from her bag and ruffled its pages. 'Yes, that should be fine, I'm on earlies. I wonder if I could invite Polly?'

'Akh, Polly? Why would you want to do that?' Valya flexed her shoulders under her mountainous green jumper and clucked her tongue. 'It's not like she's your *friend*, is it?'

'No . . . but her mother is, and I said I'd keep an eye on her. And . . .' Alla sniffed, and inspected a piece of cabbage. '. . . I only managed to get to the pharmacy once last week, and she wasn't there. I need to speak to her about my stomach, you see. Say what you like, but she can always supply the medicaments, even when they're, you know . . .' She squinted over either shoulder in a conspiratorial manner. '. . . officially out of stock. When I had that trouble with my you-know-what last month, she was right on the button, came up trumps. Best in the pharmacy—'

'I wouldn't know. You wouldn't catch me in that place.'

'No, well, you're healthy. Look at you: such colour in those cheeks.'

Valya's cheeks glowed with a hue bordering on crimson.

'That's what everyone says. I get to work on a Monday

morning, and they're all sitting behind the counter like a crate of anaemic lemons. I walk in, and the place lights up.'

'Well, it is a bank, Valya. It's not difficult to light up a bank.'

'Says she, who works in the world's darkest department store! It's like a cave! When are they going to buy some light-bulbs, eh? It's not 1991 any more, you know! Tell them, tell them to give you light! Anyway: Friday, eight p.m.'

'Who is the guest, do we know?'

'You'll never guess.'

'No, I won't.' Alla stabbed a piece of bendy cabbage with her fork and looked away from her friend's annoyingly healthy face.

'Well, have a go!' Valya bellowed after a brief pause.

'I don't know!'

'It's only Papasyan!'

'Who's he?'

'Oh, you know—' Valya's brow descended, nearly meeting her lips as she tutted and added more sugar to her tea. 'The bank boss.'

'I don't think I—'

'I used to work for him, up in Rostov. I've told you about him a thousand, million times. Everyone knows about him: snobby; miser; magician; tall; dark; ugly.'

'Oh, wait a minute! They say he's got gold . . .'

'Hidden in the toilet! That's the one. Always miserable.'

'Well, if he's had a death in the family—'

'He hasn't. He hasn't got any family; no excuse to be miser-able. Just always is.'

'Well, that's interesting, I wonder why he wants a séance then? I remember when—'

'It's all nonsense, anyway, of course,' Valya cut in, slapping her hand on the table.

'What is?'

'The séances: they never helped me.'

'No, well, your husband was always very quiet. He——'

'All nonsense!' Valya slapped her hand on the table again and slurped her tea decisively.

Alla sipped her hot water and eyed her friend. 'You were scared last time.'

'I was not!'

'You seemed scared to me. You were shaking.'

'I was coming down with something. I felt awful. Sweating all over.'

'But you're never ill!'

'I was then! Anyway, it'll be interesting to see the old goat, and find out what's his trouble. I always thought he was a sceptic, like me.'

'I'll give Polly a ring. She came once before, didn't she? And it's my . . . duty, really, isn't it, to invite her out occasionally? It'll give me an excellent opportunity for a chat about my——'

'You'll be lucky. She's been very *busy* lately . . .' Valya pronounced the word with heavy emphasis, 'with my Vlad.'

Alla wrinkled her nose. 'Do you think she's avoiding me? I mean, she used to come into the store on Fridays to say hello, on her way to the folk-art souvenirs counter——'

'Folk art!'

'Each to their own, Valya.'

'Pah! If you're going to invest, do it in something proper: diamonds, gold, or oil – like me! I've bought four barrels, got them stored at the *dacha*! Ha! What's the point investing in those trinkets? All those lacquered Palekh boxes.' Valya waggled her plump fingers across the table. 'Miniature art? Silly!'

'It's a good investment! And it's sweet!'

Valya sprayed a film of tea across her friend as she choked. 'Sweet? *Polly?*'

'At least they're something solid in your hand, a real piece of Russian heritage! Not like those, what do they call them – shares? I mean, what are shares? Just worthless paper!' Alla pushed the remains of her cabbage away. 'Did you hear, the whole of School No. 4 was invested in PPP?'

'The pyramid scheme? You're joking?'

'The headmaster thought he could triple the budget if he invested . . . they found his body washed up in the creek last Friday. He'd jumped off the bridge.'

'Stupid man, God rest his soul.' Valya rolled her tiny eyes as far as they would roll, and blotted her brow with a crinkly serviette. 'Maybe Vlad could come too. I'd feel safer with him there.'

'Safer?'

At the counter a broad woman in a stained white overall and a chef's hat began shouting at the customers while brandishing a slotted spoon.

'Time to go?' asked Alla.

'Time to go,' nodded Valya. 'Cook's been at the home-brew. I'll see you on Friday . . . if you live that long.'

She laughed deep in her chest and knocked Alla on the back with her fist. Alla coughed, and did not laugh.

'I'll phone Polly.'

'Please do. Try to peel her away from my poor Vlad's side. She's a bad influence on him, you know. I can see the difference

118

already. And it's not good.' She dragged her heavy autumn coat over arms bursting with flesh. 'Ooh, that's tight!'

'A girl always spoils a man, that's what I say.'

'Well Alla, that's a stupid thing to say. I didn't spoil my husband: I improved him.'

'Improved him into the grave.'

'Now then! I didn't know he had a weak heart. But Vlad . . . he was such a sweet boy. I know he's not been with me long, but he was so attentive, so chatty. And now – he's always on the phone, hardly eats a thing, constantly coming and going. And getting through so many pairs of underpants! He's got huge bags under his eyes, you know.'

'He's young, Valya. Maybe you should have a motherly word?' Alla smiled as she pulled on her gloves.

'Motherly? I hardly think so!' Valya's cheeks flushed deep vermilion as she fanned herself by the open door.

Alla applied her bobble hat. 'Then maybe we should ask Madame Zoya, you know, to ask the spirits . . . The departed often have a point of view, don't they? They can tell if a romance is going right.'

'Romance? It's lust – that's what it is! Come along, Alla. The poor boy's being led by his—'

The door slammed on the words as the two ladies stepped into the street. Alla trotted quickly towards the bus stop, eager to get home and issue her invite, pleased at the prospect of discussing her digestion with a more qualified ear than Valya's.

Valya herself waddled a few steps behind, the bright blue headscarf clinging tightly to her orange hair. She thought back to her days in the bank up in Rostov, and the curmudgeonly boss who had, just the once, taken a boiled egg from his lunch box and made it disappear. He'd shaken off their amazement, turned his back on calls for more. He'd been such a closed man, firmly sealed in his shell. Maybe now he was opening up? And who knew what pearls might lie within this old clam. She smacked her lips in anticipation.

YOU CAN'T PICKLE LOVE

Gor realised it was a Tuesday when the day was half-way through. He'd been caught up by Mussorgsky roaring from the record player. Mussorgsky always stirred his soul; both a pleasure, and a pain. This Tuesday, bright but with a chill, it was regret that bubbled to the surface as he tried to remember a trick, the 'Sands of the Nile'.

The trick was a good one, when it worked. He would reach into a giant bowl of murky, swirling water and, with a grand flourish, extract perfectly dry piles of brightly coloured sand. Children always loved it. He remembered, suddenly, how Olga used to dangle her fingers in the bowl as he practised. He couldn't believe he'd forgotten how to do it.

After she'd gone, he'd still been full of himself, forty-five years old and intent on success. Business had boomed, and he'd grown fat and busy, obsessed with his creature comforts. He'd guzzled the fruit of the orchard and sat back in his chair, enjoying the view of autumn days stretching ahead, content in the knowledge that he'd stored up for the leaner times and had it all bottled and pickled, everything he needed, at the back of the cupboard. But he'd forgotten his soul. And as he'd sat feeling smug, the material possessions he'd stored up so carefully were silently eaten away, as if by mice. Only then did he realise you couldn't bottle happiness, you couldn't pickle love. Now here he was, scavenging on the dust pile, seeking out scraps – and this time, all alone.

Old age had him by the scruff: he could barely walk without coughing, the legs were going too. The middle years, so important, so busy, had disappeared like so much melted snow, no more than a puddle on the mucky floor of his life. Where was the time? Where was the laughter? Where was his family, more to the point? Marina, his wife, Olga his daughter, even funny little Tolya? He had focused his energies on forecasts and fixed assets, budgets and bureaucracy. The wind buffeted the windows as he chewed his lip, pencil sleeping on the paper. How different life might have been, it whispered.

He looked up at the calendar: Tuesday 11th October. His mouth twitched, and he sprang from his chair. Rehearsal day! Sveta would be coming over. She would be limbering up at this very minute. The cabinet had to be readied, and a little bite of something prepared. He shushed Mussorgsky and headed to the bedroom to change. He would venture to the market. Tuesday was a good market day, as far as they went. And he would invest in some treats, in recognition of Sveta's good comradeship.

As he stood wondering whether to opt for two sweaters, or one sweater and a jerkin, he heard a sound. It slipped into his ear: nothing much, just a tapping – fingers on glass, quiet, insistent. He held his breath and listened: it echoed around the empty flat. Hardly threatening, stealthily soft, but it squeezed his heart.

tap-tap-tap

It was the sound of loneliness, the sound of cold nights. The tick of the clock, the beat of the heart; the tap of time, marching onwards. Beads of sweat formed on his forehead. As if the intervening sixty years had not happened, he smelled pine needles and mud, machine oil and wood smoke. The wind whistled in the pines.

tap-tap-tap

He cried out, not a word, just a sound, a half-choked plea to no one. He knew that sound, it was familiar, like a half-remembered, recurring dream.

tap-tap-tap

Dasha, the queen cat, stepped silently through the door and four fluffy white kittens mewed their hellos. The spell was broken. Gor gulped in air and flung the wardrobe shut, cursing himself for a fool and stamping into his boots. How could he be scared of a little tapping! Where was his logic? Had his brain turned to fluff? There was no such thing as the supernatural! There were no such things as ghosts!

The kittens watched him, blue eyes wide, pretending to be brave with their backs arched and paws prancing. He apologised for the noise, smoothed down his wiry hair, and slammed out of the flat.

He found he needed some company, and the streets would serve very well.

Azov's market was a modern structure: solid and unfussy on the outside, warm, dark and smelly on the inside. Clear plastic panels in the high-pitched roof let light into the centre, but the edges were folded in shadows: it was best to visit during sunshine if you wanted to see what you were buying, and how much change you got. The scent of overripe fruit swung sweetly, heavy in the air. Glowing persimmons and fiery pomegranates lay in pyramids side-by-side with precious local honey and bags of winter grain, while on the floor sacks of potatoes and turnips lounged in lumpen splendour. Gor ploughed along the narrow aisle, blind to the rough-skinned stallholders as they called to him, thrusting out samples, flashing gold teeth and knife-blades as they cut cubes of melon and blisters of pomegranate seeds. He needed no fruit.

He stopped at a dairy stall for a small cube of cheese: whiter than snow, it was solid and salty, with the supple, rubbery texture he liked. Next he bought flat-leaf parsley, richly scented black bread, and a tiny pat of soft, salt-less butter that came wrapped in brown paper. He had his own aubergine spread and salted tomatoes in the store cupboard, the result of sweaty summer labours at the *dacha*. The snacks he would serve would be solid and unassuming. Savoury was required. Sveta's warmness towards him, her sunny openness, made his palms sweat. There must be no hint of intimacy today: sweetmeats were out, as was anything pink, red or yellow. Bread and cheese would do: theirs must be friendship in the face of adversity – and nothing more. He could not and should not encourage closeness.

Gor's old string bag was almost full and it pulled at his shoulder. He was sniffing a tea sample, long nose buried amongst the pungent black leaves, when he had the distinct impression that someone was staring at him. He turned to his left, tea still in hand, and scanned the blur of faces and hats: brown, pink, sallow, fiery, knitted, woven, peaked; there was no one he knew, and no one was staring. He began to screw the lid back on and felt a sharp dig in his ribs. The tin dropped from his hand, showering leaves over the stall, his coat and the floor before clanging to the ground. The stallholder fell upon him, clucking her tongue and waving him away. A snigger slinked around his elbow and he turned to challenge the culprit, but there was no crowd behind him and no laughing faces: no one, in fact. He dusted down his coat and moved slowly on down the aisle, eyes roving restlessly between the stalls.

At the butcher, pigs' heads laughed at him from hooks in the beams, dribbling blood onto the sawdust below. In a cage on the floor jostled half a dozen rabbits with whiffling pink noses. They regarded him with trembling intensity: white rabbits, exactly like the one he had found on his doorstep. A chopper whacked a knuckle of pork from its trotter, sending silver bone splinters and globules of fat high into the air. Gor jumped. The butcher laughed and bellowed something he did not understand. He shook his head and hurried down an aisle where the empty eyes of a hundred fishes watched him from brown bowls of salty slime. An old woman with two teeth stepped before him, waving a handful of cod roes under his nose. He felt bile rise in his throat and lurched for the exit.

He slammed through the door into an alley and leant momentarily against the bulk of a bin, breathing deeply, eyes shut. When he opened them, a stray dog, jaws clamped on a fish tail, was standing before him, growling softly. He began walking. He knew you should show no fear, but found it easier said than done. He could almost feel the mutt's teeth ripping into his tendons, and broke into a trot, the string bag bumping uncomfortably on his hip. His footsteps echoed as he skipped around piles of leaves shifting on the paving slabs. He heard a whistle behind him: a familiar tune – Mussorgsky, the very notes he'd enjoyed at home this morning. He looked around, ankle turning in the leaves. The only movement was the limping, empty-eyed dog. He hurried on to the main street, relieved to join the bodies shuffling to and fro.

He passed a thick queue snaking around the corner. The face of each queuer was tormented, their voices calling out to no one, spitting shards of harsh words about robbers, thieves, the government, empty bellies and despair. No one listened, not even the other queuers. Gor walked on.

The head of the queue rested at a closed door: the local PPP Invest offices. A doorman shaped like a bullet stood immobile behind the glass. Someone threw a bank book and it bounced with a thud on the glass just left of his head. He put a hand inside his jacket where his heart should have been, and the crowd drew back, gasping. Gor hurried on and crossed the road, looking over his shoulders this way and that, without meaning to.

They were still trying to get their money out. Life savings invested in nothing but stupidity: PPP Invest – a classic pyramid scheme. More and more people paid in – an entire week's pay, or a month's pension, or a lifetime's savings, or even . . . and the ridiculous dividends were paid out, week on week. But at some point, the fever had to break, didn't it? That's how it worked: at a certain point, maximum capacity was reached, the promised dividend became simply unimaginable: as big as the moon. That was the point when the bosses snuck across the border with lorry-loads of dollars, and the investors were left behind – with nothing but paper and despair. Just paper, fluttering in their hands, their plans of a happy retirement, or building their own house on the weekends, or buying a new fridge and TV so much salty water on their cheeks.

He stopped to cough into his handkerchief, eyeing the queue from around its edges, and felt a creeping in his neck. Someone was following him. He twisted around, eyes raking the crowd: a head turned quickly, a woman moved away. Gor checked his pockets, patting for wallet and keys, and whistled with relief: nothing missing. She was weaving through the crowd now, vaguely familiar. Did he know that girl? Did she know him? Maybe she just reminded him of someone? There were so many people now – a forest of faces.

He looked at his boots and pulled the shopping bag higher on his shoulder. He was in need of a soft-boiled egg – a cross-word – tea – Tchaikovsky. And maybe, yes, maybe a chat with Sveta. Maybe he didn't have to wait until the rehearsal. Maybe he could give her a ring. He could ring to discuss the mild weather, and the order of rehearsal, or the situation in Chechnya, or a recipe for borscht. Perhaps he would do that. He hurried for the trolleybus stop.

THE PRINCESS

Polly studied her reflection in the window. There were grey smudges beneath her wide, black eyes, and her cheekbones shone sharp white against the frame of her hair. It had been a late night and an early morning. She wouldn't be surprised if she'd caught a cold; it was getting late in the year to be making out on park benches till midnight, after all.

She hadn't really had much choice. Vlad had been so full of himself, of long words and crowing exclamations and full-blown doctor-bluster; she'd had to stay. He'd repeated to her, almost word for word, the story the old man had told him, and his conclusions on his health. She hadn't asked any questions at all. Moth boy, the burning cottage, the sparks in the night sky, the ravaged faces of the family and neighbours; all had been presented to her in tableau, and she'd had a good look as she shivered. People were wrong when they said vodka warmed you from the inside.

'And his cousin – you know, who loved to scare him, who told him these old stories – is the old Armenian! What are the chances? Anatoly Borisovich is in there, all on his own in the Vim – and he's never come to visit him, not once!'

She took a gulp from the bottle and passed it to Vlad.

'That surprises you? It doesn't surprise me. He's better off without him.'

'Well, from what you've said, you might be right. But still . . .' Vlad took a sip and grimaced. 'Okh, next time, can we get some Coke with this?'

'You and your Coke!' She leant in and licked his spirit-burnt lips. 'You know it's full of sugar, as well as chemicals?'

He chuckled as he pushed his hand down the back of her trousers.

'Do you think . . . do you think you can cure him, Vlad?'

The hand squeezed her buttocks. 'I don't think "cure" is the right word, princess. He's remembered a lot, but he's old, frail – and there's a blank where his recent past should be. I will make a diagnosis, recommendations, you never know – but I doubt he will go home.' His other hand squeezed into her trousers. 'Dr Spatchkin has concerns about his heart, too.'

'There was nothing in his notes about his heart!'

The hands stilled and he pulled back to look at her.

'How do you know what was in his notes?'

She met his gaze, raised her chin, and decided to tell the truth. 'I read his file.'

He almost jumped off the bench. 'What do you mean, you read his file?'

'Don't look like that! It was when I came to see you, the other week. You fell asleep. I was bored. And, well, I'm studying gerontology too, you know. I read a lot of the files. You were catching flies, at the time.' She mimed a snore and shrugged, passing him the bottle.

She'd had to work quite hard to make him forget about it.

That was unusual. He had been like a dog chewing a baba's leg, not her usual billy-goat, easily led by his horns. She'd eventually got to her bed with numb fingers and toes. But it had been worth it.

And now she was admiring her reflection in the dusty windows of the pharmacy, where normally she'd have clocked on that morning. The blue-faced boredom of the early shift had spoilt her days all through the summer, had ground her down almost to nothing. How she'd enjoyed skiving today. She resisted the urge to spit in the doorway and instead focused on the positive; her intelligence, her beauty and her resourcefulness. She rearranged her hat, the rich red of the knit complementing the black-earth glow of her hair. She had told them she was sick, but now she didn't care if they saw her.

She smiled serenely as she walked on. It was funny how you could put up with almost anything, any kind of daily drudgery, desertion, or despair, once you saw a clear way out, gathered your courage, and took those decisive steps.

She stopped at a bank of grey public pay-phones glistening like giant slugs in the autumn sun. There would be more privacy here than at her student hostel. She chose a phone for inter-city calls and heaved out her purse, fat with brown plastic phone tokens. It was followed by her notebook, where she had hurriedly scribbled down the number and address of the flat – the same night she'd read his file. The same night she'd taken his key. She grinned again at her own cleverness and punched in the digits. The pips pipped, and she pushed in the play-money.

'Is that Babkin? Yes, it's Polina. I . . . yes, don't worry about it . . . the carpet tiles come up, I'll replace it. It's fine.' Babkin's voice slurred through his leathery gums. She really didn't want the detail. She decided to talk over him. 'Listen, I have good news: the problem at this end is totally resolved, and I can extend the lease indefinitely . . .' She paused until the grateful babble at the other end subsided. 'But I'm sure you'll understand, as the circumstances have changed for the better, I now need three months' rent, in advance . . . cash, dollars.'

Babkin didn't like it. He squeaked fiercely. She was unmoved. 'I'll explain again. When it was a short let, you could have it week on week, but now, well, it will be a long let, and I must ask the market rate. I can't thieve from myself, can I? And the market rate in Rostov is a three-month deposit.'

She waited for silence, and let a pause inch by.

'Then you leave me no choice. If you won't pay, you must go. Two weeks; it's in the contract . . .' Babkin turned ruder, but she knew he would go. He didn't have residency papers, he wouldn't dare go to the police. He didn't have a leg to stand on, really. She reminded him of the fact, and replaced the receiver. Twin plumes of steam fired from her nostrils.

Babkin could go. If the old man was now long-term at the Vim, she could accommodate a more solid tenant, someone semi-permanent, who could pay upfront. Someone with teeth and a job. A working family, maybe. Her cheeks swelled in a grin. Perhaps she could advise the good doctor Vlad on the old man's treatment? Use a little psychology . . . And perhaps she would ensure that he never made it back to his flat in Rostov, at all.

She puffed on a Pall Mall as she walked. She would have a proper clear-out once Babkin was gone: she'd only had time to shove a few boxes into cupboards so far. The tenant was

131

camping amid collections of paintings and paper, mountains of books, a mangy sheepskin, an ugly mannequin, and who knew what else. The place had been a state: that's why he'd had a good rate. She caught sight of herself in a shop window, and caught her breath: that smile was beautiful, audacious even. The smile of a winner.

On she walked, heading for the bus stop but somehow unable to resist the call of the White Flamingo department store and its folk-craft collectibles. For most of her youth its shelves had lain half-empty and uninviting. How she'd detested it. But things were changing: enterprise had the upper hand, in retail as in all areas of life. The tubes in the neon sign had been replaced, and now the White Flamingo had found itself. Oases of interest now sparkled within its walls in place of endless dusty textbooks and single sets of Czech make-up that you could look at but not buy. Even the sexless mannequins that had stood guard over the fall of the Soviet Union had been re-born, now crookedly resplendent in garish Lithuanian polo shirts, Capri shorts fresh from Turkey, and lacy Chinese knickers.

One section alone fascinated Polly, and it didn't feature a single imported item. She pushed open the dented metal door and hurried past Counter No. 1, Stationery and School Products, which had always been a desert to her, and made for her treasure trove, her Shangri-la: Counter No. 2, Gifts and Souvenirs.

In a glass cabinet with a scratched top that none were permitted to lean on, there sparkled a myriad of rainbow colours, shiny shapes and glistening figures. Crystal, porcelain, bark-work and lacquer: intricate, beautiful, tiny and valuable.

Polly leant her hands on the impenetrable glass and stared down, mute black eyes digging into every curve and notch of each folk-work collectable. Her favourite was the Palekh work: dark lacquered trinket boxes, each with a scene from Russian folklore depicted on the lid in tiny, glowing brush strokes. Each with a value of over 150 dollars. Each a solid investment, the real black gold. She counted out the boxes, recognising the fairy-tale scenes depicted on each one: the firebird and the grey wolf; Ruslan and Ludmila; a troika of long-limbed horses with flowing manes like cresting waves; the plunging magic pike; Father Frost in his fur coat and boots, and her favourite – the brave and fearless Frog Princess. She gazed at the tiny pictures on each side of the box, losing herself in them, like a child. Here was Princess Vasilisa the Wise, holding her discarded frog skin; Vasilisa performing magic; her husband the Prince seeking her salvation from Baba Yaga, and the final defeat of her evil master, Kashei the Immortal. Polly stood, impervious to the jostles of the shoppers around her, her senses filled with the heaving black forest, the smell of the swamp, the hut on chicken legs, and the power of magic.

She felt comforted: at one with Mother Russia, if not with her own progenitor. Wasn't she following in the footsteps of her distant forebears? Who needed family when you had ancestors?

The folklore princess had grabbed her happiness: made her own fate. Vlad called her his princess. And she would be. But princesses needed money.

She felt rest in her soul and a calm on her brow just looking at the boxes, safe in the knowledge that soon, very soon, another would be in her possession. Little boxes to tell her she wasn't stupid. Little boxes to tell her everything would be fine. Little boxes that were her friends, and her security. You could never have too many Palekh boxes.

'Girl, move out of the way, would you, I can't see the porcelain!' An underfed man with a sharp nose and the flat, grey eyes of a shark breathed lunchtime's omelette into her face as he leant across to examine a ceramic representation of the folklore hero Sadko, who stood like a glazed and puffy ice-cream next to the darkly delicate Palekh boxes. She recoiled from the armpit of his leather coat: it was cold and slightly slimy.

'That's a lovely one,' he observed in an undertone, licking his lips. 'For an investment, maybe, you know, longer term. How much is it, can you see? I can't count the noughts.' His nose screwed up to refocus the dead eyes, and Polly looked around, confused.

'Girl – tell me, how much is it?' he said more forcefully, finally glancing her way, spittle-flecked lips drawn back from greedy teeth. 'Can't you read?'

She didn't look at the price, but stared him straight in the eye and hissed, 'Don't bother. You can't afford it.'

On her way out, she stopped by the cafeteria, as she always did, just to look, and remember. That cafeteria: her father used to take her and her brother there as a treat, years ago, when she was shy, half-grown, and he was her tiny, rosy-cheeked clown. They would get a hard pastry biscuit and a glass of *kvas*, and Father would tell them to wait while he went and tried to find light-bulbs, or knickers, or vodka, or whatever else he had not managed to barter or borrow. Petya would sing songs with no words, his chubby hand sticky in hers, his eyes round, trusting. He would sing and sing, happy to be in the warm, happy with his *kvas* and biscuit. He was always so content. After a while she'd tell him to be quiet. She'd shush him and threaten to take his biscuit. She was trying to be cool, and he was annoying. She should have let him sing. What she wouldn't give to hear him sing again. What she wouldn't give to hear him giggle. It had been so long since she'd heard his voice. How she hated *kvas* and biscuits.

She turned and clattered out of the door, running for the 8A back to the student hostel. The smell of wet dog and the sharp stares of strangers didn't pierce her bubble. Today, the thought of the hostel, the shared room, the rubbish piled in the kitchens and the crippled kittens trapped in the stairwells did not depress her. The bus, the hostel, university, her awful boss Maria Trushkina at the pharmacy; they were all temporary. She would dig her way out of this.

Ten minutes later she was walking up the drive. Small black windows glowered at her over four storeys, flocks of plastic bags nestling at each windowsill: student 'refrigerators', flapping like tethered rooks. She smiled, and wondered if she should allow herself to buy a mini-fridge once she had her new tenant.

As she entered the foyer a hunched, spidery form shot out from behind the concierge desk and clamoured at her, waving a piece of paper over its head.

'Hey, hey!' the form shrieked.

'Elena Dmitrovna, do you have a message for me?' Polly knew a performance was coming: it always was. She tried not to scowl.

'Yes I do, and it sounds interesting,' said a voice like splintered wood.

135

'Really?'

'Yes.'

'Can I see?'

The old lady held the piece of paper to her breast and looked along her nose at Polly. She harrumphed and blew out her cheeks, and then sucked them back in, wincing.

'Akh, my sciatica!'

'Ah, I promised you those tablets, didn't I? I hadn't forgotten. It's so busy at the pharmacy at the moment . . . I have no time to myself. I'll get them for you. This week. For definite.' Polly smiled, eyes slithering shut.

Elena Dmitrovna tapped her fingers on the piece of paper clenched between her hands.

'Tomorrow?'

'Of course!'

'Very well.' The old woman handed over the paper and remained standing where she was, blocking Polly's path to the stairs.

'Well?' she said.

Polly read the message in silence.

'You see! A séance! Interesting! I told you!' The old lady danced on the spot, the ring of keys at her waist jangling.

Polly rolled her eyes.

'It was your friend Alla who phoned.'

'I can see that.' She took a step to the left. The concierge mirrored her, blocking her path.

'She sounded like she wants to see you.'

'Yes.' She took a step to the right. Again the old lady blocked her.

'She said she hasn't seen you for a while.'

'No—'

'And she's been poorly.'

'Ah?' Polly nodded and darted around the woman, jumping for the stairs.

'And your Vladimir telephoned.'

She stopped with her left foot on the second step, her hands curled into fists at her sides. She did not turn around.

'And?'

'He thinks you should go to the séance. Said it would be, now what was it . . . worth your while: yes, that was his exact phrase.' Elena Dmitrovna retreated to the dimness of her desk and the shabby armchair behind it. 'Asked you to telephone him as soon as possible.'

Polly kicked the step in front of her and marched back down the stairs for the double doors.

'We had a bit of a talk. He's a lovely young man, isn't he? A doctor! You can phone from here if you like? I promise I won't listen!'

The old lady's laugh whistled through her rotten teeth like the wind through the trees as Polly slammed back out of the hostel to find a working pay-phone. How she detested the old.

COLOURS AND CRAYONS

The grumpy orderly launched dust and noise through the air as the metal strips of the blind hit the top of the frame. Anatoly Borisovich's eyes, ravaged by time, fluttered open. Morning light pooled on his bedside table, illuminating crayons and sugar paper, almost as if they were real. He squinted and pushed himself upright, his hand drifting towards the paper; a cry of joy escaped him when it bent to his touch.

'Well, this is quite marvellous!' he said at last, shaking with anticipation as he stroked the smooth cylinders of the crayons. He could feel the colours without looking: he knew this was blue, this was red, this was yellow. They gave off energy, a frequency that tingled on his fingertips, pulsated up his arm to tickle his heart. He giggled and patted at the bedsheets with excitement.

'Now these might save my life! Oh, yes!'

'Are you going to draw us something, then, eh?' asked the orderly, her back to him as she ladled the buckwheat porridge into a dented aluminium bowl.

'No, I'm going to eat them!' replied Anatoly Borisovich with a laugh that erupted from his belly and danced around the room. The orderly sniffed. He apologised and agreed, of course he was going to draw something.

She placed the bowl and a spoon on his bedside table, and snorted.

'And what are you going to draw, if it's no secret?'

'Well, I don't know, we'll have to wait and see. When I take up the colours, they will tell me what to draw. It's impossible to plan . . . you have to go where they take you.'

'You could draw that tree.' The orderly stared out of the window with her hands on her hips. 'It's the last one. The rest went rotten.'

'If all else fails, I could draw that tree,' Anatoly Borisovich replied as he caressed the yellow crayon, and then the red. 'Did Vlad get me these? I told him I wanted to draw. It was Vlad, wasn't it? He understands me . . .'

'Vladimir? The student? You must be joking. He's too busy with that fancy girl of his. Do you know, I caught them at it in the office the other week. He's obsessed—' she broke off and straightened her tabard as Anatoly Borisovich stared, open-mouthed. 'Anyway, Dr Spatchkin got you the crayons: he over-ruled Matron. He thought drawing might help with your confusion. And the nightmares.'

'Nightmares?'

'We hear you crying out at night, you know. You make a lot of noise. We have to report it.' She folded her arms and sighed. 'I'd say you've taken a turn for the worse. You're off your food again.' She nodded at the bowl.

Anatoly Borisovich put down the crayons and regarded his porridge with a complete lack of interest. 'There is nothing wrong with my appetite that reasonable food will not fix.' The sudden spurt of energy was trickling away. He lay back against the pillows, too tired to move, almost too tired to breathe. She was right about the nightmares.

But still, like a voice far away, he heard the green crayon calling to him.

'I'm sorry for the disturbance. Sometimes I feel I have remembered too much, and it all comes rushing . . . it scares me, confuses me.' He raised a hand to tickle the green crayon and then caress the sugar paper. 'Drawing is my love. It has always helped me straighten my mind along life's higgledy-piggledy road. I remembered a lot with Vlad the other day. Maybe too much? He hasn't come back, and since then I—'

'Forget that Vladimir! Who does he think he is, telling me to wash my hands between patients? Such a know-all. You shouldn't eat cheese at bedtime,' said the orderly, and puffed into her chest, chin down, to push the porridge trolley towards the door.

'This is also true,' said Anatoly Borisovich after a moment, with a kindly smile. 'Not that cheese is a staple here. But I wish he would come back.'

She shrugged and turned back to the trolley, the wheels clacking as she heaved. 'He's around. He's probably finished with you for the moment. Enjoy your drawing.'

He listened as the wheels trundled under their weight of porridge to the next room: the peremptory knock, the vague sound of voices as the door opened and she went in. He had never met his neighbour. He still couldn't remember how he had come here. He couldn't remember the journey, or what the outside of the building might look like. He couldn't remember the summer even. Sixty years ago, yes, that was clear

140

enough, but six months ago? Three months ago? He had yet to fit those pieces into place. He scanned the grey horizon, the mud flats, the tree, and shoved the ugly porridge aside. In its place he laid four sheets of paper and all the crayons. He started with circles, squares, geometric patterns, thinking hard and not at all, his hand shaking with the effort.

He began with the easy: remembering where he lived. It wasn't out here by the sea though. It was in the town: in Rostov! Of course, how had he forgotten that? Rostov was his home town now! His fingers curled around the blue crayon. He gradually recalled his apartment, his home for many years, and the lovely things he'd filled it with. A jumble of furniture and long-forgotten artefacts dropped into his mind like rain into a bucket, getting steadily stronger, the surface of the water dancing. He could see them: the sheepskin on the wall, the mannequin in its shaman's cap, the books across the shelf, his easel, the maps and papers sprawling on his desk, and best of all, his shoe box, home of special treasures, hidden beneath his chair. He remembered the view of the trees in the courtyard: a proper copse, right by his window. He remembered its still-ness. Cats and crows, chessmen and playing cards; he remembered them all, piece by piece, putting together the puzzle. His hand moved on: more patterns, bigger, bolder. He could smell the wallpaper now, and feel the fuzz of the carpet under his toes. He sensed the creaking of the shoe rack in the hall, and the lazy buzz of flies in the kitchen. He caressed the cracked plastic receiver of the phone that never rang, and heard the hum of the lift out in the hall.

It was all there. The tick of the heating system, the crackle of the radio. The tin of lemon sweets on the side by his hiking sticks. But something was wrong. He tried to think and etched big circles, circles over circles, ripples in a pond. He recalled the maps had become prisons, the chessmen his enemies. They'd laughed at him, tortured him: the wiggled lines and hard faces had eaten into his mind. There was medicine: it came to him, the sour taste of the syrup, the bottle smashed on the floor. He'd had a fever! That was it! He'd lain in his apartment, glued to the sofa, unable to walk, sweating and shaking. He'd stared at the calendar, the harsh, stand-offish numerals, and he'd known . . . something. He had the expectation, he'd waited and waited. Someone was coming. But . . .

Eventually, a neighbour had thought it odd: he had not called for promised vegetables, had failed to collect his post. There were raps at the door, tap-tap-tapping, but he couldn't answer. All he could do was rave. He was afraid. Alone and forgotten, feeling abandoned, he'd waited for death as the sun rose and set, and the trees tapped on the window.

Instead of death, an official had come, with dirty shoes and a big black briefcase, the caretaker in tow. They'd let themselves in and covered their noses as they spoke. The doctor had been called, the union, and more.

The leaves had still been on the trees, there had been warmth in the air, the sound of bees . . .

So he'd let them take him, like a child: a brown-paper label tied around his wrist, they had packed him off, no goodbyes or hellos, to a place with mud and wind and salt marshes, and a lone pine tree. He'd lost himself along the way, like a leaf blown on the wind. The crayon rubbed the paper. He could smell the wax.

Shortly before supper, he dropped the crayon stub, exhausted.

There it lay before him, the map of his recent past. He could follow it, tracing with his finger, right up until Vlad.

Vlad, who had let him speak, who had nodded, smiled, questioned, and most of all, listened.

When would Vlad come back? He had a tickling in his bones, a clawing in his brain, something trying to get out. The story wasn't quite finished; it wasn't quite right. If only he could work it out!

The door scraped.

'Do you need the toilet?'

Anatoly Borisovich did not turn his head.

MY NAME IS SVETA

Sveta regarded herself in the full-length mirror of the bathroom as the horizon swallowed the sun. Electric light was supposed to be flattering, but the black polyester dress stuck to her every dimple and bulge. A slip would be unavoidable.

'Mama! Come out of the bathroom! You've been in there for ages!' Albina shouted, hammering at the door with her fists. Sveta smiled: the door had been closed for no more than twenty seconds. The child was a live-wire. Such spirit!

'Yes, baby-kins, I'm coming.' Sveta's sweetness at home, around Albina, was a secret she treasured closely. By day, in her persona of Svetlana Mikhailovna Drozhdovskaya, part-time teacher of English, she was strict, often demanding, blessed with an eagle's glare and a sigh of admonition that could knock a goat off its feet. She took her teaching seriously. After all, Years 2–6 presented a critical stage in pupil development: they could still be encouraged, their horizons expanded. Occasionally she scared the more timid ones with her passion: she could see their bottom lips trembling, their brains churning to butter as she demanded more of them than they were used to. But they would thank her when they were older if just a grain of that passion was left imprinted on their souls. Sveta knew she did a good job. She received the largest bouquets on leavers' day, as well as the best fruit each new term. And, of course, a large dollop of the children's respect, which was at least as important.

She leant towards the mirror and applied a rich clot of lipstick. She considered its effect, head on one side, and decided it would do very well. In her bones, she knew her talents were wasted. It was all very well making future plumbers and book-keepers recite Shakespeare with something approximating a British accent, but it lacked challenge. There was a hole in her life. Not a man-shaped hole, but a hole, nonetheless. Maybe that was why she loved mystics and psychics, and maybe that was what had made her answer Gor's advert. The excitement of . . . something else. She gazed into the mirror and imagined the fit of the bodice, the feathers at her shoulder, the glint of the tiara. The magician's assistant, or the acrobat's assistant: this was the life she had not lived, yet.

She had not lied when she told Gor she'd made her acrobat go. She had no regrets. But she needed a teaspoon of the extraordinary: a chance to be brave and to feel mystery, whether it lay in the bottom of a teacup, flitted around a candle, or was secured in a magical cabinet.

She dotted powder on her nose as Albina rained blows on the door. Tuesday's rehearsal had been very strange. Firstly, Gor had telephoned her in the middle of the afternoon to remind her of their appointment, something that was clearly unneces-sary. Secondly, he had insisted on staying on the line for a further ten minutes to lecture her on the drought in Central Asia, while she was in the middle of trying to set her hair. And thirdly, when she'd actually arrived, he'd been by turn aloof and excitable, rushing from one trick to the next, from room to room, darting between the lights and the props, hands shaking. There had even been a flush of colour in his cheeks, at times. Strangest of all though, he'd attempted to smile – a number of times. She didn't yet know Gor like a brother, but she knew him well enough – smiling was a bad sign. She had been tempted to telephone him in the intervening days, just to check that he was alive. But he was unlikely to answer the telephone, or even the door. She dearly hoped Madame Zoya would be able to give him the comfort he needed tonight.

She opened the bathroom door.

'I don't know why you bother with that lipstick, Mama. You still look old,' the girl smirked, pushing past to take her place before the mirror.

'Albina, that isn't kind. I am forty-three, and I look forty-three, that is all.'

'You look old. Look at me! I'm young and . . . and . . .' Albina regarded her body, twisting and turning in the mirror. 'And . . . fat!' She stuck her tongue out at her reflection and puffed her cheeks. 'You feed me the wrong food, Mama. You're making me fat. We should have Danish yoghurt every day! Why don't we have Danish yoghurt? That's what the other girls have.'

Sveta smiled as she walked towards the bedroom. 'We don't need imported food. Those yoghurts are full of chemicals. And think about the kilometres they have to come.'

'You're so old fashioned!' Albina followed her from the bathroom. 'Just because it's imported, it doesn't mean it's bad.'

'Yes, but it doesn't mean it's good either, *malysh*. When I was little—'

'Boring!' bellowed Albina, 'Boring, boring! Why are you always talking about *you*? You don't care about *me* at all! You won't even buy me yoghurt!' She stomped from the room, feet thudding on the parquet as she headed for her lair. 'You won't buy me anything!' she added, slamming her door.

Sveta looked after the girl and breathed out slowly. She hadn't thought having a daughter would be like this. She could dimly remember her daydreams from before Albina was born: she'd envisaged a companion, with similar tastes, who would help with the cooking, go to dance lessons, enjoy the poetry of Pushkin and the pop of Alla Pugachova. Someone who would cherish her, and read to her in the evenings. Not someone who would teach a parakeet to swear. She smiled and wriggled into her slip, patting it down this way and that. You never knew what you were going to get. That was half the fun.

She renewed her lipstick for luck, and went to the hallway for her galoshes. She could make out Kopek saying something disgusting and her daughter humming a TV jingle for processed cheese.

'I'll see you later, sweet-ums!' she called out. 'Auntie Vera from next door will be here at seven, so not long to wait. Make sure you take your bath.'

Albina's head poked through her doorway at the end of the corridor. Kopek was sitting in her hair. 'Tell Mister Papasyan . . . tell him I hope he feels better.'

Madame Zoya's apartment sprawled on the top floor of one of Azov's oldest buildings, right in the town centre. The four flights of stairs up to it were wooden, steep and uneven. Sveta passed bricked-up doorways, crooked nooks and niches, and the banisters themselves resembled sinewed, twisting snakes. She puffed, cursing the slip that stuck to her tights, threatening to bind her legs as she moved, and her hand trembled as she pressed the perished buzzer of Flat 13. After a long wait, silent but for her panting, the door opened a crack.

'What business?'

'The spirits!'

The door creaked open a few centimetres. Before her in the half-light stood a tiny, wizened woman, her puny body entirely swathed in shiny purple, including her head, where perched an attempt at a turban. It sat upon her strangely solid hair like a purple hen on a blue-black nest. Piercing black eyes, accentuated by a smudge of violet eye-liner, peered out around a long, sharp nose.

'Madame Zoya.' Sveta took a little curtsey. 'Thank you for arranging this.'

The eyes crawled over Sveta. There was a grunt and a yawn, and the head craned forward, the light from the stairwell throwing its contours into sharp relief: a face ancient and creviced, like Mount Elbrus. 'My dear, my dear . . . erm, dearest. I have just woken from my preparatory nap. Who are you?'

Sveta's cheeks wobbled with confused indignation as she introduced herself, adding, 'I am with Gor Papasyan, of course. You recall? We spoke on the telephone. We have met many times before, Madame.'

'Of course! I recall everything, child, there's no need to explain. It is an honour to be of assistance to the gentleman, and indeed, your good self. I have heard so much about the gentleman – at the library, in the theatre, when I go to collect my pension, and of course at the Elderly Club. Sadly, he is not a member. I am thrilled, I must tell you. He is of a more interesting quality than most I get around my table.' She cackled, and paused, head snapping from side to side, her hen-turban quivering. 'Where is he, anyway?'

'He is making his own way here, Madame. I did offer a lift, but he wanted to be alone.' She leant forward. 'It is his pride, I think. You'll have heard about his pride?'

'Yes, and I hear he keeps himself to himself.' She crinkled the corner of an eye at Sveta, holding wide the door. 'Come in, child, and make yourself comfortable. I am expecting a crowd tonight. Oh yes, everyone wants to know what is troubling our mysterious Armenian. I think they're interested in his money, to be frank. There are stories of gold. You know he was a bank manager?'

Sveta's previous contact with Zoya was limited to a series of unsuccessful try-outs at the Amateur Dramatics Society, and various psychics' meetings at a friend's house, where the lady sometimes turned up and scared them all to death. Being received in the doyenne's dominion gave her a frisson of excitement. She was led into the salon, large and high-ceilinged, with long, curtained windows all across one wall. Her first impression – that it was impossibly dark, over-filled with furnishings of every era and studded with horrifically stuffed animals – was swiftly overtaken by the smell. The air that hung between those ancient walls was heavy with incense, rich tobacco and a noxious spirit: rum, perhaps. It smelled like the kind of place where things happened. Sveta's hands were clammy with excitement.

Zoya hopped around the room, her spidery fingers rearranging half-full ashtrays and ugly ornaments. 'I need to concentrate!'

She stopped to sniff at a half-smoked cigar. 'Ah! Yes, I am recalling.' Her eyelids fluttered. 'Our cast of characters: here's the run-down: we've got Alla from the White Flamingo – she's poor at channelling energy, a bit floppy all round, but she gives me discounts on rum, so it's a benefit to have her. And there's Masha from the Palace of Youth – she's very keen on dance and men; but then, aren't we all?' She stopped to wheeze. 'Then there's Nastya from the library, who has a thing for elderly folk: she's quite nosey, fairly experienced and . . . erm, hang on.' She lit the cigar and puffed a smoke ring into the air. Sveta coughed. 'Where did we get to? Oh yes, of course! There's Valya, from the bank. She is a sceptic, but she frightens easily. She's been coming for a while. Her husband passed away but he won't talk to her. Now . . .' She fixed Sveta with a bright black eye. 'Valya will be bringing her lodger, the handsome Vlad – he's a medical student, works at the sanatorium. He's new. Came round the other evening to introduce himself: helped out with some DIY – I have to check new sitters' credentials, you see. He was most helpful . . . really quite delicious.' She shut her eyes and pouted. 'And he's bringing Polly. She's a friend of Alla's . . . sort of. Troubled background, she's been once before, but . . . we'd best not . . . She's a medical student also, works in a pharmacy – good for supplies!' Zoya cackled, cigar smoke erupting from her mouth and rising lazily to the ochre ceiling.

'But I haven't a clue what their souls are like! Ha! Now, can you tell me more about Papasyan, before he gets here? I've done a little digging, but . . .' She clawed at Sveta's sleeve with her sharp fingers.

'Well, no, Madame, not really. He is a very private person. But the silent telephone calls, noises in the hall, the headless rabbit, the moth sandwich, the face at the window: all these things suggest, to me at least, magic, or spirit movement, or some other—'

'—manifestation of evil intent?'

'Yes.'

'Yesss!' Madame Zoya stretched out the word as a snake hisses in its coils. 'Hey ho! We must get the table out, and put up a barricade – to stop the smokers from collapsing the balcony. Believe me, it will be necessary. Here, pass me that stool, will you? And the bookcase, just shove the bookcase over here,' Zoya commanded in her curious, gravel-crunch voice.

Sveta was momentarily immobile, utterly surprised at being commanded to shift furniture while wearing a slip. 'Shouldn't we wait, Madame, until a man gets here . . .'

'Why?' demanded Zoya, her head cocked to one side. 'You look strong, I'd give you at least seventy-five kilos, no?' Sveta blushed. 'Don't doubt your own abilities! Take that end, and on my count: ready, heave!'

The ladies shifted the fully laden constructivist bookcase across the wooden floor and into the doorway to the balcony.

'There! That should prevent any accidents,' Zoya laughed. 'Now, let's make sure we have the lighting levels right.' She flicked a switch and they stood together in total blackness.

'Madame Zoya? I think that is a little dark.'

'Aw . . .'

'No, really, Madame.'

'Nonsense! How am I to concentrate if we have light annoying my eyelids! I think that is about right.'

'But Madame Zoya, I cannot see anything.'

'That's the point.'

'Don't the spirits seek the light, Madame? Just gentle light – candles?'

'Candles?' Zoya considered. 'Ahhh! Yes, I think you're right. I will find some.' She flicked the light switch and went to rummage in a drawer that sounded like it housed a thousand jigsaws, all with no lids.

A buzz proclaimed the arrival of the first guest. Zoya hopped back to the room, three red candles in her hand. 'Look, new ones, still in wrappers! Right, erm . . . sorry my dear, what was your name?'

'Sveta,' said Sveta flatly.

'Don't be offended, Sveta dear, it is my age. Now remember: for the séance, it will be your job to ensure there is absolute calm. I will be otherwise engaged.'

'Yes, Madame Zoya. All will be calm,' said Sveta seriously. She would employ her teaching skills to ensure the conversation with the spirit world was orderly. She flexed her hands and cracked her knuckles.

A procession of young and curious, old and experienced presented themselves at the door. Sveta took coats, smiled and tried to imbue calm into every handshake. Her own hands felt sweaty. When would Gor arrive?

The bell buzzed. She leapt to open the door, expecting Gor's morose features, and stood transfixed, the breath solidified in her throat. Before her stood the beautiful young man she'd seen at the Palace of Youth.

'Good evening,' he murmured, grey eyes caressing hers.

'Yes?' said Sveta with a breathless smile, her eyes moving to his parted lips as her heartbeat fluttered beneath her breast.

'We're here for the séance,' the tall, dark girl at his side spoke. Sveta jumped at the words: she had not noticed the girl. Dark eyes assessed her.

'Ah, Vovka, you made it then?' Valya cried from across the hallway, bustling forward, gold teeth flashing, her plump hands extended in welcome.

Sveta stood her ground. She wanted a proper introduction.

'My name is Sveta, I am assisting Madame Zoya this evening. And you are?'

'Vladimir Petrovich, but please just call me Vlad.'

'Oh, how modern!' Sveta held out her hand. He took it in his, and placed his lips to her skin.

'Polina,' said the girl, 'people call me Polly.' She smiled, her eyes gazing over Sveta's head, and pushed past into the flat.

'Shoes off!' Sveta commanded as their heels tapped over the threshold.

'I thought you'd got lost,' said Valya over her glass of compote. 'Alla and I waited on the corner for ages, but we had to give up: she was getting her trouble.' Valya gave Polly a meaningful nudge, and the girl grimaced, moving swiftly into the next room.

'I am so sorry, Valya,' Vlad took up her free hand and kissed that too.

Her face glowed. 'Let's go into the salon. You met Madame Zoya the other night, didn't you? You'll have to show me your handiwork!'

'By all means, but one moment! Let me get rid of these boots.'

Sveta's lips twitched as she patted her hair in the hallway mirror. Behind her, Vlad's buttocks curved like twin moons as he bent to slide off his boots.

'It was nothing,' continued Vlad. 'I did a little inventory of work that needs to be done, took a look at the balcony.'

'You're such a good boy!' smiled Valya.

Gor was the last to arrive. He paced about the hall and said little, trying to ignore the curious eyes that blinked at him around the doorpost of the salon. He clutched his coat to him and would have kept it on if Sveta had not insisted.

'Oh come now, Gor, the spirits will not come if they think you are about to leave!'

'The spirits will not come, full stop! Sveta, listen.' He stood before her, pale and miserable. 'This is all nonsense, and I should not have come. I was wrong to let you think this could help, but I did not want to hurt your feelings. I—'

The words disappeared as Madame Zoya swept upon him, as far as a tiny woman with a purple chicken on her head could sweep.

'My dear Gor!' she clasped his hands to her bony bosom.

'Madame Zoya,' he eyed her carefully, 'I don't think we've met?'

'Not in person, as such, but I feel I know you: your aura is so strong, Azov positively reeks of it!' She grinned, showing twin rows of tiny brown teeth book-ended by sharp canines. 'Let me assure you, it is never too late to wrestle with fate. I am thrilled you have chosen me to help you tonight!'

'Lord give me strength,' muttered Gor.

ZOYA ASKS THE SPIRITS

Gor was led into the salon a little like a man to the gallows. After considerable fuss and argument from the women gathered around him, he was placed opposite Madame Zoya at the solid, oval table. His eyes glowered fiercely, black and frightful under bushy brows, as Vlad attempted to help him into his chair.

'I'm not an invalid, you know!'

The other sitters took their places, Vlad busily pulling out a chair for each. Sveta placed herself between him and Polly, although she had to tussle quite forcefully with Valya to do so. She eyed his graceful form as he sat down next to her: his grey checked trousers could barely contain his thighs, and his upper arms flickered as he poured out water. She was very aware that his knee was resting against hers. Never before had she seen a man like this at a psychic's evening: the usual males were pale creatures, reminiscent of bent sticks. This Vlad was no bent stick. His eyes lingered on each woman in turn, and he listened, intently. Sveta sighed.

The three candles were lit and persuaded to stay upright as the women twittered and grimaced, their faces all wide eyes and mouths. Hair was flicked, and make-up reapplied.

'I'm glad you could make it, Polly, it's so long since I've seen you,' whispered Alla across the table, patting the younger girl's hand. 'Ooh, you're freezing! Do you want my cardy?'

'No!' Polly shrank into the back of her chair, pinching her nose and grimacing as Alla leant forward to envelop her in a miasma of coal-tar and polyester. 'It's only been a month or so, hasn't it? Not so long. I've been busy studying.'

'Studying?' echoed Valya loudly, waggling her head like an angry bull. 'I can't guess what subject.' She hissed out a laugh and grabbed a handful of sunflower seeds from her handbag, proceeding to shell them expertly between her tongue and teeth, showering husks to the floor.

'I just wanted . . . well, to check there were no hard feelings.' Alla's voice dropped to a pantomime whisper as she leant further over the table, her breastbone almost touching the tablecloth. 'You know, about lending you that money . . .'

Sveta's cheeks wobbled with interest and Valya inhaled a seed husk as a hush dropped across the salon. Polly glowered into the top of Alla's bent head, willing her to shut up, as the latter continued, oblivious.

'And I wanted to talk to you about my stomach. It's been very bad, and I—'

'Indeed!' nodded Polly. 'Maybe later though? We must concentrate on the spirits now, Alla. Vlad, you couldn't get me a little vodka, could you darling? I think I have a sore throat coming on.'

Vlad jumped soundlessly to his feet, smiling as if nothing could delight him more. Seven pairs of female eyes followed his progress intently. When he returned, Polly gulped the dose down in one, eyes closed.

Gor observed the girl as he waited. She seemed strangely familiar: that face, the dark eyes and hair, the pale skin with a peppering of freckles, the softly feline smile . . . but then the stout orange-haired woman with the sunflower seeds also looked familiar. He glanced in her direction, and swiftly looked away.

'He's pretending he doesn't recognise me,' Valya hissed to Alla, who was now leaning away from Polly in case of infection. She pulled her mouth up close to meet her brows. 'Not a single hello, not a word. He's such a snob! He deserves all he gets!'

Zoya, meanwhile, was enjoying Gor from across the table. She had observed him in the street and the library many times, of course. He reminded her of an old piece of bark: brown, knotted, woody, but strong. Tonight, she detected, maybe a little dry rot had set in. Maybe he was a little frayed at the ends.

'Excuse me, ladies, gentlemen, and those of you who are neither! We are gathered this evening for important work. Our esteemed friend and colleague here, Gor Papasyan,' Zoya indicated to Gor with a wave of her matchstick hand, 'a man of substance and good standing—'

'Substance all right,' said a voice, with a snigger.

'Has been experiencing strange occurrences. Occurrences, we could say, that are unexplained, and frightful. Items have been appearing and disappearing, and a headless rabbit, no less, turned up on his doorstep.'

'But he has cats, surely,' whispered Alla.

'Yes, but they are fluffy and white – they never leave the apartment!' Valya replied.

'I continue . . . headless rabbits, and a partially eaten moth sandwich.'

'Yuck!' shuddered Valya. 'But if he ate half of it, why not the other half? Well, you may as well!'

'Is that paranormal?' whispered Masha from the Palace of Youth. 'Eating an insect? Cats do it all the time, after all.'

'Moths? In a sandwich?' said Polly slowly, her black eyes wide in her face. 'I hate moths, don't you, Mister Papasyan?'

She slid a languorous gaze up the table to where the old man sat. Something about the candle-light captured in her irises sent a shiver up Gor's spine.

'Ladies please!' Zoya croaked. 'I will continue! Our dear friend . . . akh . . .'

'Sveta,' said Sveta loudly.

'Sveta, here, asked me to help. Where there is mystery, Madame Zoya is all. So I said yessssss. Now, Gor,' she skewered him with a look. 'You are attracting a deal of negative energy. Therefore, I must ask you: is there anything you need to tell us, before we start?' Her right eye twitched.

He dragged his eyes to her face, 'Um, no, Madame, I have nothing to add. You have the facts. There have been bothersome calls, tappings, rappings, hateful letters—'

'Who from?' tutted Nastya.

'Hate-mail!' exclaimed Valya. 'It's always anonymous, chicken-brain!'

'Maybe he imagined it all?' suggested Vlad. 'He is elderly, after all?'

Gor shot him a look overflowing with disdain.

'Aren't we all experts?' said Polly quietly with a smirk.

'Hush!' screeched Madame Zoya. 'Now, Gor, you say we have the facts? Some, at least . . . But, I meant . . . you have no secrets?'

'No.'

'Hidden tragedies—'

'Nope.'

'Love affairs, other indiscretions—'

'None.'

'Business failings—'

'Well really!'

'—Anything you feel you ought to share before we open up to the spirits, to ease their access this evening?' Madame took a breath and raised a straggly purple eyebrow in a regal manner.

Quiet descended, thick as porridge. Gor looked at his hands, the lines etched dark with dirt from the *dacha*, oil from the car, dust from his books and music. 'No, Madame, there is nothing you need to know.'

Zoya nodded and scratched her head with a dry, scraping sound under the turban. She sighed and tried again. 'If there is anything you know of in your past that ought to come to light now, in the open, for your own good, and of your own will, would you share it with us, please?'

Gor looked at her, puzzled, and wrinkled his forehead. 'Madame Zoya, you confuse me. Is there something specific you would like me to admit to at this point? If so, just ask.' He smiled a taut, humourless smile.

'No!' she cried. 'Of course not! But perhaps you might want to share with us – your friends here – your own family circumstances, for example? Have you ever been married, or had children, for instance?' It was like pulling teeth, Zoya acknowledged to herself, but less fun. She smiled encouragingly, the edges of her mouth curling like a sandwich left out too long. They grimaced at each other across the shimmering tablecloth.

'Well now, of course I can enlighten you there.' Gor drew a breath. Every face around the table turned to him, every nose quivering with anticipation. 'I was married, once, a long time ago.'

'Ah-ha?' Madame Zoya's smile broadened and she nodded encouragingly. 'And?'

'And nothing.' Gor shrugged, black eyes boring into the table top. 'She left me. It's common enough. Will that do?'

'Well,' began Zoya, flummoxed by her combatant's resolve, but refusing to be beaten, 'that tells us a very little. At least she's not dead, I assume?'

'Surely you could tell me that?' he murmured acidly.

The pursing of Madame's lips was almost audible. 'Dearest Gor, I will do my best. But you must trust me first; you must share a little more. Do you have offspring, a wider family perhaps? In Armenia? Or America?'

'Dearest Madame, I have a daughter, Olga.' A chorus of gasps echoed around the room. Sveta felt the blood drain from her face. Why had he never mentioned this child? 'She was a sweet thing, as I recall. Ringlets, pom-poms . . . She'd be about your age now, a little older perhaps.' He frowned, flicking his fingers dismissively towards Polly. 'But I have seen neither her nor her mother for twenty years. She took up with a pastry chef – a high flyer, in the Party hospitality world. They made Moscow their home . . . the leafy suburbs. Apart from them, and they don't count, I have very little family. A cousin, in Rostov.'

'A cousin?' pressed Zoya.

'Yes. An artist; an eccentric. We're not close. I see him once a year, on his birthday—' Gor broke off, his gaze fixed on the candles. He pulled sharply on his goatee.

'And who else?' Madame Zoya waited. 'Who else, Gor? Can you hear me? Are you unwell?'

His black eyes slowly raised to hers, and he drew a breath. 'No one else,' he said quickly. 'The Armenian side of my family – if indeed it still exists – I have no contact with.'

'You are very alone.'

'Alone? Why, I have a whole town for company, Madame! Indeed, it feels like the whole town is tapping at my door and phoning me at night! Alone would be good, believe me!' Gor glared around the table at the faces staring back. Sveta pursed her lips fiercely. He dropped his eyes to his fingers once more.

'Very well. We will begin,' proclaimed Zoya, after a short pause. 'I can feel a presence, and we don't want to keep them waiting. Hands on the table, everyone, and cross fingers with your neighbour. No, don't hold hands, you girl!' She pointed a gnarled finger at Nastya from the library, 'Not necessary! Just put your hands on the table, and empty your minds! It can't be hard! Empty your minds, and let us welcome them in!'

The candles flickered as Zoya's head flopped forward to her chest and the turban wobbled. The nine around the table touched hands and crossed fingers as Zoya began a low moan, her head swaying from side to side, eyelids twitching. Sveta's hands felt wet. Polly, to her left, seemed to be pressing her fingers into the table with super-human strength, while Vlad, on her right, was all twitches. She could feel pins and needles beginning in her little fingers as the moaning floated upwards, gradually filling the room.

Gor linked fingers with the orange-haired woman and Vlad, and looked straight ahead, feeling utterly foolish. He'd spent the last few days assuming he would think of an excuse not to attend tonight, but then, when it had come down to it, he was surprised to admit he had almost wanted to come. The events of the last few weeks had left a stain on him, and he had felt perturbed – no, more than perturbed, exhausted – by it all. He needed the reassurance of knowing it was all nonsense, to prove to himself that the laws of physics and nature were in control, and nothing supernatural could exist. His comfort would be in sniggering, inwardly, at the séance, finding it totally empty and inept, and going on his way, safe in the knowledge that he was sane, if nothing else. He graced the sitters around him with a slightly condescending, paternal smile, and closed his eyes as the incantation undulated like phlegmy waves on a care-worn, polyester sea.

'Is anybody there?' moaned Zoya softly. 'Good spirits, come forth . . . Guide us.'

Silence followed, deep and dark.

'Good spirit, come forth, guide us, we beseech you! Beloved spirit, commune with us, and move among us. Help us in our misery! Will you help us?' They waited, eyes shining, willing something to happen.

Gor shifted in his chair and tried to look at his watch without lifting his hand from the table top. It was impossible: the light was too dim, and his wrist too stiff. This was insufferable. He decided to start planning the morrow's jobs at the *dacha*, in order to keep calm while being forced to sit. The double-digging of the main potato patch should probably be put off no longer, back-breaking as it would be. He had better take a substantial packed lunch with him if—

A jolt cracked through the table, followed by a sharp knock, right in front of Gor. The candles flickered and his head snapped up, eyes probing the shadows to make out who was moving.

'Ah! We are joined! Oh spirit, we thank you! Are you willing to help us?' said Zoya, triumph underlying her voice.

There was a pause, a twitch, and again the table jolted.

'Ah, I think that's a yes, don't you?' she smirked. An uneasy murmur went around the table and frightened eyes met in the candle-light.

'Keep calm everyone, keep calm!' muttered Sveta, cheeks wobbling as Polly squeezed her fingers into the veneer. 'Young woman—' she began, but was cut off by Zoya.

'Our friend, Gor – he's the bony, old one, by the tallboy – has been suffering strange occurrences, spirit. Manifestations born of the animal kingdom – unwelcome appearances of headless creatures, winged creatures, and the like. What does this mean, oh spirit? Is he in danger?' Zoya's voice rose, 'Tell us, is he in danger?'

Silence shrouded the table as they waited, and waited, and waited for a response. Gor's nose began to itch.

A dreadful knock thudded out, rattling the candlesticks and the windowpanes.

'Yes!' hissed Zoya, her eyes watery slits in her face as she stared at the candles, nodding. 'You are in danger! We must find out more.'

Gor's lips twitched, but he said nothing.

'Oh spirits! What is the threat to our friend Gor? Can you give us more?'

The candles flickered and began to fizz and pop, as if some sort of gas was being exhaled into the air around them. Grey ghosts of smoke rose in curls and collected as a fog above the

163

sitters' heads. As the candles guttered, a host of shadows twisted across the ceiling, wrestling with the bookshelves and startling the rows of stuffed birds. The room seemed much fuller than before. Sveta gazed about her in awe, brought to life by the chill of exhilaration and fear. The spirits crowded into the room, the air moving with them.

Gor wrinkled his nose and sniffed, his face hard as teak.

'Ooh, the spirits want to enter me, they want to show me something. I must let them in,' Zoya croaked, and pulled her hands from the table towards her face. She closed her eyes and began to shake, tremors running from the folds of her enormous turban through to her fingers and down her spine, shaking the chair where she sat. She mouthed sounds that never should be heard, and made striking, round movements with her hands as if swimming, gasping for air every so often and then going back under the imagined, shiny surface. Finally, she dived lower, reaching the depths and bowing her head before, vertebra by vertebra, she raised it again as if it were a periscope, the whites of her eyes gleaming in the candle-light. She whimpered.

'Ah! The smell – wood smoke! It's coming to me! Through the trees . . .' Her head twisted as she spoke, the neck bones crunching like twigs under foot. 'Such awful heat!' Her hands clawed at her bosom.

'Fire!' Sveta heard a whisper to her left. Her head flicked around to make out who was speaking, but in the next moment the table bucked under their hands and a knock cracked out, right in front of Gor. His stony face broke into a grimace and he went to pull away, but Vlad tugged his hands back sharply. 'Don't break the circle!' he hissed. 'We must hear more, no matter how scary!'

164

'Ahhh! Now I see it – fire!' Zoya rose to her feet, eyes wide and mouth stretched into a sickening, mirthless grin. Valya flopped back in her chair, mouth open, and began to whimper, while Masha and Alla crossed themselves with swift movements.

'I can see it – terrible fire!' Madame brought her hands to her face. 'Smoke and flames, burning everything up! Burning you!' She flung her purple-veined arms in Gor's direction and shook like a tree in a storm. The air whistled in her puny lungs and was expelled in a shriek, 'Heed your warning!'

The glassy eyes rolled and she collapsed back into her chair, teeth bared and chest quivering.

'Fire!' yelled Valya, grabbing Gor's hand and leaping to her feet as the table rocked ferociously, its legs coming off the floor. 'Fire!' The other sitters quickly lost control, pushing back their chairs to escape the terrible wooden creature as it bucked and twisted in the centre of the room. 'Fire! Fire!' The shouts were coming from every corner as the candles toppled with a volley of bangs, hot wax spraying bloody arcs across the walls. It seemed to Gor they actually believed there was a fire. It was panic, pure and simple, but still, the scream that rang out as the room plunged into darkness prickled his skin. There followed thuds as heaving, panicking bodies collided across Zoya's astral plane. The table crashed to the floor.

Fire! The word shivered down Gor's spine and he backed away, removing himself from the noise and tumult. He found a corner, and before he knew what he was doing, he bent to a squat, hands clasped over his ears.

Fire! Fire! Fire!

It was the way the fizz and crackle of the flames had been on the edge of his consciousness, almost there, almost tangible, as if they were just out of sight, just up the road, on the edge of the village, on the edge of the forest . . . but he could hear them, felt their heat, and saw their glow in the winter sky. The smoke was rising, the smell of it was in his nostrils.

'Fire!'

He shook himself, blinked his huge, sad eyes and looked around into the darkness. This was no good. He needed order, and he needed the light on. He would have to take charge. He stumbled up from his safe place, and as he rose, collided with a lamp, the frill of the shade feathering his face like soft, flapping wings. He cried out and batted it away, his hand slapping a face. A hand lashed out in return, grabbing a clump of his hair. There was a scream and he felt something sharp digging into his forehead.

When Sveta turned the light on, a matter of seconds later, Gor discovered he had been wrestling Valya. At this close range, and with her orange hair disguised by the shadows, he saw, finally, that he knew her. Many years before, and as a brunette, she had been one of his most reliable and accurate bank clerks. How strange life was, and oddly comforting at times. 'My dear Valentina Yegorovna!' he said, voice shaking as he sat back on his knees. 'Forgive me, if you are injured?'

He felt a pang of guilt as she remained heaped on the floor, crying and laughing at herself. She had broken a nail on his forehead, which was bleeding.

'Be calm, everyone! There is no fire here!' Sveta's voice rang out from the doorway, where she panted. She steadied herself, and took in the situation, looking for the helpers, and the ones who needed help. 'Vlad, Polly, please right the table – carefully, beware of Madame Zoya's toes, I think she is still in a trance. Alla, please assist Madame Zoya, we must ensure the spirits have left her and that she is unhurt. Nastya, please help Gor and Valya to their feet, and apply a cold compress if necessary. Breathe, Valya, breathe, that's it! She looks a little . . . Oh, really now, please stop crying! Anybody would think you were afraid. There is no need to be upset. We've just made a little mess here, that's all. There's no harm done. All will be well.' Her tone warmed, as if she had been talking to Albina, and her tight smile was replaced by one that held genuine warmth. 'I have to say, it was a very . . . energetic spirit—'

'Energetic? It was evil!' Polly's words rang out loud as she stood at the head of the table, hands on hips.

'—but I'm sure its intentions were good!' Sveta countered. 'There is nothing to fear!'

'Nothing to fear? I'd say *plenty* to fear!'

Sveta's brow furrowed. 'Come now, everyone . . . help your neighbour, and take your seats quickly! Hush now!'

Polly and Vlad righted the remaining chairs as the other sitters collected themselves up and shook themselves off, some having a glass of water, and some wishing for something stronger. The broken candles were scooped up and put away, and the ruined tablecloth bundled into the bin. Valya squared her shoulders and wiped her nose, laughing a little at her own nervousness as Gor apologised to her again for their coming together. She nodded and smiled, looking down into the yellow spotted handkerchief he offered her. Perhaps he wasn't so bad.

Zoya alone did not move, still seated in her place, staring at the opposite wall. Her chair had been knocked backwards and now rested, two legs on the floor and two legs in the air, against the rococo chest of drawers behind her. She reclined with a far-away look in her eyes, murmuring something, finger-nails gently scratching at the purple material covering her thighs. Polly pushed Alla aside and flicked the chair back upright, catching Madame with her forearm as she slumped forward. Leaning over, she peered into her irises and tapped at her cheek with sharp, insistent strokes. 'She'll be with us shortly.'

'You're such a professional, Polly,' muttered Alla.

'Here, Madame, have a little sniff of smelling salts . . . that's the way.' Polly smiled.

The circle reconvened, the glassy-eyed sitters taking their seats, and a cold quiet descended over their heads. Down in the street a cat screeched. All eyes were on the table, and Gor shivered.

Etched into the shiny black wood in a large, childish scrawl, there was one word:

FIRE

SUSPICION

'What else can I get for you, eh?'

'Nothing, really. I am quite all right.'

Sveta poked her head into every recess in the kitchen, turning up a cheese rind, the end of Friday's now exceedingly hard loaf of bread, and two gherkins. Gor ignored her and stood in the hallway, pressing the buttons on the telephone, once more trying the now-familiar number. The line clicked through with thumps and bumps, the telephone at the other end eventually buzzing, on and on. But still his cousin did not pick up. Where could he be? Out drawing, no doubt. But for three days running?

'Gor, people who are quite all right don't hide away in their apartments all weekend. You've nothing in the fridge! We can't have you fading away. We've got magic to make, and rehearsals to hold and . . .' She employed her sweetest cajoling tone, but Gor simply shuffled past her and folded himself into his armchair, immoveable as the war memorial glowering over Azov from the hilltop. Sveta persisted: she needed him to show some life, to react with some warmth. It would make her feel better. He drummed his fingers on the arm of the chair as if drilling holes.

'Thank you for your concern, but all is well. I appreciate you . . . dropping by, but it's not necessary.'

'Well, Albina's at karate club, so I just thought—'

'And you don't need to call me every morning either—'

'But it's no trouble at all!' she cut in. 'And I do feel responsible, for the fright you had—'

'I did not have a fright.'

'You did!'

'I was alarmed by the other people, and the noise, and that stupid woman grabbing my head—'

'Yes, Valya left you battered: what nails she has! I can still see the marks.' She plunged forward to fuss over the scabs at Gor's temple as he drew further back into his chair. 'It wasn't deliberate, I'm sure.'

'Yes! No! Of course not! But that's not the point!'

'So, you're not hiding away because—'

'I'm not hiding!'

'So, you're not staying in, because you were scared?'

'No! I needed time . . . to think!'

Sveta returned to the kitchen. 'You must have some ham around the place?'

'The séance was a trick, of course: nothing but a sham. Knocks and candles! Spirit writing! What rot!'

She poked her head around the door. 'But you saw it yourself? No one could have forged the writing – there was no opportunity. And what about the smoking candles – supernatural, you must admit?'

Gor shook his head. 'Sveta, you think that because it excites you: you lack logic!'

'And you want to explain away everything, when sometimes it's just not possible!'

'Think about it!' He pushed himself from his chair and began to pace the room. 'The table was under a cloth – the writing was already there. It could have been done at any time. And the candles – that was some sort of powder, added before they were lit. I've been smelling smoke around here for days . . .'

Sveta stood in the doorway, mouth puckered as if eating something unpalatable: half a lemon, or some imported yoghurt.

'Well . . . if you're going to be stubborn about it, I suppose it could have been a trick . . . But why?' Sveta laughed at the possibility and clutched at the fat plastic beads at her neck. 'Why would Madame Zoya write fire on her table? Did it mean anything to you, the message?' She cocked her head.

He hesitated.

'Gor?'

'No!' he snapped, striding past her to the kitchen. 'What has Madame Zoya against me, eh?' He stared at the calendar. 'Is this all linked? The séance was just the culmination of all this . . .'

'What, what? More horrid things?' Sveta's cheeks wobbled as she clucked around him, eyes on the calendar and the peppering of Xs that ranged its dates like pock marks on a teenager's skin. 'Are these all . . . ?'

He nodded. 'Yes. All unpleasant events. The letter . . .' He pointed at a date two days before. 'The letter was very odd: no words. Just . . . just a dozen dead moths. And tapping.'

'Tapping?'

'On the windows . . . As if someone . . . as if someone wants to get in.' Gor scrunched up his face and rubbed a hand over his tired eyes. 'Started a few days ago.'

'Scary!' said Sveta with a shudder.

'There is no such thing as the supernatural! I will not be cowed!' He shook a fist to no one. 'The séance was arranged as a consequence of strange events, and now they are multiplying. But what's afoot?' His eyes slid to Sveta. 'You . . .' he said, 'you are keen on all this nonsense! Did you have a hand in this?'

She looked over her shoulder. 'Who? Me? Why would I want to scare you?'

'Huh! Well, I don't know, Svetlana Mikhailovna! You tell me?' He took up pacing again. 'You seem very keen to get to know me, to involve me in your family. And this all started when I met you. Maybe you're after something, huh? Making yourself indispensable, in my hour of need?'

Sveta's jaw dropped. 'After something? With you?'

'Well, why not? You're not a stupid woman, and it takes all sorts!'

'All sorts?'

'Why did you answer my advert?' He stopped before her.

'What?'

'The real reason?'

'I wanted to be a magician's assistant, you stupid old goat! I don't need or want anything else – not from you, not from anyone! I just wanted a little razzmatazz.'

'Ha!' He stared at her, eyes drilling into her soul. 'Not for the money, but for the "razzmatazz"! Unbelievable!' He shook his head and slowly walked away. 'So now you know there is no "razzmatazz", why are you still around: bringing me cutlets, cups of tea – checking up on me?'

'Well, this may come as a surprise, but it's because I feel sorry for you! Yes – sorry!'

He turned, nodding violently. 'Ah! Sorry for me!'

'Yes!'

'You, sorry for me?'

'Obviously.' She folded her arms. 'Perhaps I should go.' Sveta put the cheese rind on the sideboard and smoothed her cardigan. When he said nothing, she turned for the hall.

'Wait!'

She turned back.

'What else do you know about me, Sveta?' He thrust himself into his armchair and eyed her suspiciously.

'What do you mean? Only what you've told me. Only what you said at the séance.'

'Is that all? Albina, when we first met: she asked if I was a millionaire.'

'Yes, but that's just . . . gossip.'

He raised an eyebrow.

'Everyone knows you were a bank manager . . .'

'And it follows that I'm a millionaire?'

'Yes! No! Oh, Albina was just repeating what she's heard. It means nothing. She meant no harm. You are being rude, Gor!'

He bit down his reply, eyes bulging, and blew through his cheeks, mouth slack. 'You are right!' His head dropped into his hands, and he seemed to crumple. 'I am sorry, Sveta. I . . . forgive me. I was rude. I don't think you're . . . the one. But you are the connection in all of this!'

'Nonsense!' She squared her shoulders. 'You are! All I did was set up the séance.' She smiled, her blue eyes silvered with tears. 'I'm not a bad person. I am your friend.'

'Maybe,' he conceded, with a tepid smile. 'Maybe. Don't get upset! Here—' He passed her a spotted yellow handkerchief. 'But how do we make sense of all this? What does it mean? Tell me more about Madame Zoya? Does she often host séances?'

'Every few months, when there is demand.'

'And . . .?'

'She relays messages, gives people signs. The people who come are lonely, or feeling guilty, or maybe just sad. She gives them a chance to talk, to share, and, you know . . . hope. I hear she reunited Alla – the woman from the White Flamingo, you remember – with her cat.' Sveta smiled with a hint of self-mockery. 'It gave great comfort to Alla.'

'A cat. I see. The others there . . . that orange woman, Valentina—'

'Valya, yes?'

'I know her . . . she worked under me at the bank. And the dark girl . . .'

'Polly? From the pharmacy?'

'Yes. I recognised her from somewhere. I can't put my finger on it—'

'Azov is a small place, Gor. There is no strangeness in you recognising these people, surely?'

He was silent a moment, eyes intent on the wall, and then shook his head. 'You are right. I am suspicious of everyone, and where's the point? But tell me: this séance was . . . an oddity – more violent than usual?'

'Yes.'

'It was a show for me, then?'

'You don't think someone – linked to banking – might be holding a grudge? I don't know, maybe . . . if you didn't give them a loan, or something like that? Revenge?'

'That kind of thing was extremely regulated. It was not a world of intrigue, believe me.'

'So, you didn't make any enemies?' She smiled slightly and raised her eyebrows, as if talking to a child.

He passed a hand across his eyes and hunched away. 'I don't want to discuss it.'

She frowned. 'Very well. Let's talk about something else. Don't upset yourself.'

The clock ticked.

'I think the "sawing me in half" trick is a great one, don't you?' Sveta began.

'Yes,' he nodded.

'And do you think my assistant-ing is improving?'

'It will do, very well.'

'I think it's just as well we have chosen not to do the Wheel of Death, don't you?'

'Yes . . . it seems to have dry rot.'

There was a pause before they both spoke.

'Let's go and talk to Madame Zoya!' said Sveta.

'I really should be going to the *dacha*,' said Gor.

'*Dacha*? It's getting dark, and it's raining!' Sveta was firm. 'Have the silent phone calls stopped, hmm? And the burning smells?'

'No.'

'Are you sleeping better, with this tapping going on?'

175

'No.'

'And the horrid letters, the headless rabbit – you enjoy all that?'

'No.'

'So: you say Madame Zoya is a fraud, and I say that she isn't, but either way, we must talk to her: if she is trying to scare you, we must know why! And if she is sincere, we must ask for her help. She might know something we don't.'

'It's all so black and white to you, isn't it? She might know . . .' He closed his eyes. 'Sveta, there are things you don't know,' he said slowly, 'about me. Things I have done . . . shameful things, terrible things. I . . . It's not so simple.' He opened his eyes and stared at the calendar.

'That's as maybe.' Her chin tilted as she came to stand before him. 'But I know one thing, Gor: deep down, you are a good man.'

She held his eyes until he looked away.

THE IDEAS INCUBATOR

Polly hurried along the creaking corridor. The hand-written posters advertising the flat were finally done. They had taken longer to copy out than she had expected, and she still wasn't ready for her shift at the pharmacy. She would be late. She smiled to herself: it didn't matter.

She stood in the doorway to the wash room. Every one of the working sinks was taken. Girls chattered and argued as they scrubbed, their pants around their ankles, flannels, soap and towels balanced in hand or hanging from string bags. How she loathed the wash room. But the shower-block was worse with its blatant peep-holes and green-algaed floor. A voice in her head asked if she wouldn't rather live in the flat herself. It whispered of quiet and solitude. But she knew it couldn't be: only hard cash and Palekh boxes could buy tomorrow. A girl pushed past her into the hall, and she dashed forward for the vacant basin.

Stripped to the waist she bent over to swish her hair under the tap, her spine knobbling the moon-washed smoothness of her back. The Turkish shampoo smelled like jam and lathered like it too. She'd pinched the bottle at the pharmacy, and now wished she'd chosen with more care. No doubt Maria Trushkina only ever pilfered the best.

The pharmacy: incubator of her clever idea. She had thought of it over the summer, during those endless, airless afternoons when they trailed in off the streets and stood at the counter, chattering about how they wanted to live at home but needed some help with the toilet and washing, and those sores, and sometimes they couldn't remember what day it was or if they had taken their medicine and sometimes, yes they took too much. And yes, they never slept at night because of all the funny noises and the criminal gangs and the fear of theft. And they really missed their no-good children and their no-good grandchildren – because they never came to visit any more. They had all this space, all these rooms, all these things, and they all needed cleaning and dusting and winding and mending, and wasn't it a bother? And no, they didn't keep their money in the bank any more because the banks were full of thieves and the money was worthless and instead they bought jewellery and trinkets and cameras and chocolate and hid it under the bed. Speculating: they were investing for a future that simply wasn't theirs, and in doing so, they were stealing hers.

It was a good idea, a big idea. She just had to make it work. So far, the results were mixed.

She returned to her room, dressed unhurriedly, put her damp hair in a taut bun and set off down the gritty staircase. In the foyer, black leaves blew in at the door as girls huddled around ancient, half-dead radiators waiting for their dates.

'Hey, Polina!' She heard the screech before she registered the dark scuttle across the floor. The concierge was at her side as her foot touched the floor. 'How was the séance on Friday?'

'Scary, Elena Dmitrovna. Very scary. The spirits turned the table over.'

'Never! Did they have a message for you – any warnings?'

'Me? Well, the way I interpreted it, they said that I would be very rich, some day. But I knew that anyway. As for the rest . . . they said old people shouldn't be nosey. Do you have a more meaningful message for me – via telephone, perhaps?'

Polly held out her hand.

'I haven't been paid since August, you know,' said Elena Dmitrovna.

'That's a shame.' Their eyes met. 'The message?'

Polly stretched to take the paper from the old woman's hand, but she snatched it away, huddling into the corner.

'Don't push! I won't be bullied! Stay away!'

Lisping conversations were broken off and girls' heads turned to stare.

'I'm not pushing,' Polly hissed between her teeth, her hand closing around the paper. She tugged hard. 'You'd know if I pushed you, you old witch.'

Elena Dmitrovna watched Polly's face as she unfolded the note.

'Caller: Maria Trushkina, Pharmacy No. 2. Message: Student has been late for work placement or absent without reason four times in the last fourteen days. Case referred to University Sanctions Board; employer seeking dismissal, recommends removal from course.'

Elena Dmitrovna's shoulders shook as she laughed silently into the knot of her headscarf and turned away. 'Rich, eh? I don't think so, the way you're going. On the streets, more like!'

Polly scrunched the paper in her fist.

179

SUPER RUSH

Madame Zoya was not keen to answer her door. Light seeped out around its rim, but it took several raps and a threat of calling for the ambulance and/or her landlady to make her move.

'What is it you people want?' she rasped as she pulled it open a fraction and her beak protruded. 'I am trying to sleep.'

'Madame Zoya, we are sorry for the intrusion,' said Sveta. 'But we must talk to you about the séance.'

'Oh, not you two,' she grumbled, wrinkling her nose, 'my table is ruined! Ruined! I am upset.'

'Oh,' said Sveta, 'that's most unfortunate. May we come in and observe: we may be able to offer compensation?'

Zoya's eyelids fluttered at the words, and she wobbled gently away from the door towards her salon, waving her arm in a welcoming gesture. The visitors followed, bumping into furniture and tripping over fallen stuffed animals.

Zoya collapsed in the centre of her ornate French sofa, forcing Gor and Sveta to choose a moth-eaten armchair each. The curtains were tightly closed and the chamber felt forgotten: a long-buried time-capsule. Their host wore a ragged silk kimono draped loosely at the front, which revealed a scraggy breastbone clad in sagging violet flesh. She winced as she breathed.

'Are you well?' enquired Sveta brightly. Gor coughed and Zoya laughed from the pit of her shrunken stomach.

'No, my child. I am not well. I've had an awful headache since Friday. I can barely move. I've hardly eaten. But you're not interested in me. What is it you want?' She took a deep drag on her smelling salts, and issuing an 'ahhh!', closed her eyes.

'Well, we wanted to talk to you about Friday, that's it, exactly, isn't it Gor? We want to know how . . . everything occurred, and how the table came to be scratched . . . Madame Zoya?'

'Huh?' She opened one sticky eye and regarded Sveta, mouth sagging.

'Did you hear what I said?'

'Erm, yesssss, I think so. Hnnnk.' Again her eyes slithered shut.

'This is a waste of time. She's . . . unconscious!' Gor said.

'Not!' replied Zoya thickly. 'Don't be so rude, you!'

'Is she always like this?'

'No! Not at all. I mean . . . she's a character, of course. But—' Sveta hesitated, and then in a louder voice, 'come, Madame, wake up! Speak to us!' She pushed herself out of the armchair and crossed to Zoya, taking her ashen face between her warm hands and rubbing swiftly at her cheek.

'Gerroff!' rasped Zoya, pushing her away, her hand landing with a smack in the middle of Sveta's surprised face, the fingers smudging the raspberry lipstick and pushing up her nose.

181

Sveta staggered. 'Now really, Madame Zoya! There's no need for physical attack! What is wrong with you?'

Zoya opened both yellow eyes, and closed them again. 'Self-defence,' she muttered. 'This world is full of . . . hate.' Again she reached for the little bottle around her neck, but was too weak to raise it.

'What is that pouch, Sveta?'

'Smelling salts. She always has them with her: for low blood pressure, I think. It certainly seems low at the moment.' Sveta was attempting to take the woman's pulse, and looked alarmed.

'May I see?' Stepping forward, Gor swiped up the pouch.

It contained a small glass bottle with writing on the side, but without his reading glasses he couldn't make it out. He raised it to his nose and inhaled. 'Oof!' he exclaimed, leaning back into the armchair, and then 'Aaargh!' He closed his eyes as the room turned to crystal and then shattered within his head.

'Gor?' Sveta dropped Zoya's wrist and leapt to his side, scowling, her face hovering just above his. His muscles had relaxed and fallen away and he seemed to be melting on the chair while his mind floated above it.

'I don't know what's in that bottle,' he said a few minutes later, after Sveta had brought him a reviving cup of tea, 'but it's not smelling salts. I strongly advise you, Madame,' he pointed his bony finger at the old woman, who was now also fully conscious, 'to cease sniffing whatever it is, immediately.'

Sveta examined the label with Madame's magnifying glass. 'It says "*Amyl Nitrite Super Rush*". What is that?' Her brow wrinkled.

All three shook their heads.

'Well, to rush is to hurry . . .' mused Sveta.

'It's not spirit of ammonia, which is what it should be,' said Gor.

'I'll tell Vlad,' said Zoya, with a sigh and a far-away look, 'that his smelling salts are bad.'

'Vlad got them for you?' asked Sveta.

'Yes, he brought them last week straight from the pharmacy. Or the sanatorium. I don't remember. Or Polly recommended them. When I was checking his credentials. It's all a bit fuzzy. He's a lovely boy.'

'Imports, Madame Zoya,' said Sveta with a knowing smile, 'Not everything they're cracked up to be! You'd be better off with proper, home-grown remedies!'

'Akh!' groaned Zoya.

'Now. We need to talk,' said Gor.

'The séance table,' said Sveta.

'The table, indeed,' echoed Gor.

'My table,' cried Zoya, 'totally ruined!'

'What we want to know is . . .'

'How did you fake it?' cut in Gor.

'Pardon?'

'How did you do it? And why?'

'I don't know what you mean! I never fake anything!' the old lady hissed, fingernails scratching the chintz on which she reclined.

'Akh, Zoya, you are well known in the district as a . . . as a . . .' Gor hesitated.

'Yes?' Her bird's-nest hair vibrated with indignation.

'A person of good spirit, Madame, and strong views. And a lover of the arts, and culture, and the paranormal. You are sincere. We know that,' said Sveta.

'I do my best. It's not easy, in this town. Philistines, the lot of them! If only I lived in Moscow, or St Petersburg: somewhere where the arts really mattered! Where the intelligentsia—'

'Can we talk about the table now?' said Gor.

'The spirits did it!'

'Come come, we all know—'

'The table has never been scratched before!' she insisted. 'Look at it – go and look! The woodwork was good as new until last Friday. Why would I ruin my own table?'

She struggled off the sofa, herding them to where the table stood folded for storage. 'See!' She twisted a lamp to its surface. They could see the lettering, could smell it even: freshly scratched, small splinters of naked wood still protruding. 'You have my word: I had nothing to do with this. I was as amazed as all of you when it was revealed. I was in a stupor!'

'The spirits have never written on your furniture before?'

'No, child.'

'Why do you think they did it this time?'

She shrugged and looked at Gor. 'To make a point.'

'And what was that point?'

'You should be afraid, Gor! Very afraid! It's obvious, isn't it?'

'And why?' he persisted, his tone soft but frosty.

'Search me!' She cackled, holding on to a stuffed woodpecker for balance. 'I've never been able to work out what they're trying to do. Not a clue, ha!' she laughed and then winced. 'But it can be fun. You learn so much about your fellow humans at a séance!' She limped over to the sofa, where she lay down, her head on the arm and her feet tucked under her hips. She nestled in as if to sleep. 'I have to rest.'

'A couple more questions, Madame Zoya, if you please. The people who were with us on Friday: how did you select them?'

'Select them? They select themselves. The girls . . . well, originally I sewed for them – dresses and the like, or met them in the theatre. They're all friends of friends. They're sweet creatures, in the main. Curious, but sweet.'

'And Vlad?' Gor asked, one eyebrow raised.

'Vlad? Oh, well . . . he's Valya's lodger. She brought him for security. He and Polly are . . . an item. He was good for getting drinks and . . . well, for looking at, if you see what I mean. The other ladies liked him.'

'It struck me as quite unusual,' Gor broke in, 'his type, at a séance.'

'Type?' asked Zoya innocently.

'What is his profession?' Gor asked.

'He's a doctor. Working in a sanatorium while he studies.'

'A student then?'

'Yes.'

'He's very well presented for a student, isn't he?'

'Yes! I thought he was very smart. And did you see his watch?' said Sveta, nodding. 'Modern! Imported!'

'And his sweater,' said Zoya, 'real wool, Italian.'

'So, he's unusually well-feathered for a student on a stipend,' said Gor.

'Perhaps his parents do well?' mumbled Zoya.

'Or maybe he has a . . . a benefactor, of some sort,' added Sveta.

'A benefactor? Yes, maybe. How many times has he visited you here?'

185

'What are you getting at? Are you suggesting I am his *benefactor*?'

Gor's whiskers twitched.

'Once, last week, like I said . . . so that I could get to know him a little before the séance. He offered. He had a look at the balcony, gave me the smelling salts, and made me a lovely cup of tea. We had an interesting chat.'

'Chat? What about?'

'Um . . . you know . . . this and that. I'm not sure . . . I dozed off.' Her forehead creased as her eyes flicked around the room, avoiding Gor's stare. 'He's a lovely boy. Very strong. Lithe, also—'

'Yes!' said Sveta, 'I noticed that.'

'Bit of an athlete. You can tell from his—'

'Ladies please! Did you leave him alone at any time, when he was here?'

'Of course not. I mean, I didn't trail around after him the whole time . . . I took a rest in my boudoir. He tucked me in. Home repair is very tiring. Life is very tiring,' she added pointedly.

'Ah! That would give him long enough . . .' said Gor to himself.

'For what?' Sveta and Zoya asked, in unison.

'Well, he's the face that doesn't fit, isn't he? He's the odd one out. He could have scratched the word, meddled with the candles—'

'It was the spirits!' growled Zoya.

'But he seems so, so . . . respectable,' added Sveta, 'He's a vigorous man: a doctor! A strong, healthy body . . .'

Her words died as Gor's black eyes squinted at her.

186

'Humour me, ladies! Suspend your belief in the spirits and the healthy body, healthy mind fallacy. Ask yourselves: who had the opportunity, and strength, to carve into that table? Who had the opportunity to prime Madame here, with suggestions . . . maybe as she slept? Who don't we know? Who doesn't fit?' Gor's eyes probed into Madame Zoya's as she lay on the sofa, head lolling.

She sucked in some dribble. 'Well, when you put it like that . . . But, why?'

'That . . . is something I don't yet know. But I'll find out!'

'Ooh, a mystery!' the old lady squealed, briefly looking half alive.

'Yes, but not for you, my dear,' said Sveta. 'You must take bed rest and a little soup. And no more of those smelling salts!' she added sternly. 'You have been very helpful, but we must leave you in peace for the moment.'

'Yes, I think you may be right,' Zoya croaked, lifting one claw-like hand to her forehead. 'I feel totally ship-wrecked. You must leave me, I am washed up.'

Gor snorted. 'One last thing, Madame, if I may,' he asked from the doorway.

'Oh, if you must!'

'The sanatorium, where the young man works: the name, if you'd be so kind?'

'The Vim & Vigour: out by the creek.'

'Vim & Vigour,' Gor repeated slowly. 'I see.'

'I know it!' said Sveta. 'I had a friend who attended there. It's a lovely place! Indoor pool, saunas, massage cabinets . . .'

'They tried to get me to go,' said Zoya. 'I saw them off with my pepper spray. It's full of old cabbages.'

187

Sveta laughed a tinkling, jowl-wobbling laugh, not sure if the old lady was joking or not. She said her goodbyes and hurried after Gor.

'So, we will pay a visit to this Vlad, then?' she asked, her voice eager. 'Friday is best for me! I have a busy few days at school, but the autumn holidays will have started by then.'

'We, Sveta?' Gor eyed his shoes intently as their footsteps clip-clopped in the stairwell.

'You don't want me to come, do you?'

'It's not that.'

'Well, what is it?'

She stopped still on the step, hands on her hips.

'Sveta . . .' He turned to face her, and searched her face for the words. 'It's me that is the focus for all this. It's me . . . It's me they hate—'

'What do you mean?'

'I don't want to involve you.' He looked down into her eyes. 'You are a good woman. Avoid trouble if you can. And avoid me. I'm not worthy of your help.'

She was surprised by his sincerity, the unexpected thoughtfulness. 'I'm a big girl: quite able to defend myself. If someone is mocking the spirits, I want to know. And if someone is trying to scare you . . . for whatever reason, I feel offended. I can't stand deceit. And if this Vlad, handsome and strong as he is, has been deceitful, trying to hurt you through trickery and falsehood – I'll be wanting a word with him! A big word! Both on your account, and my own.'

'Ah . . .' Gor fell silent. They passed under the dilapidated arch of the building's rear entrance and stepped into the chill of evening. 'In that case, I would be most comforted by your presence, on Friday.' He smiled softly: a true smile that transformed his face, briefly, from the depths of a glacial winter to a sunny June morning.

'That's settled then,' she beamed in return.

'We will set out at ten?' he asked.

'Ten! Good. Oh,' she hesitated, 'there's just one thing.'

'Yes?'

'Albina.'

'Eh?'

'She must come.'

'What?' The rays of the smile disappeared. 'No, really, Sveta—'

'It's the school holidays! She can't sit at home alone all day with only Kopek for company!' Sveta smiled up at Gor.

He sighed and regarded the black, leathery leaves sticking to his windscreen. 'The parrot doesn't have to come too?' He lifted an eyebrow.

'Akh, no!' Sveta laughed. 'It's a parakeet, actually, Gor. They are quite different.'

BETWEEN PINK SHEETS

Two days later, in a hermetically sealed apartment above Grocery Shop No. 6, a pool of sweat was collecting in the small of Polly's back. She could feel it trickling towards the cleft of her buttocks as she moved. Her face, broad and pale, captivating yet detached, registered nothing, eyes closed as Vlad's fingers pulled her down harder onto his hips, nails digging into her flesh as he tried to keep a grip. He was writhing. She sighed inwardly and glanced at the bedside table: seven o'clock already. She would have to go soon. She increased her speed, thigh muscles searing then numbing, her mouth moaning like she'd heard her room-mate do, hoping it would hurry him along. It did. He twisted and shuddered beneath her, swearing, making a sound like a choked rabbit.

A moment later he subsided into the pink sheets, becoming still, just a pulse in his neck flicking as his chest rose and fell. The clock ticked. She scratched her head, smiled down at him briskly, and began to look around the room for her clothes.

'Polly,' he muttered through sticky lips, twisting his fingers into the coils of her hair and pulling her down to lie on him, chest to chest, her face pressed into his shoulder. His hand was heavy on the back of her head as he attempted to nuzzle her hair. 'My princess. I've missed you—'

Her tongue clicked against her teeth and she pulled backwards, bringing her hands against his shoulders to push up and away. The room was stifling. He was stifling.

'Don't mess up my hair,' she said with a shrug, softening it a breath later with a half-smile aimed centimetres behind his head. His hands fell back onto the sheet and she dismounted gracefully, as if from a pommel horse. With a flick of a long leg and a twist, she was sitting next to him, one foot beneath her, the other dangling towards the floor, swinging rhythmically. 'I've got things to do,' she said, turning away from the injured look that crept across his face, 'and I can't do them with matted hair. If there's one thing my mother taught me' – the features twisted momentarily, eyes clouding – 'it's that I must be neat. Appearance is all, Vlad.'

'I thought you said your mother wasn't around enough to teach you anything.' He smiled and threaded his fingers into the ends of her hair. She pulled away, tutting.

'It wasn't always like that.'

'I'm sorry.' Again he attempted to touch her, leaning forward, his hand stretching for her thigh. 'Maybe you could stay here, with me, and have something to eat? There's no hurry, is there?'

She sprang from the bed and bent low to pull on shiny red knickers in one deft movement. Ex-gymnasts always had that feline grace, that controlled power. He watched her.

'You have a one-track mind. I have to go: business calls!' She pulled on thick black tights. When she stood, her legs looked like wire. 'All you think about—' she pointed a long finger, 'is sex.'

'Really?'

'Yes, really.'

He shrugged. 'That's not true. I think about other things. Plenty of things.' He scratched his balls. 'But I like touching you. I love it. I thought you loved it too. But sometimes . . . recently . . . I think you can't bear it.'

'I just did, didn't I? You touched me quite a lot, eh? I bore it. You can't complain!' She said the words softly, smiling over her shoulder and nodding her head, but still she didn't look him in the eye.

Vlad lay motionless and watched her dress, the movements hurried and exact. She zipped up her skirt and fastened the button like she was turning a chicken's neck. She never stayed. She came and went and left him by turn surprised, delighted, angry or empty. He would have liked to have held her for a while, maybe gone to sleep with her head on his shoulder, her dark hair across his chest, her graceful, fragile-boned hands stroking the hairs around his nipples, her full mouth wet against his skin. Their breath would slow and mingle as they subsided into sleep. But she never stayed.

'I'm very busy, and you should be too. We've got lots to do. How is your case study going? Good progress?'

He looked at her blankly. He'd been staring at her breasts while she twisted into her bra. A sweat broke on his brow.

'I can still feel you all over me, Polly, smell you in my nostrils, and you can't wait to talk about my patients.' He turned his beautiful grey eyes to the ceiling with a sigh.

'Your patients? He's not your *patient*, is he? You're a student, like me. Don't kid yourself with that doctor-speak. You're no more a doctor than I am.' She collected herself, and began to tug on a chunky-heeled boot.

'He *is* my patient, Polly! I'm not pretending to be a doctor, you know! I've been helping him! It's not like I'm working in a shop!'

She took two steps towards the bed and Vlad pulled the pink sheet up over his torso.

'What did you say?' Her bottom lip quivered as her eyes pinned him down. 'Did you . . . imply, that I'm just a shop girl?'

Vlad swallowed. 'No, I didn't mean that. You made me angry, I—'

'I thought you believed in me, Vlad! I thought you got it! How could you—' She took another step towards him.

'I do! I do believe in you. I love you. It was a stupid thing to say, I'm sorry.' He sat forward, hands raised in supplication as she stood over him. 'I was angry. It's . . . I just wish you'd stay.'

She turned away, head down, and sank onto the shaggy pink stool by the dressing table. Her breathing slowed and she caught his eye in the mirror.

'I feel so good now, you know.' Her tongue flicked over lips, a smile flowering briefly. 'Don't make me feel bad. It always feels so good with you. You're a sexy boy.'

He looked away. She turned to him.

'Look, I'm sorry I have to go. I'll stay another time.'

Still he didn't look at her.

'Am I the only one, Polly?'

She made a moue and returned her gaze to the mirror. 'Of course you are! You mean . . . so much to me. You're my Vlad!

My partner in crime!' She picked up a compact and dotted powder on her nose. 'I rely on you. I need you. And I know sometimes I can be a little . . . sharp. But you know how difficult my life has been—' She turned to him, face white, eyes intense.

'I know, I understand—'

'How can you understand?' Her voice wobbled as she turned back to the mirror. 'And it's all Papasyan's fault! But I'm changing it, aren't I? Life can be good, can't it?'

'I know, and I'm helping you as much as I can, Polly. You know I am. I'd do anything for you—'

'And I'm good to you, aren't I?' She came over to the bed to lean over him, her fingers gripping his thigh. His eyes followed the movement, the muscles in his leg quivering under her touch. He reached to clasp the hand.

'You are.'

'You liked that sweater I gave you, didn't you?'

'Yes, but Polly—'

'It looks so sexy.'

'You think?' He smiled into her eyes.

'And how about the watch? I know you love it: you always wear it.'

'I do love it.'

'I bought them for you, didn't I?' Her fingers dug into his leg.

'You did.'

Black eyes stared into his.

'And I have nothing. I'm clever, you know. And that's your proof. They're the best. Really expensive. And they prove that I love you.'

'Yes.'

She flopped onto the end of the bed and ran her fingers through her hair. The air prickled with the sound of a thousand tiny rips. He reached out a hand. She took it in hers, turned it to her face and licked the palm.

'You can help me so much, Vlad. You're brave and caring, and you have such talent: you can ask people anything, and they tell you, because you're handsome and strong, and they think you're a doctor.' Her gaze flicked up as her teeth dug into the pad of his thumb.

'Yes, but . . .'

She sucked his fingers one by one, tongue flicking under the nails, up and down the joints. He groaned as his brain emptied.

'Humour me. Tell me how old crinkle-cheeks is doing, since your miraculous diagnosis. It was quite a story. Has he been sleeping well?' She was leaning over him now, breath hot on his face, her voice a whisper.

'I don't know. I haven't seen him. I've been discussing my report with Dr Spatchkin, and writing bits up.' Vlad was pushing his hand into her bra and struggled to keep his mind on the words coming out of his mouth as her breast spilled out above him. 'I heard his nightmares have started up again, and his appetite is patchy.'

'Ah? So he's bed-ridden now? Definitely too poorly to go home?' She straddled him.

He couldn't believe talking about his patients was turning her on, but was happy to go with it, if that were the case. 'Well actually . . .' her nipple was in his mouth, muffling his voice, 'I heard Spatchkin gave him crayons . . . and he's making progress.' He attempted to push his other hand down her tights. 'He's remembered everything now. So he might go home soon.'

She turned to concrete in his touch, hovering above him.

'What are you talking about?'

'He might go home.'

'He can't go home!'

'Why not?' A puzzled smile creased his face.

'I . . . He . . .'

'Well?' He touched her cheek.

'I took his key!' she blurted. 'I mean . . . I've been doing up his flat. For us!'

'What?'

She gazed down at him.

'I . . . that day in your office, when I read his file . . . I saw he lived alone, in Rostov, and I just . . . the temptation was too much. We need a love-nest, Vlad!'

'Well,' he closed his eyes as he searched for the right words. 'That's a sweet idea, Polly, but it's completely crazy!'

'I've been making it nice for you!' Her smile curled into a snarl. 'I've been making it ready!'

'But you can't do that – it's not your property!'

'So what! Why should it be his? He doesn't need it!'

'He does! I mean, he will do! And what if Matron finds out?'

She jumped up his body, buttocks thrusting against his neck, pushing his chin up and back. Her face hung above him, eyes stark, lips drawn back in a wild grimace. Nestling down hard, she gripped his head between her thighs until he felt the blood pulsing in his temples. 'He can't go home.' She pronounced each word slowly, as if talking to a particularly stupid child. 'Do you understand? That's the whole point! He's got to stay at the Vim!' She didn't blink as she glared into his face. He felt the veins swell under his eyes. 'Don't ruin everything, Vlad! Don't ruin *us*!' She released her grip and sat back on his chest.

She was smiling again now. It was not a friendly smile. He had the feeling she might just as easily try to break his neck as kiss him.

'I'm sorry,' he said quietly, clearing his throat. 'I didn't realise it meant so much to you. You want him to . . . stay there – in the Vim?'

'That's right.' She kissed the end of his nose, stroked his cheek and then jumped away from the bed to stand giggling before the dressing table, once again running her fingers through her hair. 'My Vlad, you are so slow!' She picked up her leather coat from the floor, shrugging her shoulders into it. 'He doesn't need that flat. We do! Don't you want a love-nest?'

He frowned and nodded wordlessly.

'So, do as I say. It's easy! I'll get a spare key cut and return the original. Matron will never know.'

'Right.' Vlad rubbed his fingers up and down his frown-line, eyes shut. 'It's just . . . You know – it doesn't seem right. I think I can help him, Polly—'

She sauntered back to the bed to stand over him, hands on hips.

'Don't waste your time, honey. You've done enough for him already.' She smiled and shook her head, then bent to place one finger to his lips, while the other hand cupped his balls. 'You want to make love in our very own little heaven, don't you?' Her hand squeezed. He nodded. 'And it will be our secret. I won't tell Matron . . . if you don't. You're in this with me, aren't you, Vlad? After all, you let me read his file—'

'I was asleep!'

'So you were – after we'd made love across Matron's desk. You know, that won't look good, if it gets out. You gave me access to his personal effects, after all. You've come this far . . . So just do the paperwork; make sure he doesn't get discharged. I'll do the rest. That's OK, isn't it?'

He nodded and she released her grip. A dull realisation trickled through Vlad's brain.

'Was it a coincidence, Polly? That Anatoly Borisovich turned out to be the cousin of the man . . . the man who—'

She smiled. 'Of course. Sometimes life's like that. The man who no longer needs his flat, is the cousin of the man who doesn't deserve his flat. Pure coincidence.'

'You didn't read it in his file?'

She giggled and shook her head. A shiver passed through him and he sat up to look for his clothes. His pants were still hanging from the lampshade, his trousers trampled in the middle of the floor. As he stood to collect them, they heard the slam of the front door.

'Shit! She's early!'

Polly grabbed up her bag.

Vlad scrambled around, sweat-stained sheet wrapped around his middle, scrabbling into his jeans, one leg still inside out, while grabbing for his pants and socks.

'This is what you're in it for,' Polly taunted in a whisper as she watched him twirl and stagger. 'You can't live like this! You know you can't! I'll see you later in the week.'

She opened the door, poking her head around it, and then looked back at him. She watched him struggle, blew him a kiss and made a dash across the hall, jumping silently through the front door. It clicked behind her.

Vlad could hear his landlady in the kitchen, clanging pots and pans on the table top, switching on the radio, preparing for an evening's baking. She called out something sharp as the front door closed. He reckoned he had sixty seconds before she came through the door to get washed and changed. He still hadn't found his shirt. He could hear her calling now, stomping up the hallway, her hand reaching out, opening the door . . .

THE KINDLY ORDERLY

'Citizen patient! Where are you going?'

He froze, fingers twitching in the folds of his robe. He could see the end of the corridor clearly now, the doors to the communal sitting room. He heard the tread of a rubberised sole and his head retracted into his shoulders. He wanted to look back, to see who was following him, but he felt stiff, as if he might snap. He pulled up his pyjama bottoms with shaky hands.

'Back to your room, Anatoly Borisovich.'

The warmth of a body brushed his side, the smell of bottled roses filled his nose. He relaxed. It was the kindly orderly, the one with the blue-black beehive and friendly eyes.

'I thought I'd stretch my legs,' he said in a soft voice. 'Is it late? I can't tell: I seem to have lost my watch.'

'You old men,' she said, winding her arm around his, supportive and controlling. 'Of course it's late – almost eleven.' She gently turned him around and looked into his face. 'How did you lose your watch?'

'I don't know. I'm sure it was in my cabinet. But it's not there any more.'

'Hmm,' she frowned, 'that's a shame.'

She held his arm as he slid one foot in front of the other, Siberian moccasins gliding on the pale lino, skating in easy, stubby strokes back along the corridor.

'I'm wide awake now – out of routine!'

'Because of all the drawing?'

The other orderlies had been in and out of his room all day, clucking over his sketches and interrupting his thinking.

'Maybe. I have remembered, you see, and, well . . . my brain is on fire, sometimes.'

'But it's good to see you up. You're making real progress, aren't you?'

'I think I am.' Five more doors to pass. Snores and squeaks, sighs and buzzes came squeezing under the doors of his neighbours' rooms and fluttered off down the corridor behind them. On he skated, hands making little twirling movements at his sides, like a pot-bellied dancer. 'It is night now, and I know who I am, and where I am.' He smiled at the kindly orderly. 'I know who you are.'

'That's very good. Here we are, nearly back.'

'Where do you roost after dark, my dear?' He raised enquiring eyebrows and crinkled the skin of his cheeks. 'You don't patrol the corridor all night, do you?'

'No. Up there,' she nodded down the corridor, the opposite end from his foray. 'There's a camp bed in the office. I was just going to turn in when I heard you.'

'And what's up that way?' he nodded in the direction he had been going.

'The sitting room, and beyond that there are offices, the library, and the main entrance hall. You might be able to go to the sitting room in a few days, if you feel up to it.'

'That would be wonderful.'

He gently swished into his room, the ligaments in his legs regaining long-forgotten elasticity. He felt almost human.

'Goodnight,' nodded the orderly as she held up the blankets for him to slide inside. 'Sweet dreams. And no more wandering.'

He snuffled his thanks and lay back on the bed, concentrating on pulling air into his lungs. It was a long time since he had walked. But he had done it. And he would do it again.

Green eyes flicked towards the black glass of the windows glinting behind the blinds. Somewhere in the trees, he knew, there was a sound, ancient and familiar; the distant flapping of wings spangled with snow crystals. There was comfort in the sound. There was comfort in the knowledge. How could he ever have forgotten?

His eyelids drooped as his breathing relaxed, the thrill of exercise leaving his bones warm. He was falling into sleep, patting Lev's velvety head as they sat together under the table on a long-lost Siberian evening. The stove roared in the corner. His head nodded. Soon Baba would return, and there would be sausage and cheese, and stories.

Then the sound came. Not out in the forest, not on the cottage window. Somewhere altogether closer. Somewhere on the biting green corridor outside his room. The sound of fingertips, tapping.

He curled the pillow over his head, pushing his hands against his ears. The sound got louder.

'Go away! I'm trying to sleep!'

He listened to the roar of the silence, and then:

tap-tap-tap

'Is there to be no peace?'

202

He pushed the pillow to the floor and heaved himself to sitting, but stopped as a pricking in his nose sluiced sleep from every cell of his body.

Smoke!

There was nothing to see, no fug, no yellow flame, but he could smell it all the same. It gave him a nasty feeling, sick and wicked like a belly full of spoiled meat.

A SUBDUED TROIKA

A subdued troika set off for the Vim & Vigour sanatorium on that shivering Friday in late October. Sveta was quiet, the raspberry lipstick failing to camouflage her pallor as she wrapped her arms around herself. Gor observed it and threw caution to the wind, setting the car's heating system to three.

'I didn't sleep,' she said in reply to his enquiring eyebrow. 'All kinds of dreams. I ate cheese after dinner . . . never again.'

Albina, meanwhile, was in rude health, but filled with disgust at having to sit in the back. She flung herself down, pushing both knees into her mother's seat as she did so.

'I'm actually taller than her now,' she said, jabbing a finger towards the back of her mother's head. 'And I get sick in the back. It's so unfair!'

Gor said nothing, but hummed a little 'rum-pum-pum' and pulled out of the courtyard with a jerk. He too had not slept well. Rapping at the door had woken him early, and although it did not go on long, sleep could not be retrieved. Another anonymous letter telling him death awaited himself and his cats had also done nothing for his mood.

'Albina, darling, it won't take long to get there. Please sit up properly. You agreed to be a good girl, didn't you? Remember your promise?'

'Yeah!' Albina snapped forward and pressed herself between the two front seats, grinning into Gor's cheek. He could smell her breakfast. 'She bribed me! If I behave, whatever that means, she's going to buy me some Danish yoghurt!'

'Darling, I'm sure Gor doesn't want to hear—'

'Don't interrupt me, Mama, I—'

'Ladies, please!' He held up his hand, a slim barrier between his ear and Albina's mouth. 'I must concentrate on the road. Let us have hush at this early hour,' he spoke firmly, but not unkindly. Albina flopped back onto her seat.

A few minutes later Gor gave into habit and began pressing the buttons on the radio. It clunked into life, and after a thorough search, Stravinsky's 'Rite of Spring' roared through the speakers, rattling the windows with a metallic buzz.

'Ah! Classical!' Sveta winced. 'How lovely.'

Albina glowered from the back, radiating disgust.

They crossed the bridge over the wide, black river, headed for Rostov and then turned off, taking a deeply pot-holed road to the left, following it out into the country. An assortment of broken-biscuit buildings and the occasional battered wooden cottage passed them by. Chickens quivered at gate posts. Dogs in empty yards scratched fiercely at their fuzzy necks. The car slowed to a crawl as the lane narrowed and the pits and furrows in its surface widened. They bounced over hardcore and swallow-holes of mud. No one spoke, but the radio could not drown out Sveta's yelps and the thuds as Albina's head collided with the passenger window.

'I'm sorry,' muttered Gor. Checking the rear-view mirror, he caught Albina's eye. She had become bored with being disgusted, and now mouthed something at him that he could not make out. He ignored it. He heard shouting, and looked back.

'What?' he mouthed over the music. She repeated it. Still he couldn't hear. She was filling her lungs to bellow once more when Sveta's finger shot out and prodded the radio into silence with a single jab.

'Oh!'

Sveta smiled. 'My head, Gor.'

'Were you a bank manager?' Albina shouted over both of them. 'A long time ago?'

Gor winced. 'Yes. As you know.'

'Did you like it?'

'Yes. I—'

'It sounds boring to me.'

'Ah, well, you'll forgive me for pointing this out, but you are fortunate enough to be young, Albina. Many professions must seem dull to you, at the moment, when life is a blank sheet ready to be coloured. I expect you want to be a ballet dancer or a scientist or a cosmonaut when you grow up?'

'No,' said Albina, frowning. 'Why would I want to do that? Loads of work, no money. I want to go into business: import-export, you know? I'm going to make a bundle. So that I can buy whatever I want.' Then she added, with a sly smile, 'Just like you.'

Gor glanced over his shoulder, surprise elevating his eyebrows. 'Like me?'

'Come on, Mister Papasyan, everyone knows!' Albina's eyes were wide, but her mouth curled to show her blunt white teeth.

'Now, *malysh*, you're not being polite,' Sveta cut in, a dull blush patterning her cheeks.

'Knows what?' asked Gor, his eye twitching.

'That you've got gold hidden in the cistern of your toilet!'

'What?'

'And shares in all the oil companies! And jewels hidden under the bed! And—'

'Albina!' Sveta's voice cracked across her daughter's babble. 'Enough!'

Gor smiled, using only half his face. 'Everybody knows this, Albina?' he asked softly.

'Oh yes. Mama told *me*, but . . . everyone in Azov knows. Probably everyone in the world.'

Sveta squirmed in her seat. 'I didn't *tell* you that, did I, Albina? You were listening to my private conversations. And that was before I'd even met Gor. Oh look, baby-kins! Some rabbits! And a goat!'

'Is that a fact?' Gor did not look at Sveta, and ignored her pointing finger. He observed Albina in the rear-view mirror. 'What else do you *know*, Albina? Any other pearls of wisdom you would like to share?'

'Nope,' she said, and then, after staring at a chewing goat for some moments, added, 'only that we're all going to die, so we may as well make money in the meantime.'

'Well,' Gor said, 'that's a point of view. But—'

'Because of the hole in the ozone layer, I mean. That's the layer of gas that protects the earth from the sun. And it's being destroyed by rockets and space ships going through it all the time to get to the moon and stuff. It's full of holes, like a sieve. So we're all going to fry.' She shrugged. 'You may as well get spending, Mister Papasyan.'

'Ah,' said Gor, 'wisdom indeed.' He folded his lips, eyes on the road, shoulders hunched. Sveta said nothing, her gaze scanning the foamy grey sky as if looking for holes.

The road followed the steep bank of a tidal waterway. Silence filled the car as they zig-zagged on. Up ahead crows crowded around a crumpled, brown-furred body reclining on the verge. Sveta turned away as Albina pressed her nose to the glass to examine it. The crows barely raised a tarry eye, and Gor had to swerve to avoid them. A few minutes more and the water emptied out into wide, khaki flats shining like a greasy pan under the autumn sky. They had arrived: here before them on the open plain, looking out towards the brown, windswept sea, rose the pitted cadaver of the Vim & Vigour sanatorium.

Gor slowed the car to a crawl, observing the faded warning symbols depicting residents intent on jumping into the road. Not a soul stirred. Not even a crow. He parked the car on the muddy gravel space at the foot of the building's crumbling concrete steps, and Albina jumped out. The adults sat side-by-side, surveying the grey façade, its entranceway hung with aged red flags that were now no more than tattered ribbons, trembling silently in the breeze.

'I'm very sorry, Gor.'

'Don't be.'

'Albina was rude.'

'Children repeat what they hear. And evidently, that is what they hear about me.'

'Well . . .' she began to shake her head and pursed her lips, but deflated suddenly, her ready denial pricked by Gor's single, raised eyebrow. 'I am sorry. I *was* one of the gossips that spread tales about you. But that was before I'd met you. And, well

208

. . . everyone thinks you have . . . wealth, and gold and jewels . . . and things. Hidden.'

'Gold and jewels? Ha!' He slapped his hands on the steering wheel and snorted, before taking a long, slow breath and turning to her. 'And what do you think now, Sveta? Now you know me better. Do you think I have hidden treasure?'

'Well, um . . .' Sveta's eyes darted across the windscreen, her hands, the floor of the car and the windscreen again. She recalled the worn shirts, the empty cupboards and lack of light-bulbs in his apartment. 'You told me you're not a millionaire. It seems to me that you have nice things, but that you have to . . . live within your means. And your means are not terribly considerable.'

'Hmmm!' he nodded his head. 'Well, you are more astute than the rest of Azov.'

She smiled.

'"Not terribly considerable" is a fine phrase.'

'Gor, I didn't mean to—'

'I can barely scrape the roubles together to buy bread. In fact, you should know, as a person, as a citizen . . . I am ruined.' He continued nodding his head but his eyes, dark and wide, never left her face. Sveta swallowed.

Twin fists hammered on the window behind her head. 'Are you ever going to get out of the car, Mama? I'm getting a cold! Look – I have no gloves!' Albina brandished her pork-chop hands in the autumn air.

'We should get out of the car,' Gor said.

The Vim & Vigour sanatorium had once been a Soviet jewel: a fitness hotel, a health spa of the workers, designed to give rest and rehabilitation to those who toiled hard, paid for by

209

councils, employers and unions alike. Now they could no longer afford it, and it received guests on a thoroughly haphazard basis: it had become a cross between a holiday camp and an asylum. In the off-season, most of it lay empty. Only the truly frail remained.

'Look at this place,' gasped Gor, scratching his head as he squinted up at the three-storey casket. 'Just imagine ending up here.'

The colour palette in its design had heavily utilised shades of grey, varying from cemetery grey to November grey to sewage grey. It squatted like a concrete coffin on the edge of the creek, broken nets fluttering between the flag-poles above its entrance: no fishermen's nets, they were there to protect visitors' heads from falling masonry.

'I'm sure it's not that bad on the inside,' said Sveta, although her face puckered as she looked up. 'I know people who have holidayed here. Yes, it's true!' Gor was shaking his head. 'Yes! It was a few years ago, but people used to come. There is a mini-cinema, and a masseuse, and they did sketching and keep-fit and all sorts. It was quite desirable.'

'Maybe, Sveta, back in the "good old days", but who would want to stay here now? Party has-beens who've gone gaga: people abandoned by their families. No one comes here on holiday.' Gor shuddered under his jerkin, and turned to Albina. 'Take note, Albina: if you waste your youth, and do badly at school, you might end up working in a dump like this.'

'No way!' cried Albina, stomping off along the bottom of the entrance steps, her boots crunching on the gravel. 'I told you, I'm going to be rich!'

'I think it's just a phase,' said Sveta quietly.

Gor blinked slowly and nodded. 'Well, let's find our friend Vlad, and see what he has to say for himself.'

They started up the steep bank of crumbling steps with quick strides and had reached the darkened glass of the entrance doors when a familiar shriek made them pause.

'Good Lord,' murmured Gor, 'what is it now?'

'Mama!' Albina appeared from the far end of the building, running, her rubberised legs threatening to tangle at any moment as the gravel squirmed under her feet. 'Stop!' Her face glowed red, the breath coming in steaming gasps. 'Help!'

'Oh goodness! What is it?'

'Look!' she galloped to the foot of the steps and skidded in a shower of muddy stones to point back the way she'd come.

'Oh *malysh*, that's just the rubbish dump. Nothing to be scared of. Although there may be rats—'

'Not there,' persisted Albina, 'there!' The girl pointed upwards, towards the far end of the building.

They trod back down the steps to crane their necks in the direction Albina was pointing.

'Is it a bonfire?' Sveta's voice trembled.

'No bonfire,' said Gor.

A thick black snake of smoke was writhing into the clouds. They heard a crack of breaking glass followed by a cry.

'Oh!' Sveta began to push Gor in the direction of the car. 'You must get away immediately! Remember the warning!'

'Now Sveta—' he began, but the smell of the smoke had bled his face white and his hands, raised in protest, were shaking. She propelled him backwards.

'Albina, go with Gor to the car, and make sure he stays there. I will raise the alarm.'

211

The girl stood stock-still. 'But Mama!' She frowned. 'It might be dangerous!'

'There are fragile people in there, Albina: I must do my duty, and make sure the alarm has been raised. I won't do anything dangerous.'

'But Sveta—' Gor took a step towards the building.

'Don't tempt fate, Gor! I will be back almost immediately!' She smiled her best and bravest smile and, without a further word, trotted up the steps. She did not look back.

It took a moment for her eyes to adjust to the dimness of the entrance hall. She made out a mosaic covering one wall, depicting workers and peasants engaging in recreation, their jaws square around smiling, ruby lips. She spied the reception desk at the far end. There was no one there. No alarm was ringing: she heard no scurrying. The only sound was the muffled clack of a typewriter, coming from a doorway behind the desk.

'Coo-eee!' The typing continued. 'Hey! Emergency!' Sveta crossed to the desk and shouted over it. The clattering of keys continued. She scanned the hall, eyeing the doors leading off from each corner to who-knew-where. All was peace. Her hands hammered on the desk. Still there was no response. She noticed a small brass bell, like those they have in hotels. Under it read the legend 'Ring for attention'. She patted the bell and it let out a mournful ding. The typing stopped and an anaemic-looking administrator sauntered through the door in her slippers.

'You're on fire!' cried Sveta, jigging from one foot to the other.

The administrator looked down at her legs and over her shoulder.

'Not you – the building! There's smoke – in that wing!' Sveta pointed, now jiggling on the spot.

'I don't hear the alarm,' said the administrator, and pushed her glasses back up her nose.

'Go and look if you don't believe me. But hurry! People may be trapped!'

The administrator sighed, undid the latch on the counter and scuffed her heels towards the main doors.

'I don't see anything,' she intoned, poking her head out of the door. A blob of ash fluttered around her face like a charred butterfly and stuck to her glasses. 'Oh, over there?'

She scuffed back to the office and grabbed the handle of the fire bell, cranking it in slow motion. 'It needs oiling,' she said, 'I've told Ivan a hundred times . . .'

Sveta stood open-mouthed as the girl struggled to get more than a clank out of the bell.

'No one will hear that! Shouldn't you go down the corridor and warn the staff? Lives may be at stake!'

'You do what you like. My role is to ring the bell. It's in the regulations.' She jabbed her elbow at the small print plastered to the wall behind her.

Sveta's eyes fell on the reception desk bell. The wood cracked as she ripped it from its moorings and then bolted for a corridor she guessed would lead her to the fire.

'Hey!' shouted the administrator. 'You can't—'

Sveta prised open the creaking door, took a deep breath and plunged on.

The corridor was badly lit, windowless, and long. There was no sign of life. She trotted down its middle, filling it with the sound of her steps, the dinging of the bell and her alarm call.

'Fire!' she yelled in a voice loud enough to wake the dead.

'Fire!' There was no reply.

'Fire!' The lights before her flickered gently in the gloom, and went out.

Ding-ding-ding went the little bell on her palm as she hurried on, confused there was no one to save, and no one came running. Where were all the guests, all the staff? Her boots echoed. She pushed out a fist and rapped on a door marked 'Dietary Advice and Monitoring'. No one answered. She felt foolish.

'Fire!' she yelled, and dinged the bell. Now her voice wobbled, and she coughed as the smoke began to bite the back of her throat. She stopped and looked around, wondering whether to turn back. She thought of Albina waiting at the car. She thought of Madame Zoya's warning. The burning smell was strong now. Was that a cry she heard, behind the far door? She was sure she had heard a shout. Someone was trapped, scared. Maybe they were becoming unconscious down there, in the dark and the smoke? They were probably elderly, immobile, alone. If she turned back now to fetch help, it might be too late! She squared her shoulders, dinged her bell, and ran down the corridor.

VIM AND VIGOUR

'Let me out!'

'Mama said to make you stay in the car.'

'I have to go and help!'

'But what about your warning?' She arched a dark eyebrow and waggled her finger at him from the other side of the glass.

Gor had allowed himself to be returned to the car and had sat immobile behind the wheel, face grim as he watched the black smoke pulse like blood into the insipid sky. He couldn't make out the source: the broken window must be at the back. But now he couldn't sit still. He should not have let Sveta go. He had been a coward.

'Albina, move away from the door. I must get out.' The girl's reply was to lean her hip even more heavily against it. There was nothing else for it: Gor pushed with all his might, an 'akkhh!' croaking from his throat as he did so, the veins standing out on his forehead. She squealed as he heaved, but after regaining her balance, simply pushed back, effortlessly. The situation called for more than brute force. He rolled down the window a couple of centimetres.

'Albina, I have to go and help your mother. I cannot sit here and watch a catastrophe unfolding.'

'No way! Mama told me to make sure you stayed here, and that's what I'm going to do. But if you want to fight about it . . .' She shifted her weight away from the door and stood back, flicking the pigtails out of her eyes and pushing up her sleeves. 'Karate: do you think you stand a chance?' She drew back on her tiptoes, hands raised, face perfectly serious.

Gor regarded her for a moment and rubbed a hand over his eyes. He opened the window further, so that he could lean out.

'Albina, I'm not going to fight you. I'm an old man, and you're a girl. But listen to me. You have a choice: either way, you must be brave, and make the right decision. I have to go into that building, and I think you know that. Your mother has not returned. I have to make sure the fire brigade has been called, and your mother is safe. You can either stay here at the car, which is the safest option, or . . .' he took a breath '. . . you can come with me, and help. Just promise to stay by my side. And do what you're told.'

The girl looked hard into Gor's eyes, and turned to examine the building. She nodded. 'Let's rescue the people. And Mama.' Gor rolled up the window and unfolded himself from the car.

'Come!' he said, taking her hand, and her pigtails bounced as they hopped up the battered stairs into the smoking building.

'We will tell your mother I overpowered you: that you could not make me stay in the car,' said Gor as they headed for the empty reception desk.

'She won't believe you.'

Gor nodded.

At the desk the administrator, in the process of oiling the alarm bell, sulkily confirmed that she had called the fire service. When Gor inquired about Sveta, she waved him away with an impatient flap of the hand. 'She went off down the corridor before I could stop her! I told her not to! I told her it was dangerous! It's Communal Sitting Room No. 2 that's on fire,' she added, as Gor and Albina made for the corridor, 'right at the end.'

'You stay here,' said Gor.

'No!' Albina gazed up at him, eyes fierce. 'She's my mother!' She sprang through the door, Gor scrabbling behind her.

'Breathe through your sleeve!' he shouted as they stumbled along, eyes scanning the floor and doorways for obstructions or casualties. 'Check all the doors, just in case!' he added. There was no noise, and no heat, but the smoke reeked with a chemical intensity that turned Gor's stomach and made Albina cough. He grabbed her hand and they crouched low. The way towards Communal Sitting Room No. 2 was a dark, sooty clot.

Gor closed his eyes for a second against the sting of the smoke. His mind filled with the impression of a village in Siberia, dark pine trees swaying in the air above a straggle of warped wooden houses. It was night-time, the sky a deep blue, and the frost was crackling under his felt boots as he hurried up a track. Orange sparks were shooting and snapping into the air above a roof. Dogs were barking, frenzied in their yards and kennels, as ashen-faced villagers fell from their doorways, pulling on boots and coats over their night-clothes. They were running up the track to the edge of the village. He was running, the cold biting his lungs, stealing his breath. He was crying. Before he even saw the fire, he knew. He knew whose house it was. He knew they were too late. And he knew it was his fault.

He opened his eyes and tugged hard on Albina's hand. 'Let's hurry!'

He saw the door when they were a dozen steps away. He fumbled for the metal handle, and sagged with relief when its coldness struck his palm. He listened, and sensed the vibration of voices. Someone had got there before them.

Sveta stood amid a scene of dripping, blackened chaos, directing a pair of smut-stained orderlies who were damping down what had once been a wing-backed armchair. They sloshed water from dented buckets as steam rose off it, hissing with a dangerous pungency that brought to mind a nest of freshly singed rodents. Above the chair, flames had reached fingers to the ceiling, melting the polystyrene tiles and sending them dripping back onto a nearby table, the telephone, another armchair and the lino-covered floor. Small patches of burnt plastic still smoked. The windows had been smashed open but the air was thick and sharp. Gor placed his handkerchief over his nose and mouth and stepped hesitantly forward.

'Sveta? Are you all right?'

Sveta tutted and shook her head. 'It looks like a seat for the devil himself, doesn't it? It's a miracle no one was harmed!' She was talking to herself.

'Mama! What are you doing? Come out of there!' Albina pushed past Gor and leapt forward, arms outstretched. She stopped when she saw the odd way her mama was holding herself. 'What have you done?'

Sveta smiled at her daughter with puzzled eyes, and looked

down at her hands, which she was holding in front of her, as if she had Kopek cupped there. The hands were shaking, shiny and swollen under a layer of soot.

'I don't know, baby-kins. What have I done?'

'She has burnt her hands,' a voice cut in from the opposite doorway. Vlad strode forward, wet sponge in hand, his eyes darting from Sveta to the new arrivals. 'And suffered some smoke inhalation. But it's OK. I'm here.' He towered over Sveta, jutting his chin towards her as he took her hands and gently dabbed at the soot. She winced.

'I thought someone was in the chair!' she said, eyeing its twisted remains once more and smiling apologetically. 'Ooch, that hurts!'

'No one was in the chair, dearest Sveta,' said Vlad, concentrating on her hands. 'Everything was under control. You gave me a fright, rushing in like that . . .' he tutted and surveyed her swollen palms. 'You're lucky we were here.'

'Sveta?' said Gor.

'I . . . I can't remember what happened. I ran in . . . I was getting scared; it was very smoky. I saw the flames, and heard a cry. I tried to put it out . . . with my hat. There was someone here . . .' Sveta swayed and smiled up at Vlad, her eyes glazed. Gor and Albina frowned to each other.

'It was staff, doing their jobs,' he said quietly, holding her hands and the sponge in one of his, and wiping his brow with the other. 'It's a good thing there are no guests on that corridor, the one you came through. They might have been . . .' He looked away, through the window into the grey morning.

'How did it start?' asked Gor gruffly.

Vlad shrugged. 'I don't know . . . these things happen so

219

often, you see it on the news every month: a spark from a plug, a short circuit, something over-heating, a stray cigarette . . .' He held Sveta's hands up to the light, his eyes flicking across them.

'Why no alarms?' Gor persisted.

'Maybe they're broken. More likely they were faulty and someone disconnected them: you know how people are. No one thinks a fire might happen to them.' His tone was matter-of-fact, but his face was grim.

'Sveta could have been killed!'

'Oh, no! I am fine,' said Sveta, her face stiff.

Albina looped her arm through her mother's and rested her head on her shoulder. Sveta was gazing at the charred armchair, chewing her bottom lip. 'I wouldn't have come in, if I'd known it was empty. It was all on fire.'

'She's in shock,' said Gor. 'Sveta, you've been very brave, but now you need to go home and lie down. We will come back and speak to Vlad another time.'

'Actually, I'd like to suggest she be seen by our resident doctor, Dr Spatchkin.' Vlad turned to Sveta. 'You could stay here for a night or two, Sveta – in the ladies' wing, of course! Just for a rest, and to let your hands heal. I don't think the wounds are serious, but . . . we will take good care of you. It's nice here: far better than Hospital No. 4. You need to rest, and I can get you anything you need,' Vlad added as she was about to argue, and a boyish smile flitted across his face. 'Just ask.'

Sveta nodded. 'Maybe I should stay. I do feel . . . odd.' Small beads of sweat stood out on her forehead and on the hairs of her upper lip. 'Perhaps I should have a rest.'

'But Mama—'

'She will go to the Tereshkova wing,' Vlad addressed Gor. 'For ladies. She will be in good hands. It is very peaceful at this time of year, and it's on the other side of the building so . . . no smoke.'

He held her arm as she was lowered to a stretcher that had appeared by her side, carried by another set of smut-spattered orderlies.

'Perhaps you should go with your mother, Albina? She will need you for comfort and support,' said Gor. 'Don't worry. I will come along in a while to take you home.'

The breath caught in Albina's throat and she stared at her mama. 'But there'll be no one at home! Mama will be here! And I will be all alone!' She grabbed the stretcher, her grip threatening to flip her mother onto the floor. 'Mama! Mama! What am I to do! Don't leave me!'

'Oh, *malysh*, careful with Mummy's hand!'

'Be calm!' Gor pressed Albina's shoulder. 'We will sort something out. Is there a neighbour you can stay with?'

'Only Auntie Vera, but Mama, don't make me stay with her! She drinks vodka and beats her cats!'

'Akh!' moaned Sveta. 'My hands! I can feel them! Oh, that hurts.'

'Don't make me stay with her!'

'Hush child!' Gor cut in. 'Very well: if there is no one else, you can stay with me until your mother is rested. There is no need to howl.'

'Are you sure that's wise?' asked Vlad. 'When there are strange things going on at your apartment?'

'And what business is it of yours, Vlad?' Gor struggled to keep his tone even.

221

The student sucked in his cheeks. Around them orderlies bustled and grumbled, scratching over shards of burnt armchair and blobs of charred ceiling tile. The two holding the stretcher shuffled their feet and coughed loudly.

'It's not my business.' Vlad smiled. 'I don't know why . . . anyway, Sveta, please be on your way. I will pop in to check on you in a day or two.' He crinkled his eyes at her.

She smiled back, and turned her head to her daughter. 'Be a good girl for Gor, Albina. I'm going to have a little sleep now.' She kissed the hand still gripping her shoulder, and yawned. She was borne off, back down the dingy corridor. Albina went to follow, but was stilled by Vlad's single raised digit.

'No visitors today, young lady,' he said softly. 'Your mama needs silence, and rest. You can visit her after the weekend.'

'But my mama!' she wailed.

The doors swung shut with a sudden, echoing clunk. Vlad pressed a hand against them.

'Ah! The security doors have locked,' he said with a frown. 'That's unusual! I don't have the key for this one.'

Gor shook his head. 'By all that's holy! First the alarms don't work, and now we're locked in!'

The younger man turned to him with a stern face. 'We do the best we can, in the circumstances. Why are you here anyway, Papasyan?' He raised an eyebrow. 'Ah, you've come to visit, at last?'

'Visit? Pah!' Gor made a face of distaste. 'We came to talk to you.'

'Me?'

'We had some questions, about the séance.'

'Ah! I see. But wait!' Vlad opened his eyes wide. 'Madame

Zoya warned of fire – and here you are, and there's a fire! That's scary, isn't it?' He looked from Gor to Albina and back again, nodding.

'I'm not scared,' Gor said tetchily.

'Me neither,' said Albina.

'Oh? Right . . . well, that's good. But I'm sorry – I can't talk now. I'm on duty, and as you can see, we have mess to clear up, and elderly residents to reassure. They're roaming the corridor, all out of sorts. They don't understand they're safer in here than on the marsh.' He shrugged his shoulders. 'I suppose I'll have to let you out this way. Please follow me!'

Vlad set off through the door from which he had earlier appeared, slapping his feet on the floor in precise strides.

'All guests to their rooms, please!' he called out. 'No need for alarm! The fire was very small, and it's out now. All is well!' He coughed as he spoke. 'Close the sitting-room doors,' he barked at an orderly, 'the smell is making them worry.'

Gor and Albina followed. Doors stood open as staff tried to reassure the confused and infirm that the emergency was truly over and bed was the best place to be. Their efforts weren't helped by the wail of a redundant fire engine floating up from the marshes as it picked its way along the creek towards them. Vlad slammed doors energetically as he progressed.

A broad orderly, face glistening with sweat, stood hands on hips in a doorway arguing with someone who very much wanted to go outside. Vlad looked in, and Gor heard raised voices.

They waited in the corridor. Gor felt the weight of claustrophobia in his chest. He was impatient to leave now: it had a strange atmosphere, this place, threatening and close, despite the high ceilings. The smell of new paint didn't help. He started walking for the doors at the end of the corridor.

'Come, Albina!'

The girl was standing at a doorway half-way along, peering in.

In the flicker of a strip-light she saw a figure standing at the end of a bed: an old man, short but wide, with wild grey hair. He swayed on his feet, trembling and muttering.

He was facing the door, but his eyes were shut. Both hands were held stiffly out in front of him, the pudgy fingers tightly crossed. His mouth was moving. Albina leant forward to hear. A hurried whisper escaped his mouth, high and thin.

'Comrade Stalin, protect me! Protect me, Comrade Stalin!'

She squinted. Her initial reaction – to giggle – was displaced by something deeper that made her stomach clench. The man was terrified. His mottled eyelids fluttered and one bright green eye peeled open. A high-pitched shriek escaped his mouth.

'I'm sorry!' she mumbled as she backed away, hurrying out into the corridor, stumbling to catch up with Gor. She jumped as Vlad slammed the opposite door and leapt up the corridor behind them.

'Time to go!' he smiled, pushing Albina along in front of him and grasping Gor's arm above the elbow. 'Matron is angry!'

'But when will we speak? I—'

'Another day, please! Just phone first, yes? You understand: I can't always be available.'

Vlad stopped before the dusty double doors and twisted a key in the lock. 'Take the stairs down, go left along the corridor and out at the door with the push-bar. Come back and knock loudly if it won't open.'

He propelled them through the door, nodded to both and slammed it shut, locking them out.

Albina pushed her face against the grimy glass, following the student doctor's progress back up the glowing green corridor. She watched as he stopped at the doorway to Room No. 6. He looked in for a long moment, shook his head, and then shut that too.

'That was scary.'

'Come, we must go home.' Gor's boots echoed on the concrete steps. 'You will be needing some milk and biscuits.'

Still the girl stood looking down the corridor. 'I'm not hungry.'

'Don't be alarmed, Albina: your mama will soon be well, and I'm sure this place isn't as bad as it seems.'

Albina's chin was on her chest. 'That old man . . .'

'What old man?' Gor waited as she caught him up.

'In the room. He was creepy!'

'What do you mean? I'm sure he was just an elderly guest, left here to rot by his family.'

'You didn't see him.'

'And what could be so creepy, Albina?' Gor's whiskers twitched. He found Albina's penchant for melodrama wearing.

'He was standing with his eyes shut and his fingers crossed, as if he was praying or something!'

'That's not how you pray, Albina.'

'He was praying to Stalin, though!'

Gor stood still on the bottom step.

'What do you mean, child?'

'He was standing with his fingers crossed and eyes closed saying "Comrade Stalin, protect me!" – over and over.' Albina mimicked the scene.

225

'But that's . . . impossible.' He stared at her open-mouthed for a moment, then shook himself and hurried on down the stairs. 'No, no! It can't be. Come, Albina, time to get home. Enough for today. Enough!'

The girl gave Gor a long sideways look. His voice was too loud, the pitch too high, and his tight-skinned face was glowing pale yellow. It was almost as if he was scared. As they hurried down the last few steps, her hand slipped into his. He glanced down, and then, without slowing his pace, turned to look back up the way they had come.

'There's no one there,' said Albina.

ICE-CREAM

ping-ping-ping

The alarm on his Tag-Heuer had gone off at least half an hour ago. He'd put it on snooze, couldn't work out how to turn it off entirely. Now it pinged every few minutes. He'd set it so he would know exactly when she began to be late, and now it reminded him, endlessly: she was not there; she had not come.

He sat alone, twirling a spoon in his empty cup, long legs tucked uncomfortably under the warped plywood table. His thigh twitched and his heel bounced on the floor. The sugar shivered in the bowl. He knew the girl behind the counter was looking at him. She was pretty, but he wasn't in the mood. Why hadn't Polly come?

Polly, who had taken his breath away, stolen his soul: so unexpected, so exciting, so other. Here was someone who didn't giggle or simper, or pretend to be stupid: she was powerful, animal. Her intent had pinned him down, and he had been content to be contained by her, forever, he had thought.

It had started late in August, as the flies died and the sun steamed. He'd been watching girls as they filtered into the hall,

227

sun-kissed, newly shod, a brood of horny hens. Something had made him turn his head and look into the shadows opposite.

She was tall, athletic looking: a high-school runner or a floor gymnast. Standing on her own as the other girls giggled and chatted, she looked as if she couldn't hear them – as if they weren't there. She had stared across the hall as though the only thing she could see was – him.

He had glanced down at the notepad, the forms he was supposed to be filling, empty spaces littering the page. When he looked up she was there, sliding down beside him into the faded plastic chair. He looked into her face, a surprised smile on his lips.

Without looking at him, she reached out a long-fingered hand and took a tab of his chewing gum, throwing it into her mouth.

He shifted in his seat, the joints cracking, and opened his mouth to speak.

'What's your name?' she asked in a cool voice, still looking straight ahead, before he could start.

'Vladimir. People call me Vova.'

'I will call you . . . Vlad.'

'Oh, you will, will you?' Still he smiled but his eyes were puzzled.

She turned her head and raised a fine, dark eyebrow, then looked away.

'And you are?'

'Polina. You'll call me Polly.'

'Are you a second year?'

'Yes.'

'I don't recognise you.'

She popped the gum in her cheek. 'I took a year out. Family problems.'

'Ah. All happy now?'

Her lips twitched. 'Yes.'

'Do you like my gum?'

'Yes.'

She turned to him. There was no make-up on that face, and her hair hung long down her back. Her cheekbones were broad, the nose small, scattered with golden freckles, but it was her eyes, those dark, curving eyes . . . by turn frank, otherworldly, motherly, blank, that fascinated him.

'Where's your work placement?' she asked.

'Vim & Vigour sanatorium – care wing. Worst luck. Lots of geriatrics. And you?'

'Pharmacy No. 2, Azov town centre.'

'A pharmacy? You won't get much practical there.'

A cloud passed across the eyes.

'I've been there all summer already. I don't think they like me.' She nodded towards the table at the top of the hall where a clump of administrators argued over sheaves of paper and rubber stamps. 'But never mind.'

'Don't take it personally. It's only for a short while.' He observed her thighs under her short summer skirt. 'And what do you like, Polly, besides being a medical student – and my gum? Music? Dancing? Ice-cream?'

She turned to study him, her head on one side.

'Come here: I'll whisper it to you.' A lock of hair fell over her brow.

He had leant forward, and closed his eyes to listen. When he opened them, nothing could be the same.

At each lecture on the 'Advanced Years' course they sat, thigh pressed against thigh, strolling through the decay of old age, words about dementia and tissue degradation flitting around their heads like butterflies. They learnt what it was to age, and together they laughed at it, disdained it, rejected it, enraptured by their youth. Those sad stories with forgotten endings would never be for them.

ping-ping-ping

Time had done strange things since they had met: lectures could take a lifetime, each breath a slow, sweet torture. Each night without her was an endless death. How he writhed. Valya had noticed; she'd sat him down and tried to have a word: 'Don't take on so,' she'd said. 'She's just a girl. It's just a romance. What do you know of her? Go to a few dances, watch a film, play football with the lads.' She hadn't understood. He didn't want to know about her family, her pets, her previous boyfriends or her favourite reads. He didn't want the distraction. He just wanted to touch her.

He'd never had a girl like this: instantaneous and wild, making love in the dusty grass on the river-bank or in the clattering store cupboard at work. Sometimes he felt too exhausted to get up in the morning, too exhausted to sleep, eaten up as flames twitched from his groin into his belly and his blood sang with desire. He was ravenous, but unable to eat. He'd wanted Polly to devour him entirely and spit out his husk. If only life could be as simple as sex.

ping-ping-ping

That night, back in early September, he'd been on lates, still nervous and new at the Vim, trying to please, being responsible. She'd thrown a stone at the office window, giggled up, and then climbed right through when he'd opened it. He'd been scared and thrilled. Wordlessly, she'd locked the office door, sat before him on the desk in her mini-skirt and stockings and slowly undone the buttons of his shirt. He'd wanted to say stop, but didn't really want to say stop. She hadn't stopped.

ping-ping-ping

And when he'd fallen asleep, she'd gone through the patients' files. That hadn't really worried him at first. After all, she was studying with him, and it was only natural, he told himself, that she should be interested. The pharmacy, after all, didn't give her much opportunity for practical work. He'd put it to the back of his mind. But then she'd told him about taking the old man's key.

He'd always known she was different. He knew her emotions governed her actions, and her emotions could be very strong. Take her plans for Papasyan, for example. But this was different. She had not understood his disquiet, in fact she'd ripped through his objections with frightening determination. She had been so emphatic the old man must stay at the Vim, he had felt threatened. Ridiculous, maybe, to feel threatened by a girl who claimed to love him. But hadn't she threatened blackmail? Was that the word? And for what? The idea of them bedding down amongst the old man's things sent a chill along Vlad's spine. How could they make love on his sofa with the whispering trees of Chernovolets, the wood spirits and the stories flying all around them? The whole idea was . . . monstrous.

And then there was the fire.

ping-ping-ping

So here he was, spending Friday night sitting in the Northern Star ice-cream parlour, waiting for her, to talk it through.

231

Waiting for her, watching the pretty blonde serving girl at the counter, and wondering; maybe he really just wanted something, someone . . . a little softer?

Maybe he could change her back into the person she'd been before, at some point in her past. He was convinced, once upon a time, she'd been a good girl, a princess – before life had made her hard. He could see it in her face, and sometimes when she spoke: she hadn't been the type to nail birds' wings to the fence post. Had she?

The door opened and he looked up: not her, again.

His stomach growled. The blonde smiled his way as she chewed her nail polish. He swallowed the lump in his throat, smiled back, and returned his eyes to the menu.

'Can I get you anything?' she called over.

'Do you do anything savoury?'

'We're an ice-cream parlour,' she replied with a smile, tucking a lock of stray hair behind her ear.

'No then.'

'We do a lovely hazelnut?'

'Uh-huh.' He unfolded a bigger smile, but she'd turned to walk to the other end of the counter and the old lady who stood at it, counting out piles of change.

As Vlad pushed back his chair, to leave or to talk to the girl at the counter, he hadn't decided which, the door opened and in jumped Polly, shopping bags flicking around her ankles like small dogs. The smell of rain and leaves and clouds came with her through the door.

'Akh, there you are! Have you been here long? I'm sorry!'

She sat down in a flurry of energy, the bags bouncing and rustling. Her cheeks were almost russet from the cold, and her

232

mouth was working hard, chewing something very minty and white.

'I've been in Rostov, just got back. It's really changing! Have you been recently? I bought some gum,' she added unnecessarily. 'Want some?'

Vlad shook his head, eyeing the bags at her feet. 'And not just gum. Had fun?'

'Business,' she replied, peering solicitously into one of the bags as if checking on a sleeping baby. 'Good business.'

'Oh?'

'I've had a lovely day: very busy, and very productive.' She smiled and, to his surprise, leant forward to run her fingers from his cheekbone to his jaw. 'And you? How was work?'

'Work?' He shrugged. 'I don't recall: I've spent most of the day waiting here, for you. Would you like a drink?'

She pulled a sorry face, grinned, flipped over the menu without reading it, and popped a bubble in the gum.

'No, I'm not thirsty. Was there something specific you wanted to see me about? It's just that I've got a lot on.'

'What do you mean?'

She stopped chewing.

'Why am I here? Was it something—'

'It's a date, Polly!' he almost shouted, before recovering his calm. He took her hand from the sticky table and rubbed her cold fingers. 'A date: I wanted to see you . . . to chat to you, and see how you are. Because I . . . I care about you.'

'Ah?' She raised her eyebrows, smiling open-mouthed. 'You're sweet. I've been busy.'

'And I wanted to talk to you.'

She waited.

233

The blonde at the counter looked across. Vlad cleared his throat. 'What have you been up to?'

She looked past his shoulder to the street beyond. 'This and that. I told you – taking care of business.' She winked. Vlad closed his eyes. 'Apart from that, I've been at the pharmacy working like a slave, trying to placate that fat bitch Maria—'

'Ah. Everything OK there?'

She chewed fiercely for a moment, and stopped. 'Actually, no. They want to get rid of me. She's threatened me with sanctions; wants to take it to a university board.'

'What do you mean?'

'She hates me! Just like everyone else! I've missed a few shifts: I've been so busy with Papasyan and doing up old crinkle-cheeks' flat—'

'Don't call him that!'

She stopped chewing. Shock flitted over her face. Their eyes locked as silence pressed on the booth, the tinkling of cutlery fading away. 'You're sensitive today, Vlad. What's the matter? Something you want to tell me about?' She smiled, but her tone was poisonous.

He shrugged. 'He's my patient. I don't feel it's right to . . . to mock him.'

Her brow puckered as dark clouds filled her eyes. He could almost feel the storm whipping up inside her. An A-board outside the window tipped over in the breeze and went flipping down the pavement.

'I'll get some drinks. Tea, was it?'

She stared out of the window and didn't answer.

He returned two minutes later with tea and a dish of ice-cream. Polly had not moved.

'Please eat it. For me?'

She stared at the ice-cream. He tried to catch her gaze.

'Do you like me, Polly?'

'Like you?' She tore a corner off a serviette and folded her gum into it. 'Yes,' she said eventually, biting out the word.

'I don't feel very . . . liked. You don't kiss me, or hold my hand when we walk down the road.'

'We don't walk down roads.'

'You're right. We meet in borrowed bedrooms, or office cupboards, or on park benches.'

'I thought you liked that?' She frowned.

'Well—' the spoon clattered in his glass as he stirred. 'Maybe . . . but I think I want something more . . . more like other people have. Talking to Anatoly Borisovich, getting to know him, and then . . . and then you telling me you'd taken his key, so that we could use his flat. It's not right, is it? And all this with Papasyan. I don't like what we've been doing. It made me think.'

She stared, open-mouthed. 'Think? Think what?'

He looked into her beautiful face, the swirling darkness of her irises. 'I think I want some . . . normal.'

'Normal?' She sneered. 'What's so good about this "normal"?' Her face was hard.

'I don't know! We need to have conversations; talk about things that aren't money or business or patients; go on dates – do things that aren't work, or—'

'Ha! Now he wants to talk! Before, all he could do was shag!'

'I want to be your friend, Polly! We can't carry on like this! Look, I think . . . I think Papasyan has been scared enough,

235

don't you? I think we should stop now. If revenge is what you wanted, you've certainly had it. Did you see his face at the séance? And he looked terrible when he turned up at the Vim today.'

'Ah? Really?' She was smiling, but her tone was dangerous. 'You've been thinking a lot, haven't you, Vlad? I didn't know you had it in you. You didn't say anything?'

He shook his head.

'I can't believe you've had enough already.' She leant forward. 'He's miserable, and that's what I want. But he's still not as miserable as my father was, when we had no food for a week, thanks to him.' Her eyes bore into his. 'He ruined my family, don't forget, turned us out on the street—'

'I know. And I understand why you wanted revenge for that. That's why I agreed to help you. But he's just an old man, Polly. Just a miserable old man. What's the point—'

'Why should he be rich when I'm poor? Eh? Why should he have that flat, and cats, and friends, when I have nothing?' Her voice rose as her fingers gripped his. 'He's a filthy old miser, and he deserves what we're giving him!'

Vlad swallowed. Customers were turning their heads to stare.

'Eat your ice-cream, Polly, and stop shouting. It's hazelnut: the best,' she said.'

Polly placed a tiny spoonful of ice-cream on her tongue and chewed on it, surveying the bags strewn at her feet. She thought about the new tenant for the flat, whom she'd shown around that day as Babkin packed his things, and whose deposit – the whole three months – she had taken and already invested. He'd be moving in within a week or so. She thought about the money that would come in every month, once that happened. She thought about Papasyan's gold hidden in his flat, nearly within her reach, if she could just keep up the pressure, and get him out of there. He would soon be at the Vim for a spell under Doctor Vlad. She thought about a job at the Vim that she would ask Vlad to get her, which would give her an endless supply of affluent and confused elderly connections. She thought about the pleasing range of opportunities for theft and fraud that this would bring. And she decided she could ease up on Vlad. She had it all under control. He just had to love her.

'But maybe you're right. It's all been pretty stressful.' She took his broad hand in hers and squeezed the ends of his fingers. 'You don't need to worry. Don't do anything more. Leave Papasyan to me. You've done enough; you must be a master of the silent phone call by now.' She kissed each fingertip and looked into his eyes. He snorted.

'And the rest.'

'You're a good boy. Do you want to see what I bought?'

He shook his head. 'I don't think so.'

'No, really, have a look! Share my interest! You've never seen such good quality. I was really lucky . . .'

She dipped into three bags before eventually, very carefully, raising a tiny lacquered box wrapped in green tissue paper to the table. She placed it in front of Vlad and slowly peeled back the layers, her eyes intent. 'This one's by Manezhnik. You won't believe how beautiful it is. Such work!' Her hands shook as the paper fell away and her voice dropped to a squeaky whisper. 'Look! It's the Snow Maiden!'

She leant down so her eyes were level with the table and

gazed on the tiny black box, shiny as jet in its pool of green paper, her eyes devouring the topaz blues and frosty silvers of the minutely painted portrait.

He reached out to pick up the box. Her hand clamped over his instantly.

'Don't touch!' The glinting in her eyes reminded him of something small and fierce.

'As you wish. How much was it?'

'It was well priced.'

'How much?' He leant forward and twisted a finger in her long, brown-black hair. 'Tell me.'

She hesitated, and he wound the lock of hair again around his finger so that it was taut.

'Eight hundred . . . thousand.' She carefully enunciated the words.

Vlad swallowed.

'It was a good price. For the quality. That's a solid invest-ment. It will only appreciate.'

He released her hair and she began re-wrapping the box, fingers hurrying, fumbling over the rustling paper, tearing at it.

'Where did you get the money?'

She smiled, but her mouth remained closed.

'How many did you buy?' Vlad took in the bags. 'These aren't all Palekh boxes?'

'Ay-ayayaah! That would be telling!' She carried on wrap-ping. When he continued to stare, she added, 'Of course they're not all Palekh boxes.'

'Where is the money coming from, Polly?'

'Are you fed up because I didn't get you anything? You've

238

already got the watch and the jumper. I'll get you something next time.'

A cold sweat broke on his forehead.

'Have you . . . have you been ripping off Anatoly Borisovich? Selling his things? Is that what's going on? Is that why you stole his key?'

'His things? Pah! You wouldn't get fifty roubles for his things!' she hissed scornfully. 'Let a girl have some mystery!'

'It is, isn't it?'

'No, Vlad!' She was smile-frowning, shaking her head.

He gazed at the watch on his wrist, the smooth progress of the second hand moving across its face. It was an international icon. She followed his gaze.

The watch slipped onto the table with a clunk.

'You're crazy. This is all crazy. Take the watch. I don't want it. I didn't realise—'

'What do you mean? I gave it to you. You can't give it back!'

'I don't want it. It . . . it disgusts me.'

A crack rang out as she dropped the Palekh box to the floor.

'But . . . I didn't sell the old man's things! I didn't!'

'So how did you pay for the watch?'

Her eyes bored into his, searching his soul. A tight smile split her face. 'I sold pills, OK? Just stuff from the pharmacy, to lonely old cows who knew no better.'

He groaned and shook his head. 'Oh God, that's nearly as bad! How could you, Polly?'

'But I did it for you! I thought you were my friend!'

'This is madness. I need to think. I'm not sure—' He sat back from the table.

She grabbed his wrist. 'You can't just drop me. You have to help me! I need a job at the Vim.'

His eyes popped. 'A job? At the Vim? After what you just said?'

'They always need staff there—' Her eyes were like Siberia; wide, cold, empty. 'And I need a job. It'll be nice—'

'No way!' He pushed himself into the corner of the booth. 'Things are weird enough there. There's gossip, Polly, about you and me. And reports to Matron . . . things going missing. Papasyan turned up to question me this morning – at the same time as a fire broke out!'

'Fire?' Her face held a strange expression, somewhere between a sneer and wonder. 'While Papasyan was there? That's fantastic!'

'No it's not! People could have been hurt! Was it another coincidence, Polly?'

'What? You don't think I had anything to do with it?'

'I don't know what to think, but you can't work there! It wouldn't be right!' He looked away from her. 'I'm not compromising myself any more.'

'You pompous pig! I *need* that work!'

The blonde behind the counter clanged a dish onto a tray and sniggered.

'I can't help you! Let's forget it, forget the whole idea. We don't need it. I don't need it.'

She gazed at him, open-mouthed.

'You mean you don't need *me*!'

'That's not what I meant.' He focused on the shiny ceiling tiles. 'Find something else. Forget revenge on old men, forget thieving keys – forget Palekh boxes! Have fun, do your college work, make dresses and, you know, talk to the other girls. Just be . . . nice!'

Polly stared at him in silence.

'You can ask for a placement transfer if you hate the pharmacy so much. Just not to the Vim. It won't work.'

Her breathing was fast and shallow.

'Don't go psychopath, princess. Can't we start again? Can't we be . . . normal?'

She said nothing.

'Eat your ice-cream?'

She fingered the spoon as her eyes looked through him, face blank.

'Polly?' He touched her hand.

'You're just like all the rest, aren't you?' She snatched her hand away and bent to scrabble up the broken Palekh box from the dirty tiles. 'You don't care about me! You don't care about my future! You're abandoning me!'

'That's not true—'

'I'll find a way. I'm clever! I don't need you!' She staggered up from the seat, bags seething around her, and ran for the door.

'Polly! Wait!'

The door slammed. Heads turned.

The blonde leant on the counter and waited for him to turn. 'Everything OK?'

He puffed out his cheeks and shook his head. 'I don't know. She's . . . there's something wrong with her, I think.' He made a screwy motion with his finger at his temple. 'But I . . .'

'Ah. And she's your girlfriend?'

His cheeks burnt. 'Well, uh, yes. At least, I thought so. I'm not sure.' He scratched his head. 'We had an argument. We study together. I'm a doctor.'

'Ah? Do you want to talk about it?' The girl fluttered her eyelids. 'I could give you another tea – on the house?'

'Well, uh, thanks.' He picked up the watch from the table and sauntered over to the counter.

'Are you looking to sell that?' she whispered, her teeth biting into the softness of her lip as she glanced over her shoulder.

He looked into the glum face of the watch, and nodded.

MOONLIGHT

Sveta lay in her bed on Tereshkova wing, the white sheets crinkled underneath her like starched waves. She lowered her book – a Soviet-realist tale of concrete production – to peek over its top. She needed to see, but the book gave her privacy: the space between her nose and its pristine, unread pages was her own.

There was something out of place at the Vim & Vigour. Her instinct for institution, finely tuned through many years' service, told her so. It wasn't her room-mates: they were both perfectly charming, in their own way. Tatiana Astafievna, the tiny, shrew-like one on the left, had once been a lawyer. She ran a sharp eye over every word that bounced around her, tasting phrases on her tongue, feeling the weight of snatches of conversation in her frail hands, but uttering not one syllable herself. The other one, long, bony and referred to by all the staff only as Klara, had once run a municipal bakery, producing over 5,000 loaves per day. Picture that! The daily responsibility of 5,000 loaves, come rain or shine, rye or spelt. Sveta admired the woman who baked 5,000 loaves each day. Klara coughed, and muttered into her hands, occasionally dropping them to issue commands to an unseen workforce.

Both ladies were regularly propped up to take tit-bits of food, but most of the time they lay curled and ragged, thin as old lace, disappearing against the white oceans of their beds. Each was connected by a tube and two wires to a machine stationed between them which, in turn, appeared to lead directly to the other old lady. It occasionally made a pinging noise, to which nobody paid attention. Sveta comforted herself: at least she was not also attached.

'So, how are your hands today?'

She held out white-bandaged hands, and concentrated on looking like they did not hurt. She moved her fingers, wriggling them as if playing the piano, and suppressed a grimace. It was lucky her burns were only minor, they said. How sad it must be to have only stumps.

And it wasn't Spatchkin, the doctor, who made her feel strange. She'd got over his appearance very quickly, hardly noticing the way his face hung from an out-sized head perched above a childlike, bent body. She could hear him coming: he wheezed as he walked. He sat on the edge of her bed, eyes intent on her face, and asked in gentle tones:

'How are your bowel movements?'

Sveta sought to express total satisfaction without going into detail.

'And the dressings have been changed? There is no sign of infection?'

'No doctor. I think I am ready to go home.' She said it each time they met.

'Ah, but it's not up to you, is it?' He smiled sadly.

244

She felt like a school girl and shook her head.

'Are you quite rested?'

'Yes, I feel . . . marvellous! The best I've ever felt.' Her pale lips stretched into a smile.

'The best ever? Well, perhaps we should have you stay a few more days, we might turn you into Superwoman?'

He patted her leg with his tiny, fine-fingered hand.

'A ha-ha-ha!'

'I shouldn't joke,' he said, coughing softly. 'Health is a serious business. How are your bowels, did you say?' He leant forward.

'Excellent.'

His eyebrows twitched.

'Can I go home now, please?'

He patted her leg with one hand as he jotted a note with the other. 'We'll see what Matron says. In principle, I think maybe, yes.'

'Hurrah!' The cry escaped her and she giggled.

'But the human organism is complex . . .'

Klara muttered something about rye, and Tatiana weighed the word, rubbing it between her fingers like dough. Spatchkin remained on Sveta's bed, silently regarding the two elderly patients from the slits of his eyes. The machine let out a ping.

'Good!' he exclaimed loudly. 'Carry on!' He stood, nodded to each of the women in turn, and shuffled away.

Vlad had not paid a visit. Maybe he only worked in the men's section. Maybe he had a guilty conscience about the séance. Or maybe he didn't care how she was: after all, there was no reason why he should. But he had said he would pop in. Those were his exact words. And they still needed to ask him about Madame's table. Fire had been the warning, and fire there had been.

245

It wasn't the orderlies, who were all the same but different, their tabards made of the same material as the bedsheets, their hair back-combed into red and yellow beehives and stuffed into tall white cotton hats. Neither the hats nor the hair moved. They served meals in the day room, cleared up spillages, propelled patients back to bed and stood in the corridor, eyes shifting, waiting for instructions. They were all normal people, as ready to laugh, cry or argue as the next person: nothing untoward there.

When the daylight faded, however, and the lights were lowered, the buzz of the hive died away. The last round of checks and discussions was had and the steps in the corridor faded. Then they were left alone, the door propped open with a chair, the only sounds the vague throbbing of the boiler system, and their own breathing. The older women struggled for air. Sveta could hear them: the delicate branches of their lungs weighed down with traces of yeast, books and dust: the relics of a lifetime of toil. A fear began to work its way through her veins, bringing a cold sweat to her skin. Not a fear of ageing, so much, as a fear of ill-health: the slow decline, the gradual indisposition, the loss of vigour. Had it started already?

The first night she woke before dawn, eyes focusing on the glow of the doorway. She had heard a step in the corridor, on the edge of her sleep. There it was again: slow, soft, coming towards her room. There was no reason for it to be menacing, but . . . She turned over carefully, bunching the sheets under her chin as she tried to snuggle down. As her eyes closed she heard it again, closer this time. She yawned into her pillow, but her eyes would not stay shut.

She felt it in the room a second later, and tried to turn her head to get a clear view. It was at this point she realised she was paralysed. A figure slid towards her, on the periphery of her vision. She willed her arms to thrash out and her legs to throw her body to the floor. Breath filled her throat with a scream. But only her eyes moved. Panic gripped her: perhaps she couldn't breathe. She was wheezing like the other ladies, bronchioles filling with fear, submerging her as if she were drowning in the bed. Her spirit leapt in the useless body.

As the oxygen ran out she woke with a muffled 'nugh!', sweat slicking her body, the sheet in her mouth. All was peace. But a feeling remained, a sense of something un-seen: waiting in the corridors after dark; under the bed in the dead of night; at the bottom of the cup at the end of the drink.

In the morning, when the breakfast bell sounded, Sveta turned tired eyes to the pillow. No amount of buckwheat porridge would dispel this feeling of disquiet. The Vim & Vigour was haunted, and if she'd had anybody to talk to, she'd have told them so right then.

The second night proved different. She had no nightmares, because she had no sleep. She tossed and turned, tangling her feet, and gave up at around three a.m. to creep along the stuffy corridor in search of air and a drink.

The light of the moon pierced a window at the far end. Sveta stared into the cosmos. She was wide awake, the feeling of confinement itching across her skin. Instead of heading back to her room, she went left up the corridor towards yellowing way-markers that pointed to invisible delights: the massage cabinet, the office of dietary advice, the mini-cinema, ping pong tables. It was strange to see it all at night, quilted in eerie silence and shadow. She wondered when anyone had last played ping pong.

She headed right along the next corridor, comforted by walls dotted with dusty needlework and faded watercolours, and then, through another set of doors, found herself in the entrance hall. This time there was no typing, no droopy administrator, no smoke. She shuffled around the gloomy perimeter, eyeing the mosaic and displays of old photos: groups of jolly factory workers and serious party officials, festival days with bunting, huge mounds of healthy vegetables. In a cabinet along one wall lay a collection of cups and medals won by the staff for their endeavours in building Communism. A wistful chuckle escaped her throat.

As she examined the treasure in the half-light, she became aware of movement behind her, reflected in the cabinet glass. A door was opening, a dark shape gliding through. She turned, ready to scream, and shoved her fist into her mouth. A small elderly gent with wild grey hair was sliding slowly across the floor on silent moccasins, heading for the entrance doors.

'Ah!' he exclaimed on spying her.

'Ah!' squeaked Sveta in reply.

He pointed the moccasins towards her, but stayed where he was. 'Good evening!' he called across the hall.

'Good evening!' Sveta's voice trembled despite herself.

'Are you . . . are you a resident?'

'I'm a guest,' she said, staring hard at the old man. 'Temporarily. And you?'

'No. Well, yes. Sort of.' He looked about him and waved his hands at the walls. 'Terrible artwork.'

Sveta nodded, deciding he was probably harmless. 'I couldn't sleep,' she ventured.

'Me neither.'

'Maybe it's the moon?'

248

'Not just the moon. This is a terrible place, for sleep. There's something . . .'

'Creepy?'

'Yes, creepy.' He nodded energetically. 'I've had terrible dreams.'

'Yes! So have I!'

'And noises in the night. I thought there was someone hiding in my cupboard.' He chuckled in his throat, but his eyes, startling green, were like a child's.

'Ah! I'm sure there wasn't.' Sveta shook her head.

'Maybe not. But there's something in the corridors. And there certainly *was* a fire!'

'Oh, I know! I helped put it out!' Sveta took a step forward and held up her bandaged hands.

'Well done!' He took a step towards her. 'I tried to do that too, a long time ago.' He stopped and scratched his head. 'But I was frightened. You know, it shouldn't have happened.'

'They said it was a workman who started it. A decorator.'

'That's not right.' He shook his head sadly. 'It was probably Yuri.'

'Yuri? Ah. Maybe that was his name.' Sveta smiled the smile she usually saved for upset Year 3s.

The old man sighed. 'Do you want to go home?'

'Yes. I am ready for home.'

'I am too. These people . . . they don't understand me.'

'No? Well, maybe home is best then, if you've had your little rest?'

'Yes.'

'You can go if you want to?' Sveta gazed into his eyes, and they glowed in response. 'If you're ready?'

'I'm ready to go. Home to Baba.'

She nodded. 'Well, I think I'm ready for bed now. I was just getting a little air, looking at the display.'

'Yes? Oh, yes. Lots of cups there?'

'Yes.'

'Oh. Well, goodnight then!' He did not move.

'You are going back to bed?' She raised an eyebrow. The old man hesitated.

'I think I'll take a look at the display too.' He skated towards the cabinet. 'I love to look at things.'

'Goodnight then.' She shuffled towards the door. They passed in the centre of the hall and nodded, smiling to each other.

Sveta headed back down the corridor towards Tereshkova wing, still smiling. How very odd, and very similar, all people were.

MUDDY GOINGS ON

Albina's pink woolly leggings were caked up to the knee. She waddled around in the rubber boots Gor had found for her, oblivious to the clinging cold and the mud that was now dropping inside, encasing her socks. Dirt covered both her hands. Even her cheeks were liberally smeared. She brought to mind a Neolithic hunter-gatherer Gor had once seen depicted in papier-mâché at the Rostov Historical Museum: squatting in the dirt, half savage, using primitive tools to scrape sustenance from the cold earth. She grinned as she worked. He smiled to himself and pulled open the door of the old wooden *dacha*, heading inside to fetch the samovar.

On days like these, out at the allotment with only the drizzle and the wind for company, he fully appreciated the piece of ingenuity that was the Russian samovar: a thing of brassy beauty, both ancient and modern, designed to boil water, keep tea hot for hours, and give a man a place to warm his hands no matter how hard the wind blew. He tugged it from the shelf and placed it on the table out on the veranda. Removing the lid, he checked inside for spiders. Next came sooty lumps of charcoal, which he piled carefully into the central chamber, interspersed with a few bone-dry pine cones. Then, with the steady hand of experience, he poured water into the kettle chamber surrounding the fuel. He lit a long match, and with a little spirit and considerable puffing, was finally rewarded as the pine cones fizzed into golden flame. Content that the fuel was lit, he carefully replaced the lid, topping it off with the teapot to warm. He took a seat on the wooden bench, worn smooth and shiny with the years of resting backsides, and looked forward to when the steam would start to hiss.

'Albina, what say you, time for a glass of tea and a biscuit?' She was across the vegetable patch, exploring the area where next year, all being well, potatoes would multiply in the rich earth. He hadn't expected her to be keen: he had, in fact, brought along a book for her to read, thinking she would choose to sit in the *dacha* and eat *pryaniki* while he dug. But although she had been sullen with the very idea of visiting the allotment, and sulked during the short car journey out of town, she had been spellbound by the smell and silence of the country-side as soon as they made their way down the steep path from the car park. She ran the final few steps, dashing between the allotments, craning into water-butts, peering into empty *dachas*, shaking gnarled trees for any forgotten fruit. When they reached Gor's plot, she leapt straight in, exclaiming over the skeletal remains of the summer's last crop, and excited to find the occasional berry or mushroom.

'Don't eat that!' Gor said sharply, automatically, as her hand reached out for a softly undulating growth, the frills on its underside bright orange.

'Eat it?' said Albina, 'Are you mad?' She giggled, and Gor smiled. Children these days were quite different . . . It had brought to mind, with a clarity that made him catch his breath, a memory of his own daughter, in the park in Rostov, one autumn morning in the late 1960s. She had been fascinated by the thin layers of ice lying on the puddles: had prodded them with sticks, flipped them over to examine the rotting leaves and twigs stuck to their rough undersides, got her tights all wet and muddy at the knees. She had been so inquisitive, and so happy just to be. He wondered if she ever remembered that visit to the park. If she ever thought of him at all.

Albina strode with splaying steps between the empty potato rows and the bare plum trees, anorak soaked through with dew and the effort of digging. It was still only eleven a.m. Despite the dark mornings and the chill in the air, a visit to the *dacha* always meant an early start. It didn't feel right if he arrived when the birds had already finished their morning chorus and disappeared into the blackthorn bushes.

'Do they have *dachas* in Armenia, Mister Papasyan?' Albina asked as she dropped down next to him on the bench, picking soft mud clumps from her sleeve as she did so.

'Call me Gor, child; I think we're past formalities now. And yes, I expect they have *dachas*.'

'What do you mean, you expect so? Don't you know? You are Armenian, aren't you, Gor?' she raised an eyebrow, tone accusatory, although she was smiling.

'I don't know that either.' Gor hummed to himself as he brought out two chipped cups, a box of sugar cubes, a bag full of *pryaniki,* and an old, mottled spoon.

'What do you mean?'

'Well . . . my father was from Armenia. But he met my mother in Rostov . . . way back, in the 1920s. They married,

253

and together, they moved to Siberia, where I was born, in the 1930s. After the Great Patriotic War, I moved back to Rostov, and that is where I made my home. In total, I have visited Armenia only once, to meet distant relatives, show off my family and discover the mountains. So you tell me: what am I? Am I Armenian? Siberian? Rostovian?'

Albina was eyeing the *pryaniki*, and shrugged. 'I don't know,' she said. 'Can I have . . . ?'

Gor passed the bag of biscuits to her.

'You see, I used to be a Soviet citizen, and that suited me quite well. We were all Soviet citizens. But they no longer exist. Now it pays to be Russian.'

'Hmmm,' she said, chewing heartily and not listening. 'So, you don't know anything about Armenia?'

'Well, I know things, I can tell you things, but it's mostly from books and papers, or the TV news.'

'It's very small, isn't it?'

'Compared to Russia, yes.'

'Tell me about your father.'

'Well, my father died when I was quite young—'

'Young like me?' she asked.

'Not quite that young. When you get to my age, anything below fifty is young. He died when I was in my early twenties. So—'

'What did he die of?'

'His heart.'

'A broken heart?' Albina's eyes widened.

'A heart attack. People don't really die of broken hearts.'

'No?' She looked disappointed.

'No. They carry on. It's miserable, but not fatal.'

Albina took another biscuit. Gor fell quiet, staring out from the bent veranda into the misty gardens. The water in the samovar began to simmer with a homely, bubbling sound, and he opened up the tap on the front to fill the battered metal teapot. After giving it a good stir, he placed it back on the flat top of the samovar to keep warm.

'There,' he said, 'now we have tea for the whole morning. We just pour a little into each cup, and top it up with the hot water as we go. There's the sugar. Just help yourself.'

'I don't like tea,' said Albina.

'Ah,' said Gor.

'But it doesn't matter.'

'I see,' said Gor. 'You can have hot water then, to keep you warm. And perhaps you'd like a boiled egg? Better for your teeth than *pryaniki*?'

The girl thought for a moment. 'Maybe,' she said at last, wiping biscuit crumbs from her lips. He drew out his ancient canvas knapsack from under the table and unwrapped the eggs.

'I have salt and pepper. I can't abide an egg without salt and pepper.' He smiled at the girl, showing his long, gnarled teeth.

Albina nodded in a non-committal way, and picked mud from her wild, shaggy hair. Gor wondered if he should have told her to tie it back. He had no idea how to handle pom-poms, and did not possess a hairbrush.

'Have you seen the disappearing egg trick?' he asked.

'No!' Albina turned to him eagerly. 'Can you really make them disappear? Is it real magic?'

'Well,' began Gor, 'it's a trick, that's the whole point. Making things really disappear would be—' He stopped, aware that her interest was seeping away. 'But, actually, yes, of course: I'm a magician. I can make all sorts of things disappear.'

She smiled and clapped her hands. He took up an egg and a chequered tea-towel, flourished the egg, flourished the tea-towel, put them together and – pop! – shook out the tea-towel with the egg nowhere to be seen.

'Ahh!' squealed Albina, bouncing up and down. He smiled, leant forward with a demonic look, shook his cupped hand by her ear, uttered the magic words 'hey presto!' and – pop! – the egg reappeared.

'Ha ha! That's excellent! Can you do it with two eggs?'

He hesitated. 'Er, no. That would be impossible.'

'No, try! I want you to!'

She forced another egg into his hand, the shell cracking as she did so.

'No, I'm afraid two eggs won't work. Stop it! But this egg is now magic.' He gave her a serious, dark-eyed look, and she stopped still, her face half scorn, half wonder. 'Are you brave enough to eat it, or shall I?'

She eyed the egg, held out towards her in Gor's spidery hand. 'If I eat it, will I become a good person?' she asked, her voice serious.

'Albina, you don't need a magic egg to be a good person. Look at you: you yourself – you are goodness. Just listen to your conscience, and don't drown it out with your own noise.' He shrugged. 'It's the same for everyone.'

She thought for a moment. 'OK, in that case, you have it. I think you need it more.'

Gor snorted and cracked the egg on the side of the table.

'Why do you like magic so much?'

He shook pepper onto the dome of the egg and took a bite. 'Oh, that's a good egg. Eat yours, Albina: eat! I love a good egg.'

She nodded and copied his actions, picking off minute pieces of shell with her grubby fingers. He took a gulp of hot, sweet tea and smacked his lips.

'Why do I love magic? Well, I don't know. When I was a boy, growing up in Siberia, the people there . . . well, there were old traditions, and beliefs. Traditions that survived the Tsars, survived the Revolution, survived Stalin even . . . just. They will survive us all, I think. The native people there – I mean not Russians exactly, but the indigenous people, the native people who have lived there for thousands of years: the Yakuts, the Samoyeds—' He broke off. Albina looked confused. 'Native peoples, like Eskimos. Anyway, where we lived, it was mainly Russians who'd lived there maybe twenty, maybe thirty years. But somehow, the stories of the native peoples, who had lived there thousands of years, had soaked into the soil, the trees, the houses. You could see it and hear it, little snippets. Especially the children: we liked to believe in magic, in spirits, special powers, special people who could talk with the spirits, cast spells, see off evil and . . . and all that kind of thing.' He stopped and cleared his throat. 'Of course, it wasn't encouraged. Our parents, the school teachers, the Komsomol: they told us it was all nonsense, told us the old beliefs were a result of the peasants' struggle for meaning under the yoke of feudal and then bourgeois capitalist regimes . . .'

'But was the magic real?' asked Albina, spitting egg into his tea.

'Well, of course the magic was real! If you sense it, it is so. If you see it and feel it, you can judge it for yourself. The wonder . . . mystery. It is very powerful, especially for children.

Sometimes too powerful.' He broke off and got up to throw the broken egg shells onto the compost heap. 'It all came back when I was working in the bank. It was like . . . the other side of the coin. I had to be very serious and straightforward at work. Bank work does not give much opportunity for the imagination, or creativity, or surprise. So I liked to study something that brought me . . . life, a little: it gave me the magical power to make things appear and disappear. I liked to entertain, to make people think, and to doubt . . . but I just do tricks. For hundreds, thousands of years, Albina, people have needed to believe in magic, in a power . . . outside themselves. And that fascinates me.' He shrugged, sighed, took a gulp of tea. 'It's much more interesting than money. Money hasn't been around long, compared to magic.'

'Ha, but people need money, they don't need magic!' the girl said confidently.

'Are you sure?' he paused, squinting at the drizzle that had begun to fall from the grey sky. 'Maybe you're too young. When you're a child, there's magic in everything. But it slips away, slowly, without you even noticing. And suddenly you're grown up, old even, and you wonder why you stopped feeling . . . wonder. What good is money, without wonder? People need both.'

'Huh! So, you need magic more than money?' she was smiling her fox's smile. 'Probably because you've got gold in your cistern and a bank full of cash!'

'That's not true, Albina.' He chewed his lip for a moment, hollow black eyes moving from table top to tree to the girl and back again. 'But we're not talking about money at the moment, are we?' He took a sip of tea. 'I loved entertaining people, stupefying them.' He drew out his handkerchief and coughed into it. 'But then . . . after my own daughter went, when she was small, I found the shows just got too . . . painful. I missed the sound of her laughter, which I used to find so distracting, annoying even. I missed the wonder on her face. I stopped doing shows. The children's clubs, the hospital, birthdays and New Year. I couldn't do it any more. I couldn't bear to see their . . . faces.'

'I didn't know you had a daughter. Did she die?' Albina frowned.

Gor was startled. 'No, nothing like that. I had a wife, too.' He looked up and smiled at Albina's shocked face. 'Once upon a time . . .'

'No! I can't imagine . . . What happened?'

'Nothing, really. Nothing dramatic. I . . . forgot to look after them. I was doing my duty – I worked all the hours in the day. It made me tired, bad-tempered. My wife decided I didn't love her. So she went away, and took our daughter with her.'

'So she's still alive?'

'As far as I know.'

'You don't even know?' Albina almost choked on the last of her egg.

'No.' Gor frowned, and knocked mud flakes from his trouser leg. 'They left. Some time later I received a letter telling me where they had gone, and that they were both well. I . . . I thought, well, she's made her choice, let her get on with it.'

'You never went after them? To get them back?' Albina leant forward, incredulous.

'No. She didn't want me. And I couldn't look after our daughter alone: I had to work. It was for the best.' He shrugged.

'What's her name – your daughter?'

'Olga.'

'Were you sad – when they left?'

Gor looked into the bottom of his mug, swilling the tea leaves around in little golden-brown clouds. 'I am sad every day that they left. And as I get older, I get sadder still. You may say that I am an old fool, but now, from this great age, I can see clearly: I let them slip away. And I shouldn't have.' Albina's hand crept out for a sugar cube, and Gor's hand joined it. Together they crunched on the solid sweetness, the sound echoing in their ears and off the veranda roof. A crow cawed in the hedgerow and flapped its damp, oil-slick wings.

'Is there anyone else?' she asked eventually.

'What do you mean?'

'Family?'

'Well, yes. I have a cousin. Actually . . .' he kicked a stone off the veranda, observed the damp patch it left on the wood. 'I'm a bit worried about him. I have been trying to phone him, but he doesn't answer. And . . .'

'And?'

'Well, at the sanatorium on Friday . . . you said you saw an old man in a room. You said he was creepy.'

'Yes – the old man who was talking to himself? The old man who was scared?'

'Yes. Well, what you said he was saying, doing . . . you know—'

'Fingers crossed, asking Stalin to protect him?'

'Yes . . . My cousin used to do that, when he was little.'

'But this man was an old, old man. He wasn't little.' Her eyes were round. 'Oh! You don't think . . . he was your cousin?'

'Maybe, yes. I'm not sure.'

260

'Aren't you going to check?'

'Well, I—'

'Go and see him!'

'It might not be him. It probably isn't. But—'

'But you're not sure! Just find out!'

'It's so simple?'

'Yes!' Albina took another sugar cube and nibbled its corner, sucking loudly. 'Go and see him when we go to visit Mama! I don't see what the problem is.'

'The wisdom of youth!' Gor snorted and finished his tea, fixing his eyes on the furthest plum tree. 'What you don't realise, is that life is full of misfortune. Most of it we create for ourselves. And as you get older, nothing is simple. Everything is wrapped up in some spider's web of . . . hurt.'

'You are very gloomy,' said Albina with a frown. 'You've really no reason to be.' And after a pause. 'Go and see him. It won't be so bad.' Her hand patted his on the table, and he looked up, startled. She smiled. 'I will try some tea. If that's OK? As long as I can put some sugar in it? Mama says I eat too much sugar, and that it's bad: she makes me have myrtle-berry jam in drinks. She says it's good for the skin. I hate it.'

'You don't like myrtle-berry jam?' Gor raised his eyebrows and looked down his nose at her. 'It could be worse: it could be turnip jam.'

'Ugh!' cried the girl, and then, 'More sugar please.'

Gor poured out the tea and pushed the sugar box towards her. She selected three cubes, dropped two into the tea and the other into her mouth, and warmed her hands on the sides of the cup. She blew into it, enjoying the blossom of steam on her face. 'Hmm, it smells OK,' she said.

261

'It is "OK", I assure you. Now, drink up, and then we'll finish off the digging, tidy up the compost, and maybe have a little bonfire.'

'I wish we had a *dacha*,' said Albina, wistfully.

Gor sucked in his cheeks. 'It's hard work, you know. Especially in spring and summer. You have to come every day, no matter how you feel: sowing, watering, weeding, cropping: it's not a hobby. I don't suppose your mama has the time for a *dacha*.'

'But I could help.'

Gor shook out tea drops from his mug onto the soggy grass. 'I'm sure you could.'

'When will she come home?'

'Well, we'll telephone to the Vim when we get back, and see what they say. Tomorrow, hopefully, when we visit?' Gor's spade bit into the earth.

'Why can't we visit today?'

'The rules: patients need a proper rest, and visitors,' he pointed at her, a mock glower on his face, 'spread infections. Especially at weekends, apparently. We all have to be brave. And she's being very brave. As are you.'

Albina sniffed and stamped her spade into the soil.

'Tell me a story while we work?' she asked.

'A story? I don't know any!' Gor found it difficult to dig and speak at the same time. The soil needed more compost: it was heavy, water-logged.

'You must do! Any sort of story.'

'I really don't know stories, Albina.'

'But it's easy!'

'Well, if it's so easy,' he said, giving up on the digging and standing up to ease his back, 'please, by all means – make one

262

up, while I'm digging this over. It will give me something to listen to, and you something to think about.'

'Very well!' She tossed her spade away and stooped to the broken earth. Carefully, she looped her gloved fingers around a shiny, purple worm, and raised it to her face. 'Once upon a time,' she breathed to the worm, 'a long, long time ago, there was a rich banker. He had everything: a car, a piano, a record-player, and even fluffy white cats. But one day, a wicked Siberian witch turned him into a sad little earthworm—'

'Albina!' Gor protested as she burst into a fit of giggles.

'No, wait! It'll be a nice story. Let me think. The witch was angry, because the banker had turned her down for a loan on a new, imported broomstick, with a turbo-charger. A BMW broomstick! One day, our poor earthworm spied a huge, magic apple, hanging in the tallest tree . . .'

Gor's eyes crinkled and he shook his head. 'This had better be a good story, Albina, with a happy ending. Don't forget – this earthworm will feed you tonight!' He was both offended and flattered, a strange mixture of emotion that made his voice creak with joy and indignation.

Two hours later, many stories had been told, and all the jobs were done. The bonfire had puffed half-heartedly in the brazier, they'd put their tools away, and the potatoes and apples had been collected from the dark store inside the *dacha*. Albina had got into her stride, recounting tales that wove together ancient folklore with modern-day advertisements: Baba Yaga had been defeated by way of Danish yoghurt and a magic sword. Kashei the Immortal had been trapped by the worm-banker and locked up in the local jail.

Gor emptied the samovar and cleared it of ash, replacing it

in the little crooked cupboard along with the teapot and cups. Finally, they swept the floor, Albina demonstrating a range of karate moves and pleading with Gor to join in.

'We won't be back for, well, many weeks, so we need to make sure everything is correct, and as it should be.'

'You don't come in winter?'

'There's no point: nothing that can be done. We leave the earth until just before spring.'

'It all hibernates?' Albina patted the side of the *dacha* as if it were a horse.

'Yes, you could say that.'

Gor put the plastic covers over the seats of the little Lada and they loaded themselves, aching and muddy, back in for the bumpy ride home.

'Do you know about Mama's misfortune?' asked Albina as they drew towards the lights of the town.

'Yes, well,' Gor paused. 'She told me about your father, and the fact that they could not be together.'

Silence filled the car, and Gor wondered if he had spoken out of turn. Then Albina laughed, the sound pattering the windows like rain.

'Nooo! That's not misfortune, silly! We don't need an acrobat Papa. He sends postcards from all over, and promised to buy us a car when he is rich. Mama says it's nonsense. No, the sad thing is about her parents.'

'Oh, really?' said Gor, briefly relieved. 'And what—?'

'She's an orphan,' the girl said simply. 'They were killed – in a fire.'

Gor bit his lip as the car rattled over a pot-hole.

A SPLASH OF ZELENKA

'So,' cried Valya, settling her bottom into the seat beneath her and drawing her tea closer to her elbow, 'happy Sunday to you!' She grabbed her friend and playfully gouged a chunk of skin in her upper arm. 'Are you real? You're so pale! I might be talking to you through Madame Zoya this time next week if you don't pick up. Now don't grumble at me! What's new this bright morning?'

'You haven't heard?' asked Alla, thin and shaggy as an upturned mop, but unusually smug with it as she stirred honey through her hot water.

'Heard what?' Valya squinted, bobbing low over her cup.

'About last night? About Polly?'

'Okh, this sounds good! How should you know something I don't? Spill the beans!' She rubbed her hands.

'Polly *and* Vlad, I should say?'

Valya's brow descended as her mouth fell open. 'But they split up! On Friday. He told me! I was cock-a-hoop. It happened at the Frozen North over a sundae – hell of a place if you ask me!'

265

'Ah, well!' Alla licked her cracked lips, triumphant. 'That's where you're wrong. They made it up yesterday . . . with catastrophic results!'

'Cata-whati? . . . How? Why? When?' Valya jiggled in her chair, her colour rising to a glowing cerise.

'I'm not sure I should tell you. It's quite shocking really, and highly personal. Maria Trushkina told me in confidence. As Polly's, you know, guardian. Sort of.' Alla looked around the empty tables and chewed the inside of her cheek.

'In confidence, eh, direct from the fat pharmacist?' Valya crouched lower to the table and pushed her bulldog head up below Alla's chin, eyes twinkling. 'So now you have to tell me, eh, All-*inka*? What's the scandal?'

'You'll never guess.'

'I won't. So tell me.' Valya slurped her tea.

'It's like this: Maria was rushed off her feet all day: elderly customers, questions, niggles, prescriptions. You know how it is: sometimes nothing is right.'

'Yes, we have that at the bank also.'

'Yes, but at the bank you don't have people wanting to show you their boils, do you?'

Valya considered. 'Not often!'

'So, Maria was dealing with this old girl. She wouldn't give up. "Really, Citizen, I cannot view your boil. You must take the ointment home and apply it. Just a pea-sized blob. No more." "But I can't reach! Believe me, I've tried! What can I do – ask the man next door?"

'You can imagine the scene, yes? It's the end of the day, everyone has had enough, and you get faced with a boil. Anyway, Maria is doing her best, and she sees Polly just standing around

266

at the other counter, gazing at the clock, looking stroppy, picking her nails – the way girls do.'

'Tell me about it! At the bank, we had one who used to read magazines—'

'Don't interrupt! So, a boy comes in, a note in his hands, and starts asking Polly a long question about mustard plasters for his mama. You know what she does?'

'No?'

'She says "No, brat! Just piss off!" – just like that! The boy stammers, but he doesn't give up. No! He sniffs and starts again. Now, Maria can see Polly's lid is about to blow – she's boiling with it. So what does she do? Bares her teeth and snarls at him like a rabid dog! Snarls! He drops the paper and runs away!'

'She needs training!' laughed Valya. 'Woof! Woof!'

'It's not funny! Maria had to have words, obviously, and Polly says it was just a joke and the boy misunderstood. But Maria *knows*: Polly is always rude, distracted, late or off sick. She's already facing a disciplinary. So Maria decides to keep an eye on her for the rest of the evening. She tells Polly she's going to get off early, and asks her to lock up. She's done it before. But this time she doesn't go home: she pretends to, but instead she hides in the back, where she takes her breaks. She's doing surveillance.'

'Ah? Sneaky pharmacist!' Valya bit into her pastry.

'So, it's five to eight, nearly time to shut up shop, and the little bell on the door tinkles. Polly starts shouting "Get out, we're shut!", but stops. Maria pokes her head around the corner. Guess who is there?'

'Well, I don't know who is there. Brezhnev?'

'It's only your Vlad, with a big bunch of roses, walking on his knees to the counter!'

Valya's jaw hit the table. 'Oh no! That stupid boy!'

'So they have some conversation, I don't know, something to do with an argument—'

'Yes, yes. He came home Friday very late and all sullen. I had to make him eat, he didn't want to. Wouldn't tell me what it was about.'

'Ah? Well, there it is. So, they were making up, and Polly starts being . . . well, being friendly—'

'Ha! I know her "friendly"!'

'The last customer slinks away, and Polly tells Vlad to go lock the door.'

'I knew it!'

'And he comes back and says, "We can start again, Polly, if you love me. Do you love me?" And she says, "Why don't you come around here, behind the counter, and I'll show you?" She raises the hatch to let him through.'

'Raises the hatch!' Valya rolled her eyes and took a serviette from the pile on the table. 'A man behind the counter? That's enough there, isn't it, for dismissal? And then?'

'It gets worse. They start . . . you know . . . kissing. Maria can't see, but she can hear. And she hears zippers, you know, zipping, and clothes . . . ripping. And panting: bottles rattling on the shelves; moaning, groaning—'

'I get the picture.' Valya's cheeks glowed as she blotted her forehead.

'And this is in the shop, with the lights on and everything! There are medicines about!'

'Exactly! Think of the medicines! What happened next?'

'The counter starts creaking. Creaking, it is! And there's rattling, and before you know it – bottles smashing! Of course,

Maria has to go right out there and shouts blue murder! Sacks Polly on the spot!'

'Ah-ha! Oh my goodness! Polly! Ha! My poor Vlad!'

'They had their pants round their ankles and their bits on display like tomatoes at the market! Doing it on the counter, with no thought for the stock!'

'Ahh, ha-ha! No! That's terrible! What is the world coming to?' Valya's laugh hissed like a snake. 'I don't know whether to laugh or cry!' She dabbed at her eyes.

'Polly starts screeching like fury, blaming Vlad and cursing him. Maria Trushkina threatens to call the police, it's that bad – she's afraid for her safety! And Vlad, of course, zips out of there like a scalded tom – away into the night.' Alla took a breath. 'So, that's it! Finished! She won't be able to get me those tablets any more, will she?'

'Oh no! That's terrible. Poor you!'

'What a hussy! She's really let me down! I helped her get that position, I did! I pleaded with Maria Trushkina. But I always knew she was a bad one. I only did it as a favour to her poor mother!'

'Well, you know my views.'

'But listen: now Maria can't bear to touch the counter, where it happened . . . she can't put tablets on it, as if it's haunted!

'Woo! Ha ha!' Valya twisted her buttocks into her seat as Alla hid her face in mock disgust.

'And worse: the place is covered in Zelenka.'

'Oh no!' Now Valya's hands flew to her cheeks. 'The antiseptic?'

'That's what was broken: two bottles of Zelenka!'

'I thought there was a funny smell in the bathroom this

morning!' Valya hissed into her tea, eyes streaming. 'You can't get rid of Zelenka.'

'Such a silly girl,' Alla coughed and wiped her eyes with a crispy serviette. 'I tried so hard to support her. She's ruined now, of course. They'll throw her out of university.'

'Mmm.' Valya slurped her tea. 'I've got no sympathy. Deserves it. And what about my Vlad?'

'Well, it wasn't really his fault, was it? She led him on. He's only a man, after all.'

'Yes. That's true. But still: embarrassing for him. Oh, poor Vlad! I hope it won't, you know . . . affect his studies. He's quite sensitive.'

The two women sipped their drinks. A young girl and her boyfriend walked past, hand in hand, laughing.

'She was useful when she got your tablets,' said Valya, 'at least we can say that for her.'

'And she gave me good advice about my you-know-what,' replied Alla. 'But I'll have to break with her now, won't I? After that? And I'll have to tell her mother.' Alla nodded into her hot water. 'Strange girl. She never seemed happy, did she?'

'No, not happy. But that's no excuse.'

'You're right. After all, who is? She's dead to me now. Dead!'

'Come on, time to go. I need to see if Vlad's all right, poor boy! At least you'll have something to talk about over the counter tomorrow, eh?'

Alla drained her hot water and pulled on her gloves. 'Oh yes. Although I don't like to gossip.'

'No. Me neither. Terrible thing, gossip.'

ALBINA GIVES CHASE

'Well, Mama seemed better,' said Albina, after they'd had their allotted ten-minute phone call.

'Yes, she's stopped coughing, did you notice?'

Albina nodded.

Gor put a pan of milk on the hob ready for cocoa while Albina released the kittens from their play-pen. He could hear their downy mews as she came back into the kitchen with them scooped up in the hem of her jumper.

'They're so sweet. I'd keep them all, if I were you. They're more cuddly than Kopek.'

Gor was about to say that things with beaks were rarely cuddly, when the telephone bleeped. He looked in its direction. Albina looked at him, but neither moved.

It rang five more times, six, seven, eight.

'Are you going to answer it?'

Gor said nothing.

'Why don't you ever answer your telephone? I'll answer it for you!' She skipped out to the phone, one hand still holding the jumper-sling of small cats. Gor attended to the drinks, keeping half an ear on Albina. She came back. 'No one there.

271

I asked and asked, but no one spoke. So I wished them luck – in Japanese, of course.' She smiled.

'You're a good girl.'

'The phone was ringing last night too, wasn't it?'

'Yes.'

'And I heard tapping on the window, when I was in bed.'

Gor sighed. 'Yes, I thought you might. I'm sorry about that.'

'Is it the spirits?'

'No.'

'I didn't think so either. Why don't you do something about it?'

'Well, Albina, we were doing something about it, remember? But your mama got injured, and now . . . well . . . What can I do?' He hunched his shoulders and turned to her. 'What can I really do? We must ignore it. I have other things to worry about.' He ran a hand around the back of his neck, dry skin on dry skin, and busied himself once more with the cocoa.

'But,' she said, kicking the door jamb, 'that's like giving in, isn't it? Letting them win.'

'They're not winning, whoever they are. And there's nothing *to* win, Albina. The whole thing is . . . ridiculous.'

A knock rang out on the apartment door. Albina's eyes stared into Gor's tired face. Together, they went to answer.

'We must be careful,' cautioned Gor.

He checked the spy hole.

'No one.'

'But they knocked.'

'Albina—'

'Open it! Don't be scared.'

'Very well.'

He released the bolts and the door creaked. No one was there. However, the dull brown light of the corridor eventually picked out the corpse of a crow, sodden, black and worm-ridden, lying on the door mat. There was a message tucked underneath it. Gor shifted the body with his foot.

'What does it say?' whispered Albina.

Your cats next – or maybe you.
Get out now, while you can!

They stared at each other.

'You see? No point answering the door!' Gor tipped the crow down the rubbish chute and bolted the door.

They sat at the little table to drink their cocoa. Albina swung her legs, rubbing her toes on the old brown lino. Outside, the wind whistled around the building, sharp edged from Siberia.

'I will fry some potatoes and cutlets. I think there's a tin of peas somewhere . . . we won't let them beat us.'

'Don't bother with the peas,' murmured Albina as she ran a determined finger around the bottom of her cup to retrieve a lick of chocolatey mush.

The tapping started after they had eaten, and as Albina gave Gor her assessment of his record collection. He was seated in his armchair by the piano, Albina huddled in a heap on the floor with the kittens and a blanket. She had brought a pair of teasels home from the *dacha* and the kittens were fighting them, the prickles sticking all over the rug.

Softly, insidiously, tap-tap-tapping scuttled through the apartment. Gor sucked in his cheeks, and Albina raised her head.

Gor rubbed his eyes. 'Just ignore it. It will go away, eventually.'

The kittens pounced, again and again, from behind Albina's outstretched leg onto the crumpled teasels, their razor-sharp claws ripping at the spiky seed heads, their backs arching, hair on end, when the teasels shook.

tap-tap-tap

Albina pushed herself up from the floor. She stood silently, listening. A kitten tried to claw its way up her tights. She shook it off with a slight ripping sound.

'I'm going to brush my teeth,' she said.

'Good girl.' Gor picked up a well-thumbed music periodical. He leafed through its familiar pages. Dust particles, illuminated by the standard lamp, circled in the air all around him like tiny, flickering moths.

tap-tap-tap

'Agh!' she shouted from the bathroom, toothbrush clenched between her teeth. She appeared in the hall, wiping her mouth on her sleeve.

'It's in the kitchen!' Her voice boomed with excitement.

'Take no notice!' said Gor from the sitting room. 'I'm not going to let it bother me. I'm taking no notice.' He hummed a little pom-pom-pom as his eyes strayed to the window.

Albina turned on the kitchen light and took a seat at the table. She listened as the clock ticked through the seconds. She counted to 139, and then it came again.

tap-tap-tap

'Gor!' Her voice was a fog-horn along the hall. The kittens scattered.

'I heard.' He turned another wrinkled page.

'I'm scared,' she bellowed.

'You're not! Well, not too much.'

She smiled in the darkness and marched her toothbrush up and down the table in time with the ticking clock, making it into an ally; keeping herself brave.

tap-tap-tap

Now she saw as well as heard. The silhouette of a long, thin finger tapping at the top corner of the glass. The blood drained from her face and collected in her legs, weighing her down. She kept her eyes on the window, blinking away tears of excitement. She couldn't hear the clock any more, only her own heartbeats. She waited.

tap-tap-tap

This time she saw it quite clearly. There could be no doubt. And this time there was a face at the window.

She shot from her seat into the hall.

'Gor!'

The note in her voice silenced his humming. He dropped the periodical to the floor.

'Yes?'

'W-what—' she stammered, tongue knotted. 'What's above us?'

'Above us?'

'Up there!' She pointed to the ceiling.

'Nothing. That's the roof.'

'The roof!'

She dashed for the front door, tugging on the lock levers.

'Albina, wait!'

'We have to get up there! That's where the tapping is coming from.'

She twisted her feet into her moon-boots as Gor looked on doubtfully.

'Whoever's doing it is on the roof!'

'But—'

'With a stick! So simple: they're standing on the roof, tapping your window with a stick!'

Gor stared at her, a confused smile on his face. 'So simple? The devil!' He stamped his feet into his boots with two loud bangs. 'The devil! I'm coming with you. The roof is no place for a child!' His blood was up. He scrabbled for keys and a torch on the sideboard and hurried out to the echoing corridor behind the girl.

In the stairwell, they stopped, face-to-face, listening: there was no sound, no one leaving the building down below, no hint that anyone was up above. They climbed, feet careful on the narrow steps, boot-toes nudging cigarette butts and bottle-tops left by the local youth. A notice on the dark wooden door at the top proclaimed: 'Stop! No Public Access'.

'It should be locked,' said Gor. He stretched out long fingers and pushed: it gave easily, opening wide to reveal three battered concrete steps up, followed by the blue-black Azov sky.

He took Albina's hand. They crouched as they passed through the covered doorway, huddling against its wall while scanning the long, flat roof studded with satellite dishes, sky-lights, rubbish and air vents. He took a moment to get his bearings. If they had come along the corridor from the apartment, and had come back on themselves on the stairs, and if that was the library building he could see over to the left, the windows to his apartment must be . . .

He shuffled round on all fours and screwed up his eyes. Was that a figure he could see, hunched over the parapet, directly above where his windows must be? Or was it some rubbish piled up, or a stray plastic bag flapping in the wind? He nudged Albina, and pointed.

'Is that . . . is that a person, there?'

She clicked her tongue. As Gor was considering the options for action, she lurched to her feet and waved her hands at the figure.

'Hey! You! What are you doing? Trying to scare a poor old man, eh?'

She stomped forward. Gor scrambled to catch up, feet slipping on the cold, wet skin of the roof, the beam of his torch bouncing. The huddled shape straightened, silhouetted against the lights of the town behind, and turned towards them.

'Yeah?' Albina's steps faltered, but she held her hands out in front of her in a karate challenge. The figure turned away, dropped, scuttled. The girl broke into a trot.

'No, Albina!'

The enemy was running towards the far end of the roof. Dodging sky-lights it scurried, turning over satellite dishes and old deck-chairs as it went. Albina leapt the sky-lights, gaining on her prey. Gor realised, with a sick feeling, that he could not catch her up.

He looked down to negotiate a sky-light, and when he looked back, the intruder was leaping onto the parapet: for a moment it stood on the wall, clear against the night sky, looking down at the earth far below.

'Hey!' shouted Albina. 'Stop!'

277

Metal scraped on concrete. The figure dropped out of view, clattering down the twisted skeleton of the fire escape.

Albina launched herself at the parapet, moon-boots squealing as she pushed herself up onto the narrow ledge. Her prey was half-way down already. She reached out.

'No!' roared Gor, 'Danger!'

She clambered onto the fire escape. It shifted in its moorings, the rusty nuts and bolts grating against the skin of the building. The ground swayed beneath her. Fear welded her hands to the cold metal handrails.

'Don't move, Albina! It's dangerous!'

'But he'll get away!'

'You cannot follow! It's not safe!'

The fire escape wobbled and groaned as the intruder hurried down. Albina stared at the gap between her feet, the earth, and the building. Her hair blew into her face and she felt the earth shift.

She shut her eyes. 'I can't move,' she whispered. 'I don't like heights.'

'It's all right. I'm here,' Gor knelt onto the parapet to face her. 'Open your eyes, Albina. I'm right here. See?' She peered at him. 'Just shuffle your feet up one step, that's it. Now lean this way, towards me, and now jump across, come on!'

One by one she unpeeled her fingers from the frame, kicked her feet and launched herself off the ladder.

'Oof!' She collided with Gor's chest, knocking him backwards from the parapet onto the flat roof behind.

'That was scary,' she whispered, and then giggled until she ran out of breath.

'You did very well,' said Gor as he picked himself up,

coughing, and then helped her to her feet. 'You are truly a brave comrade! But don't ever run off like that again! You gave me a dreadful fright.'

'I couldn't help it! I could have caught him!'

'Precious girl!' He tweaked her ear and together they leant out over the parapet towards the swaying trees. Gor played his torch across the fire escape: the mysterious figure was at the bottom, an evil shape, all shadows and scurrying. They could make out no features. The clattering stopped, there was a loud thud and a muffled cry, then uneven footsteps retreated across the courtyard.

'Huh! Did you hear that? I hope he broke his ankle,' said Albina.

'The scoundrel! He deserves it!'

'Whoever it was,' said Albina, 'it was definitely human.'

'Definitely.'

They picked their way across the roof to the spot where the figure had stood.

'What's that?' Gor pointed with a bony finger towards a swaying silver birch. Albina pointed the torch. There, in amongst the branches of the tree, hung a long pole, a plastic face mask, the kind you might buy at the flea market up in Rostov, attached to one end.

'Well, I'll be damned! There's an end to it, Albina,' said Gor with a satisfied snort and a tug on his beard. 'There'll be no more faces at the window, I feel.'

'And no more tapping,' smiled Albina.

FUNNY PILLS

Polly's nights were becoming indistinguishable from her days. She seemed to spend most of her time now walking in the twilight, or sitting shivering on a collection of stinking buses. Just a few days ago she had been a princess, ready to claim her kingdom. The keys to her future had been within her grasp. But now everything was crashing down. She could hardly move with the weight of it. She hadn't been to a lecture for days. She hadn't slept. She'd lost her job and her boyfriend. But worse, much worse, the old men, so frail, so decrepit, were just not giving in.

Her right ankle throbbed. She could hardly think with the pain of it. She felt raw, half dead, crazy with the disappointment of it all. Sparks went off behind her eyes every time she moved her foot. It might be broken. It would have to stay broken: she couldn't lose now.

Monday morning was spent staring at the walls, chewing tablets she'd stolen from the pharmacy, smoking endless bitter Pall Malls and trying to think up a plan. She had to get things straight.

Crinkle-cheeks was not nearly poorly enough. Instead of

turning to a jellified mass of ga-ga, bed-bound and terrified, he was getting better. She almost had to laugh at the idiocy of it. She had thought it would be so simple to scare him into relapse: she knew all his fears, after all. She knew the weight of conscience that pressed on him, the visions that preyed on him in his twilight days. She'd paid him a couple of visits, quietly, at night, to put the fear of God into him. It had worn her nerves, used up all her cunning. But he had proved detestably resilient; hadn't really turned a hair. And soon he'd be going home, to the flat she'd promised to a tenant; the same tenant whose deposit she had already spent. The same tenant who was due to move in within days. She would have to charm him. That's what she would do: embark on a passionate affair, perhaps; persuade him to sign over his apartment, and then hurry him on his way.

And as for Papasyan: the girl was making him brave. He wouldn't have dared go up on the roof on his own, that much was clear. But now there could be no more tapping: she couldn't even make it up the stairs. The old goat had stuck fast, and no kind of haunting had shifted him. She had to admit, her psychological approach had failed.

At about midday, long after her room-mates had scuttled away for lessons and whispers about sex and sanctions, she levered herself off her lumpy mattress, quelled the shaking in her arms and brushed her hair, the full hundred strokes. She would start with the easy, and she would be neat. The black tights went on, eventually, the wool skirt, the boots – although she couldn't fasten the right one. She applied a light powder puff, ignoring the blue-grey bags beneath her eyes and her growling stomach. There was no tea, no *pryaniki*, no bread. As she shivered on the trolleybus into town, the pills in her stomach frothed up in her bile like an evil milkshake, and she almost puked.

Her journey over, she stretched her face as she made her way around the White Flamingo's displays, practising a smile. Her skin felt odd: rubbery, heavy on her bones. Her gaze washed over the hatted heads and sloping shoulders, seeking out grey hair, pallid skin, the dead eyes that probed. Maybe it had been a mistake to be offhand with her at the séance. Maybe she would be difficult. Polly would have to flatter and woo, pet and prime. But the old bag would come across. She wouldn't abandon Polly in her hour of need.

A job at the White Flamingo would be a stopgap. It could work: there would be ailing women, lots of gossip, in-roads to people's families. The possibilities were endless – if dull. She just needed a foot in the door, and to borrow some cash.

The clunky boots dragged and her palms sweated under her gloves. She approached the counter, an approximation of a friendly smile arranged around her teeth, and raised her dark eyes.

'Alla! It's good to see you! How are you?'

Alla's head came up. She gave Polly a grey stare before turning away, hands busily writing price labels for garish Polish socks.

'You wanted to talk to me about your stomach, the other day? I'm sorry I haven't been around much. You don't look well, and that's the truth.'

Polly waited, knowing the woman would be unable to resist. But instead of snapping the bait like a piranha, Alla said nothing, simply sniffing loudly and turning away to carry on writing in her neat, looping script.

'Or was it your feet?' Polly persisted, nails tapping on the counter. She pushed her face towards the older woman and raised her eyebrows with concern. She waited. Her ankle throbbed. 'Or your you-know-what?' The words came out half garbled.

'I don't want your help.' Alla didn't look up, but her thin upper lip curled as she spoke. 'Go away.'

'What do you mean?'

'You're a disgrace!' Her head snapped back, face sharp. 'Please move away from my counter. You stink!'

A dull blush spread across Polly's cheeks. She laughed.

'You've heard, then. But, you know, you shouldn't believe everything you hear. It's just gossip. Let me—'

'How could you do this to me? How could you . . .' Alla sniffed again, her hands curling on the unwritten price tags. 'Sex on the counter. After everything I've done—'

'It was a mistake! Everyone makes mistakes! But I need your help—'

'You'll get no more help from me! I won't be seen talking to you, to be frank. I'm a respectable woman.' Alla moved away, going to the other end of the counter. Polly followed her, stumbling.

'You promised my mother—'

'I've already telegrammed your mother!' They stared at each other. 'So unless you're going to buy some socks, get out.'

Polly leant over the counter, eyes bulging. 'But I helped you! I listened to you, day after day. I got you tablets, really good deals! Now I need a job, and you can get me one. Come on!' Polly's hands closed around Alla's, but the older woman leapt away, dropping socks all over the floor.

283

'You, work here?' She stared at the younger girl, her face a smear of disgust. 'Leaving prints of your backside all over the counters? You're joking!'

'How dare you?'

'Oh, I dare! You're not getting a job through me. I helped you before, I won't do it again!' She paced to the other end of the counter and began writing out a label. Polly watched her intently for a moment.

'You know, it's no wonder your stomach's been bad,' she said with a purr, 'when you think about what those tablets I sold you really were.'

Alla's head shot up, socks forgotten. But Polly had already disappeared into the crowd.

VISITING TIME

Sveta heard Albina before she saw her. A slamming door followed by the cheery clatter of mugs going over on a tea trolley, a flurry of voices, and . . .

'Mama! We've been having such fun!' She bounded through the door and onto the bed, flinging her arms around Sveta's neck, pressing her face into her chest before drawing back with an assessing look. 'You haven't done your hair! And no lipstick?' Albina gazed into her mother's face. 'What have you been doing here?'

'Albina, darling, do not be alarmed. I've been having a good rest, and everyone has been delightful. This is no place for lipstick!' Sveta took the bunch of crumpled roses from Albina's fist. 'These are lovely, *malysh*, and so thoughtful. How I've missed you!'

'We're taking you home today. We've decided. And you'll never guess – we know who is tapping on the windows!'

'You do?'

'A human! We saw him last night – standing on the roof with a long stick! I nearly caught him! It was so exciting!' Albina nodded her head emphatically as Gor approached the end of Sveta's bed, bag in hand, tea stain down the front of his jerkin.

'You've been on the roof?' Sveta's sharp gaze admonished Gor.

'Ha! Er, yes! It was all quite safe, of course. I oversaw the operation.' His words flowed hurriedly over her huff of disapproval. 'The scoundrel got away. We gave him a scare, and possibly an injury. All has been quiet since.' His face was lit briefly by a crooked smile. 'I feel almost . . . But no. How are you, Sveta?' He took in her dishevelled appearance and pale face. 'All mended? We need you home, you know.'

'And I am striving to come home.' She felt so much better just for seeing them. 'I have to say,' she dropped her voice, 'I don't like it here. The people are lovely, but there's an atmosphere. And I've had no access to the mini-cinema, not a whiff of a massage. Just thrice-daily visits from the doctor.'

'Vlad?' Gor's eyebrows lowered to hide his eyes. 'He's being very attentive—'

'Not Vlad.' She pursed her lips. 'The proper doctor, Dr Spatchkin. He's very able . . . and very small. He says I'm fit for home. We just have to speak with Matron. She is very busy, I hear. Can you wait?' Sveta cocked her head.

'Ah, yes. As it happens . . .' Gor hesitated, bag still in hand, 'I have to visit Gagarin wing, briefly.'

'Oh? Ah . . . To collar Vlad?' Sveta said, nodding. 'Quite right.' She frowned. 'He hasn't visited. Perhaps it is guilty conscience? After all, I am only here because of him.'

'Mmm. I'm hoping he has something more severe than a guilty conscience – a broken ankle, perhaps.' Gor smiled grimly. 'We will find out. However,' he surveyed his feet, 'there's something else I need to look into.'

'Gor's cousin, Mama!' said Albina, kicking the floor with her moon-boots and shooting Gor an encouraging look. 'Can you believe it? We think he's here!'

'Your cousin?'

Klara quivered in her bed and muttered into her hands about forty dark loaves.

'On holiday?' A bleak light in Gor's eyes told her the truth. 'Oh no! He's a . . . long-term guest? After what you said about this place!' Her mouth pulled tight. 'I am surprised at you!'

'I didn't know! It may not be him. I'm not sure!'

'Well, that's even worse.'

Gor nodded. 'Akh, maybe. As far as I knew, he was in Rostov with his paints and his books. He has a good flat there, in the suburbs. I never got a call to say he was here! But I need to find out. Albina will fill you in—'

'Prove the yeast!' muttered Klara with urgency. Tatiana Astafievna licked the air, and nodded her head.

'Very well. Go and do your duty, Gor. Albina and I will wait for Matron, and see if we can get those papers signed off. And you can tell me more about your adventures, baby-kins!' Sveta caressed Albina's cheek, and Albina rolled her eyes.

'I won't be long,' Gor stood in the doorway. 'It's good to see you, by the way.' He nodded to the two other ladies and the pinging machine, and headed off back down the corridor.

The reception area was just the same, the girl in the glasses still typing away. She ignored Gor as he hurried past. The corridor to Gagarin wing was just as long, although now there were workmen in it, splashing the walls with green paint that bit at Gor's eyes. He wished them good day as he strode on. A ghost

287

of scorched plastic still hovered in the air as he crossed Communal Sitting Room No. 2, which was also now green apart from three black scars in the ceiling, where the tiles had melted. He slowed, taking in the marks and thinking of Sveta rushing forward, trying to put out the fire with her hat, not realising there was no one in danger but herself: silly, impulsive, brave.

He thought on the fact that it had taken him several days to come and find out if the terrified inmate were indeed his cousin. He could reason this delay quite easily: the Vim & Vigour indulged in a strict regulation of visitors; he had Albina to care for; work had had to be undertaken at the *dacha*; the petrol money was no small matter. Except it wasn't just these few days, truth be told: there were years before that, dozens of them, stretching way into his past as long as he could remember, when he had actively avoided his cousin. These days were the latest in a long line of days, broken only by the annual visit on Tolya's birthday for the eating of cake and a compote salute.

And there was the worst of it. He had been so taken up with himself, he had only realised during that ridiculous séance, at the moment when Madame had dug a little deeper into his family vault, that he had forgotten Tolya's birthday. How had he allowed himself to sink so far? It was the one day when he had to perform a family duty: to make a visit and smile and talk; to show interest. And he had forgotten it.

He cursed himself for a fool and strode towards the door Albina had crept through. All was still. He knocked, waited, coughed, knocked again, and pushed. It opened with a groan. Inside lay darkness, the blinds down.

'Tolya?' he began quietly. 'I think I owe you an apology—'

His eyes adjusted to the gloom, and the words stopped abruptly.

Before him leered the sagging, stained mattress of a stripped bed. He looked around, feeling foolish, and stepped across the room to pull up the blind. Only the dust moved, circling in the air softly, lazily, falling gently on his shoe, an empty beaker, the visitor's chair, the floor. There were no personal effects.

He returned to the corridor and opened the next door along: maybe he was mistaken. Here was a man with ginger hair and a beard of soft grey, sleeping with his head lolling to one side. Gor retreated, tried the next door, and the next. He tried all the doors along the corridor in turn, refusing to give in to the fear that had bloomed when he saw the empty bed. By the end of the corridor, soft dread was reaching fingers up his throat, stroking the backs of his eyeballs. He blinked away tears. In the last room he found two patients, both awake and chatting, and an orderly who was busy at the blinds.

He intended to wish them good day, to introduce himself, but instead blurted, 'Where is Tolya?'

The orderly turned very slightly in his direction and frowned, feather duster stilled in her hand. 'Tolya?'

'Anatoly Borisovich: he was in the room a few doors up – number 6, I thought? A short man, quite round, and old. Artistic. Nervous. A cake lover. Quiet soul.'

'Ah, yes,' said the orderly, turning around more fully, her eyes curious under her blue-black beehive. 'Anatoly Borisovich. Are you a friend of his?'

'No. That is to say, I'm . . . his cousin,' said Gor, adding out of habit, 'we aren't close.'

'In that case,' said the orderly, 'you'd better speak to Matron. Go to the office at the end of the corridor and tell them who you are: they will find her for you.'

Gor made to leave, but turned at the door, his face taut.

'Has he . . . Has he gone?' he asked softly, not wanting to hear the answer.

The orderly smiled sadly, over her shoulder.

'Yes, he's gone. On Saturday night: quietly and suddenly. No suspicious circumstances. But go and speak to Matron.'

A small sound escaped Gor's throat.

The world turned grainy. The sharpness of the strip-lights jabbed at his eyes. He stumbled away through the door, back through the sitting room, back along the newly painted corridor, out into the echoing reception area, through the clanging double doors and down the rotten steps of the Vim & Vigour to the safety of his little brown car. His hands shook and he dropped the keys. He could barely manoeuvre himself behind the wheel as he tried to squeeze down, legs jarring and knees refusing to bend. Eventually his feet slid forward. He folded his elbows and leant on the steering wheel, forehead on his hands.

He did not cry. He wished he could: to cry and be done with it, to feel and express something. But he sat, brimming with regret, sorrow, relief and confusion: so many emotions boiling in his head that he felt physically sick.

In the darkness behind his eyelids, he saw his family, old and young, the people he loved and had loved for a long time. He could count them on the fingers of one hand. They were fading, fading and receding, sinking down the tunnel of time. How was it every family member seemed to slip away like this, unannounced, on a whim?

Tolya, the most difficult, needy and troublesome spirit. Tolya, whose resilience had kept him living when all was lost. After battling with life for sixty-odd years, now it seemed this Tolya had simply slipped away in the night, without so much as a tip of his hat or a wink from those green eyes.

Gor remembered: boys' eyes cold and hard as split pebbles, chests heavy, lungs burning with the effort of sucking in icy air, heartbeats aching in their throats as they watched and waited at the window, silent in the darkness of the afternoon. Lost days when the howling wind rushed spirits out of the forest like bats from a cave, straight into the blood-red minds of the boys. The boys had been cruel. A shudder threaded his spine.

The teachers had done their best to beat sense into them. It hadn't worked for Tolya. His imagination would not be crushed. He had been a kite in Gor's hand, thoughts blown on the wind. Before the fire, he'd made sense of the world for Tolya. He'd looked after his cousin, guided him. And afterwards, somehow, although they'd lived together, he'd let him go. He'd spent sixty years letting him go.

His hands clutched the steering wheel, knuckles pale as china, as he tried not to think. Fat raindrops thudded on the windscreen, mingling with his heartbeats. Mouth dust-dry, he listened to the patter and wondered when it would stop. It became too much: he broke his hold on the steering wheel and jerked his hand towards the radio dial, pressing the switches in quick, trembling desperation. Sound filled his ears and familiar notes flooded his mind. The wind chased across the car park, rocking the little car. Still he sat.

He knew he should speak to Matron and learn the dull details of his cousin's last moments. He should see the notes

291

of how he breathed, how he struggled, how the blood in his veins surged, faded, and cooled. But he had no heart for it. He opened the car door and placed his feet on the shingle. Perhaps he should return to Sveta and Albina, the only people who might care, and explain what had happened, his treachery and his loss? He stood staring into the rain as it bounced off the hedges and the gravel, and did nothing.

Raindrops trickled down his forehead and neck, soaking his collar. As time stood still, through the hiss of the rain and the buffeting of the wind, he eventually became aware of uneven steps, crunching closer. Someone was trudging up the drive. He ran his hands through his wiry, wet hair and reached for his handkerchief.

It was a woman. She was hunched over, wire thin, her black coat billowing in the wind and a scarf pulled close around her face. As she got nearer, Gor saw her clothes were spattered with mud all the way up to her knees. She did not look up, but scurried on, talking to herself in a low monotone, boots clunking. She went to mount the entrance steps and Gor looked into her pale face.

'Polly?'

She jumped sideways as her face twisted to him, fingers clinging to the scarf flapping at her neck. Dark eyes squinted at Gor from a rain-washed face.

'Papasyan?'

Even her lips were white, barely moving as she spoke. They stared at each other for a moment.

'Is everything all right? You're soaked through!' Gor's arms came up as if to touch her, and she backed away, stumbling up the first step.

She stared, her broad, beautiful face otherworldly, almost like a painting. But the eyes were empty, and the lips gnawed on each other. She glanced down at her sodden clothes and nodded.

'The bus broke down. And I must visit . . . I must visit—'

The wind whipped at her words and Gor leant forward to hear. He smelled stale vodka on her breath and something else, something sharply medicinal.

'You don't look at all well. Let me—'

'Time is running out. I have to sort out his affairs.' He felt vaguely queasy as her pupils dug into his for a second and then swam away.

'I see.' He nodded. 'A relative? Can I help at all? Maybe a lift back to town when you've finished?'

'No,' she said on a sigh, a sad smile splitting her face. 'No, no. I'll be some time. But it has to be done.' Again her eyes dug into his.

'If you're sure? Good luck to you, Polly. You're doing the right thing, you know.' She started up the steps. 'I have just lost my cousin!' he called after her in spite of himself. 'Care for your loved ones while you can!'

She stopped and turned. 'Your cousin?' Her voice was a whisper.

'Yes. He . . . he died on Saturday night.'

'No!'

He stared at his boots, touched and shamed by her concern.

'I'm afraid so. I left it too late to, to put things right with him. So you run along – go to your relative! Good girl!' He looked up and smiled, eyes filming with tears.

She stared into his eyes, her face wild and bleak.

'No,' she mouthed.

He went to touch her arm but she turned away, the wind whipping long strands of brown-black hair around her face as she hobbled up the steps towards the glowering glass doors.

This was how good people cared. This girl had walked half-way from town to make a visit, while he had waited, nurturing his excuses of Albina and the petrol cost. He leant on the car, legs refusing to move. He could no more look Sveta in the eye than he could coax his cousin back from the dead. The grey sky beat against his head as the world shifted with the wind. He stared out to the flatness of the estuary, where sky and earth and sea met in one muddy brown line.

A WINDSWEPT PLACE

Sveta's head snapped up. 'What time is it, baby-kins?'

'I don't know, Mama.' Albina was tracing patterns in the dust of the windowsill with her finger and spit.

Sveta put down her book and eased herself upright.

'Gor has been gone a long time.'

'Yes.'

'It will be dark soon.'

'Yes.'

'Fire the ovens,' cried Klara from beneath her crackling sheet. Tatiana Astafievna sniffed the air loudly, and licked her thin, grey lips. Sveta nodded.

'Something is wrong.'

'What do you mean?' The heat in the room was making Albina drowsy. Not a single thought rotated in her head.

'I don't know. I have . . . a sense. Why would he be gone so long? Gagarin wing is only fifty metres that way. He could have orbited the moon by now.'

Klara nodded busily to herself, and the machine let out a prolonged ping. Sveta looked to the window and the green-grey light beyond.

'Maybe he got lost,' suggested Albina, rousing herself.

'You're not being helpful, *malysh*. Pass me the gown.'

Sveta swivelled on the bed and eased her feet to the floor in a decisive movement.

'What are you doing, Mama?'

She threaded her bandaged hands through the sleeves of her gown. 'Foreboding! That's what it is! This building is full of it! I'm going to look for Gor.'

'But what if Matron sees you?'

'I don't care if Matron sees me! I've been waiting for Matron all day.' She stood so that Albina could knot the belt at her waist. 'I'm beginning to think she's a myth. Slippers, please.'

Albina shrugged and stretched under the bed for the slippers.

They marched on soft feet down the corridor, Albina opening the doors and Sveta hopping through. Glancing over their shoulders, they skipped past the nurses' station and eased down the stairs. It was easy: no one paid attention. They heard the echo of the mini-cinema, and headed for the entrance hall and its confluence of corridors.

The administrator was arguing with a visitor, hunched and dripping over the counter.

'I cannot give out confidential information!' she roared. 'How much clearer do I have to be?'

There was no option to scuttle unnoticed across the hall, so they set out at a march, backs straight and heads high. They nearly made it.

'One moment! Citizen . . . Woman! Patient! Where are you going? You can't go through there!' The administrator was outraged.

Sveta did not stop. 'I have lost my friend. He came this way.

I have to find him.' They made directly for the door to Gagarin wing.

'I know you! You were here on Friday! You're the citizen who burnt her hands!'

'Uh-huh!' nodded Sveta with a smile, waving her hands and still making for the door.

'You're looking for that man, aren't you?'

They slowed.

'The tall, dark, miserable one?'

They stopped.

'You won't find him.' The administrator pushed her glasses back up her nose triumphantly. 'He ran out of the door half an hour ago.'

Albina and Sveta swapped glances.

'He hasn't gone. He wouldn't do that,' whispered Sveta.

She took Albina's arm and they swerved for the entrance door.

'Hey! You can't go outside! Matron will—'

It slammed behind them.

The little car stood forlorn in the car park, door open and keys in the ignition. There was no sign of Gor.

'Something terrible has happened! Look, the seat covers are all wet. He wouldn't leave it like that. There's evil at work here!'

They called his name, voices carried on the breeze to the edges of the estuary. The only reply came from the wind whistling around the corner of the building, blowing salt and drizzle on them from the sea.

'Has he been kidnapped, Mama?'

'Kidnapped? Well . . . Who knows in this crazy world! We

must search for him. You go that way, *malysh*, quick, scout around, look for clues, but keep away from the water. I'll go around the other side. If you need me – scream.'

Albina nodded earnestly.

Sveta lurched towards the building, the open flats and sea beyond, while Albina headed along the drive towards the road, following the edge of the creek. At the top of the entrance steps a dark, dripping figure watched them.

Sveta's progress was slow, hampered by treacherous slippers that were quickly water-logged. She rounded the building and found herself in the back yard. Here were the kitchens, warm scents of cutlets and buckwheat streaming through the door to lie heavy on the damp air. Voices came, the sounds of people carrying on their afternoon patter. A dog sat in the yard, well-fed and shaggy, ignoring two bright-eyed cats churning in a bin beside it. It yawned as Sveta stepped over uneven paving stones and through a broken wooden gate, out to the grass and mud of the world beyond.

She spotted a tall figure in the distance, clambering over tussocks of sea grass, wobbling towards the lone tree that stood stark against the sky.

'Gor! Gor Papasyan! Come back!'

He didn't hear. She bumped and stumbled across mud streams, old wooden buckets, rotten car parts, ancient broken nets, bones bleached white by the sun. 'Gor! Wait!' she shouted into the wind.

The figure stopped, but did not turn.

Sveta panted. Her slippers had disappeared into the mud, and the bottom of her gown slapped wetly against her calves.

Her bandaged hands were smeared brown and gritty, and her hair fell into her eyes. She squinted up at the figure by the tree. It was looking out at the water, watching as the light began to fade. The wind whistled in her ears.

'What are you doing?' she bellowed.

He turned, his gaunt face twisting.

'I . . . I needed some air.'

'Air? Huh!' She gathered up the flapping hem of her nightie to clamber over the last mud-dune and reach Gor's side. 'Well, there's plenty of air.'

He stumbled backwards as she stood to face him.

'What's wrong? You didn't come back!'

'I . . . oh Sveta, I'm sorry, look at you! Running out here . . . worried about me. And I . . . He . . . Oh it's too much!'

'It's just mud! I'll get over it. But you—' She looked into his face.

'Sveta, don't! I'm not worth your concern! I am a failure, not a human being!' He threw himself to the ground, shrinking before her eyes, hands grasping tufts of grey grass as he knelt in the mud and growled out the words.

'Is it your cousin?'

He shook his head. 'I've . . . I've gone wrong. It's all wrong. So many . . . I don't know . . . what to do.'

'Is it . . . is it to do with the . . . the shameful thing, you once mentioned? The thing about you . . . that you said I don't know. Tell me?'

'Ha! Just one shameful thing? Just one, you think?' He looked up, baring his teeth in a grimace fuelled by laughter and tears, and spat into the mud. 'Dear Sveta, curl your toes! This will be the end of our friendship. I don't even know where to start.'

'Start with whatever comes out first.' She crouched down next to him and took his hand. 'We'll make sense of it.'

'My cousin has . . . gone.'

'Gone?'

'He is dead.'

'Ah!' Sveta nodded slowly. 'I'm so sorry, Gor.'

'Not as sorry as I! I didn't want to come, you see; I troubled over the petrol – no, really! Any excuse to avoid . . . finding out. And finally I came, to spout platitudes and say sorry, and ask if he needed cake. And his room was empty! He's gone.' The words came out clipped, staccato. 'Without me. I wasn't there with him! After all that time . . .'

'You weren't to know.' She reached out to him and squeezed his fingers, but he pulled away, eyes trailing to the pine tree swaying with the moaning wind.

'I *should* have known! Mama told me to look after him. She told me to be kind. But I failed. I even forgot his birthday! I *never* forget his birthday! It is the one thing . . . I failed him. Not once but many times. No surprise to you, surely?'

'Oh no, Gor. You're being hard on yourself. You did your best—'

'No Sveta, I did the bare minimum!' He pushed away her hands as his eyes blazed. 'Forget kind words. I did what I could get away with. I did not love him as I should have.'

He pressed his hands to his mouth and closed his eyes.

'But that's human nature! Heaven knows, you can't choose your family! But . . . we do our duty. I'm sure you did too.'

'Ah, family duty? I assure you I have *not* done my duty. I have failed, Sveta! In everything! Do you understand? In

300

e-v-e-r-y-t-h-i-n-g. The people I should have loved and protected . . . My Marina!'

'Marina?'

'My wife. Beautiful, sweet little Marina. She chose me, you know. I was too shy, when I was young, to ever . . . But she picked me out, and she loved me, she really loved me . . . But what happened? After a while, I didn't notice. I was busy, always busy with the stupid things in life; loans and savings accounts! And when she left, for better love, I sneered – who needs love, eh? And who deserves it? Not me! I buttoned up my skin, and pretended she had never been. Just like Olga.'

'And Olga is—'

'God's gift to me! My child, my daughter!' He raised his hands heavenward, fingers curled.

'Ah. Of course, I remember now.' Sveta's face wrinkled. 'But how is she involved?'

'She's not! She's not involved in anything. She's not in my life! I didn't realise . . . I tried not to think! I put her to the back of my mind, when they went. But Albina asked me . . . at the *dacha*, she said, "Did she die?" And I thought – no, of course she didn't die! How could you think that? She just went away.'

'Yes?' Sveta was confused.

'So why did I act like she was dead?' Gor shouted. 'It didn't have to be forever, did it? Why didn't I write to her, phone her: go and see her in the holidays?'

Sveta's mouth opened to speak, but he carried on.

'I'll tell you why: because I was a coward! Because it would have hurt too much: because I would have felt everything, and suffered every time we said goodbye. I would have had to

301

pretend that I was strong! And I couldn't do it! So I put her out of my mind, and turned my back. It was all too painful. Just like Tolya, just like Baba, just like families . . .'

Sveta's bottom lip protruded as she scanned the sky. 'That's so sad, Gor. So very sad. But it doesn't have to be like that. We can make happiness as well as misery. You made a mistake, but it's not too late—'

'Save your gentleness, Sveta. It is very much too late. There is nothing left in my life. Nothing to share, with anyone. I am a shell, a thief with nothing to offer. I lie to myself and I—'

The earth shivered. Albina was bounding towards them, moon-boots snagging in the grass, floundering in the mud.

'It's all right, *malysh*! I've found him!' Sveta waved. She turned to Gor. 'What do you mean – a thief?'

Albina flung herself to the ground next to them, panting and red-faced, before Gor could answer.

'Why are you sitting in a field?' Her voice held an edge of scorn. 'We were worried about you, you know!'

'Hush, *milaya*. Gor is feeling bad.'

'Aaah?' She turned to look into his face, her hair wiggling like worms in the wet air.

'Not feeling bad. I am bad! Oh yes. The more I think about it, the more squalid I become: mean – ridiculous—'

'What?' Albina was incredulous.

'Listen,' he spoke with slow deliberation, 'these people: my cousin, my wife, my daughter . . . they were my treasures, my responsibility, all these three. And I failed them. I forgot them. I conjured them away, out of my life. Even you, my dear friends: you who cared for me. How did I repay you? I let you run into a burning building, Sveta, and I let you run about on

302

a roof, Albina. I put you in harm's way, while you strove to protect me.' His yellow teeth shone in a sickly grin. 'My shame is complete, and absolute. I am a failure as a human. What is a little theft against that?'

'Theft?' Albina pushed herself up to crouch next to Gor, her eyes wide, considering. The smell of mud and salt and weeds blew through her hair.

'Money. It took over my mind: I let it. After all, it was money, not love, so I fretted over it. Just money.'

'You stole some money?' Albina's smile was gleeful.

'Oh yes, I who lectured you on the importance of being a good student and getting good grades. I am a common thief.'

'Fantastic!'

'Gor, you are never common. But tell us – a thief, really?'

'Did you rob a bank?'

Gor hesitated. 'Do you really need the detail?'

'An orphanage?' she snorted.

He sighed. 'No. Not an orphanage. I abused the trust of those who respected me . . . I—' He raised his sorrowful eyes to gaze at Sveta and shrugged with a defeated air. 'I took the Magic Circle money. I could almost laugh now. But . . . I was desperate.'

'Ah?' Sveta's eyebrows corrugated her forehead. 'Magic Circle?'

'I am the treasurer. I meant to borrow it, you see, to invest. I was desperate. I lost my life savings – to inflation. There, in the bank.'

'Inflation?' Sveta looked doubtful.

'They keep adding noughts to the rouble bills. Doesn't it make you wonder what happens to the roubles in old savings accounts? I can tell you; wipe-out. I had nothing. I sold things

303

off to make ends meet, but I struggled. Then it came to me . . . the Magic Circle interest account: I could invest it, quadruple the money, replenish my savings, and replace the principal. If I played the market right . . .'

'Not PPP Invest?' whispered Sveta. 'Tell me you didn't—'

'The very same. It's almost funny, isn't it? The PPP pyramid.'

'Oh Gor!' Sveta pressed her cheeks, shaking her head. 'You silly!'

Albina frowned and surveyed the horizon with a serious eye. 'An unwise investment. How much did you lose?'

'About . . . about a million roubles.'

She brightened. 'Oh, that's not so bad then.'

'It seemed like everything – like the end of everything. I was so wrapped up in it . . . so wrapped up in money! The day I stole it . . . the day I went to the bank . . . was my cousin's birthday. That's why I forgot it! Don't you see? I was wrapped up in money, and I forgot about him – for weeks! If I'd only remembered, I'd have known he was sick. I could have helped! My greed killed him, as surely as if I'd stuck a dagger in his belly!'

'No, no really, this is ridiculous. First a thief and now a murderer! Gor, this is not you!'

'He's dead?' Albina's face paled. She leant forward, putting her arm around Gor's shoulder as he huddled on the patch of sandy mud. 'I'm so sorry.'

Sveta blotted her eyes on the back of her bandages and sniffed hard. 'No matter what has happened, not matter what you say you are, Gor, I believe you are good, and we are here to help you.' She put her arm around the other shoulder. 'We are your friends. We will sort all this out. We will not abandon you.'

Gor sat head down, nodding gently to himself, dry-eyed, his back bent with the weight of his thoughts, as the drizzle sheened their skin. High above, a gull hovered on the air.

'Ahoy!'

The cry came from the direction of the Vim. Sveta raised her head. A figure was stumbling towards them, hopping over pot-holes and long grasses. Someone in a house coat, with lank hair and glasses. She looked cross.

'What are you doing out here? Elderly citizen: really, sitting on the wet ground? Citizen patient – you should know better! Child, you too! Are you all mad? Matron has seen you from the tower – and she is very distressed. You must come in at once! At once, she said!' The administrator pointed towards the dull grey tower on the end of the building. They saw a figure at the window move away into the shadows.

'Oh dear,' said Sveta ruefully, 'we'd better go. Come, Gor.'

They rose as one, and as one, each arm in arm, they made the journey back to the hulk of the building. Mud oozed through Sveta's toes and she shivered. The shaggy dog watched them as they straggled back through the yard, thumping its tail in greeting.

'So, Sveta,' said Gor softly as they reached the bottom of the entrance steps, 'go and make yourself ready. I should speak to Matron about my cousin, but I don't have the strength. At this moment, I can only think of going home. We will wait for you here.' He could barely lift his feet, one after the other, up the crumbling entrance steps.

'Well, Gor, I'm afraid . . . Matron hasn't yet signed me out,' Sveta said in a small voice. She glanced up at the doorway where an orderly with a blanket was pushing through the glass, eyes fixed on her. 'And I don't think she will now.' She turned to Gor. 'Tomorrow is another day.'

'Akh, Sveta . . . if you think it is for the best, to stay another night? I will come back tomorrow lunchtime.' He looked deeply into her eyes.

'Thank you, Gor.' She pressed her bandaged hands onto his. 'Today is a turning point. Just a turning point on your journey. When I am home tomorrow, we will talk it through. We will set you right. And all will be well. But for tonight – rest and sleep. Quiet sleep.'

'You are so very brave. Thank you, Sveta. Go in now. We can't have you . . .' He did not finish his sentence; the orderly had enveloped Sveta in the blanket.

A DISAPPEARING GIRL

'Kalinka, Kalinka, Kalinka, moya, rum-pum, pum-pum . . .'
Albina whisper-sang as she waggled the paws of the smallest
white kitten who lay supine, lost in rapture, gazing into her
eyes as if they were stars in its heaven. They sat on the old
red-brown rug in the middle of Gor's living room, the other
kittens scattered under the piano, lovingly clawing up the sheet
music. This kitten was special. Albina had christened him
Ponchik, or Doughnut, because he was so sweet. Her fingers
lingered in the silkiness under Ponchik's chin, and she tickled,
laughing as he stretched out his neck, giving himself up to her
completely.

She glanced at the clock: still only one p.m. Gor had left
her in charge of the kittens: he said the cats could look after
themselves. All had been calm, but Gor was not himself. When
they had returned late the previous afternoon, he had gone
straight to his room, and had stayed there for two hours. She
had taken him tea, played with the kittens, and waited. There
was no tapping. There were no phone calls. An absolute hush
had descended on the flat.

Eventually he'd emerged, worn slippers shuffling on the lino, and cooked up a cutlet for her. He did not eat. They had sat side-by-side on the old yellow sofa, the radio humming in the background, and spent the evening sorting through old photos Gor had tugged from the back of the sideboard. Here was Tolya as a youth, fresh out of military academy, a bemused look on his face as he stood skinny and pale, stiffly holding his diploma. Here was a wedding couple, jolly in a restaurant: Gor dark as ever, but with a light dancing in his eyes, his bride looking both proud and self-conscious. Here was Olga as a toddler, all chubby arms and freckles, playing with a ball at the beach. Here was Olga, a serious, dark-eyed girl, tall and slim with plaits down to her waist, on the first day of term. Here were mother and daughter either side of a wiry, sharp-toothed monkey on a chain. The photos ran out around 1975. Albina told Gor he should put them in a photo album. He had blown his nose and said perhaps, perhaps.

His plan this morning had been the grocer's and the dairy, and then to motor over and collect Mama, no matter what Matron said.

He said he wouldn't be long, but he had been ages, and time was dragging, despite the kittens and the radio. Albina was learning that she didn't like being on her own, although she didn't like company either. Gor had suggested she go for a healthy walk, but she had laughed. She didn't like walking. She didn't really like being outside: people looked at her, and it made her feel stupid.

Her eyes wandered to the glossy, muscular body of the piano. It called to her, and the day was too silent. She pushed herself up from the floor with Ponchik still on her shoulder, his tiny claws curled into the knit of her jumper. Raising the lid, she looked down at the perfect pattern of black and white keys. When Gor had played it, the melody had been immense, cascades of notes spilling out of its body like water from a fountain. He said you had to be careful with grand pianos, especially baby-grand pianos. She reached out and touched the key that was middle C, pressing gently. No sound came. She pressed harder and jumped back as a note rang out, clear and cool. She played her fingers across the keys and listened to the tinkle, the tones dropping and pinging like rain on a pond. She laughed, played louder, pressing keys with her fists, her elbows, her forehead, rolling her hands up and down, to and fro, creating thunder and rainstorms, dew and snowflakes. Ponchik silently mewed for his mother, who slinked nonchalantly past on her way to the kitchen.

Hammering at the front door eventually silenced her playing. She leapt back guiltily from the piano. Was she in trouble for the noise? Should she answer? She returned the kitten to his siblings and trod quietly into the hall. She knew how to handle angry neighbours. She would be firm, and blame the little cats. She would not swear.

'Hello,' she said to the door without opening it, her voice bouncing, sounding silly, like a child. She stood on her toes to look through the spy hole, losing her balance and squashing her nose. She couldn't make anything out. More blows rang out. She struggled with the lock, tangling her hair into it as her fingers slipped. Finally, she pulled it open.

Gor and Sveta arrived home half an hour later after a largely silent car journey. Sveta had tried to begin some jolly chat, but the old man was not ready for it. She was looking forward to getting back. When they arrived, the kittens were asleep in a bundle of old shoes, Dasha and Pericles happy and relaxed lying on the sofa. All was well. But Albina was not there.

Gor stood perplexed in the hall as Sveta scooted from room to room calling her daughter's name with increasing volume. She returned to him, open-mouthed. Gor's bag of *pryaniki* slipped to the floor. They checked the cupboards, behind the doors, under the beds; they even opened windows to look out and call. Perhaps she was on the balcony? Only a deep stillness greeted them there. There was no girl, and no note. After whirling through the flat with increasing fervour, room-to-room-to-room, they stood together in the kitchen, panting, and noticed two cups of tea with a pink flowery pattern standing untouched on the side, next to a half-empty box of sugar cubes.

Sveta swooped on the cups, pressing the back of her hand to one. 'Warm! Not even sipped! What does this mean?'

Gor shook his head dully. 'Someone was here?'

'Two people!' Sveta nodded. 'Albina doesn't like tea!'

'She does if she's allowed sugar.' He smiled sombrely, and stepped forward to taste from each cup. 'That second one,' he coughed, 'Albina's: sweet enough for bees. Perhaps you should go and check next door – Galina Petrovna on the left, Baba Krychkova on the right. Maybe she's gone to them? Or left a message? I will investigate here: there will be a note – we must have missed it.'

Gor began another search of the apartment, eyes scavenging the living room, picking apart the ordinary, looking for something wrong. The girl's things were all still in his former dining room: a tangle of clothes, books and homework, and a dog-eared teddy. Her purse lay abandoned amongst the rubble.

He stood in the hall and scratched his head. Two cups of tea in the kitchen, and not a sip drunk. He returned to stand over them, examining the rims and the ring of brown left on the side by a spillage. He picked up the kitchen cloth to wipe away the mark, and caught a whiff, the shadow of a smell. He sniffed his hands, and then the cloth: yes, it was definitely there, a distinctive medicinal tang pricking his olfactory nerves. He frowned: he'd smelled that smell recently, somewhere else. Was it at the Vim? The nurses? Or maybe Madame Zoya?

He heard steps in the hall and Sveta appeared in the doorway, her worried eyes glassy.

'They have no news. Baba Krychkova reported hearing the piano being played very loudly, and a banging, which she assumed was a neighbour complaining. Galina Petrovna could offer no help at all – she's just got in from a dance class. I've looked out at the courtyard too: no sign.'

Gor shook his head. 'I've found nothing. Only this – a funny smell. Can you identify it?' He raised the cloth with an outstretched hand. She took a doubtful sniff, frowned, and pressed it closer to her nose.

'That's Zelenka. What of it?'

'Of course! That's it!' He clicked his fingers, and shook his head. 'I don't have it in the house.' Their eyes met. 'And I've smelled that smell just recently. I can't put my finger on it—'

'Well, think Gor!' Sveta's eyes bulged. 'It might be important!'

'I'm trying!' He screwed up his face in concentration. 'It was a vague smell . . . akh, maybe if I sit. My mind is so fuddled, I hardly know what day it is.'

He sat heavily on a stool, the cloth still clutched in his hands, sad eyes dim. 'Where can she be? She promised . . . promised to be good. She wouldn't go anywhere, when she knew you were coming home.'

'She would not. She's a good girl.'

'Yes. She is a good girl.'

'Someone was here . . .'

'Yes.'

'A friend?'

'Sveta, you know me better than that.' He frowned.

'I don't like it.'

'Me neither.'

'What shall we do?'

'I don't know.'

The telephone bleeped from the hall. He opened an eye and observed it from where he sat.

'Answer it, man!'

'But what if—'

'You're not scared, are you?' Sveta's eyes glowed as still he sat.

'No. I'm not scared. I will answer.' He pushed himself up from the stool and hastened for the receiver.

'Papasyan!' he barked.

'You're back! I'm so glad!'

'Albina! Thank God!'

His legs buckled beneath him and he sat down with a thump. Albina's voice was loud, lisping, full of life, and only a little wobbly. He waved his arm wildly to Sveta, beckoning her to the phone. Their heads bent together as they listened. 'Where are you, child?'

'I'm in a flat, it's smelly, and I think it's in Rostov. That's what she said, anyway. And I've got some Danish yoghurt! Raspberry flavour—'

'Wait—'

'Mama's here, *malysh*!' Sveta's voice broke over Gor.

'Oh Mama! I'm glad to hear you!'

'Who is this "she", baby-kins? Who are you with?'

'Oh, it's such good news! Gor, are you listening? You'll never guess: it's Olga! Yes, your long-lost Olga!'

'Olga?' Gor cried. 'My Olga? But that's not possible! I don't understand!'

'She came to the flat while you were out! I guessed it was her — I just knew! She is tall and dark, just like you! I made her a cup of tea and scalded my hand and everything, but then she said we had to leave for a family reunion. We're here now, and you're not. Why aren't you here?'

'Where is here, *malysh*?' Sveta's face was white, but at least she could form words. Gor sat with the kitchen cloth still pressed to his lips, eyes haunted.

'I told you: Rostov. She told me to phone you. I miss you. Why aren't you here?'

'Let me speak to this Olga!' said Sveta heartily. 'What does she think she's playing at—'

'Oh, no, Mama, she doesn't want to speak to you. She only wants to speak to Gor—'

There was a clunk as the receiver was grabbed, and they heard Albina being shooed away.

'Papasyan?' came a rasping, whispered voice at the other end.

'It is I. To whom am I speaking?'

'Don't ask. Just listen. I have the girl. If you want her back, give me your gold.'

313

'My what?'

'Gold, miser! Your gold!'

'Akh, what lunacy is this? I have no gold! You are no Olga!'

'You lie! I don't know where you've hidden it, but I know you have it! I need it! Time is running out, Papasyan!'

As Gor listened, he closed his eyes and buried his nose in the kitchen cloth still held in his hand. A face materialised in his mind's eye, lashed with rain, a face with dark eyes, and a twist of ruthlessness. And he smelled a smell, medicinal and sharp, carried by the wind.

'Oh no! It can't be! Why would she . . . ?' He dropped the cloth as his hand flew to his mouth. 'I thought she was . . . a good girl.'

'Gor?' Sveta's cheeks wobbled. He put his hand over the receiver.

'I . . . you won't believe this . . . The smell, yesterday – the Zelenka – it was Polly!'

'What? Vlad's girl?'

'Papasyan!' the voice in the telephone crackled. 'Are you listening?'

Sveta's blue eyes shivered with recognition. 'It could be!'

Gor did not hold back. 'Is that you, Polly?'

There was a roar of sound, animal and wild.

'It is, isn't it? I am . . . I am astounded! Why have you taken Albina? What is the meaning of this?'

The line crackled with static, but no words.

'Polly?' Sveta broke in. 'How could you? You've taken Albina . . . for what? Gor has nothing, you wicked, wicked child!'

'Shut up!' shrieked the voice.

'What's going on?' Gor growled. 'What are you playing at?

Is someone . . . is someone controlling you? Is that it? Is it Vlad?'

'That idiot?' The voice cracked with indignation. 'I did this all myself! And it's very simple – give me your gold, and you get the girl!'

'But I have no gold!' rattled Gor into the mouthpiece. 'I'm no better off than you!'

'Oh, of *course* not! That's why the whole town knows about you! You moved it to spite me, didn't you? You hate me, just like the rest! But I won't be beaten! You better go and dig it up. Bag it up: everything you've got!' Her voice dropped to a snarl. 'If you won't pay for her, I won't wait: I'll find someone who will.'

'Oh!' cried Sveta and bit on her knuckle.

'Get the gold. I'll phone at six with instructions. And don't even think about the police: I'll know – I have connections!'

There was a click and a hum as the line went dead. Sveta and Gor stared at each other.

'The girl is . . . quite mad!' said Sveta.

'I thought . . . I thought she was a good girl.' He hunched forward and pulled on his beard. 'I saw her yesterday, at the Vim . . .'

'A good girl?' Sveta raised an eyebrow. 'We know nothing about her, Gor.'

'She was visiting a relative.'

'What rot! Visiting Vlad more like!'

Gor staggered back to the kitchen and folded himself onto a stool. 'She reminded me of Olga.' He rubbed a shaking hand over his eyes. 'Oh, this is all too much. I can't take it in.'

Sveta placed a mug on the table before him. 'Drink the sweet

tea, Gor, drink it quickly. It will revive you. I need you revived.'
She began to pace. 'We need to think. Where do we start?'

He looked away, towards the window and the pale sunlight
brushing the tree tops in the courtyard. He remembered the
hateful note at the Palace of Youth, left crumpled on his chair.
He remembered walking in the market, feeling watched, and
being shoved. He took the mug and slurped at the tea. The
recollections bloomed like mushrooms in his brain, gaining
form and clarity. On both those occasions, he realised, Polly
had been present. That was why she was familiar. He shut his
eyes. Going back further, back to August, maybe early
September . . . he remembered a visit to Pharmacy No. 2, to
collect something to help him sleep. The girl had been very
helpful, asked questions about daily routine, support at home,
friends and neighbours. He scratched the back of his head.
'Maybe that was it, Sveta – all along?'

'What was it?'

'You know, the occurrences . . . the letters, the rabbit, the
calls. The tapping. Maybe it was . . . her?' He stood suddenly.

'Be calm, Gor.' Sveta took his hands and held them firmly.
'Tell me more.'

'She . . . and he? Tolya was in there, after all! That's it!' He
pulled away from her to pace the room.

'I don't know what you're talking about.'

'The tapping, woman! The moths! Maybe . . . Tolya
remembered? But of course he remembered!' He whirled away
from her, addressing the window and the leaves heaving
through the autumn air. 'Albina told me he was praying to
Stalin. And why would he do that? Because he'd remembered
– remembered the scary things! The tapping and moth boy!

The fire!' He turned to face her. 'I wasn't going mad! There is no supernatural!'

'I don't understand.' She shook her head till her cheeks wobbled. 'Not a thing do I understand. Gor—'

'Akh, we don't have time. It's an old story, and a tragedy – my family tragedy. They came together—'

'You didn't tell Madame Zoya of any tragedy!' Sveta's eyes and mouth scrunched with disapproval.

'Pah, Madame Zoya! They already knew, these blackguards! And they used that knowledge – to get at me!'

'How?'

'At the séance, at home! It all fits! They knew about the tapping! We used to do it, you understand – when we were boys! We scared each other.' He looked into her eyes. 'I thought I was going mad. But it was them . . . they tried to drive me mad!'

'But why, Gor? Polly and Vlad – why?'

'Why?' He stopped dead in the middle of the kitchen floor, black eyes wide. 'Because they hate me, of course!'

'Akh! Why would they hate you?' Sveta jumped up from her stool. 'They don't even know you.' They stared into each other's eyes, face-to-face across the kitchen table. Sveta raised her chin. 'Unless . . . Oh yes, it's clear, really.' She nodded energetically. 'Oh yes! Gor, everyone who doesn't know you, knows you are a millionaire . . . with jewels under the pillow and gold in the cistern. They don't hate you. They wanted to rob you!'

The great black eyes opened and his head tipped back. 'You think? You really think?'

'Don't you? They are young, stupid . . .'

'The gold in the cistern? You think they believed . . . Hang on!'

They jumped up as one, Gor dashing before Sveta into the hall and through the bathroom door.

'I don't believe it! You're right! Come and see!'

He stood like the Grim Reaper, bony finger pointing to the lemon-yellow toilet as he panted. Sveta saw, and nodded, lips pursed: the lid of the cistern was crooked, clearly replaced by an inexpert hand, and on the floor tiles, dotted around its foot, were splashes of water, muddy boot marks pressed into them.

'Gold in the cistern,' said Sveta quietly. 'She didn't even put on slippers: wasn't here long enough.'

'Akh! Greed and gossip!'

He dashed to the bedroom, searching with fresh eyes.

'Yes, yes – I see it now! The drawers are crooked, and the pillows! Look with the right eyes, and all is clear. She was searching for treasure! But she got nothing!'

'She got Albina!'

'Well, yes.'

'We must find her!'

'And the police?' Gor frowned.

'You heard what she said.'

'So we must do it ourselves. But how?'

'Vlad?'

'Vlad.' Gor nodded.

THE BROKEN ADONIS

Vlad was easy to locate. A phone call to the Vim found him on a week's study leave, so Sveta tried Valya, who informed her with quick pride that he was performing community volunteer work – at Madame Zoya's apartment.

'She's not answering her phone though: I've already tried twice. I need to know when he's coming home for tea. I've made a vanilla sponge, specially, since it's Tuesday.'

'We'll take the car,' said Gor, as Sveta dropped the receiver.

Madame Zoya hovered unwelcomingly behind her door, spectre-like in a grey gown, the outline of her scrawny limbs clearly visible.

'We are busy,' she grumbled, 'you cannot come in. I have done with you! I helped you as far as I could. Do you want blood?'

'Cut the drama, Madame Zoya. We know Vlad is with you,' said Sveta firmly. 'Our business is with him, not you.'

'Please, Madame!' added Gor. 'This is urgent. We believe a child may be in danger!'

The door creaked inwards, and Zoya curled her lip below her sharp, beaky nose.

The interior was lit by a spotlight, its beam trained on a naked body reclining on a pile of Uzbek cushions scattered on the floor. The light threw shadows across biceps, a pair of broad shoulders and the tightest stomach muscles Sveta had ever seen. She averted her gaze to a stuffed woodpecker.

'I'm sorry, Vlad, we must end our session. I have guests . . . well, you do.' Zoya trailed her fingers across the polished-concrete of his shoulder as she went to collect her pencils from the easel. He stood, stretched lazily and reached out for a robe.

'I do?'

'You do,' said Sveta, raising her eyes from the woodpecker to his chest.

'Sveta! You are all recovered?' He smiled and bowed. 'And Papasyan!' His face fell. 'This is unexpected.'

He threw on the robe and headed for the sofa, bare feet slapping on the floor. 'What's up?'

Sveta and Gor stood in the spotlight, their faces stark in its beam.

'You know very well! You're in this together! You . . . you criminal!' Gor pointed a long, accusatory finger.

'Criminal? I've done nothing criminal, as far as I know.' He attempted nonchalance, issuing a bored sneer in Gor's direction over the mound of his raised knee. 'I was helping a friend, nothing more. There's no harm done.'

'Helping a friend? No harm done? My daughter's been kidnapped!' Sveta's voice echoed off the walls.

'What?'

Madame Zoya turned to him, blinking. 'What is this, Vovka?'

'I don't know!' The nonchalance was gone.

'Tell us where Polly is!' demanded Sveta. 'We must find her, and quick.'

'How should I know where she is?'

'You are her beau.'

'Not any more.' Vlad shone a sad half-smile on Sveta, and then Zoya.

'Poor boy,' muttered Zoya, a hand on his arm. 'They had a falling-out.'

'Since when?'

'Since Saturday,' said Vlad. 'You haven't heard? You must be the only people in Azov.'

'We do not gossip!' said Gor acidly.

'And I have been unwell,' added Sveta.

'Yes, I—'

'You were in cahoots though?' she interrupted him.

'I don't know what "cahoots" are, forgive me? We were going out together. She's a . . . a strange girl. She asked for my help with a . . . a project. But tell me: what exactly do you think she's done?' Vlad looked from Sveta to Gor.

Sveta jumped forward clutching her brown handbag to her chest. 'We don't *think*, we know! She's kidnapped my daughter!'

'But when? How? Why?' His face was incredulous, a laugh lurking in the back of his throat.

'She thinks I have gold . . . like half the town. She's been trying to scare me out of my flat, make me go mad, so that she can break in there and steal it. Don't pretend you don't know! You've been in on it with her! Plotting!'

'No! But, really? This is . . . incredible. She was after your money? She believed all the gossip?' The laugh was bubbling in Vlad's throat. 'I never knew that! That's ridiculous—'

321

'This is no laughing matter. If you don't stop, I will slap you.' Sveta stepped forward, her hand outstretched. The laugh subsided and he grabbed the crimson velvet cushion next to him, hugging it to his chest with a puff of dust.

'I knew nothing of this,' he said.

'Then do your duty, and tell us anything you can – quickly.' Sveta hopped over a floor cushion to kneel before him. 'We will treat anything you say in the strictest confidence.'

He sighed and rubbed the soles of his feet together.

'I'll tell you what I know . . . Just one moment. I must collect my thoughts.'

'Collect your lies, more like!' Gor muttered.

'Come, come, old man, that's rather harsh. After all, you're the biggest liar here!' Vlad's words came out in a bellow. The accusation hung in the air.

'What do you mean, Vlad?' asked Sveta.

'He told Madame Zoya there had been no tragedy in his life. That wasn't true, was it?'

Gor's face shone like a yellow skull in the beam of the light. 'I don't know what—'

'Polly told me everything.'

'What are you talking about, dear heart?' Madame Zoya gripped his arm.

'About him—'

'We are here to find Polly—'

'—and how he destroyed her family—'

'Polly has Albina—' Gor's voice faltered.

'Refused them a loan, kicked them out of their workshop—'

'What?' The haunted black eyes came up, confused.

Vlad leapt from the sofa and faced the old man. 'They ended

322

up on the streets, her mama in an asylum!' His chest heaved. 'Yes, she wanted revenge. Yes, she wanted to scare you. To repay you for ruining her life! And I thought, why not? You're a bastard, Papasyan! And you deserved it.'

Madame Zoya's spidery hands reached out to clutch his fingers.

'Vlad, *petuchka*, I think—' she cocked her head, 'you are confused.'

'He may not look evil, Madame Zoya, but . . .'

'Vlad,' she jumped up next to him, tiny but insistent, reaching up to turn his face to hers. 'Dearest, listen a moment. Polly's mama is not in an asylum. She is in Florida. With her little brother. She has been for a year now. She married a Yank, you see: an investment banker. Met him in a hotel in Yalta . . . Polly was left behind, with Alla to watch over her. Alla told me the whole story the other day. By all accounts, the mother lives on a fancy yacht.'

Vlad blinked his beautiful grey eyes.

'But that can't be! What about her papa – Papasyan kicked him out of the bank, spat at him in the street! He became an alcoholic! She told me!'

'He works on a rig, *malysh*, in the Caspian Sea. Always has done. It seems our Polly has spun you a line.'

She squeezed his huge hands. His firm, sensuous lips flapped uselessly as a rich guttural sound escaped them.

'Oh Vlad!' Sveta's fingers tugged at her face. 'Oh no! You terrorised Gor, set up a bogus séance, all for that – for a lie!'

'Phoning me up, tapping on the windows, leaving dead animals?'

'I didn't know!' Vlad's face was pale.

'I never kicked anyone out of my bank! Or denied them means to make a living! I may not be perfect, but I am a human being!'

Madame Zoya guided Vlad back to the sofa, where he sat dejectedly, his head in his hands.

'She used me! That's all she did: used me!'

'There, there, don't upset yourself! Cuddle up with me and we'll have a vodka. All will be well.'

'All the time . . . she lied. And just because she believed some stupid gossip about gold!' He started to pull on underpants over the firm, creamy legs. 'Those stories about how hard her life was! Her struggle!' He tugged on trousers. 'Reminding me how she'd suffered whenever I disagreed with her, making out how much she needed me—'

'And you were very ready to believe!' ground out Gor from the corner. 'With not a jot of proof!'

'She said I was the only one.'

'It was a despicable thing to do.' Sveta stood before him, hands on hips. He looked up into her eyes.

'But I thought I loved her. I *did* love her!'

'No excuse.' Sveta wagged her finger.

'I wanted to make her happy!' Vlad spoke to her receding back. 'It seemed to make her happy!'

'Twisted!' Gor muttered to a stuffed badger.

One shoe was on. With surprising agility, Madame Zoya knelt on the floor beside him and gently ushered his foot into the remaining shoe. 'There now.' Her fingers remained on his ankle, softly rubbing the wool mix of his sock as she sat back on her heels.

'So, now you know what Polly is, and what she has done,

will you tell us where she is?' Sveta raised an eyebrow from the doorway.

'Well . . . she shares a room in the student hostel on the edge of town.'

'Try harder,' said Gor from the shadows. 'She's in Rostov.'

'Rostov?' He sat open-mouthed for a second. 'I suppose . . .' he began sheepishly, 'I suppose she could be at Anatoly Borisovich's flat.'

'What?' Sveta's cheeks wobbled violently.

'Well, erm . . . She knew he had an apartment there: she talked about us using it, if you must know. We didn't! But . . . She had a key. She's been there.'

'Akh!' Gor hissed, striding into the light. 'Your job was to help my cousin, and instead—'

'How could you?' Sveta's face crumpled.

'I told her it was wrong! But . . . she threatened me, she was going to make things really difficult for me, if I didn't do as she wanted.'

'Oh dear, Vovka!' Madame Zoya flopped onto the sofa and took a sniff of her smelling salts. 'You have been a silly boy.'

'Rostov!' said Gor, jumping the mound of cushions in the middle of the floor.

'Rostov!' echoed Sveta, as she opened the door.

'I'm sorry!' cried Vlad, as it slammed. 'It wasn't me, Madame Zoya!' He turned to her, grey eyes pleading. 'I didn't know what she was going to do! I thought she just wanted to scare him a little.'

'I believe you, Vlad,' said Zoya, grasping his fingers and looking into his face. 'I believe you. She led you astray, and

325

she lied to you. She is clearly . . . unbalanced. Now, what about a little vodka, for medicinal purposes?'

'No, Madame! I can't stay. I have to help – to try and sort all this out! She's kidnapped Albina, for heaven's sake! And I know what she's like . . . She can get . . . carried away!'

'Ah, me, yes, I suppose perhaps you should go. I am sure all will be well, though. The spirits would have alerted me, if something too catastrophic was going to occur.'

He was half-way to the door, striding over the cushions.

'*Bon chance, mon brave!*' She blew a wobbly kiss across the room. 'Come back soon though – the portrait is only half done, and I haven't paid you yet!'

CUCKOO!

'I'm out of yoghurt, Olga.' Albina lay on the couch and burped into her cupped hand. Her stomach didn't feel good, maybe because of the yoghurt, maybe because of the strange mixture of boredom and anxiety within the flat. She looked up at the other girl, the 'Olga' girl. She didn't seem much like Gor.

'Stop calling me Olga.'

She was standing at the window, looking out into the court-yard and the mass of skinny birch trees huddled there: so many you couldn't see the other side of the yard, could hardly make out the neighbours' windows reflecting the fire of the setting sun. There was only the darkness of the trees, their shadows knitting into a perfect stony grey. Every so often she muttered to herself.

'Olga, no more yoghurt!'

Albina rubbed her feet against the armrest of the sofa and picked at the split ends in her hair. The clock on the wall, shaped like Sputnik 1, gently tocked towards four.

Still the girl scowled into the courtyard.

'Olga, you didn't buy enough! I'm starving!'

'You can't be hungry! You've just eaten.' She turned on Albina. 'And you're fat.'

Albina's mouth stretched into an offended 'O'.

'You said this would be a party, Olga. This is a rubbish party. And where is my mama?'

Polly pressed her forehead to the cool glass and shut her eyes, trying to shut out the fat girl and the voice and concentrate instead on why she was here, what it was all for: her future; a life worth living; to show them that she could. This flat should be hers. She'd worked hard to secure it. But with the typical selfishness of the old, crinkle-cheeks had gone and died before she could persuade him to sign it over. All she was left with was his scrag-end souvenirs and old clothes dank with must. Anger flamed in her cheeks.

'This isn't a party. Where are they? Why haven't they come?' Albina flipped herself over to lie face-down and pretended to cry for a while, her shoulders shivering as she inhaled fluff and crumbs from cracks between the cushions. 'I don't like you! I want my mama!'

'Shut up! Oh do shut up! How can I think when you're howling like this?' Polly twisted around and threw the first thing that came to hand: a heavy metal ashtray missed Albina's head and hit the door frame with a thud.

Albina broke off crying, surprised, and looked over her shoulder. 'I hate you!' She began hammering her fists and feet on the couch. 'I hate you!'

Polly's lip curled. 'And I you!' She limped around the sofa and into the tiny kitchen, pulling shut its ancient sliding door.

'I hate you!' cried Albina even louder.

Polly slammed shut the little serving hatch, cutting her off.

Exhausted and ignored, Albina sat up and looked about her properly for the first time. The flat was small and dark, and stuffed full of strange objects: a bedraggled sheepskin here, a silky tapestry of a bear family there. Poker work and bead work, books and balalaikas, glasses and bottles all crowded the shelves. In the corner stood a desk covered with drawings and maps, and behind it a tailor's dummy dressed in a peasant shirt, mangy fur stole, headscarf and a funny-looking hat. She stood to better examine the treasures, starting with the hat.

'What's this?' she shouted over her shoulder, so that the doors on the serving hatch rattled in their frames. The hat was not a hat: it was a gnarled leather headdress, in faded red and brown. It crinkled as she ran her fingers across its folds. The head piece was tall, with fragile leather strips protruding from the top. Across the front was sewn a long fringe of multi-coloured beads that would fall into the wearer's eyes. Along the bottom there was another fringe, this time strips of leather knotted with tiny bells and wooden carvings. It felt like the most ancient thing in the world; older than life itself. She leant forward to sniff it, and the scent raised the hairs on her neck: it was forgotten-familiar and vaguely threatening, like a recurring dream, or nightmare.

The serving hatch flew open with a bang and the other girl's head poked out.

'Don't touch!' her voice lashed the air.

'But I'm bored, Olga!'

'Don't call me Olga!' The hatch doors slammed shut again.

'But why shouldn't I, Olga? When is the party starting, Olga? Where is my mama?'

'Shut up!' the voice came back, barely muffled by the closed doors.

Albina flung herself back on the sofa.

'Valentina Yegorovna, I have done a bad thing.' Vlad stood in the hall of the flat above Grocery Shop No. 6, eyes earnest, impervious to the scent of vanilla sponge wafting towards him.

Valya waggled her head. 'Look, we've discussed what happened at the pharmacy, and I told you: you are forgiven. She led you astray, and now it's over. We won't talk of it again.' She went to turn away to the kitchen, intent on making the young man sit down long enough to have a slice or two.

'No, you don't understand. Things have got worse.'

'Worse?' She stopped, intrigued, and shone her piggy-bright eyes at him from beneath navy-blue lashes.

'Yes.' He cleared his throat. 'It appears . . . it appears Polly has kidnapped Sveta's daughter.'

'A kidnap!' Valya clapped her hands and jiggled up and down on the spot, earrings swinging. 'That's terrible!'

'Yes. But I think I know where they are. Sveta and Papasyan have gone already . . . I want to help. It's sort of . . . my fault. And she might be dangerous. I need you to drive me . . . to Rostov.'

'Eh?' The jumping stopped and she pushed her orange head towards him, squinting. 'You want me to drive? To Rostov? I only drive in the summer, and then only when it's light. And I've baked a cake.'

'Please Valya?'

She looked from his handsome face to her driving gloves on

the sideboard, and back again. He took her hand, his Adam's apple bobbing as he swallowed.

'We can take the cake with us?'

She screwed up her mouth. 'Very well. Hand me my scarf, yes, and the driving gloves. Give me the keys to the garage, there on the shelf. Do we need anything else?'

Vlad thought for a moment. 'Courage?' He smiled.

'Courage. And Alla.'

'Alla?'

'She's the girl's guardian – and a very poor job she's done of it too! She ought to come. Perhaps she can talk some sense into her? We'll grab her on the way.'

'I don't think you *are* Olga, are you?' Albina said loudly into the silence. 'I don't know who you are, but you're going to be in big trouble.'

Polly clambered from her stool in the kitchen and heaved on the sliding door: it produced a horrible metal-on-metal squeal, but did not budge. She pulled again: again the squeal, but no hint of movement. She tugged and tugged, hair sticking to the spittle flying from her mouth as she grunted and swore. The door was stuck fast, caught at the top: derailed. She had slammed it too hard. She punched open the serving hatch and out shot her head. Albina giggled.

'Cuckoo! Cuckoo!'

Polly's eyes burnt in her face and her mouth grimaced, but no sound came out. Fury had stolen her words.

'Cuckoo! Ha! You look funny!'

'Shut up!' she eventually spluttered, and pulled the hatches shut.

'I think I'll dress up.'

'You won't!' Again the hatches flew open and her head popped out.

'Cuckoo! I'm bored, Olga!' Albina returned to the ancient leather headdress hanging on the mannequin in the corner. 'I'm going to wear this hat—'

'No! That's old! It's worth money—'

'Ah! There we go!' Albina carefully untangled the headdress from its resting place and knocked dust from its grainy surface. She looked up into it and carefully placed it on her head.

'Idiot!'

'Well,' sighed Albina, 'what do you think?'

The girl pushed her head and shoulders further through the serving hatch, her voice the scrape of nails on a blackboard. 'Put it back. If you break it, I will break you!'

'Is it yours?' Albina's eyes were sly.

'It's all mine!'

'Oh really?'

Somewhere outside, beyond the window, amongst the restless wind and the shivering trees, there was a faint scratching, like claws on bark.

'Take it off! It's not yours!'

'Cuckoo! I will in a minute. I have to make a phone call first.' Albina smiled, feeling less frightened. In fact, she felt quite comfortable; almost as if she were in control.

'No calls! Who said you could call?'

Polly slammed the hatch and stumbled back to the door, pulling with all her might. The bottom moved a centimetre or so as the top clung with sharp steel fingers to its mooring. Hopping back to the hatch she went to thump it open, but her hand collided painfully with solid wood: it too was now stuck.

Albina trotted to the telephone and gulped down the lump in her throat.

The girl in the kitchen howled. Albina dialled Gor's number and waited as the line clicked through invisible connections. The girl in the kitchen roared. Eventually the call connected. It rang, long and low, over and over. She willed him to pick up. The ringing carried on, calling into the cosmos, calling to nowhere, until the connection terminated and pips told her the line was dead. She tried her mama: the hum, the hum, a thousand whispers across the mud flats, the river, the fields and pastures, the trees and crows. No one picked up.

She dropped the receiver and pounced on the front door. It was padded with black faux leather, and was locked. She tried every key in the basket on the telephone table: not one fitted. She beat her fists on it, banging as hard as she could, shouting out, the fringes on the headdress flying around her shoulders. Only the softest thumps escaped the blackness of the faux leather, her voice drowning in the darkness of the hall. She dropped to her knees, panting, hands over her ears to muffle the screams from the kitchen.

'Help me!' Polly was becoming frantic. 'Pull the hatch! Pull it! Where are you?'

Albina observed the stuck sliding door and the stuck serving hatch. She picked her nose nervously. 'I don't know who you are,' she said eventually, 'but I don't think you're Olga. I want to go home. So I won't help you, unless you tell me where the keys are.'

'They're here, you little cow, in my pocket! So open the damned hatch!'

Albina considered for a moment. If the keys really were in the girl's pocket, there was not much she could do. She flexed her arms and tugged at the sliding door, pulling this way and that, easing upwards and downwards. It did not move.

'Try the hatch, pull on the hatch!' The voice was becoming hoarse.

Albina tried the hatch.

'It's stuck! You've slammed it too hard, cuckoo!' She heaved on the little plastic handles once more. One snapped like a dry wishbone. She closed her eyes and wished.

'Ay-ayayah!' the voice inside the kitchen moaned. Albina backed away, pressing her shoulders to the window. She heard the wind moan and the trees rustle, leaves fluttering on the breeze.

There was a yell of pain, a thump of feet on floor and a crash as the girl came smashing through the hatch head-first, splitting the wood as she sprang, arcing in the air before Albina's eyes like a salmon going upstream. Her graceful flight was halted as she hit the back of the sofa. The crunch sent a shiver down Albina's spine. Polly fell limp to the floor.

'Phewee,' muttered Albina, tucking the headdress' beads behind her ear as she bent down.

'Olga?' she whispered, prodding the girl with her toe. 'Cuckoo?'

She was out cold, or dead, Albina was not sure which. She reached shaking fingers into the girl's right trouser pocket and was relieved to feel a metal key ring. She pulled gently. Freedom was hers. She tiptoed to the front door.

As she raised the key to the lock she heard a noise. Another key was turning in the lock, retracting the bolts. She stumbled back, her mind flicking through versions of what could be on the other side. None of them were good. With seconds to prepare, she turned off the light, flexed her fists and braced her legs: a good stance might help. She would go in low, try to knock her opponent to the floor, and roll them over using their own momentum. Her heart beat loud in her chest as she waited, terrified, and licked her lips.

A LONG JOURNEY

'Is this the quickest way to Rostov? Are you sure?' Sveta's eyes roved the window, trying to make out the lights of the city. All she saw were murky fields, thickets of trees, the occasional concrete shelter and desultory roadside kiosk. The light was almost gone. The anxiety that she'd worked so hard to keep in check now wormed through her body.

'Sveta, believe me, I have tried every route to the city, and this is the quickest, especially for this time of day, and the prevailing weather conditions.'

'And you're sure you remember where the apartment is?' Her fingers felt into the crevices around her lips as she spoke, muffling the words. She could taste fear on her tongue.

'Yes. I have been there many times. Unless they have moved the street into the air and yanked it down somewhere else, I know where it is.' He nodded and drove on at a steady forty kilometres per hour.

'You're always very sensible Gor.' Sveta was irritated by his calm.

'Ha!'

'Don't you get tired of being so sensible?'

He picked up the acid in her words. 'I am no automaton, Sveta, as you know. I feel the same as everyone else. The events of this week are grinding my soul, believe me. But at the moment, I am trying to help in the way I can, and that is by driving the car safely, so we arrive at our destination and don't spill off the road.'

Sveta nodded, but her stomach churned. 'I know. I'm sorry. It's my nerves.' She fiddled with her handkerchief, pulling threads from a seam. 'So, what's the plan?' she asked suddenly.

'Plan?' Gor's face was grim.

She gave him a sideways glance. 'What's our approach to be? Good cop, bad cop?' She spoke through stiff lips. 'Or both bad?'

'I think we have to go up there and demand Albina's return.'

'But what if she won't open the door? My goodness, we have no plan!' Sveta's voice rose. 'She will check, won't she, and see it's us. Unless you pretend you've brought the gold?'

'She will want to see it. We could say it is in the bank, and she must come with us to get it?'

'She won't do that. We need a way of guaranteeing she will open the door. Maybe we can get a neighbour to call on her . . . I don't know, we tell them it's a surprise visit or something, so could they please just check that she's at home . . .'

Gor's mouth was pulled into a grimace and he raised an eyebrow.

'Well, I don't know! Don't look at me like that! I think it is a reasonable plan.'

'Yes, it is an idea, Sveta. Or maybe, for simplicity's sake, I should fetch the axe from the boot and simply break down the door, if she doesn't answer?'

337

'Ah! Now, that's a superb idea!' Sveta beamed. 'Yes, I think that's the one.'

'Agreed.'

She wiped condensation from the window with her woolly hat, smearing it to a mess of streaks and fibres. 'Is it far now, Gor?'

'Far enough. Try not to worry.'

'Try not to worry, he says!' Sveta smeared imaginary lipstick marks from the corners of her mouth, and set her jaw.

Beyond the windows, the inky clouds parted and the sun smudged the horizon like blood.

'Take my mind off this interminable journey, Gor. Tell me something of your cousin, if it's not too painful?' She turned to him in her seat.

'Well—' He swerved to avoid a black truck chugging down the middle of the road towards them, and his eyebrows twitched. 'We were close, when we were very small, living out in Siberia.'

'A long way away . . .'

'I looked out for him. I wasn't much older, but I was taller, bigger . . . I hesitate to say cleverer, but it was the case. He was . . . he was a character, even then: funny, cheeky, silly. He lived with his baba, and his father stayed there some of the time . . . when he was sober. I'm afraid he was a difficult man. His mother, my aunt, was already dead. I don't remember her at all.'

Sveta nodded. 'And?'

'He was always . . . eccentric. He could be in the room with you, but not be aware of you. His imagination was very strong. He loved to draw, and he drew stories. He always wanted stories. And he believed the stories told to him. If you said "Tolya,

338

there's a witch in your yard!" he would jump and turn to look, would always believe you. Those big round eyes of his . . .'

'Innocent?'

'Yes, no – more than that. I'd call it gullible: too willing to believe – in anything at all. A bit of a . . . fool. The boys at school – me included – told him about this local legend, a monster living in the forest: moth boy, we called him. All so much nonsense . . .'

'Oh yes, you mentioned moth boy this afternoon. And?' Sveta frowned.

'It was an old story. We embellished it, updated it, as children do. We told Tolya this moth boy tapped on the windows at night, trying to get in. We told him about cold, dead eyes and fluttering wings. He took it to heart and . . . and we encouraged his belief. Because we could laugh at it. We . . . were cruel.'

Gor sighed. Sveta turned to look at him.

'He became obsessed. Scared to be at home on his own, too scared to come to school sometimes. He believed moth boy was visiting him, tapping at the windows. And . . . he started blaming moth boy, for bad things that he'd done. His baba didn't know what to do. He had nightmares . . . wouldn't sleep without a lamp burning. That was the . . . the cause of the tragedy. He always had to have a lamp burning. And that's not safe, if you live in a timber hut, with a thatched roof.'

'No.'

'No. There was a terrible fire. Tolya's house – it just went up, one night.' Gor paused and coughed into his handkerchief. 'We all went to help. The sky was orange. I remember running, running down the main street, shouting, hearing the roar, knowing whose house it was. There were some brave souls that night. They battled to get into the house. But the heat was so strong . . . it singed the hairs in our noses as we stood. Only Tolya escaped the flames.'

'Oh, my! That's terrible. His baba?'

Gor shook his head. 'It was a tragedy for the village.'

'How awful.'

'Tolya was in a fever for days. They thought he might die. He didn't recognise me: looked straight through me. In his fever, he . . . he said moth boy had done it – had been in the house, had taken up the lamp and dropped it. Blamed moth boy!'

'But this moth boy was just a story . . . ?'

'Exactly! We had to assume that Tolya had taken up the lamp, to look in the windows for moth boy, and had dropped it, starting the fire. But when he awoke from the fever, much, much later, he remembered nothing. He asked for his baba, as if she were alive.'

'That's so sad!'

'So it was decided never to speak of it again. He came to live with us, but it was not a happy time. He was changed. He was afraid of everything, howled all night with nightmares – I remember the sound. It makes my skin prickle. My father decided it would be better if he went away, so he was enrolled in the military academy in Krasnoyarsk. It seems ridiculous now, but they hoped to toughen him up. My parents were simple people: they could not cope with him. They did what they thought was best.'

'And you?'

He turned to look her in the eye. 'I was pleased, truth be told: I did not like him in my home, sharing my room, plaguing me with his terrors. I was glad when he went.'

'That's understandable. You were a child too. So – how did he end up here, in Rostov?'

'My mother felt badly for him. She insisted we look after him, and I promised to do my best. When we moved back to Rostov, we invited him to join us, and he eventually followed. We didn't think he would come. We had only a two-room apartment, and he stayed with us for over a year. In the end, he gained an apartment of his own. I married, began my own family . . . and he had his books, his art, and a view of the trees.'

'You weren't close?'

'No. Separate lives. And . . . I had loved his baba. I wanted good memories. I didn't want to think about the fire, the lamp. He had scars on his face, they always reminded me . . . But he never talked of her after he was told, you know?'

'He must have been traumatised?'

'That is true. But . . . it was all too complex for me. Too many emotions. You know me: it was easier not to feel.'

'That's not really you.' Sveta shook her head.

'I used to see him every September, on his birthday,' Gor's eyes dipped from the road and he sniffed.

Sveta chewed her bottom lip.

The road became wider, smoother, with blocks of flats, workshops and garages appearing at its sides, set back behind tangled hedges and breeze-block walls.

'It's not far now.'

'I'm ready,' said Sveta.

The nerves pulled tight across Gor's neck and shoulders as the tower blocks rolled by. It was too late for Tolya, too late for regrets. But maybe . . . maybe he could begin to put things right, if he could save Albina?

PRYANIKI FOR TEA

The door creaked, light from the corridor seeping in around its edges. Then it thrust open. Albina glimpsed a shoulder, a dark coat. It was not Mama. It was not Gor. There was no time to think. She pounced, going in low, shoving up and back as hard as she could.

'Oof!'

The shock of her head hitting solid flesh snapped down her neck into her shoulder. The body under the coat was round and solid. She pushed. It staggered, wobbled on its feet, but did not go down. Cold hands shoved at her shoulders, unpeeling her grasp and she reeled backwards, knocking her head on the wall behind. She cried out as the door was slammed shut.

'Oh dear!'

She scrabbled the hair and fringes out of her eyes.

'What a surprise! I didn't expect . . . no, whatever, else . . . I didn't expect *this*.' It was a man. He flicked on the light. She saw a puffy rabbit-skin hat, dishevelled clothes. 'You're playing the giddy goat! You're . . . hmmm, I don't know . . .' He squinted down at her, a shaggy black silhouette. 'A shaman?'

'I'm not a she-man,' huffed Albina as she scrambled to stand.

The figure held out a hand to pull her up. She wondered if she should bite it.

'Don't be afraid, little shaman.'

He was dressed in a khaki coat, patterned all over with dead leaves, the ghostly remains of wet cobwebs and dry mud. It was thrown over pyjamas. Albina sniffed an odour of trees and mulch, rainy nights and dark days. The liquid silver trail of a snail glistened on his lapel. The perpetrator itself sat upon his right shoulder, munching on a rotten leaf.

'I'm a girl,' she said firmly.

'But what a surprise! So tell me, do you wish *pryaniki* for tea? I do! I am quite giddy, I tell you, to be home!' He squirmed out of his coat and hung it with some difficulty on a black hook by the door.

Albina did not know what she wished for, apart from to go home. She stood in the doorway to the living room, feet square, and twisted her hands together.

'I think you should. Who doesn't love *pryaniki?* And after all, we are celebrating! I am home!'

He went to go past, but she did not stand aside. Instead, she stretched out her arms, stubby fingers touching the brown-papered walls on either side of her.

'Who are you?'

He made a fish-face of surprise.

'I am the man of this house!' he said, nodding. 'Stand aside, please.'

'Tell me who you are!'

'Asks a man who he is! What a cheek!'

He pulled the hat from his head and held out broad arms as if to enfold her in a bear hug. Albina backed away. Under the

343

wild grey hair she made out green eyes glinting amid broad cheeks laced with lines.

'Oh no! You're . . . you're the man from the Vim! The cousin! But you're . . . you're DEAD!' Her voice rose in a squeal.

'Who, child? Me, child? I'm not dead. Well, you can see . . . here, touch me!' He reached out to touch Albina's arm with his blueish fingers, laughing. She shrieked and drew back.

'I'm not dead! Not dead at all! I've had a long journey, I must admit – a ride in a truck, a ride on a bus, a sleep in a shed and a long, long walk . . . but it wasn't fatal.' The bench in the hallway creaked as he lowered himself onto it to remove his boots.

'No, you don't understand—'

He peeled off socks that hit the floor with a slap. The feet beneath were pale and swollen. A strong smell of cheese and mushrooms, churches and the dead seeped into the air.

'Gor Papasyan thinks you're dead!'

His head snapped back. 'Cousin Gor? He's alive?'

'Of course he's alive! He went to see you, at the Vim – but they said you were dead!'

'How I missed him on my birthday! He never came, you know. I waited and waited . . . it broke my heart! It was the end of family. The end of everything, I thought . . . But you? Wait! You must be . . .' he peered up at her, wrinkling his cheeks as he squinted '. . . his Olga, yes?'

Albina glowered. 'I am not Olga! Olga is a grown-up! I am not Gor's daughter! I've been staying with him, because my mama is ill.'

'Ah? So you are—?' he shoved his crinkly face towards hers, eyes enquiring.

344

'Albina!'

'Albina?' He stretched his mouth over the word. 'If you say so. But I still think you make a better Olga,' he added, muttering into the lino. 'So, where is my cousin? Is he here? Is he well?'

'Well enough.' Albina shrugged. 'But not here. I really—'

'If he is alive, and well, it must mean . . . he forgot me. Like I forgot myself.' The old man put his hands in his lap and stared at the floor, a sad expression creeping across his face.

'Listen, please!' Albina shook at his shoulder. 'Can you help me? I thought the other girl was Olga. She brought me here. She said she was Olga. I don't think she is. And now I'm all confused. And . . .' Albina pointed to the living room '. . . and she's in there.'

'Another girl, you say?' He looked up slowly. 'She is very quiet.'

'Yes. She's a mean girl. She smells of antiseptic. And she shouts. But I think,' Albina paused, her face serious, 'I think she might be dead.'

'Ah!' The green eyes lit up, and he nodded. 'Did you use magic?'

'No! It wasn't like that.'

'No? But you're wearing the shaman's cap?'

'Dressing up!'

'Ah. Disappointing.' He pushed himself up and peered into the living room.

'I suppose we'd better take a look. She can't scare us if she's dead . . . can she?' He smiled and propelled Albina forward into the living room.

Albina shrugged. 'She told me there would be a reunion with Gor, and yoghurt, and my mama. But there's only me . . . and now you.'

345

'Ah, well, that is still a reunion, to be fair.'

'But I want my mama!' moaned Albina as she stood over Polly's prone form.

'Well, we all want our mamas, don't we? But unfortunately, yours is in Moscow, and mine is in the grave.' The old man made straight for the desk in the corner, scraping up papers and pencils from its top and hugging them to his chest as if they were children. Then he tutted over the tell-tale gaps on the dusty shelves. 'My things, my lovely things,' he muttered. 'Someone has been here, disturbing my things. Where are the oil paints, Olga? Where is the book of nudes? Not here!'

'My name is Albina, and I don't know anything about a book of nudes.'

'Ah?' He gave her an assessing look. 'Very well. You are my welcome guest, as long as it was not you who ransacked my home.' He looked again to the shelves, and sighed. 'I am Tolya. Your father may have mentioned me?'

'Akh, he's not my father! But yes, he has mentioned you. Quite a lot.'

'That warms my heart a little. Good.'

'Not really. As he thinks you're dead.'

'Oh-ho!' Anatoly Borisovich tripped on Polly's foot, protruding from behind the sofa. 'And this is . . .'

'The scary girl.'

'Indeed?' He shook his head and prodded the body with his naked toe. There was no response. He looked up and smiled. 'I'm sure it's nothing to worry about. Tea?'

'The kitchen door is . . . stuck. She got it stuck. She was angry, and slammed it, and then it got stuck, and that made her more angry, and she got more stuck. Look!'

The old man circled the body on the floor, padding around on soft feet, leaving wet marks from his trailing hems on the carpet tiles. He approached the sliding door and gave it a gentle nudge in the middle with his hip, followed by a double-knock at the top with his knuckle and a quick kick at the base for luck. It squeaked, then slid open with a sigh.

'Oh!' exclaimed Albina. 'Magic!'

'As I said, this is my apartment. And I have *pryaniki*. Hurray! At least,' he patted his pockets. 'I did have *pryaniki*. I think, ah, maybe in here. It was a long walk, and can you believe it – all I had for sustenance were these biscuits.' He brought out a soggy paper bag from his trouser pocket and popped a biscuit in his mouth.

Albina watched him chew and felt an odd, lonely sensation in the pit of her stomach. Perhaps tea was a good idea. But she didn't want to get too close to this Tolya. He had strange eyes, and a strange smell, and he really wasn't anything like Gor. She waited until he moved into the living room, his pudgy hands stroking the sheepskin on the wall, and hurried through. A wet munching sound emanated from the old man's cheek.

'Why aren't you dead?' she called through the hatch as the kettle began to hiss. He looked up from the book he was holding.

'I don't know,' he replied, his green gaze on her forehead. 'Do you think I should be?'

Albina twisted her hands behind her back. 'I didn't mean that. I didn't mean anything. I just meant . . . Gor thinks you're dead, and he should know. They told him you'd gone!'

'Well, quite right! You have the evidence before you! I am no longer there. I escaped, in the dead of night. I couldn't bear it!' He approached the hatch. Albina handed him a biscuit, and he padded on. 'It was very easy in the end, once I remembered about clothes, and shoes, keys and offices. That grumpy orderly slept like a rock! And out I crept, like a little mouse. I couldn't stay any longer; they were trying to kill me. And my new friend didn't visit any more.'

He wiped his eyes and whiskers on his sleeve and then, with great care, rolled the girl's body over with the side of his foot. 'How did you do it?'

'It wasn't me!' cried Albina. 'She did it herself. She just came flying through the hatch and—'

'Ah, magic then?'

'No, not actually flying—'

'But she came through there? That little hatch hole? And what propelled her, eh? If not magic?'

Albina thought for a moment. 'Well. I don't know.'

She crept forward to take a closer look. 'She's breathing.'

'Very good,' said the old man. He shuffled over to a drawer in the sideboard, and laboriously pulled out a blanket to lay over the unconscious girl. Returning to the kitchen, he pulled out two stools, sat on both of them and spread out the remaining *pryaniki* before him.

'Come, eat, Olga! Share with me. We need sustenance.'

'I'm not Olga! She's the Olga! But what shall we do,' asked Albina, 'with her?'

'With her?' He shrugged. 'Let's wait. Wait . . . and eat.' He shoved a biscuit into his mouth and chewed enthusiastically, eyes glazing over. 'Mmm, these are good. A little damp, but—'

Albina's eyes were drawn to a moth on the windowpane. Night was gathering in the corners like sooty cobwebs. The kettle boiled with a scream.

'We'd better get the lamp lit,' said Tolya.

'But we have electric light. We don't need a lamp.'

He crossed the living room, lumbering for the sideboard. Old sketch books, paint brushes and colourful, crumpled hats rained to the floor around him as he rummaged about. Eventually he stood up straight, a battered paraffin lamp held in his outstretched hands.

'Here we have it! Fetch the matches, Olga!'

Albina rolled her eyes, but did as she was asked.

He lit the lamp with a hiss and a pop, and the air filled with the scent of burning paraffin and dust.

'Such a happy glow!' He peered into the light of the lamp as it burnt first white, then yellow, then a honeyed orange as he adjusted the wick. 'It scorches my old eyes,' he chuckled. 'Now I see nothing but white and green and red! Look!'

Albina frowned as he flicked off the light switch. The glow of the lamp did not make her feel safe at all. Shadows shifted in the corners of the room and it felt to her as if another person had joined them. She fiddled with the fringes of the shaman's cap. When were Gor and her mama ever going to arrive?

The old man seated himself behind the jumbled desk and hummed as he sifted through piles of softly crackling papers. 'I thought I had a picture, of me and Lev in the yard.'

Albina decided to check on how Olga, or whoever she was, was getting on behind the sofa. Perhaps they should call an ambulance? Or better still, tie her up? She bent down and reached a hand to touch the girl's shoulder. The blanket collapsed under her touch, and the breath caught in her throat. She dared not move.

'Tolya?' she whispered.

Albina patted all over the blanket, her hands meeting the floor.

'What is it?' He didn't take his eyes from the papers. 'Is she dead?'

'She's . . . she's gone!'

'Dead gone?'

'No!' Albina wailed, leaping up from the floor to press her back against the window behind her. The shattered doors of the serving hatch swayed on their hinges and she squealed at the black shadows leaping in the kitchen beyond. 'Just . . . gone! She's not on the floor! Where . . . where is she?' Her eyes flew around the room. 'Put the light on!'

'Magic! It's wicked magic!'

'She's not magic! She must be here – somewhere.'

'But I have only these rooms!'

Their eyes met across the shadowy darkness and, as one, they looked towards the black hole of the doorway into the hall.

Tolya stood and lifted the lamp, the sallow light splashing over the floor and up the walls in waves as he moved. Albina jumped behind him. They stood together, pale faces turned towards the doorway, their round eyes staring, straining to make out a form.

'I am afraid,' whispered Tolya. 'Help me.'

They crept a tiny step forward.

'Olga?' called Albina.

'Scary girl?' whispered Tolya, eyes shut.

They stood as statues and held their breath, straining their ears: the human hum of a neighbour's TV; the grinding of wet trolley-buses beyond the birches; a crow cawing its evening call.

Beneath the everyday noise, there was something else, subtle, low, threatening; the beast of winter creeping across the eastern plains.

They took another step and the lamp shook in Tolya's hand. 'Shhh!' breathed Albina. She sensed something in the hall: rhythmic breathing mingling with the darkness, vibrating in the space; a slight creaking on the floorboards, a breath stirring the dust. She peered blind into the blackness.

'Do you hear that?' whispered Tolya. 'It is the sound . . . of wings.'

'Wings?' Albina screwed up her nose.

'Giant wings, flapping. Listen . . .'

Albina listened. As she concentrated on the silence, beyond her own heartbeat, the blinking of her eyelashes, somewhere in the air of the flat she felt an oscillation, a flutter . . .

tap-tap-tap

'Moth boy!' Tolya's hand gripped hers.

'It's her!' whispered Albina. 'It must be her!'

The tapping had come from the hallway, nails on wood: an empty sound.

tap-tap-tap

'She's trying to scare us! Don't be scared!'

'You don't understand,' he waved the lamp around his head. 'He comes in the night. He is my friend!'

tap-tap-tap

'It's not a spirit! It's her!'

'Come in, Yuri! Where is Baba?'

tap-tap-tap

Tolya took a step towards the darkened doorway, arms held wide. The light from the lamp swung over the walls, washing

351

into the hall. Albina pushed back the fringe of the headdress. She thought she saw a face, just for a second as the lamp swung up. A glowing pale face with huge, moonlit eyes. The face grinned. The lamp swung back, the hall melted into darkness, and she cried out for her mama.

A rush of air feathered her face as something leapt past, springing into the room, smashing into the lamp swinging from Tolya's hand. Fire flashed as the old man windmilled his arms, flailing at his attacker, slamming the lamp this way and that.

'No!' shrieked Albina, cowering against a wall as the glass of the lantern shattered. She heard a thud and saw Tolya lurch to one side, falling like a rotten tree. Burning paraffin spilled from the lamp onto the floor in snaking, livid trails. She saw a boot raised to kick, a fist to punch. And she sensed the wind rushing through the black arms of the forest, the silver moon riding high. Tolya's hands reached out, fingers gripping the air, as the shadow of his attacker loomed large against the wall.

'Baba!' he cried.

Albina leapt, hands, arms, thighs ready as the blood sang in her ears.

SPECIAL MEASURES

An elderly man, tall, skinny and nut-brown, chased up the corridor, a short, well-built woman with curving eyebrows and a very blonde bob just behind him. He reached out a bony finger, and depressed a doorbell very hard. Their eyes locked as they stood panting.

'I didn't hear anything. Did you hear anything?'

'I did not hear anything. But it might be one of those bells that rings in the depths.'

'It's a one-room apartment, you said?'

'Ah.'

Sveta applied her finger to the bell, repeatedly and for a long time.

'It doesn't work.' She began rapping her knuckles on the door, the pain creasing her face.

'No, no, Sveta; rest your hands.'

Gor bunched a fist and hammered. The noise echoed down the corridor. No one came.

Sveta bent to put an ear to the keyhole. 'I can hear . . . things!'

'And?'

Her eyes bulged.

'It doesn't sound . . . thudding – fighting!' Her voice rose. 'And burning! I can smell burning! Oh Gor! Quick!'

He dropped the string bag from his shoulder and carefully unwrapped the axe. Its blade shone.

'Time for special measures?'

She nodded.

He drew himself tall, creaking at the joints and sucking in a big breath. The axe wheeled over his shoulder and down onto the door with a clank. Shock pinged up his arms and wobbled his eyes in their sockets. The axe clattered to the floor as he bent double in pain.

'Akh, metal?' observed Sveta.

Gor grimaced and gripped his right shoulder. Down the corridor a neighbour peeped silently around the edge of a door and hurriedly shut it again.

'Here, let me try.' Sveta rolled up her sleeves and wrapped her sore, red hands around the handle. The blade glinted as her hands shook above her head.

A door slammed and riot of footsteps echoed up the corridor.

'Wait!' cried a voice. 'Let me help!'

Sveta turned to see an unlikely trio dashing towards her: one tall and handsome, one thin and grey, and one squat and orange, carrying a cake.

'We're here to help!' puffed Valya. 'Give me the axe, come on! I'll manage that better than you!'

Sveta put the axe behind her back.

'Have you spoken to Polly?' asked Vlad.

'Spoken to her? We can't get in! What do you think the axe is for?' cried Gor.

'I knew something like this would happen!' wailed Alla, tissue to her nose, sniffing wildly. 'I was just saying in the car, I always knew—'

The door vibrated as something hit it from the inside.

'Sveta, I think maybe—' Vlad held out a hand, and she placed the axe handle in it. 'Right! Stand back ladies! And you, Papasyan! I'll sort this – I'll take it sideways – slice off the handle.'

They spread out down the corridor in a straggling horseshoe. Again something heavy thudded against the door and the handle rattled.

'Hurry!' cried Sveta, fingers pressed to her throat.

Vlad wiped his palms on his trousers, wrapped them around the handle of the axe and planted his feet wide, side-on to the door. Smooth muscles bulged as the axe flew into the air over his head, only to be brought down softly, slowly, as a golfer might, practising his shot.

'Oh, come on!' cried Gor.

'Hit it!' shrieked Sveta.

Once more he swung the axe above his head. This time he arched backwards with a sharp grunt to scythe the blade down in a swift, slashing stroke.

But as Vlad arched backwards and the blade began its descent, the door itself was opening, pushed from within. Tolya had never locked it. Gor and Sveta had failed to try it. And now something was escaping. There was no time to shout. Eyes popped and mouths grimaced as smoke belched from the doorway. They heard the crunch, and they felt the thud as the swinging door pushed the air from Vlad's chest. It hit him in a neat line from nose to sternum and hip, throwing him backwards. The axe flew from his hands, rotating through the air, the blade sharp and shiny as a shard of glass.

As the axe somersaulted, something came cannoning through the door, a blur of movement, big and fast as a train bolting the tracks. The axe flew, the body charged. A roar echoed around them, followed by a scream. The axe fell. Sveta threw her hand to her mouth and screwed her eyes shut. A thump rang out, a splitting sound . . . and the clang of the axe blade as it bounced and hit the tiles.

Something strange and terrible rolled unevenly across the floor, coming to rest at Gor's feet. He looked down, and hopped sideways.

It was a head.

NOT DEAD

Valya's scream was the shrillest sound Albina had ever heard. More shrill than Kopek on a bad day. More shrill than Albina, when bitten by Kopek. More shrill than Albina at that very moment, issuing her battle cry as she charged forward through the entrance hall toward the light of the corridor beyond. It was a sound that would stay with her always. It pierced her mind as she careered after the mannequin, thrown out through the door by the scary girl, after Albina had charged her with it for the seventh time. It had served Albina well, and now it led the way to freedom. The ribbons of the shaman's cap streamed behind her as she dashed forward, coughing smoke and wiping smuts from her eyes, life a blur around her until she came into the light. She heard the scream, saw a fat woman faint – straight into her mama's arms. Her mama staggered, holding the weight and controlling the fall, her eyes pinned on Albina.

Gor was nearest: he reached out when he saw her. She flung herself into his wiry arms, half laughing, half sobbing, not even looking around for Olga, not caring, knowing the fight was over. The touch made it real.

'You're safe!' he roared. 'Tremendous girl!'

'*Malysh!*' Sveta leapt Valya's prone body to dash forward. 'Oh look at you, poor baby!' She squeezed her daughter to her chest. Albina unpeeled her face.

'Don't fuss, Mama, I'm fine. But we must save *him*!' She pointed to the open doorway into the darkness beyond.

'Who, baby-kins?'

'The old man! She's still in there with him! Olga!'

A figure in black came plunging through the smoke-stained doorway, dashing at full-pelt, cat-like, feral.

Polly streaked through the door. She swerved around Vlad's outstretched hands, past Gor's braced arms, straight down the corridor, eyes like car headlights, mouth twisted with pain as she leapt the headless mannequin and the struggling Valya. She sprinted for the doors. Sveta looked to Gor, Gor looked to Vlad, still leaning against the wall trying to stem the bleeding from his nose. Vlad shrugged: it was too late.

Alla bided her time. She was standing half-way down the corridor, almost invisible in a doorway. All it needed was a few centimetres, the raising of her toe at the right moment, and she felled Polly like a child in a sack race. With barely a murmur, the girl slowed from twenty kilometres per hour on the straight to zero kilometres per hour flat on her face. The slap of the impact echoed up the hall as she slid to a halt.

'That's what you get,' hissed Alla, 'for trying to help someone. I get her a job at the pharmacy, and she turns to kidnap!' She bent over Polly's groaning form. 'I'm going to tell your mother all about this, you know. She won't be pleased. How could you do this to me?'

Polly's response was muffled by the floor tiles.

A noise in the doorway brought their heads back around. Out of the billowing darkness emerged a man: smallish, plumpish, rocking on his feet, green eyes blazing in the half-light as he held a smashed lamp to his face, as if its blackened glass and broken wick could make sense of the scene around him. One eye was swollen and there were claw marks across his cheek.

Gor dropped the little string bag from his shoulder, face ashen.

'Wha . . . ?'

'Not dead!' cried Albina. 'Just gone! That was it! I'm sorry she's not Olga, but he really is—'

'My cousin! My cousin! This is . . . a miracle!' Gor wobbled forwards to take his cousin's hands and led him out into the light. 'Saints be praised! I can't believe it!'

Tolya's eyes streamed from the smoke and it took him a moment to clear his mind and see who held his hands. He stared into the face of his cousin. 'You've come at last!' he beamed. 'How I hoped you would!' The broken lamp dropped to the floor as he enfolded his cousin in his arms, his head resting on Gor's chest. 'All is well. All is well! We are home. Here we are. Come in, cousin, come in everyone, please! There's been a fire, I'm afraid. I broke the lamp. But it's mostly smoke. All is well.' Together the two old men began to shuffle through the apartment door.

'That's cousin Tolya?' Sveta's chin wobbled with curiosity and she laughed into her neck.

'He came home – he walked, Mama! Well, some of the way. He just left. He wasn't dead.'

'So he got home . . . bravo!' Sveta smiled into Albina's hair and kissed her forehead. At the door, she turned and called in a louder, authoritative voice, 'You'd better phone an ambulance, Alla! Master Tolya looks concussed. And so perhaps is Vlad. And maybe Polly. And possibly Valya. Oh, and the police; we must call the police, I think.'

'Very well!' Alla hopped up the corridor to give her friend a prod. 'Valya, come on now, pull yourself together.' Valya groaned and waved her arms as though swimming up the hallway. 'You're never ill! Rouse yourself and guard that Polly – although I don't think she'll be going anywhere for a while.' Alla snorted. 'I must call the services. And you're just lying about dribbling. Come on now, friend!'

'Akh, but . . . the body!' Valya's tiny black eyes reappeared above cheeks still the colour of alabaster. 'The head! Oh . . . it rolled at his feet! Urgh!'

Alla knelt. 'Valya, *milaya* – borrow my glasses. Look, eh? Where is the blood? A mannequin: that's all. You fainted over a few splinters, my sturdy friend. Maybe it's *you* who needs the vegetarian diet?'

Valya pushed herself up, scowling. 'Devil take it! Splinters? Wood? How was I to know? It came shooting out like a demon – straight for me! And the axe . . . oh my God, that came straight for me too! And the head!' She crossed herself with jerking movements.

Behind her, Polly groaned.

'Come on, now – guard the prisoner! Do your duty!' Alla pulled Valya to her feet and stalked off to find the telephone.

'I have to keep you here. Understand? I don't want to do this, but I must.' Valya bent her knees to rest on the other girl's chest. 'Don't squirm now, Polly. It would be better for you if you just did as you're told, for once.'

The girl groaned as Valya shifted her weight. 'Don't even think about it!'

Vlad limped up the corridor to crouch by the pair. He reached out a hand to Polly's brown-black hair.

'How could you, Polly?' he asked in a soft voice.

Her eyes, flat and black as a shark's, were on the mannequin, silent and lifeless, still wearing its peasant shirt, splinters massed where its head had been. Her gaze slithered to him.

'Idiot,' she mouthed.

Sveta opened the windows and watched the smoke trickle away towards the stars.

'There now!' huffed Anatoly Borisovich in joyful tones, pleased to have guests on his homecoming. 'We must have tea!' He began to pick his way over broken pieces of serving hatch, heading for the kitchen. Gor took his arm and gently diverted him towards the sofa.

'Let us sit, cousin. Have a little rest. It's a long while since I have been here. It's a long time since I saw you. I see you still have the sheepskin.'

'Oh yes. My lovely things.'

'And the easel.'

'Yes, yes. And my treasure box.'

They sat side-by-side on lumpy cushions, arms entwined. Tolya leant his head on Gor's shoulder as Sveta tidied up around them, unobtrusively sweeping yoghurt pots and broken glass from the floor.

'The police and ambulance are on their way,' she said in an undertone to Gor.

'Cousin, cousin,' murmured Tolya. 'I'd given up hope! I thought you were dead! But here we are, and I am home.'

Gor patted his hand. 'I'm sorry you had to wait so long. And I'm sorry I didn't come before . . . on your birthday. I will explain everything, and I will make it up to you. I . . . I was confused. But things are clearer now.'

'I know about confused, cousin. I know about confused. But I am so glad you are here, and little Olga too!'

Albina rolled her eyes and removed the shaman's headdress, placing it on a dusty shelf.

'Cousin, we must talk.' Tolya pressed Gor's arm with firm fingers.

'Yes, we must, dear cousin, but maybe not now? There is no hurry. You must get those wounds looked at. Have a little rest. We will talk when you are mended.'

'Mended? Ha! I just walked half the way from Azov! You think I'm infirm? I'm a tiger!' Again the shaggy head lifted and Tolya grinned into his cousin's face.

'Of course! But I am not.'

'No, you're more of the night-time? Something winged?'

'What do you mean?' Gor frowned.

'An owl, maybe?'

A smile warmed his eyes. 'I see. But Tolya, even tigers and owls needs rest. These few weeks, for you and I . . . have taken a toll, I fear. Get your wounds looked at. Have a rest. We can talk any time.'

'I wanted to call you, you know. I wanted to see you. I remembered, you see: Vlad helped me. But you never came,

362

and he never came, and then I thought I'd better just get on, and come home.'

Gor's eyes met Sveta's over his cousin's head.

'Remembered?' he asked, rumbling deep in his chest.

'Everything!'

'Everything?' Gor's eyes shone.

'Everything!' Tolya giggled. 'We were nothing but boys: you, me and moth boy.' Tolya nodded his head energetically. Gor's right eye twitched. A siren wailed in the courtyard.

There were voices in the doorway, and Vlad stepped through, swallowing uncomfortably and looking around. He stood before the two old men on the sofa, one hand feeling the scabs forming on his nose, the other held out to Anatoly Borisovich. The old man clasped it.

'You got home then, Anatoly Borisovich?'

'I did! I did! And here we are. It's so good to see you, Vlad. But, forgive me, why are you . . .?'

'Polly.'

'Polly?'

'The dark-haired girl. Out there. The girl who—'

'Ah! The scary girl? That was . . . your great love? Apart from BMW?'

Vlad's cheeks burnt a dull red. 'I think I got it wrong, about that.'

'Oh? We live and learn, eh? Even doctors?' Tolya winked, and then winced.

'I hope so.' Vlad nodded.

'But listen Vlad, I must correct you!'

The young man narrowed his eyes. 'About what?'

363

'It's been bothering me so! But you never came back, so I couldn't tell you!'

'I'm sorry. But—'

'The case study, Vlad!'

'What about it?'

The old man's eyes grew wide. 'The trigger – for everything coming back – my memories of the fire. Remember you wanted a trigger?'

Vlad nodded slowly.

'I was wrong!' Anatoly Borisovich grinned. 'It wasn't the tapping. It was never the tapping, you see?'

'So – what was it?'

'It was my dear cousin here. Or rather, his absence. He didn't come, on my birthday. I waited and waited and, in the end, I decided he must be dead. It made me so afraid, so lost and afraid, and then . . . it all came back, in my fever here, ragged patches, like leaves in the wind!'

Vlad squeezed the hands that held his. 'Don't worry about it now, Anatoly Borisovich. I'll come and see you next week, and we'll get it all straightened out.' Grey eyes met green. 'And I'll try to make it up to you.'

The old man patted his hand.

Vlad turned his head. 'I want to apologise to you too, Mister Papasyan.'

'Just go away.' Gor folded his lips and looked towards the window.

The police arrived ten minutes later, scratching their heads over the scene of domestic chaos. Furniture lay broken and overturned on carpet tiles that were scorched and blackened, curling like dry scabs on the floor. Witnesses chattered incessantly, or silently stared into the depths of the yellow-brown ceiling as if star-gazing. The alleged criminal, who had at some point been handcuffed with knotted sheets by one of the witnesses, sat head-down in the corridor, black eyes burning, refusing to speak. She was guarded by a square orange woman eating vanilla sponge and drinking tea.

'One more time, so I can get this straight,' said the police officer. 'You were all here because you believed the girl had been kidnapped?'

They nodded.

'But not one of you called the police?'

They looked at their feet.

They shuffled into the hallway, heads bowed, to wish the police officers and paramedics a goodnight.

'Of course, she was unbalanced,' said Vlad, as he watched Polly being escorted along the corridor, hands cuffed behind her back. 'I can see that now. Only interested in herself – no sense of shame, no conscience. She would make an interesting case study. I wonder if I should ask—?'

'Just forget it!' Valya snorted. 'Get on with your life. Study hard. And get some cake down you!'

'She's always been the same! And to think, I used to take her into my confidence. All the intimate details I told her. I have medical conditions, you know. There was the time—'

'Goodnight, cousin Tolya. Sleep well,' said Gor. 'We'll be back in the morning, to start putting things right. No more *pryaniki* now, just sleep. Quiet, velvety sleep!'

Tolya nodded his goodnights, kissed his cousin's cheek and shut the door.

Gor, Sveta and Albina took the little car home, back through the rolling fields and the stark little villages, the breeze-block shanties and the mud flats of the estuary. In silence, they drove through the outskirts of Azov, the car picked out by the fuzzy orange street lights, twinkling as it crossed the town, oblivious to the late-night drinkers and fussily dressed party-goers. They crossed the bridge spanning the deep blackness of the River Don, and rounded the block, heading back to the squat concrete building that Gor called home.

They closed the curtains and switched on the lamps. Gor sat before the piano, regarding it lovingly for a moment as he cracked his knuckles. He began to play, and he played as if his life depended on it, choosing music to enrich the soul, and music to soothe. Rachmaninov, Rimsky-Korsakov, Mussorgsky. He closed his eyes. Albina sat in his armchair, blanket around her shoulders and four fluffy white kittens in her lap. Her mama curled on the sofa, feet resting on Dasha. Pericles sat atop a pile of books balanced at the end of the baby-grand, and slowly-slowly blinked his sapphire eyes.

Eventually Sveta yawned and stretched. 'Let's have a feed. Everybody? We need to eat. I haven't eaten all day. Albina, you must be hungry, baby-kins?'

'Mmm, actually, I had quite a lot of yoghurt . . . and *pryaniki*. But if you're making something?'

Sveta went to the kitchen. 'To start, I will put the kettle on, and we will have tea. Now, Gor . . .'

She came back to stand in the doorway.

'What a wicked girl: all those phone calls, all that mischief; and all for nothing! I still can't believe it!' Gor stared at the piano keys.

'Greed,' said Sveta, 'that's what it is. Gets hold of a person . . . when there's not enough love.'

'Ha! Only a woman could believe the bad turn bad due to lack of love.'

Sveta raised her eyebrows and pursed her lips.

'And only a man could be too blind to see it. Now — have you any cutlets about the place?' She trotted back to the kitchen, opening first the fridge and then the freezer compartment. 'Oh, you have! How marvellous!' She brought out a brown paper parcel, wrapped with string.

'Have I?' He began polishing the piano keys with spit and his handkerchief, rubbing at the ivory till it shone. 'I didn't know. What a fine piano!' He stood back smiling to himself, and patted the piano's lid.

Sveta cut the string with Gor's sharp red-handled scissors and pulled open the paper.

Her shriek filled the apartment, echoing off the ceiling, jumping into the cats' ears, making them hiss and arch their backs.

Gor dashed to the kitchen. Sveta was standing over the parcel, one hand to her throat. Inside lay the frozen remains of a headless white rabbit.

THE BIG SHOW

On a grim day in December, Gor looked from his little kitchen window, and smiled. Life was perking up. A rosy-cheeked glow had spread among the residents of the southern Russian town of Azov, and it wasn't from the cold. School was out, the Year 2s still did not know the Roman alphabet, and Kopek had learnt a new song. Albina had settled down and was no longer being over-polite to her mama, which Gor reckoned was a good thing. The nights were long, the frosts hard, a promise of snow watched from the shoulders of the Urals, and New Year beckoned with glinting fir-tree fingers.

Gor had long-since torn the X-bespeckled calendar from the wall and shoved it down the rubbish chute with a 'rom-pom-pom' and a flourish. He and Sveta had embarked upon a series of serious rehearsals, even hiring a room at the House of Culture. And while he had resisted Sveta's initial costume sketches, he was not equal to the task of putting her off completely. Eventually, he had agreed to both ostrich feathers and sequins, for her at least.

They were striving for normal, pushing the events of the autumn far behind them, like swimmers in a pool, pushing away the water, stroke by stroke. When he wasn't visiting cousin Tolya or rehearsing magic tricks, Gor spent a lot of time thinking. He and the kittens held a series of long communions. He told them his troubles, and they listened attentively. In turn, they told him they were ready for new homes.

And today? Today was show day: the Fund-Raising Spectacular, or FRS. It had started when Albina had asked again about the Magic Circle money. He was trying to teach her the notes on the piano, just the basics. She was like a dog with a bone; all she wanted to hear about was his crime.

'But what are you going to do?'

'You don't need to concern yourself. Now, this is middle C—'

'Seriously! They could kneecap you!'

'No, no! They are magicians! I will sell the piano. That is the answer. This note is D—'

'You can't sell the piano! It's your only joy!'

Gor sucked in his cheeks and nodded. 'Well, maybe I can sell the car. This note is E—'

'Nooo! If you have no car, how will we get to the *dacha*? How will you eat?'

'Well, if I can't do that, I may just go to the police and admit what I've done.'

'But they'll put you in jail with murderers!'

'Albina, I don't really care. So next to E comes—?'

'But what about cousin Tolya, if you are in jail?'

'You really are tiresome, young lady!'

'You said a million roubles? That's only about . . .' She screwed up her nose and counted on her fingers. '. . . Two

369

hundred and thirty US dollars. That's not a lot. Not worth jail.' She fixed him with a straight look.

'I have three dollars,' she said. 'I can put that in—'

Gor shook his head. 'Thank you Albina, you are most generous, but—'

'I was thinking of it as an investment, not a gift.'

'Either way, I cannot take your money. The piano must go—'

'There has to be another way,' said Albina, finger in her nose.

'The accounts are due in January. There is no other way.'

'Ooh! But wait!' Albina leapt from the piano. 'What about the spectacular? Eh? Eh?' She looked from Gor to her mother.

'Hmm?' Sveta roused herself from her magazine. 'The spectacular? But that's just an idea, Albina. I don't see how it could help.'

'Spectacular? Spectacular what?' Gor asked.

'Oh Gor, you must remember – the idea I had for a variety show.' Sveta's eyes turned misty as she stared into the middle distance. 'Something the like of which Azov has never seen: a glittering cornucopia of light entertainment.'

'Mama, we will do it, and make it a *fund-raising* spectacular!'

The magazine dropped to the floor. 'Tell me more, baby-kins?'

'Imagine: the spectacular of the year, a glittering event: we charge for tickets to cover our cost, and use the profit to clear Gor's debt.'

'Ooh! That sounds—'

'We charge two thousand roubles per ticket, give some to children's homes and hospitals to make it look good . . . It's so easy!' She giggled.

'Well, I have to say, Albina, I think you've had a marvellous idea!'

They jiggled up and down together on the sofa squealing with excitement.

'Right!' Albina clapped her hands. 'Let's start with the programme, then the marketing strategy, and then the budget.'

'Ah-ha,' said Sveta, 'and the costumes. Don't forget the costumes!'

Gor stared at the bowl of toffees on the table, and wondered if he should try one. After all, he would not need to speak now for at least an hour and a half.

'We could have acrobats. You know we have a certain circus connection?' Sveta gurgled. 'Well, maybe I could use him—'

'Oh no, Sveta—' Gor coughed out the toffee.

'Don't worry, it will be very tasteful! He can get his hands on all sorts, believe me! The stories he used to tell: the Cossack troupe, the strongest man on earth, Rudolfo the Clown. Oh, and they had trained piglets, can you believe that? Piglets pushing cats around in prams! That would be super-fantastic, wouldn't it?'

'Kopek can sing, Mama. Kopek can be in the show, can't he?'

'Absolutely, *malysh*! He has to be in the show!'

'I could teach him a new song—'

'And if we get the piglets—'

'I'm not sure about piglets,' Gor cut in.

'We just have to do it! It will be marvellous, piglets or no! We have had more than our fair share of misfortune. It's time to make us some luck!'

Excitement sizzled through the corridors of the Palace of Youth. Chattering school children, young couples with fingers interlaced, big-bellied local dignitaries and wizened old ladies with apple-pip eyes tussled one after the other with the stiff double doors, intent on the event of the year.

Intriguing posters plastering every bus stop, bottle-exchange and bread shop had promised the townsfolk an extravaganza they could not resist, and the great and the good had sallied forth, proud to pay up. Even the Deputy Mayor was in attendance, a tall blonde dripping diamonds by his sweating side. He'd insisted on paying double the going rate, on principle.

Valya and Alla surged into the foyer, sheathed in matching creations of shiny, flower-spattered viscose. Thrilled with their free tickets, they had told everyone who would listen, for two weeks in a row, what a lovely man, and fantastically talented magician, Gor Papasyan was.

'We went to his séance, didn't we?' said Nastya to Alla from the corner of her mouth as they waited to stow their coats. 'Did anything come of it, do you know?'

'Well,' said Valya, leaning in and shaking her head like a terrier with a rabbit, 'let's just say it was nothing but a con, as I always said! Smoke and mirrors, nothing more!'

'But what about Polly?' pressed Nastya in a stage-whisper, suppressing a grin. 'There have been rumours! Didn't she bite the head off a chicken?'

'You shouldn't listen to gossip!' snapped Alla loudly. 'I did my best. I gave her so much support, and what did she do? Theft! Menaces! Kidnap! But no chickens, wool brain. Where did chickens come from?'

'It was all her! My Vlad was just . . . just putty in her hands. Her filthy hands! She used him abominably,' said Valya. 'He's still suffering now! Anyway, she's off for a little correction, and let's hope she comes back . . . corrected. Or not at all.'

372

'Huh!' huffed Alla. 'Her mother's very cross. Blames me! Might impact on US immigration, apparently.'

Valya pulled a face. 'I wouldn't know. East, west, home is best.'

'Exactly.'

'When are the piglets on?' asked Valya, squinting at the programme.

Cousin Tolya had been brought by taxi all the way from Rostov. Gazing about him as he took his seat in the front row, he wondered at the babble, the hum, the busyness of it all. It was a long time since he had seen so many people. He had wondered about the noise, but as he sank into the velvet of his seat, he felt a flutter of calm, a murmur of excitement; he liked it. He heard the thousands of words, saw the flashes of smiles, and felt at home. The bag of cake in his lap added to the comforting effect.

'Eat! Eat and enjoy, Anatoly Borisovich!' Valya had said as she helped him to his seat.

Life could be magical.

In the foyer, several former bank clerks crowded around Gor, mumbling quietly and shaking his hand in the gloom, making diffident remarks about how fit and slim he looked. He rebuffed their compliments and managed two jokes in the six minutes he gave it before pretending he had business backstage. In fact, he had no business anywhere in the building. So he checked on his cousin and made for the dressing room, for a little meditation before curtain up.

Sveta, meanwhile, was in her element. The programme had been a joy to put together, and the costumes were all that she had hoped for, if not more. Hers had been hanging on the back of the bedroom door for a week, sending tingles up her spine each time she looked at it. Now, she gave a yelp of pleasure as she zipped up the bodice in the honeyed light of the dressing room, the gold sequins sparkling like a sky full of fireworks.

'Sveta,' she murmured to the full-length mirror, 'you are indeed a cracker.' She blew herself a kiss and carefully hoiked up her fishnets before slinking through the door. She would stand in the wings, feeling the buzz, watching the audience . . . living the show.

First up there was dancing, supplied by the nimble fairies of Albina's school. No one was sure who had devised the work, which was, as the audience discovered, an interpretation of 'the meaning of milk products in modern society, and the life of a cow'. Interesting in the extreme, they had no clear clue as to whom out of the dozen or so dancers was the cow, who was the milk, and who was the butter. It received a standing ovation nonetheless.

Next came Albina. She had worked up her own composition on Gor's baby-grand, and proudly took to the stage, all notes memorised, with Kopek on her shoulder and a framed photo of Ponchik in place of sheet music. Notes pounced from her fingertips like kittens on teasels and the audience sat, spellbound and afraid to move, as the piano howled and mewed in turn. Sveta wiped away tears of pride when her daughter left the stage.

Bogdan had been unable to supply a Cossack trapeze troupe, and had also failed to come through with the piglets pushing cats in prams. What Sveta had managed to bag, however, was Rollick, the King Singing Billy Goat. A hush descended across the auditorium as Rollick bleated the opening bars to 'Moscow

Nights', followed by a snatch of the national anthem, and finally the rousing and almost recognisable chorus of 'Kalinka'. The goat brought the house down and fans showered the stage with flowers, many of which he promptly ate.

'Ah, Mama! Perhaps we could get a goat! It could live at Gor's *dacha*, and I could teach it to duet with Kopek!'

'Yes, *malysh*, that's a fine idea. Let's talk about it later.' Sveta was dancing on the spot; nerves were getting the better of her.

Finally, it was time for magic. They took to the stage: Grand Master Papasyan and Sveta, his Magical Mistress. The old man, dressed in a suit of dark green wool with a ruby bow-tie at his throat, was confident, assured, mysterious and kindly. He grinned at the front row, and waggled his ears. Sveta concentrated on sophistication meanwhile, her arms and legs slow and graceful, her smile poised. She ignored the ostrich feathers sticking to her lipstick.

They began with card tricks, picking audience members to join them on stage, then progressed to scarves which appeared out of a hat or Sveta's ear. Next came flags, knotted and un-knotted, and balls that appeared under the cup you least expected. Nothing was dropped; not a thing got stuck. The audience gasped as the magical cabinet was wheeled onto the stage. It glistened, caramel varnish liquid under the lights. They had practised the illusion many times, but still, as Sveta lay back in the cabinet, her thoughts returned to the first time she had met Gor, not so very long ago. She remembered how frightened she had been, how everything seemed strange. Now he took up his saw and bent over her, and she smiled. All was vibration and illusion. The lights pulsed and she heard the audience release a communal 'aahhh!' When she was invited to, she wiggled her toes inside their fishnet stockings. The audience gasped anew, and Sveta giggled.

Small children lined the foot of the stage to pass up sweet-smelling waves of bouquets and boxed chocolate. Sveta curtseyed, blowing kisses to the balcony. This was what she had been looking for when she answered Gor's advert. This was the spark that had been missing from her life. She floated back to the dressing room, arms heavy with gifts.

'I cannot thank you enough!' said Gor, his long face bent into a smile as he hurried back from the box office. 'I have checked the figures, and, indeed, my debt is cleared! We can also make a donation to the orphanage. You are an angel! You have rescued me: you have salvaged my life! I can never repay you.'

He took her hand, bent low and pressed it to his lips.

'Ah Gor, it was a pleasure! You were wonderful tonight, I have to say. I'd love to . . . to do it all again!'

She gazed into his eyes.

'You . . . you, of course, were marvellous too: the perfect assistant! A vision of loveliness, combined with an aura of mystery and, um . . . well . . .'

He still held her hand. She went to pull it from his grip, but his fingers held her wrist. He coughed, pulled out a spotted silk handkerchief with his free hand, mopped his brow, and returned it to his breast pocket.

'Sveta, I was wondering, well . . .' he straightened and his huge, dark eyes flickered around the ceiling, the steamed-up windows, the feathers at her neck '. . . whether we should consider . . . becoming . . . becoming a couple. I mean, along-side the magic. Not just a double act: I mean, as far as our social dealings go. You know. I feel, I mean, I get the impression, you are eager for a mate in life, and I, well, although I am older, I wondered—'

'Oh Gor!' Sveta's chin wobbled. A shadow passed over her blue eyes, and he thought for a moment she was going to cry. Instead, her face broke into a tender, puzzled smile.

'No, Gor. I mean, oh no!'

He dropped her hand.

'I am your friend; your very good friend. Your best friend, even!' She giggled. 'But that is all. I am sorry if . . .'

She swallowed and dropped her eyes, shaking fingers wiping away imaginary lipstick lines from the corners of her mouth. Stillness enveloped the dressing room.

There came a choking sound from Gor's throat, followed by a creaking, tumbling, thundering, like flood water on dry rocks. Sveta looked up, alarmed. It was a sound she had never heard.

It was the sound of Gor guffawing.

He threw his head back and roared, eyes staring wide-open into the grimy ceiling and then squeezed tightly shut as he bent double, clutching his sides. The veins in his temples stood out as his shoulders jerked. Tears squeezed from his eyes and his ribs ached as his laughter rang out. It was infectious. Albina left off talking to Rollick the King Singing Billy Goat, giggles bubbling. Tolya toddled through the door, and started to chuckle, wide-eyed. Sveta herself could not resist, a chortle rising in her ample, elastic throat. Gor gasped for breath. Even Rollick stopped chewing, regarding Gor with his chilly, rectangular irises. Soon the entire dressing room fell about in a circle, laughing with Gor.

'What's so funny?' Albina asked eventually, gasping for breath as a frown-smile creased her face.

'I am just so . . . so relieved!' he croaked, wiping his eyes with his handkerchief and patting the goat.

'Relieved?' said Sveta, the smile stilling on her lips.

'Akh, that is to say, happy! I am so happy – with everything! With life! Everything is resolved: life is simple again! We must celebrate! A weight has gone from my shoulders. Or several weights! We should go to the bar! Let's have a toast! Come, we'll go up to the bar.' Gor rubbed his hands and grinned.

'The bar? But Gor, I'm all in sequins!' said Sveta, delighted at the thought.

'Sveta, you look divine! Come Tolya, come Albina: we must celebrate my new chance at life. Lead the way, and I will treat us all to a little Soviet champagne!' Gor bowed low, allowing Sveta to pass him. She led them up the polished concrete steps to the circle bar, her skirt swaying to the swish of satin and beads.

Gor's eyes swept the glowing metal and concrete of the foyer below. 'It's been such an evening! I feel a lightness in my bones, Albina, as if I could just direct my thoughts, and fly!'

Albina kept her eyes on the stairs and shrugged. 'Where would you fly to?'

'To Armenia, maybe? Or perhaps north, to Moscow? Or maybe . . . I could travel the whole world!' He bared his long, yellow teeth as they threaded their way into the brown velour dimness of the bar.

'But you'd come back, wouldn't you?'

'Oh yes, yes!' he looked down tenderly. 'Of course.'

The champagne arrived and, with a flourish, Gor popped the plastic cork into the ceiling, releasing a shower of dust and paint flakes, met by Sveta's squeals.

'I must propose a toast: here's to you, dearest Sveta! You are a true friend; a forgiving friend. No one could ask for more. I thank you from the bottom of my heart, and I wish you good health, happiness, love and fortune in the coming year, and all your years!'

Albina raised her orange compote, her lips sealed as the grown-ups talked and laughed and planned. Her mama looked so content. They all seemed so happy. Maybe she should say nothing at all.

'All is well, *malysh*?' Sveta leant over to smooth her fringe and pat into place the huge frilly pom-poms that stood at each corner of her head.

'Yes, Mama. I was just thinking.' She could not meet her mother's gaze.

'What about?'

'About a moth.'

'Ah, baby-kins, I know it's difficult, but that's all over now. We have a new beginning – all of us! So we're going to forget about the past and go forward, yes?'

'Yes, Mama,' the girl nodded and took a sip of her orange. Life was all about the future, all about happiness. She twirled the straw in her drink. They carried on talking. But she couldn't be happy with this feeling like mud in her guts.

'No, Mama, I have to . . . Gor: listen to me.' The chat died away and his eyes met hers. 'You have done bad things in your life, as you say. You have also done good. And you have taught me . . . to face up to the bad. And now, I have to tell you: I did a bad thing.'

'Oh? Well, don't worry—'

'It was me: you weren't going mad.'

He raised his eyebrows. 'The moth, Albina? In the sandwich?'

She nodded, face glum.

'I don't know why I did it. Just to test you. But I felt so bad, when you said . . . said about all the scary things that were happening, and then Mama made you go to a séance and it was . . . a joke. I didn't mean to harm you. Can you forgive me?'

'I forgave you the minute you did it.' His mouth twitched into a smile. 'But I am so glad you've been able to tell me.'

'So am I.'

Gor looked into the bubbles in his glass, and then across at his cousin, who sat oblivious, eyes sparkling, filled with the simple joy of company.

A NEW YEAR GLIMMERS

The kittens were gone, the apartment was quiet. A snow-bound, downy stillness ruled the air. For the first time since he could remember, Gor dragged the little tinsel tree from the back of his store cupboard, and wiped it with a damp cloth. He placed it in the corner, where it shone with an ancient, plastic mystery. Dasha and Pericles sized up its glinting baubles. It had last come out . . . December 1974? His whiskers twitched. He wished he had a photo of that last New Year. He could not even remember it. Had he been there?

The letter to Olga had been written on thin blue paper, a lettergram folded over and over, covered in his precise scrawl. The cover bore a colourful representation of the hydroelectric dam at Krasnoyarsk. He had practised the words on old napkins three times beforehand, to get them right. Still, it lay sealed on the sideboard. He had reached for it several times, got as far as putting it in his old string bag ready to post. But then he had hesitated, and taken it out again. It probably wouldn't reach her anyway. Whoever opened it would laugh at him: writing after twenty years? What a fool. Or if she did receive it, perhaps she would simply tear it up in disgust. He couldn't blame her. Did he, really, deserve her to read it?

He sat in the hall to don his boots. Ponchik had departed for Sveta's the day before. He missed the skittering, the chorus of mews, the attention when he did up his laces. He smiled to himself as he tidied the shoes on the rack, putting away the fluffy orange slippers, Albina's pumps, his old galoshes that the kittens loved. His hand brushed something cold, the fleeting feeling of something round and smooth. He stopped and pushed his fingers inside the perished rubber galosh. There was no mistaking . . . his hand closed around a perfect white hen's egg. The one he'd lost that day, back in early October. He must have put it down, and it had ended up in a galosh, a toy for kittens. A low laugh escaped his throat. Wait until Sveta heard about this. She would find it most amusing. How she would chuckle. Carefully, he removed the egg and placed it in the kitchen bin.

He arrived at seven p.m. precisely. 'Cousin, cousin, come in, let me take your coat. How was your journey?' Tolya fussed about, taking Gor's things in the half-light of the hall. A single lamp burnt in the sitting room. His breathing was laboured, and Gor noted how he moved with stiffness, like a clockwork soldier.

The flat was cosy, redecorated in reds and greens to remind Tolya of forests, berries and sunsets. New carpet tiles creaked on the floor and the comforting smell of old clothes and cooking fat now included a top note of fresh varnish and virgin plastic. Gor's gift – a small tinsel New Year tree like his own, stood on the shelf in the corner, glinting merrily.

'And how is it here, Tolya?' Gor's eyes swept the room, 'All peaceful?' He took in the papers on the easel, the open books scattered like giant butterflies across the shelves, seats and floor.

'Calm, Gor. So calm. I have been drawing. You see? And reading. So much to do.' He rustled through soft pages stacked on a corner of the desk, picking out a few pastels for Gor's perusal. Swirling patterns in greys, greens and blues were studded with silver-gold stars.

'I can almost feel the breeze.' Gor smiled. 'And smell the pine cones.'

'They are my joy.' Tolya nodded. His green eyes looked sharply into Gor's pale face. 'Something is wrong, cousin? You look . . . frayed. Be careful you don't snap! Let me fetch cocoa. Maybe cocoa will bring some colour to those cheeks? And you can tell me all.'

'I'll do it, Tolya. You rest. And when was the last time you saw colour in my cheeks, eh? All is well, don't fret.'

Gor slid open the door to the tiny kitchen and busied himself with milk, a pan, the gas.

'There is some cake, if you are willing? That lovely lady – the orange one with the bulldog's face—'

'Valya?'

'Yes, Valya bakes me one every other day. Vlad brings them himself. Last time it was fruit cake. Today – walnut. They have both been very kind.'

'Ah, good doctor Vlad!' Gor squeaked the hatch open and bent to stick his face through. 'You know, the police have pressed no charges against him? In fact, he is now almost a local celebrity, it seems. Modelling for Madame Zoya.'

'Ah, I know. It's lovely; he should feed his artistic side.'

'It doesn't anger you? It angers me!'

383

'He is young, but he's not bad. It takes time, sometimes, for the goodness in people to get the upper hand, don't you think? I enjoy talking to him. And he listens to me.'

'If you say so. Here! *Na zdarovie!*' Gor sat beside him on the sofa and carefully handed him the cocoa and a slice of cake.

'We've been discussing his case study . . .' Tolya stopped, a sad smile stilling his lips.

'And?'

'It has been revised. He had a long talk with Dr Spatchkin and . . . it appears . . . well, they think I may have . . . dementia.' Questioning green eyes turned to Gor. He scowled in response and slammed his piece of cake onto the table.

'What rot! Absolute rot!' He ran a hand over his goatee. 'You're just a little confused, cousin. It happens to all of us as we get older!'

Tolya examined his slice of cake.

'Maybe you're right. We are all confused, to a greater or lesser degree. But it doesn't worry me, you know.'

Gor shot him a sideways look. 'Good!'

Tolya raised the plate to his chin and sprinkled chopped walnuts onto his extended tongue. 'Mmm, that is delicious.' He chewed. 'If only I had learnt to make cakes!'

'You wouldn't fit through the door, dear cousin, if baking were a skill of yours.' Gor's eyes glinted as Tolya snuffled with laughter. He stared into his cocoa. 'But Tolya, you know . . . whatever happens . . .' He looked up. 'I will take care of you. This dementia, if that's what it is; it changes nothing. We will be strong – together.'

Tolya nodded and wiggled his toes in time with Rachmaninov seeping from the radio on the wall.

384

As they sat, arm in arm, a large brown moth drew circles around the light fitting, fluttering a shadow onto the new brown carpet tiles below. It reminded Gor of childhood, of Albina, and of duty. He took a deep breath.

'I have something . . . there is something I must tell you, Tolya. It's been bothering me, and now is the time. It's been in the back of my mind forever, but . . . until recently, I thought it was a dream. I thought it wasn't real.' Gor hesitated and Tolya looked up, still happily chewing. 'But it was. When I thought . . . when I thought I'd lost you, it came to me forcefully, with clarity. And then when Albina . . .' Tolya issued a quiet burp. Gor plunged on. 'I finally saw it for what it was. I don't want to upset you, but it must be told.'

'My dear Gor!' Tolya smiled broadly, eyes sparkling, and wiped his mouth on his sleeve. 'Speak, speak and get it out! Don't suffer!'

Gor licked his lips.

'I know you have remembered that night . . . at your baba's? And it is good, in a way, that you can . . . face it. But, I wondered, have you remembered . . . how you woke?'

'Yes Gor. It came back when I was ill.'

'On your birthday?' Gor's face was drawn.

'Stop feeling it, Gor. I have. You explained what happened. We each have our own worries . . .' He squeezed his cousin's hand. 'It was a jumble. Telling the story . . . it's always the story, isn't it? Life is full of stories. Family is a story. Friends are a story. It was all in the story . . . and telling it to Vlad got it straight. I remember . . .'

'Yes?'

'Waking in my bed, in the dead of night. The smell, the

taste of the smoke . . . fire everywhere, eating up the cottage.'
He thrust more cake into his mouth.

Gor frowned. 'No, Tolya. Don't you remember . . . tapping
on the windows? Being afraid?'

'Tapping?' The old man's face hung empty. 'No. There was
no tapping.'

'You must have been frightened, by the tapping—'

'No, Gor! You are mistaken. No tapping woke me. I woke
because of the roar, the smoke. The fire woke me.'

Gor's face remained stern. His gaze fell to the floor.

'You are not remembering correctly. I must go on. That
night, Tolya, I visited your cottage. For a dare.' Gor's voice
cracked.

Tolya's eyebrows rose a fraction, his tongue stilled, but his
round face remained calm.

'Why?'

'To prove myself . . . to the boys at school: you remember,
the big boys? They teased us, used to follow us home from
school.'

Tolya nodded.

'They told me . . . they said if I went at midnight, and
tapped on your window, they would let me be one of their
gang. So I did it. I tapped on your window in the middle of
the night! It was me who scared you!'

'No, no cousin.'

'I made you drop the lamp! It was . . . it was me who killed
Baba!'

The great black eyes filled with unshed tears. Tolya shook
his head and leant forward, his hand on Gor's. They sat nose
to nose.

386

'You have it wrong, cousin, you have it wrong. Did you see me, when you came?'

'It makes no odds—'

'But did you see me?' The green eyes shone.

'No! All was dark. I tapped, and tapped again, and ran away back home like a scared dog. I ran back home and bundled into bed, shaking with it; shame and pride and fear. I was just dropping into sleep, dreaming about school, when . . . when the alarm came. It was me!'

'Ah, cousin. You still don't understand. Don't cry!' Tolya stroked his bowed head. 'There's no need. It wasn't you. Really.' Gor raised his eyes. 'And it wasn't me.'

'But—'

'It was Yuri, the moth boy, my poor, poor friend. It was an accident! He always loved the lamp. But he wasn't careful – he just wanted the flame. He dropped it. Baba let him stay, it was so cold. But she fell asleep with the lamp still lit. She fell asleep . . .'

Gor took his cousin's head in his hands and looked deep into his eyes. 'Tolya, you don't understand. That is your imagination. This Yuri was not real; moth boy was not real! We told you about him! We made you believe the story, but he wasn't there! You imagined those memories: you blamed him, but you must blame me!'

Tolya peeled the fingers from his hair with a chuckle. 'No, no! It's you who doesn't understand. You wait! You just wait and see.' He eased himself up and tottered over to the desk. After rummaging for many moments, he pulled out a small, battered metal box. 'You'll see. You'll see! This is my special treasure. I don't open it often. It's magic, you

387

see. I can smell my childhood in this box. My happy times.'
He carried it carefully to where Gor sat. The lid came up
with a jerk. He pushed in his hand, turning over yellowed
papers, dry pine cones, ancient pressed flowers tied in faded
ribbons. He smiled as his fingers closed around something
solid.

'Here is proof, since you won't believe me. They found it
in the ruins, above the stove where I slept. The only thing.
Goloshov returned it to me.'

He pulled out a battered, rough wooden spoon. On its
handle, in blotchy poker-work, were written the words

* Tolya * Yuri * Friends *

Gor stared at the spoon and a chill passed over his skin.
'Baba told me never to tell. She said he'd be our secret. But
I don't think she'd mind, now.'

When he got home, late that night, Gor took the letter to his
daughter from the sideboard, kissed it along the seal, and took
it straight down to the little blue postbox on the corner. After
it had disappeared through the slot he stood imagining its
journey across the wide Russian countryside, speeding from
town to town, past coal mines, quarries, metal works and
factories, following the crows and the rivers, all the way north
to that snowy jewel – Moscow. His fingers lingered on the
metal of the box, sensing his letter on the inside. He wished
it well.

What would Sveta say about all this? He could hardly wait
to tell her. Fluffy snowflakes fell silently from the blue-black

sky as he stood. He looked up to feel them on his face. How strange and wonderful, perplexing and precious life was.

That night Tolya was alone in his room. There was no Baba, no Lev with his cold, wet nose and restful tail thump. He'd been scaring himself with stories: the stories that made his heart beat hard in his chest, the stories boys at school told him. He felt the wind rushing in the tree tops even as he lay in his bed, warm as toast, warm as the top of the stove, although a little too soft. He pressed the eiderdown to his face. If he reached out his hand he might feel a hunk of black bread and the lamp. He rolled over carefully, opened his eyes and looked out of the window. His curtains were gone.

Where, at some point, there had been a copse of birch, tussled and bullied by the wind, there now stood a forest. Dark and frost-laden, silent and watchful, it twinkled with the eyes of a thousand creatures nestling in the night-time, taking shelter in its branches. Tolya crossed the room on bare feet and pressed his nose to the glass. It was beautiful.

At the bottom of the trees, on the edge of the clearing, he could see the outline of a figure hovering in the undergrowth, almost transparent. Just the idea of a figure, the impression of a thought. Waiting for him. He turned back into the room and rubbed his eyes. Perhaps he should get something to eat. Maybe Baba had left him a sausage. She said food was important, if you couldn't sleep. He would share it with Lev. Lev would enjoy a sausage: the old dog never got much these days – just left-over porridge and scraps from the bins. Lev would like a sausage. He would look.

tap-tap-tap

He stopped in the middle of the room, hairs rising on his neck.

tap-tap-tap

He screwed up his eyes and crossed his fingers, standing there in the darkness, but the words wouldn't form on his lips. Where was Stalin anyway? Where was Baba? What was he afraid of? He took a slow, deep breath. He was afraid of nothing.

The forest scent was in his nose, he could taste it on his tongue. He relaxed his hands and stood a long moment, listening to the wind, to the air in his lungs. He opened his eyes, and turned back to the window. Someone was there.

A face gazed at him, hovering in the darkness, almost close enough to touch. He could see every feature. He stepped forward. The eyes flickered strangely, oscillated in their orbits: twin moons shining in a face as pale as milk.

'Come,' said Yuri, and his mouth spread into a wide, toothy grin. He tapped on the glass, glowing in the darkness, the long thin fingers twitching. 'Come, friend. All will be well.'

'Yuri,' said Tolya. 'My friend! Yes, I'm coming now.'

He opened the window.

ACKNOWLEDGEMENTS

I'd like to thank Mary Woodrow, Ady Coles, Lucy Du Plessis, Tim Partlett and Liz Moore for their helpful comments on the various drafts of this book. Big thanks to Cassie Browne and Charlotte Cray at Borough Press for their wise advice and patient encouragement when all seemed a bit confused. Also thanks to all at The Prime Writers for mutual support.

As ever, huge thanks to Mick James for his critical eye, good ideas and warm hugs.

And thanks to Louis and Archie, for being Louis and Archie.